Hidden

Circle
Book Two

M.A.I. Murray

Anden Jade
Published by Anden Jade
Charlottesville, VA

ISBN-13: 978-0-9966044-3-7

DEDICATION

For Mama Murray.

I hope you're enjoying
the view from above.
We miss you.

CONTENTS

ACKNOWLEDGMENTS

There are too many people to list without whom this book never would have made it as far as publication, but I will try my best. To my wonderful husband Sean, thank you for the unbelievable amount of support you have provided me over the past few years as I devoted way too much time to writing (among many other creative pursuits). To Lauren and Britt, thank you for helping me refine all my ridiculous ideas into a coherent story (well, as coherent as anything coming out of my brain could be). To Mom, Dad, Teddy, and Jess, thank you so much for your invaluable feedback on the early drafts, helping me find all the plot holes, and, of course, for your years of friendship. Those who dislike the ending can blame Jess in particular. Lastly, a huge shout out to Rob Vega Jr. and Josh Lintz of True Sounds Audio, who turned my dream of hearing *Destined* as an audiobook into a reality; I do hope you'll help me bring *Hidden* to life as well.
All of you are amazing.

PROLOGUE
My family would not understand

It was the silence that woke her.

He always brought the silence with him when he came, as if it clung to his person like a spider to its web. He did not visit her every night, but as soon as the sun dipped below the horizon, she could tell the nights that he would. She had known long before she laid down to sleep that he would arrive with the midnight and enfold her in blessed silence.

She shoved the blankets back and braced herself on her elbows. Squinting, she could just make out a shifting shadow in the corner of the cramped room. She knew the answer already, yet like a ritual she asked, "Who's there?" The shadow moved closer, bringing with it the scent of cloves, myrrh, and a sickly sweetness. It was the scent of flowers left too long in the vase, of lilies at the edge of a grave. She inhaled the familiar, bittersweet perfume. She exhaled, "It's you."

"Of course," the shadow whispered. "I have returned to you as I promised I would." He perched on the edge of her bed in a rustle of cloaks.

She sat up higher, fumbling towards him. "Returned from where?" she asked with the softest of sighs. "You never tell me where it is you go when you leave. I want to know. I have a right to know." She reached out an arm to him; her fingers fell just short of the distance.

"I never leave you, not truly. I just cannot risk being seen by anyone else," he whispered, taking her hand and stroking the callused skin of her palm. "Not yet, at least."

"Then where are you during the day?" she persisted.

"Where I have to be."

"And now?"

"Where I want to be."

She closed her eyes, mulling over his response and enjoying the sensation of his cooling touch. "Come closer," she pleaded. "You're still too far away."

He slid along the covers, the thick quilt giving way as he moved toward the head of the bed. He came to rest beside her, his back against the headboard. When he finally spoke again, his voice was the barest breath, mere inches from her ear: "Anything you wish, my love." His lips against her neck left a trail of winter shivers.

"I wish to see you in sunlight," she replied, the request nearly inaudible. "I wish to walk down the street holding your hand. I wish to know who you are."

Although she could not make out the details of his face through the gloom, she knew his brow wrinkled in frustration. The air thickened around her, constricting her throat, but just as quickly the pressure dissipated in time with his frustration. By the time he replied, his voice was as calm as ever. "All you need to know is that I remain yours. Here, I've brought you a gift." He deposited a scrap of knotted velvet in her hand. "Open it," he commanded.

"What is it?" Her jeweler's fingers, normally deft, hesitated and tripped in the dark. When she succeeded in untying the slick fabric, those same fingers recognized the object within at once. "A ring," she announced. "I bet it's beautiful. I can't wait to see it in the morning."

"It holds but a fraction of your own beauty. Wear it always, and I will always be with you," he explained. He plucked the ring from her palm and slid it into place along her middle finger. "If you are ever in danger, day or night, I will know, and I will come for you."

At first she felt a spark like a needle prick where the ring rested against her knuckle. Peering down at her glimmering hand, she asked, "What is this stone? It's so black I can see it even now. It feels odd." She flexed her fingers. "Heavier than it should be."

He brushed her hair over her shoulder and said, "It's a special stone, one native to my birthplace."

"Everyone will wonder where I acquired such a ring," she commented softly. "Bits of wood and scraps of metal, even bone, those I work with. But this…"

"Tell them anything you like," he whispered, planting another chilling kiss on her neck. "The truth, perhaps."

She turned to face him. "The truth?" she scoffed. "That three years ago I found a wounded angel who stole away my heart? That he gives me jewels yet never shows me his true face?" She laughed hollowly and shook her head. "You know perfectly well why I can't tell them the truth. My family would not understand."

The glint of his grin flashed. "Then tell them nothing."

"I will think of something, my angel."

"I never said I was an angel."

"You never said you were not," she countered, a touch of humor brightening her voice. She placed her hands on either side of his face, stroking the sharp bones she had come to know so well by touch, if not by sight. Not since that first night had she seen her visitor clearly, and even then, the moon revealed only so much. "And I know what you really are, deep inside."

In the morning, when the rays of sunlight broke through her window, she was unsurprised to find herself alone. She closed her eyes, memories swirling through her brain. That night in the forest, the arrow, the bones.

She nearly forgot to breathe.

As she opened her eyes again, she whispered, "No demon can love, not truly."

The ring on her hand glittered, its polished gold framing a sphere hewn from the emptiness between stars.

The Fifth Spinner paced back and forth in the weaving room. In the corner the Loom lurked, its threads tangled in the frame. Half-spun threads waited on a wheel in another corner. "Something's wrong," Laria muttered as she picked up a book from the desk to the left of the Loom. She flipped it open and squinted at the tiny script, scrawled there by one of her predecessors in an ancient language she had only just begun learning to decipher. Many of the words remained a mystery to her, but she could recognize enough now, at least, to know that the pages contained no mention of the topic she sought.

An equine snort at the window interrupted her silent studies. Laria held up one slender finger in the direction of the disturbance. Once she had finished scanning the page, she shut the book and raised her gaze to see Micaleth pressing his long, white nose through the shutters. His horn glistened as he rested his chin on the window sill.

"Guardian Hal has the rest of the books you requested," he announced. Though his words were formal, his tone was anything but.

"Thanks, Mickey," Laria replied, forcing a smile.

Micaleth snorted again. "I still don't understand that name, but since you are the Spinner, you may call me what you will."

Laria smiled, genuinely this time. "I'll look at the books this evening," she said as she turned back to confront her burden and her gift, the enchanted item that allowed her to peer into the past and present and future of the three worlds. The Loom. The timelines wove and unwove, revealing patterns spun along lines of prophetic probability that no other could decipher, that no other could control, but the reigning Spinner. The power within the Loom itself came from another, but the duty of interpretation fell to her. She could see anything she wished in the fabric.

Anything, that is, until now.

She grasped either side of the wooden frame, concentrating on the colored threads, and a trickle of magic coursed through them. The fabric unraveled and wove back together to form a neat pattern. Gradually the pattern evolved into a picture, and a distant city spread across the fabric, red and green lights blinking in the twilight as buildings climbed toward a mundane sky. "It works fine if I look literally anywhere else," she mumbled underneath her breath.

"What's wrong?"

"I'm still not sure," Laria replied with a frown. "Could you go get Gryndonmin? I think it's time I asked for more help with this than just books."

Micaleth quirked his head to the side, but then nodded. "You know," he tentatively suggested, "you still have friends outside these walls, too. Maybe they could see what you cannot."

"That's not a bad idea," she mused as she returned her attention to the Loom. The urban scene danced across the woven threads. Laria almost thought she could hear the horns of the cars singing in the streets. If she focused on the scene much longer, she knew she would hear them and a great deal more besides. She waved a hand in front of the Loom, and the scene faded.

The threads tangled.

CHAPTER ONE
Certainly took you long enough

Gren squinted at a blueprint as he trudged down a darkened corridor with Mari a few steps in front of him and Ruv a few steps behind. The rosy light of either a motion sensor or a camera—they were not quite sure which, although they were at least fairly certain they had successfully disabled the overall system as evident by the general darkness—blinked in the far corner. "According to the printout, it's two more lefts, then three cells down on the right," he reminded his friends. His boots made the softest of clicks along the tile floor, but despite his efforts to remain otherwise silent, every few steps his bow and quiver of arrows rattled under his trench coat.

Mari spun around fleetingly to respond, "Good." As she neared the end of the hall, she dropped to the floor. She kept low and darted her head around the corner. Seeing no one, she hopped back on her feet and adjusted her own long coat to cover the bejeweled sword at her hip. "Ruv, still got those keys?"

He chuckled quietly, hazel eyes sparkling with mischief as he replied, "Of course! I only lifted them from the front desk five minutes ago. Even I cannot lose something so quick." All the same, he checked his pocket and let out a silent sigh of relief when his fingers brushed metal. He spared a glance behind them to ensure no one followed.

So far, so good.

Suddenly Mari held up a hand to halt their progress, scooting closer to the wall and pressing herself as flat as possible. Her companions followed suit. "I think I heard something," she mouthed. She glanced about them, scouring the darkness for a possible attack.

Gren's shoulders drooped. "No," he whispered with an embarrassed half-smile. "That was just me. I stumbled when I was putting away the map, and it echoed weird in here," He shrugged, the leather of his coat and quiver rustling again. As if to emphasize his words, the folded blueprint stuck haphazardly out of one of his pockets.

Mari relaxed as she continued down the corridor. "I don't know why I bother with you two," she lamented. "If I were by myself, I'd already be—"

Her thoughts were unexpectedly dispersed by the telepathic intrusion of Laria, who asked, *Hey, you busy?*

Mari suppressed a squeal at the invasion of her brain, but since she had grown more accustomed to the fatestone link, it took only a few breaths to recover. She reached for the anchor that allowed such communication: a pendent of faceted jade, carved into the shape of a crescent moon, suspended perpetually from her throat. "Holy hell, girl!" she answered, mentally directing her words toward the Spinner's sanctuary where Laria had resided for the past several years. At least, years had elapsed for Mari since she had seen her friend in person. She suspected only a handful of months had passed from Laria's perspective. Time became a funny thing when you traveled between dimensions. "You know damn well I'm busy."

Gren and Ruv, all too familiar with witnessing spontaneous, seemingly one-sided conversations (and, in Gren's case, participating in his own), resigned themselves to the inevitable break. Gren moved forward to keep watch around the other corner, while Ruv took a few paces back to better guard their rear. As he moved into position, Gren prayed that this time his own brain would remain clear of any thoughts that did not belong to him.

Mari rolled her eyes as she listened to Laria's telepathic response. *I can't watch everything you're doing every minute of every day, you know,* she was saying. *Besides, I don't particularly want to see what you and Gren get up to in your free time lately.*

"Well, we're in the middle of an operation," Mari replied with a vague wave of her hand, even though she knew Laria could not witness the action unless she happened to be actively watching her in the Loom. Since Laria seemed to possess limited knowledge of their present circumstances, Mari suspected the Spinner's attention must have been focused elsewhere as of late. "Sam got caught. Long story."

Ah yes, the thieving panther twins, Laria rejoined. *I thought you all were still in Scotland with that wicked smart geologist? The one whose circle you fell through?*

Mari allowed herself a soft smile as she repeated, "Like I said, long story. Short version: Sam's chilling in a jail cell, and Sarah's about to drive the getaway van."

And the geologist?

"She's tagging along for the ride."

When Mari, Gren, and Ruv first met Sarah and Sam near Kupala's waterfall while attempting to fulfill the task the goddess had set before Gren on their first trip to Aorea, they never dreamed they would spend the ensuing weeks cleaning up the various messes the twins left in their wake. They were suspicious of the siblings to be sure, considering their reluctance to answer direct questions with direct answers, but curiosity at meeting another set of shapeshifting humans outweighed that suspicion. That the twins were clearly so comfortable shifting between their human and panther forms intrigued them. More intriguing still, the existence of traveling circles was not exactly common knowledge on Earth, and their operation required magic limited to a select few in each generation, and especially few among humans. Gren possessed such magic; the twins did not.

So when Sarah and Sam's path disappeared as soon as they reached the Birch Forest circle, they took a chance and followed them. The trail led them through the rainforests of Southern Faerie and into a hidden cave, where they ended up rescuing the twins from the vengeance of Kutkah, a shapeshifting god of trickery and mischief who also happened to be Sarah and Sam's erstwhile employer. He had used the twins to acquire various treasures to add to his collection. Now, however, Kutkah was safely contained by his fellow lanti, and thus, unable to cause further mischief.

Yet here they were, just a few weeks later, cleaning up another mess the twins left behind. This time, they did not have Kutkah's orders as an excuse. The theft was entirely of their own volition.

Mari could practically feel Laria's arching eyebrow through her response. *Sounds about right for those two.*

"Get to the point, please," Mari admonished, fingers still firmly laced around her fatestone. "We are kinda on a time crunch."

Right, sorry, Laria replied. *I need you to come back to Aorea, and you might want to bring the whole crowd with you. Twins included. Got a bit of a problem I'd like you to look into. I'll have someone meet you with the details at that tavern up in the Alpines that Ruv always talks about. What's the name again? I know he knows it, at least. The one whose owner has all those daughters.*

Mari frowned, concentrating, then suggested, "The Tipsy Turtle?"

That's the one!

"Sure thing," she agreed. "Now if you don't mind, I've got a jail break to complete." Mari released her grip on the jade crescent, letting the connection between them fade once more to the back of her mind. The fatestone link lingered only as a dull hum, imperceptible unless she actively thought about it. Mari ran her fingers through her hair, as messy as ever and, unbeknownst to her, every bit as tangled as the threads in Laria's Loom.

Observing that Mari's thoughts had returned to the present, Gren and Ruv collapsed their positions. "What'd she want?" Gren queried, adjusting the belt that strapped an ornate knife to his thigh. He then adjusted his coat again since the previous movement had caused his quiver to slip off his shoulder. "Damn arrows," he muttered with a grimace, shoving one of them back in place. "I really wish we could have just left these with the girls."

Mari flicked Gren halfheartedly across an ear while resuming her position as point of their miniature assault party. "Considering they had to move the van after we hopped out, you know that wasn't an option."

"I know, I know," Gren whined, his voice louder than discretion might deem wise. "Worked great for holding Kutkah's cave in place, not so great for an automobile. Emphasis on the *mobile* part. Stupid binding."

"Please, keep it down," Mari reproved. "We don't have time for any of your lame puns, let alone to argue the merits of enchanted weapons. We may have temporarily taken out the security system and knocked a guard or two unconscious, but we only have a few minutes left before the emergency generators kick in and someone realizes we're here." She gestured around the ostensibly empty halls to emphasize her point. "I'll tell you what Laria said later. She probably wants us to the save the worlds or something. But first, we need to finish saving a sanguine," she finished with a flourish, grinning at her own alliteration and daring either of her companions to comment.

Gren just sighed, murmuring something about how he was supposed to be the poet, not Mari, but she chose not to acknowledge it. Ruv, if he heard, wisely kept silent.

The trio slunk through the corridors, naught but the faint glow of the emergency lights along the baseboards and the blinking red of the motion sensors (or possibly cameras; they remained undecided on that front) to illuminate their careful steps. They could hear muffled voices echoing from around the next bend, signaling they had finally reached the primary cell block.

Stopping outside the third cell on the right, Gren rapped his knuckles across the bars. "Hey, brother, how you holding up in there?"

A shadow stirred in the far corner of the cell, accompanied by Sam's velveteen voice. "It's about bloody time. A fellow could rot in here. In fact, I think one of my neighbors already did."

Ruv began fumbling with the lock while Mari said, "Sorry we left you so long. We had to get all the details ironed out first. Shift changes, security measures, when they're down to minimal manning. You know how it is. Plus it's not exactly like any of us have done this before."

"Well," Ruv cut in, "I have."

Gren snorted. "Jails have changed a lot since, what, eighteen-something-or-other."

"Just unlock the damn door before the guards come back, will you?" Sam growled, his inner panther bubbling beneath the surface as he approached the cell door.

Ruv, still searching for the correct key on the welded ring, asserted, "We've got a little time. The guards are, how you say, indisposed."

Sam sighed. "There's video surveillance, you ninnies."

"Ha! I knew they were cameras!" Gren said with a triumphant smirk.

Mari rolled her eyes at the gloat but kept her attention fixed on their imprisoned friend. "The cameras are disabled for the time being as well," she explained. "Also, we figured you might be wanting these. You'll be at least somewhat less conspicuous." She tossed him a gloomy bundle of clothing.

Suddenly forgiving the delay in his rescue, he praised, "You, my dear, are a saint." Sam gleefully shed his jumpsuit for his preferred black leather and mesh. He slid into the skin-tight clothing with more ease than anyone would have deemed possible had this been the first time they had witnessed him perform such a feat. Yet the life of a sanguine possesses its share of peculiarities, frequent nudity chiefly among them. "Ah, that's much better," he continued. "Though would it have killed you to bring some earrings, too?"

"Those are in the—" Mari started, but the wailing of an alarm and a flood of blinding light interrupted her as the security system sputtered back to life. Outcries in varying degrees of hostility from the rest of the prisoners further assailed their ears, and so instead of finishing her prior statement, Mari released a torrent of curses. "Ruv, can you speed things up? It's safe to say our grace period is over," she shouted over the cacophony. Instinctively her hand moved to the hilt of her sword, although she dreaded the thought of wielding it against another human, especially since that human would merely be doing his job.

And, of course, she knew full well that a sword, enchanted or not, would do her little good against a bullet.

Ruv jiggled another key in the padlock, eschewing comment while he squinted in the sudden brightness. Instead the reply came from Gren. "We should just count ourselves lucky this outdated place still uses real locks," he drawled. The fingers that hovered over the sapphire cabochon in the pommel of his dagger, however, belied his easy tone in an echo of Mari's unease.

"Success!" Ruv proclaimed at last. Mari and Gren hauled open the door while Ruv tossed the keyring around the corner from which they had arrived, safely out of the other prisoners' reach lest they find themselves swarmed by less friendly offenders as well as the inevitable guards.

"Thank the various gods," Sam exhaled as he strode into the hallway. "Let's get the bleeding hell out of here!"

The four raced away from the cellblock, this time turning down the opposite corridor from which they arrived. They sprinted past the auxiliary cells, past the stale kitchens, past a break room reeking of burnt coffee. They did not slow their pace until they reached the emergency exit at the back of the building. Considering the alarms still blared around them and probably at least a few guards— no doubt waking from their enforced slumber with angry headaches—bore witness to their hasty escape, they did not think twice about exploiting the emergency door.

Mari, the first to reach the exit, hurled a shoulder into the metal to no avail. Gren and Ruv joined her for a second rush while Sam kept an eye on the open hallway behind them. At last the hinges gave way. An empty back alley and a wind thick with smog and the threat of rain rewarded their efforts.

When they poured into the dim morning, boots squelching in the muddy street, a petite young woman in a blue raincoat stepped out from behind a rusted dumpster. Strawberry-blonde hair bound in a tight braid framed her heart-shaped face, and rectangular glasses failed to conceal the dusting of freckles sprinkled across her delicate nose. Nor could the lenses conceal the enormous eyes that made her appear perpetually astonished. Her mouth, too small for the rest of her face, broke into a smile.

Mari, Gren, and Ruv were initially surprised that their newest acquaintance, Wendy, had wanted to participate in this particular venture. Like the twins, they met her quite by accident. Unlike the twins, Wendy had never attempted to pick their pockets. Her insistence on joining them had proven invaluable. Indeed, no part of the rescue would have been successful without her generosity.

Shortly after they unbound the twins from Kutkah's service, Mari, Gren, and Ruv returned to Earth. At Sarah and Sam's request, Gren sang them through the traveling circle to Scotland. Since only three circles remained active on Earth and they had only ever used the one in Virginia before, Mari and Gren couldn't be sure where, precisely, the Scotland circle would be located. They only suspected that it would be there based on their prior research of unexplained disappearances. The twins, having never navigated the circles unassisted and having always been rendered blind during the process, could not say for sure where the Scottish circle was either, only that it was there. Kutkah never felt it necessary to share the information, preferring to keep his employees as ignorant as possible.

So when Gren's song deposited them on a highland hilltop where Wendy had been observing the autumn equinox with a solitary picnic, they were as surprised as she. A scientist by trade, Wendy adopted the notion of magic with astonishing immediacy. Magic had confronted her clear as the glass of one of her slides, she argued. She would be a fool to deny it. Instead, she chose to accompany her impromptu wards in hopes of uncovering the science underlying the enchantments.

Mari gave the diminutive woman a quick hug. "Where'd you guys park the van?"

Wendy pulled up the hood of her raincoat and pronounced, "Found a spot just two blocks away." Without further delay she dashed down the alley and onto the sidewalk that skirted the main street as the others followed, their own hoods pulled up to conceal their identities from the closed circuit street cameras. Not that it mattered much if the cameras did capture their faces; they no longer possessed identities to identify in the first place.

On Earth Mari, Gren, and Ruv had long been presumed dead.

As planned, the early hour worked in their favor. Although the tiny jail technically resided within the city limits, they encountered few pedestrians. They hurried from the alleyway to the corner of the next block, where Sarah waited in a dingy but otherwise unremarkable van.

Just as they rounded the corner, the back doors burst open, allowing them to leap straight inside. Sarah embraced her twin for only a second before scrambling into the driver's seat. Mari counted heads one last time as

Gren dragged the back doors shut. With the final headcount complete, Mari nodded to Wendy, who had hopped into the front seat next to Sarah and was watching for just such a signal, and braced herself against the chilly metal. The engine sputtered as Sarah shifted into drive.

"Certainly took you long enough," Sarah remarked, shooting a look of concern over her shoulder before turning her focus to avoiding potholes and changing gears. The traffic was still light as they traversed the side streets, but they knew it would get much worse when they neared the city center no matter what time of day they had chosen to execute the operation. "So what was the hold up in there? I was starting to fear you'd botched the whole thing and I'd have to put together an entirely new crew."

"So we're your crew now, huh?" Gren remarked.

"You know what I meant," Sarah snapped. "And my question stands."

Sam, huddled behind the driver's seat with his knees to his chest, nodded in agreement. "Funny," he recalled, "I asked the same question."

Everyone turned their eyes expectantly to Mari, who was busy rearranging the drape of her coat to cover her sword so that an unsuspecting Londoner would not glimpse a world they were not mentally prepared to encounter. When she finished her adjustments and saw her friends' anxious faces, she explicated, "Once we get out of here, we've got another mission. Laria needs us to go back to Aorea for something."

Gren, crouched opposite her, narrowed his eyes. "Surely she knows we were headed that way anyway, right? We've got to figure out Wendy's totem. Besides, with Ilya gone…" He choked back the rest of his intended statement at a flash of warning in Mari's eyes. The recent loss of her father remained taboo. When she turned her gaze out the window at the gray buildings and grayer skies, Gren felt it safe to proceed. "There isn't much to keep us here anymore."

"Yeah, but she wants us in the Alpines instead of the Birch Forest," Mari clarified, her voice strained but steady. If a wrist happened to dart across her eyes and come back moist, no one acknowledged it. She took a deep breath, and when she continued, she had her emotions firmly under control. "Or Faerie. Or anywhere else, for that matter. She said she'll have someone meet us at the Tipsy Turtle to tell us more."

Ruv, polishing the iron tips of his wooden fighting staff and ergo making no effort to hide it from any curious onlookers whose attention might stray into the back of the van, lit up at the mention of his favorite tavern. He flashed Mari his crooked grin, and her returning grin betrayed that she was all too happy for a change of topic. "Excellent!" Ruv professed. "It's been ages since I've flirted with one of Therese's girls. I do hope Therese himself doesn't remember me, though."

The three women in the van released a collective sigh of annoyance. "You never change," Mari chided.

"Well, we can't *all* have you," Ruv intimated.

Gren's attention snapped from worrying about how Mari was coping with their recently discovered loss to the thinly-veiled challenge in Ruv's lopsided smirk. However, before he could retort, Sam cut in, "Sister dear, how much further to the station?"

"Hard to say now that we've hit the morning rush. If this damnable traffic gets much worse, we may be better off just stashing the van in another alley and walking the rest of the way," she replied. Wendy, nose buried in the GPS app on her phone, quietly directed Sarah to take a left at the next intersection. The back tires skidded on the wet pavement as the vehicle whipped around the bend, bumping against the curb and narrowly avoiding a collision with a lucky signpost.

"Never thought I'd miss Hal's driving," Gren quipped.

"If you think either of you bloody Americans can do better, then one of you take the wheel. You don't even drive on the right side of the road," Sarah hissed through her teeth as she shifted lanes in preparation for another quick turn.

Gren grinned. "Actually, we do drive on the *right* side."

"You know what in the hells I meant!"

"Look, I get it, everyone's adrenaline is running high and everything is a bit tense, but we need to keep it together until we are safely on that train," Mari directed. She peeked out the back window at the retreating roadway and caught sight of blinking blue lights. Pursuit was still several cars back, but it was approaching fast, weaving in between the traffic in a delayed mirror of Sarah's driving. "Crap. I guess word's out. We've already acquired a tail."

Gren, Ruv, and Sam whipped their heads around to share Mari's view. "Bollocks!" Sam exclaimed. "How close are we now?"

Wendy, her nose still buried in her phone's digital map, answered, "Within sprinting distance."

Sarah's eyes flashed to the rearview mirror. She just managed to maneuver the van into the outer lane before careening down the next empty alley. The police car, unable to make the turn in time, sped past. The van had barely skidded to a halt before the occupants exploded from its doors. Mercifully, the alley emptied into another side street, and so the six friends bolted toward it without so much as a backward glance.

While she ran Wendy switched the settings on her app from vehicle to pedestrian, skimmed the recommended route, then tossed her phone in the next trash bin without missing a step. "The station's only about five more blocks. We should make it in no time."

Foot traffic picked up substantially as they neared the entrance to the metro, allowing them to catch their breath as they melted into the morning crowd. They kept their hoods up and weapons covered to the best of their ability, though Ruv's staff garnered a few quizzical looks, as they zigzagged through clumps of people on their way to work.

The faceless throng absorbed them, each person caught in his or her own haste. They became nothing more than anonymous members of the horde, six more strangers in a sea of trench coats. At last, they could relax. The police would find the abandoned van, and by the time they pulled the footage from the closed circuit cameras and figured out where they went, they would be safe in another world.

Well, not exactly safe, perhaps, but they certainly would be inaccessible.

Once they entered the station, Sarah and Sam took the lead, navigating the congested metro with practiced ease. Since they knew their ultimate destination would require them to return to Scotland well before the jailbreak occurred, they had purchased the necessary tickets ahead of time. The black-clad siblings searched the blinking monitors for the right track.

"Let's never do that again," Gren asserted as they boarded their train several minutes later.

Mari squeezed his shoulder. "We won't."

Gren raised a thick, dark eyebrow at her. "You can't know that for sure—unless you're dreaming again?"

She pursed her lips. "No, not yet."

They spread out once aboard. Mari determined that they would be less conspicuous in pairs, so she and Gren chose a spot toward the center of the car while Ruv and Sam staked out the back. Sarah and Wendy remained up front. Originally Sarah had argued with her reasoning, not wanting to be separated from her brother as soon as they reunited. Mari countered that, given the circumstances as well as the twins' particular history, Sarah and Sam would be the most conspicuous pair among them. Mari's subsequent recommendation that the twins should consider highlighting their naturally blue-black hair with less memorable colors than neon magenta and turquoise, however, fell on deaf ears.

Finally, the tracks rumbled, and the train took off, carrying them away from the dismal city.

Mari gazed out the window at the passing countryside. After several minutes, she said to Gren, "Laria sounded really, well, perturbed, I guess, is what I'd call it."

"Yeah?"

She combed her fingers through one of her many mahogany tangles, vainly attempting to put her hair back in some semblance of order after the dash through jail corridors and windy streets. She gave up and transferred her attention to a hangnail. "We obviously didn't have time for her to go into any details," she clarified, "but she sounded almost panicked, and she was clearly trying to hide it from me. She was way too casual. So whatever problem she wants us to look into, I got the sense it's bigger than she's letting on."

"Eh, Laria could just be being Laria, though," he disputed. "You have to admit she tends to be excitable. I mean, there was that whole thing with the dragon."

Mari snorted and poked Gren in the ribs, and he flinched. "To be fair, we were all a little dramatic during that particular event."

"Ok, yeah, but she is still only eighteen, though," he reminded her. "Time hasn't really passed for her and Hal."

"Even so," she said, drawing out her words, "this wasn't her usual tone." She paused to chew on her lip before adding with a grin, "Plus she's had a lot of weight on her shoulders since she became the Spinner. She's probably more mature than us at this point. She's certainly more mature than you."

Gren returned her mocking grin, but his soon gave way to a frown. He removed his coat with the utmost care while simultaneously slipping out of the bow and quiver, then folded the whole bundle across his lap. The rehearsed move allowed the coat to continue concealing the weapons. He stretched, yawned, and asked, "Did you pay attention to any of the news yesterday? Shit is seriously about to go haywire. It almost makes me glad we don't really have a steady home here anymore."

"I've been trying my best to avoid the news," she replied, unbuckling her sword belt and shedding her coat in much the same manner as Gren.

"It's definitely not the world we grew up in," he murmured. He glanced out the window, the movement causing a few strands of dark hair to shine copper in the fluorescent lights. When he turned back to Mari, she was staring blankly out the window past him. "Whenever you're ready to talk about it, you know I'm here."

"I know," she mumbled. "It's just...I should have been there for him. We should have waited another year before we went back."

Gren laced his fingers through hers. "He was the one who urged us to leave. He must—he must have known he was sick, and he didn't want us to see him that way." When Mari made no indication of responding, he added in a whisper, "I'll miss Ilya, too, you know. He was like a second dad to me."

"I know."

"Ruv is also upset about it."

"Can we talk about something else now, please?"

Gren gave her fingers a quick squeeze. "We could talk about the news you haven't been watching."

She rolled her eyes. "Let's try and get some rest. There's nothing we can do about the path Earth is on anyway," Mari contended. "Who would listen to us? We're nobody. Besides, I have the feeling this mission of Laria's will be a long one, so I don't know how many years will have passed by the time we come back to Earth again."

Mari's pale jade eyes met Gren's fathomless brown ones as he chuckled hollowly. "It can't be worse than playing a love song to a love goddess who would much rather be smiting you," he said.

"Oh please, that turned out just fine."

"Says the girl who did *not* have her guitar smashed on a rock," Gren remarked with a quirked eyebrow. "Although I guess we all did have to run from her wrath."

"At least we made some new friends out of the experience," Mari rejoined.

"Only if you define the term 'friend' rather loosely."

"Wendy definitely counts," she asserted. "The twins, in any case, are never boring." Then she cracked her neck and settled down to sleep, resting her head against the warmth of Gren's shoulder. Though, try as they might, sleep would not come for either of them.

The surface of the water rippled and wavered as an image fought its way through the murky depths of a gargantuan basin carved from banded black stone. The necromancer gripped either side of the bowl's rim, drawing the image to the surface through sheer force of will. At last the otherwise mundane water began to boil with the magic coursing through it.

When the surface of the water stilled once more, his desired image formed. Yet, though pleased with his apparent success, the necromancer did not loosen his grip on the scrying bowl. Instead, he concentrated even more deeply. He concentrated until the water showed him every fleck of amber in the liquid marigold of his quarry's eyes, every ebony freckle marring her perfect complexion. He concentrated until he could taste her name on the very wind that had first blown her into his life. He concentrated until reality frayed at the edges and space blurred and bent around him, the water became like a living scene, and the accompanying sounds echoed throughout the chamber.

The necromancer watched, mute, as two evrae maidens, with skin the golden-brown of fresh acorns and hair like black moss, walked hand in hand down a wooded pathway. Both girls were uncommonly tall for their people, although the younger of the two was far from done growing. As much as they shared in appearance—from their bare toes and matching leaf-green dresses up to their prominent cheekbones and the points of their elfin ears—they differed in mannerism. The younger tugged enthusiastically on her sister's hand, practically dragging her along the path as the elder shuffled forward at a sleepwalker's pace. Afternoon light filtered through the tree tops, catching a glint of midnight stone on the elder girl's fingers.

"Come on, Necria!" The younger's words echoed around the necromancer in real time as the water upon which the maidens' images were transposed wavered. He winced against the sharp whine of the young girl's voice and frowned. "We're going to miss it!" she urged, tugging yet harder on her sister's limp hand. "They're only here for one more night and you promised."

"Did I?" Necria asked in a whisper. She glanced down at her third finger where the heavy ring pressed.

Her sister released Necria's hand along with a dramatic sigh. "Ugh, it's like you aren't even here anymore! Last year you promised you'd take me to the festival when they came back and I was old enough and now I am and mother said I could go as long as you stayed with me!"

Shaking her head to clear her clouded thoughts, Necria mused, "Is it the solstice already? Naya, I'm sorry. I remember now."

"Finally!" her sister said as she retook Necria's hand and continued marching along the shaded pathway, black hair streaming behind her. "It's the last day before they leave and they won't be back for a whole year and you promised and now you are walking so very slow and if we miss the dancing I'll never talk to you again!"

Necria smiled fondly at her sister's enthusiasm, and the two girls kept walking, fingers entwined, as the trees began to thin and the wooded pathway opened into a meadow filled with brilliant, silken tents, bonfires, and the steady pounding of drums. But once the maidens approached the outskirts of the festival, the watery image flickered twice before fading entirely.

"Servorg!" the necromancer thundered, turning his back on the disappointing basin. His summons echoed around him from the walls of the hollow chamber. He cursed as he released his stony grip from the scrying bowl's rim. Whatever magic lay dormant in the water, it had been completely drained.

A heavy door scraped open at the far end of the room, and a small, misshapen creature with peeling flesh and empty red eyes materialized at the threshold. "Yes, master?" the goblin croaked.

The necromancer reached into the folds of his cloak and withdrew a handful of ashes. He breathed into his hand, and the ashes ignited in a puff of acrid smoke before evaporating. All that remained was a pile of obsidian shards. "Take these," he commanded. "Have them made into a necklace." He deposited the shards in his minion's waiting hand as he mused, "The ring can't seem to anchor the images well enough. I need more."

"Of course, master," Servorg said as he shuffled away, his right foot dragging from an injury that would not heal.

The dead could be reanimated, but they could never be made whole.

By the time they debarked the train in Glasgow, the morning had nearly ended, and there had been no more signs of pursuit beyond a halfhearted announcement, echoing over the train's intercom, to be wary of escaped prisoners. Sam stoically ignored it. From Glasgow they took a bus to the village nearest Wendy's inherited estate. The bus jolted and jounced for several hours along the winding, uneven roads, bearing them deeper north, and they used the time to catch up on the sleep they had neglected over the past few weeks of preparation.

When the bus at last sputtered to a stop, the six companions dismounted into the Autumn mist. Gren checked the time on his watch and declared, "We've got about three hours still until sunset."

"I vote we head to the pub for a quick drink," Ruv offered. "After all, it's going to be a while before haggis is on the menu again, and I've grown rather fond of it. Reminds me of a similar dish from my youth."

Sam and Sarah exchanged mirrored looks of disgust. "Why does the circle have to be in Scotland?" Sarah whined.

"London is much nicer," Sam agreed, tightening the collar of his leather coat.

"We didn't plant the circles," Mari reminded them, cramming her sword into the trunk of Wendy's car between Gren's bow, Ruv's stave, and the twins' ample collection of knives. "We just use them. And since it takes about an hour to hike up to the circle from the manor, we should probably head straight to the estate, grab our shit, change, and head back out."

Ruv's face fell, but he nodded his assent along with the rest. Thus, without further debate, the group began the last, shortest, and most cramped stretch of their escape. Wendy drove with Gren in the passenger's seat and Mari squeezed between them. In the backseat Ruv and Sarah flanked Sam, who did his best to keep out of sight in case his mugshot had already been plastered throughout the United Kingdom.

"Does it hurt?" Wendy probed after several minutes of silence.

"Does what hurt?" Mari asked.

"Going through the circle," she continued. "What does it feel like?"

Mari furrowed her brow. "It's different for everyone, I think. I mostly experience a lot of pressure, like I'm being squeezed at the bottom of the ocean, and then all of a sudden the pressure lifts and I'm floating, and then I'm just…somewhere else." She stared out the windshield at the gray road stretching before them, bordered by the sporadic gray trunks of windswept trees beneath an even grayer sky. "The first time, I felt a little nauseous, too, and I passed out, but it's gotten easier each time since."

"Different for me," Ruv said with a shrug. "I hardly feel anything, maybe just a slight tingle. Of course, I don't remember my first time going through a circle. I didn't know that's where I was, you see, only that me and my pack needed a place to sleep for the night, and one spot in the Siberian forest was as good as any other. So we went to sleep, and when we woke up, well, we seemed to have moved."

Mari craned her neck to look at him. "I still wonder how that's possible, you know? I mean, it requires a lot of magic to operate the circles, and you can't do it without a Wanderer. You definitely didn't have a Wanderer in your pack to accidentally sing in his sleep."

Ruv cracked a crooked smile. "I don't think we'll ever know. I was asleep on Earth, then I was awake in Aorea." His smile gave way to another shrug. "Maybe someone came along and opened the portal for us. It certainly turned out in our favor, at least. For the good of the pack."

"Doesn't sound so bad," Wendy supposed. "Gren, what's it like for you? I imagine it must be very powerful since you're the one who can actually open them."

He kept his gaze directed out the window while he ran his hand over his face. "Powerful is one word for it," he eventually said. "The song fills me completely, overwhelms my brain until I can think of nothing else but letting the words and the melody flow out of me. As soon as I step into a circle, I start to hear the song calling me. It doesn't even have to be near dusk or dawn. I still hear the music, all the different melodies intertwined, overlapping in endless potential." With his description complete, he leaned back, thick lashes concealing the chocolate of his eyes as his voice faded to silence.

"Your poet is showing," Sarah commented in an ambiguous tone of either derision or grudging respect; no one but Sam could be certain which, and no one desired to ask for clarification.

"How do you know which song is the right one?" Wendy pressed.

After a while, Gren answered, "It's hard to explain. I kinda just know." He shared a glance with Mari before adding, "If I focus on where I want to go, I can pick out one melody that's stronger than the rest, and then I start singing it, and the circle takes it from there."

"So it doesn't hurt," Wendy whispered. "That's good."

Mari reached over and gently clasped the driver's arm. "Don't worry, it's really not that bad. All you have to do is hold on. You excited to find out your totem?"

Wendy blurted, "I'm not sure I'm ready to think about that part just yet. Let's get there first, and then we'll see how much faith I can muster in Ruv's assertion I'm a shifter. Sanguine. Whatever the hell you call it."

Ruv feigned offense at her expressed doubt of his abilities to sniff out those who possess sufficient totem blood to shift between human and animal form, but then his lips broke into yet another lopsided smirk. "I have never been wrong," he bragged.

The rest of the drive passed by without conversation, the only sound the punctuation of the raindrops on the roof and the occasional splash of the tires rolling through a puddle. By the time Wendy pulled the car into the driveway of the estate she inherited from her uncle, the fog and rain had mostly cleared. The six friends hastened out of the overcrowded vehicle and onto the front porch. Wendy unlocked the front door then motioned for the others to enter.

"Are you sure you want to come with us?" Mari asked, lingering on the porch. "I thought we could just make a short trip, but I don't think that's the case anymore. I don't know how long it'll be before we can get you back."

Wendy did not immediately respond. Instead she contemplated the rolling expanse of her late uncle's estate, its emerald grass and hedgerows, once trimmed to perfection, fallen into shaggy disarray. She wondered how long it would remain untenanted after she left, considering she was the last MacEunrig heir. She decided it did not particularly matter. Wendy closed her eyes and sniffed the wind, then nodded. "I've already taken so much time off my dissertation. What's a wee bit more?"

Mari smiled, but it was a sad smile, full of fresh memories of friends and family lost over the decades in what had, for her, been only a few years. "You've still got time to change your mind."

Laria sat before the spinning wheel, translucent filaments flowing across her slender fingers like unfinished spider silk, winding around the spindle in a gossamer blur as the wheel spun on and on. The turn of the wheel, its monotony, its steady whirr, drew her into a meditative state that allowed her thoughts to float about her as if they were visible entities. A litany of problems, solutions, more problems, the unknown, all spiraled through the air around her head in an echo of the filaments she spun into thread, her thoughts a tangled reflection of the uncooperative Loom. She contemplated the vastness of the task she was about to lay before her friends, and she hoped that whatever they found within the shadow blocking her sight was something small. Something concrete. A glitch, nothing more.

But hoping and knowing are two separate things, and Laria knew better.

A rap at the door snatched her consciousness back from reverie. She slowed the wheel to a stop and gathered the newly finished threads. Hal entered in response to her silence. "How goes the spinning?" he asked.

Laria coiled the last bit around the spindle, saying, "This latest batch is ready. Maybe new threads will help."

"Awesome," he decreed, but the trace of a line between his brows contradicted the conviction of his tone. "Did you have any luck earlier?"

Nibbling her bottom lip, Laria replied, "Same as before. The whole western coastline is shrouded." She turned her gaze to the window to observe the niethera milling about the fields and gardens. She kept her eyes on the window as she continued, "If anything, my blind spot may be growing. This morning it looked like the hidden area might be slightly larger than yesterday."

"Well, you've sent Micaleth—"

"He sent himself, to be honest," Laria interrupted him. "I could have communicated everything directly to Mari and Gren myself."

"I know, but—"

"But I suppose I have been rather busy lately, between the Loom and the spinning and entertaining Nemini every time she gets 'lost' and lands her mortar and pestle in the middle of the garden. Plus, Micaleth was, well, bored," she finally finished. She glanced back at Hal, a formidable presence with his piercing cobalt eyes and golden curls that nearly brushed the ceiling.

"But now *I'm* bored!" he complained. To emphasize his state of agitation, his fingers twitched over the hilt of the onyx-studded sword he bore at all times regardless of the security provided by the sanctuary's unbreakable walls. "None of the other niethera will spar with me!"

Laria rose from her stool, a faint smile playing across her lips. "Nothing's keeping you here, you know." She stretched her hands to Hal, and he took them in his own. The twitching fingers stilled. "You could have gone with them as well," she added. "I know you've been itching for another adventure. Mari could use another friendly face right now anyway."

He drew her closer, crushing her in a fierce embrace before she could so much as utter a protest. "She has Gren and Ruv. They'll take care of her. And as much fun as I'm sure another adventure would be, it's not an option. You stay, I stay," he breathed into her hair.

Her reply was muffled. "So you've said, but—"

"You stay, I stay," he repeated.

"You sure?" she asked as she pried her cheek away from his warmth. "You barely know me, even now."

"I know your spirit, your heart. I'll learn the rest of you as time goes on," he replied with a warm smile. The line between his brows had faded. "Besides, we have a thousand years to do just that."

"You're going to get sick of me long before that time is up," Laria warned. "I'm not nearly as interesting as you think I am."

"I could never get sick of you."

Laria chuckled and shoved him away. "Quit being so dramatically sweet and go make yourself useful. Chop some wood or something."

"For what? We don't have a fireplace."

"Then build one!"

Hal grinned. "See? You already know me so well."

At the crest of the hilltop overlooking Wendy's estate, their backs burdened with camping gear, weapons, and extra clothes, the six friends waited just beyond the perimeter of stone monoliths for the sun to finish its daily descent. Everyone had traded the jeans and coats that allowed them to blend into the city crowd for clothing more appropriate for long days of hiking through one forest or another in unknown weather without the luxury of a washing machine.

Everyone except the twins, of course.

Sam and Sarah had stubbornly maintained their coordinated aesthetic, and so they still sported leather and mesh in a midnight monochrome, broken only by the occasional pop of neon. Their plethora of knives remained stowed in assorted locations, some of which the rest preferred not to know. Sarah had even gone so far as to pack a bottle of black nail polish and a tube of blood-red lipstick, arguing that it was her pack to fill with what supplies she saw fit, and if Mari would mind her own damn business, then everything would be just peachy.

Abandoning the gauze dress shredded by her previous journey to Aorea, Mari opted for sturdier layers for her third trip. She wore a tan suede vest laced over a green tunic, leather leggings in a dark chestnut wash (Sarah had actually helped her find those, but then lamented when Mari chose brown instead of the superior black), and waterproofed suede boots. Since it was no longer necessary to conceal her ostentatious weaponry, she now strapped her sword belt around the outside of a wool coat so the blade would remain visible as well as accessible; the accompanying knife buckled around her thigh, however, remained hidden under her tunic.

Gren, largely at Mari's incessant urging, had finally exchanged his loose jeans and t-shirt for a pair of slate gray cargo pants, hefty hiking boots, and a knitted sweater that matched the sapphire star suspended from his throat. Like Mari, he had moved his weapons to the outside of his coat for easy access, the quiver and bow slung across his torso and another knife strapped to his thigh.

Ruv, after raiding Wendy's uncle's closet, sported a buttoned shirt in the same shade of gray as the present sky along with a tweed vest, jacket, and thick linen pants he kept tucked into his boots. Wendy herself, unable to find any clothes of such resilient materials in her size, had opted for muted athletic wear and running shoes. The children's section had been a bust.

They eyed the stones, glittering in the fading sunlight, with interest and expectation. No matter how simple the construction of the traveling circles appeared to be from the outside, the power inside was palpable. The gargantuan slabs of gray stone formed the outermost perimeter of a series of concentric circles. Within the stones hid a ring of fae mushrooms, all white and pink and spotted; then an inner circle of soft, spongy moss; and finally, at the heart of the traveling circle itself, an ancient rowan tree, twisted branches ever reaching toward the sky. Even from outside the stone boundary, they could feel the magic pulsate.

Voice pitched to a reverent whisper, Gren asked Mari, "So you're absolutely sure she wants us in the Alpines?"

Mari, whose sense of the magic was present but muted in comparison, voiced her response at her normal volume: "Laria was quite clear about that, yeah."

Ruv tugged at the day-old scruff on his chin, saying, "There should be a cabin near there that the pack uses sometimes. We can bed down for the night in comfort. I know they would not mind if we use it." After a pause, he added, "That is, if the boys are not there themselves. It would be a tight fit for us plus another twelve men, but I am sure they would welcome the reunion."

"Potentially sleeping on top a wolf pack still beats sleeping on the ground," Gren offered.

Ruv opened his mouth to offer an additional suggestion, but before he could utter so much as a syllable, Sarah cleared her throat. "I hate to interrupt all the chatter," she said, although her facial expression betrayed the fact that she really did not hate interrupting much at all, "but we are wanted persons, you know. We may want to get going while the going is to be got."

Mari rolled her eyes and began a retort, but it was Gren who, adopting the pedantic tone he always acquired when explaining such things, replied, "We still need a few more minutes. I have to finish the song right at sunset. The rules for Earth-to-Aorea travel are picky, as I'm sure you remember, and we're a little too far past the equinox for me to just rely on that to thin the veils."

"All the same, may as well get ready," Sarah quipped.

"A pack should only have one alpha," Ruv observed, looking pointedly at Mari.

"It's ok, Sarah's right," she interposed. "It's time."

Gren inhaled deeply and closed his eyes, bracing against the onslaught of magic and music he knew would rip through his brain as soon as he stepped across the stone perimeter. He was the last to enter. The others followed Mari, meeting at the center and forming a circle of their own around the battered rowan tree. Mari and Ruv stood to either side of Gren, while Wendy and the twins completed the ring. Lacing his fingers through Mari's and gripping tight, he breathed, "Now."

The wind, sensing the magic about to take place, began to rise. Wendy shuddered, her fingers trembling in Mari's. "I'm st-starting to get nervous, now that it's really happening," she stammered.

"This is your last chance to back out," Mari said softly.

Wendy shook her head in response. "I'm going."

Then Gren began to sing, and the solid world fell away.

Through the mists of space and time,
The changing fabric of violet light,
Into the snow, into wind and ice,
Among the everlasting pines.

Gren's song continued as the cold wind kept rising, surrounding them in a cascade of brittle leaves and dry autumn moss. The circle engulfed them in a blur of cold and sound, symphonic synchronicity and shifting space-time. They felt the pressure of the worlds compressing them, and yet all the while, Gren's voice rang true.

Bring us where our journey begins.
Bear us through the howling winds,
Into the snow, beyond winter's eyes;
Bring us to the everlasting pines.

As he began the third and final stanza, the raging wind vanished. The only sound the humans could perceive was

Gren's melodic baritone. The sun finally dipped below the skyline, surrounding them in utter darkness.

> *Through the mists of time and space,*
> *Through dark nights and darker days,*
> *Into the snow, into wind and ice;*
> *Bring us to the everlasting pines.*

On Gren's final note, the silence shattered, and the ensuing darkness plucked them from the earth.

CHAPTER TWO
That disreputable pair of sanguines

Wendy regained consciousness amid a howling maelstrom of frigid winds and frozen pine needles, and then promptly wished she had remained asleep. Mari, Gren, and Ruv huddled around her, their expressions anxious, as she struggled to sit upright. She could not at first see Sarah or Sam, but then deduced that the two dark masses shivering to her left were likely them. Half submersed in snow and shivering herself, Wendy finally squeaked, "Well, this is certainly bracing. How far away did you say that cabin was?"

Mari and Gren relaxed as she spoke, and Ruv's face broke into a grin. "Not too far," he shouted back. "A few kilometers."

Reaching out a hand to help Wendy to her feet while simultaneously addressing the others, Mari remarked, "We've got to figure out how to time these things better."

"Don't look at me," Gren said. "I'm just the song guy. I couldn't know we'd end up in a midwinter blizzard. It was still fall on Earth. Although I suppose the lyrics this time should have probably given me a hint."

Mari opened her mouth to retort, but Sarah cut her off, growling, "Now that the little one's awake, can we just get moving? It's bloody cold, and I can barely hear myself think over this damnable wind."

Wendy assured the others that she was sufficiently recovered to walk on her own, and so they promptly began the trek from the exposed clearing that formed the traveling circle into the relative shelter of the surrounding evergreens. Ruv led the way, cutting a cautious trail through the knee-high snow. He paused every few minutes to give the wind a thoughtful sniff and study scratches on the bark that no one else could see. While the rest of the group could not discern any difference between one storm-beaten pine tree and the next, they trusted Ruv's memory and tracking skills to locate the cabin he assured them really did exist somewhere in the woods.

After one such pause, Ruv announced that they were nearly there and should arrive within ten minutes. "Well, assuming the cabin didn't move, that is," he added.

Strangely enough, no one laughed.

When they finally reached the cabin, they were too relieved to get out of the wind to complain that Ruv's designation of "cabin" may have been rather generous. With no windows to speak of and only one entrance, the squarish building crafted from interlocked tree trunks, many of which still bore shreds of bark, resembled more of a small barn. Regardless, they gratefully scuttled through the singular door.

Once they had shaken off the worst of the accumulated snow and ice, they inspected the interior. However low their expectations had been from the outside view, they were pleased to find the hut well-sealed and insulated with a rough-hewn cabinet in one corner and a primitive hearth, complete with chimney, nestled in the far wall. Ruv picked the lock on the cabinet and perused its limited contents: a sack of rice, some rotten tubers, and a small pouch of Aorean currency. He picked hastily through the coins, then stashed the pouch in his pack, assuring the others that his former packmates really would not mind, and they could always repay them next time they found each other. Meanwhile Gren and the twins, having lost a quick round of rock-paper-scissors, braved the cold once more to gather wood as Mari and Wendy unpacked their nightly supplies. After the fire at last achieved a steady blaze, Ruv set some snow to melt and boil.

No sooner had they settled around the crackling hearth, lounging on piles of blankets and travel pillows with their boots set out to dry, than Sam shot to his feet and raked his fingers through his artfully tousled hair. The disturbed turquoise highlights shimmered green in the light of the fire. "I'm going to hunt," he growled.

"In this weather? Are you crazy?" Mari exclaimed.

He waved a hand dismissively in her direction. "I'm feeling a bit restless, is all. It's been too long since I've unleashed my panther. Besides, I'll be warmer in fur."

Sarah arched a brow at her brother, studying his face. "Do you want any company?" she inquired, her voice far softer than anyone was accustomed to hearing.

"I'd rather go alone."

She narrowed her eyes at him, but nevertheless nodded her acquiescence.

Ebony fur sprouted from Sam's limbs almost faster than he could shed his clothes. By the time he reached the door, he had completely transformed, his discarded clothing scattered behind him like overgrown lumps of velvet coal. A bone-chilling blast tore through the cabin as he melded into the shadows.

Mari regarded Sarah for a few moments, but Sarah pointedly ignored the attention, her dark eyes focused on the hearth. Eventually, Mari asked, "Is Sam ok? I've never seen you two part willingly before."

"Even twins need time alone with their thoughts," she replied, her voice level. Her only outward indication of disquiet was her incessant worrying at a hangnail.

"I suppose he has had a rough few weeks," Gren conceded with a shrug.

Sarah finally drug her eyes away from the fire; they pierced through Gren's as she stated, "Believe me, he's survived rougher."

Despite the others' prompting, Sarah refused to elaborate, and so they sat in silence until the tea kettle whistled. Ruv roused himself from his blanketed nest to pour the boiling water into a brewing pot. He gave the rice a stir while he was up and announced that it still needed a bit longer to cook.

When he had resumed his seat, Wendy asked him, "So, how'd you come by this cabin?"

"Built it," Ruv replied. "Back in my pack days, before the Old Farmer's curse forced us to live only in our wolfskins, we'd wander around a lot, learning what we could about the land we'd stumbled into, and moreover, learning what we were and how we came to be sanguines. As a species, I mean. Anyway, in our wanderings, we made sure we had a safe house in every corner of the woods for whenever we needed to lay low for a bit, or just whenever we got tired of running on four paws all the time." He waggled his fingers in front of him, inspecting with particular glee his opposable thumbs. "This was our favorite one due to its proximity to our favorite tavern."

Mari chuckled. "The trail y'all leave, I can't imagine they still let you in."

Ruv winked at her, the corner of his mouth quirked in amusement. "You know how it is. No one can resist my charm for long." Arching his back in a languid stretch, he added, "Ah, it's good to be back in Aorea! No more struggling with English."

Wendy's already large eyes widened behind her lenses, making her youthful face look even younger. She pushed her glasses, dislodged by the sudden excitement, back into position. "But you're speaking it right now!" she cried. However, as her eyes returned to their normal size, she speculated, "Although you don't have an accent anymore. Come to think of it, you actually sound a bit like a Scot to me. I thought you were just mimicking my own speech."

Ruv smiled back at her and stated, "And to me, you all sound like you're speaking Serviko Romani."

Gren turned to Wendy and clarified, "Er, it's a little complicated, but basically none of us are speaking what we think we're speaking. We're all using the Old Tongue." At Wendy's sustained look of confusion, he continued, "If you just talk without thinking about it, like without trying to use one specific language or another, you can pretty much communicate with anyone in Aorea. I don't totally understand how it works, but that's how it was explained to me when we were here the first time. It's probably the most convenient thing about this place."

"That and the ability to just hop in a mushroom circle and teleport to a completely different part of the world," Mari added.

"Only if you have a Wanderer present," Gren corrected with an exaggerated bow.

Witnessing Wendy's still lingering bewilderment, Ruv returned to the original thread of their conversation. "You expect Mari and Gren to sound like Americans," he explained, "so they do. You expect Sam and Sarah to sound like Brits, so they do. But me? You hear me as one of your own, because I am no longer trying to communicate in a language foreign to me. When I first met Mari and Gren, low these many years ago—"

"Two," Mari cut in. "It's been a whopping two years."

"—they heard me as one of their own, too. It was only once we returned to Earth that I started to learn English."

"What I think Ruv is trying to say," Gren elucidated, "is that no matter what language we were raised with, when we're in Aorea, we are all native speakers of the Old Tongue. Something like that."

Digging through her bag for her notebook so she could jot down the newly acquired information, Wendy pronounced, "Simply fascinating." Having finally located the notebook, she then devoted her efforts to frantically searching for a pen. As she did so, she queried, "Now does this apply to written language, too?"

Gren's face fell. "I wish. Script is different, for some reason. I have some theories about it, but I don't want to bore everyone else. We can talk about it later."

Mari giggled until she caught sight of the solemn Sarah, who had remained silent since her brother's abrupt departure. Sobering, she asked, "Now that we've broken your brother out of jail and made it to safety, more or less, would you mind finally sharing the story of how he got there in the first place?"

"Oh, you know. The usual."

"Come on!" Gren scoffed, dark brows even broodier than normal. "The whole time we were planning you wouldn't tell us a thing. Well, beyond that it wasn't for murder. You gotta at least give us more than that."

"Ugh, fine," she relented. "As you know, we worked for Kutkah for quite a while."

"That's that trickster fellow you told me about, yeah? The raven god?" Wendy interjected.

Sarah nodded, adopting the mask of the storyteller as she opened her tale. "That's the one. Well, not everything we stole at his command made its way to his cave in Faerie," she continued. "Some things got, as you might say, relocated. And some items of power that once belonged to other lanti remained on Earth. We hid what we thought we could get away with, but over the years someone must have found our stash and divvied everything up to a bunch of history museums and colleges and archeological groups." She spat on the floor by her feet. "Rotten bastards."

Mari bowed her torso over her legs in a languid stretch. After she resumed her former position, she commented, "I see your overwhelming respect for institutions of learning hasn't changed."

"Need I remind you," Sarah retorted, "I'm higher educated than either you or that brainiac boyfriend of yours." When Mari and Gren shot her looks of equal parts irritation and disbelief, she amended, "Albeit barely. At least we finished high school. Eventually. Anyway, since we are no longer in Kutkah's employ, we thought it might be time to return the items in our private collection to their original owners." Sarah allowed herself a predatory smile. "For a fee, of course."

"If they're not actively in your possession, I'm curious how you think they're yours to redistribute," Gren interposed, suppressing an answering grin.

Sarah waved a manicured hand in an echo of her brother's earlier dismissal. "Completely irrelevant. In any case, we got them back soon enough. And more importantly, the Ianti will pay quite a price to have their artifacts returned, don't you think? We managed to round up almost everything in the first few days, but there was one that gave us some trouble." She reached into one of her many hidden pockets and withdrew a pendant the size of her palm, carved from blue lapis into the distinct shape of a scarab beetle, all set in gold with eyes of faceted topaz. "Worth it, though," she whispered. "One of Svarog's amulets. Said to hold all the power of the sun itself." She turned the pendant over in her hand, the jewels sparkling in the firelight, before passing it to Mari. "Well, maybe once. Just a necklace these days, but still awful pretty."

"I agree with you on that last point, at least," Mari breathed, admiring the handiwork. "Where'd you track this down to?"

"Egyptian display in the Museum of London," she said with a slight scowl hardening her angular features. "When we came back after visiting hours to reacquire the amulet for its original owner, well, I made it out, but Sam didn't. You know the rest of the story from there."

"I can't believe you went to all that trouble just for some jewelry," Gren remarked.

Sarah snickered. "It's not the jewel itself, love. It's the eventual payoff."

While they waited for Sam to come back, Ruv regaled them with stories of his past adventures in Po, the town that hosted the Tipsy Turtle. As the nearest settlement to the Alpine traveling circle, Po also sported one of the largest trading markets in northern Nomansland as well as plenty of accommodations for travelers. Likewise, Ruv assured them, that meant the local townsfolk were used to entertaining people of all races, even the occasional human. At Gren's raised eyebrow, Ruv amended, "Well, at least as used to humans as anyone in Aorea can be."

They had polished off the majority of the rice (though Gren took some convincing that "you snooze, you lose" was not a sufficient argument to eat the final serving when someone was presumably hunting for the good of the group) and were halfway through a second pot of tea when another icy blast of air announced Sam's return. He dumped a young buck on the cabin floor, cracked his neck to either side, and rapidly re-clothed himself. Ruv and Gren lugged the carcass to a far corner of the cabin to begin the lengthy and messy process of dressing the still-warm meat. It was apparent from the massive chunks missing from one of the deer's back haunches that Sam had consumed his portion before he shifted back to his human form.

Retrieving his dagger from the sheath at his thigh, Gren said, "I'm impressed you managed to find anything worth eating in this mess."

Sam ignored the comment and collapsed next to the fire. "Any tea left?" he queried as he wiped a stray drop of blood from the corner of his mouth.

Wendy poured him a mug while Sarah scooped up the remaining rice, kept hot in the embers at the edge of the hearth, and thrust it toward her brother. "Better yet, we saved you a bowl," she said. "You'll need carbs as well as protein."

Sam downed the steaming liquid in a single gulp, tasting nothing but its heat. He shoveled the rice into his mouth, and then promptly hid his head beneath the blankets. Within seconds he was snoring. Wendy and Sarah joined him in slumber shortly thereafter, Sarah settling back to back with her brother and Wendy scooting closer to the hearth. Ruv and Gren continued sawing at the deer carcass, adding new stains amid the old ones splattered across the floor. Mari, not wanting to sleep while her friends remained busy, intended to keep watch over the fire until they had finished stripping the deer down to the bones. However, before long she, too, had succumbed to Morpheus's somnolent spell.

As he pierced the last piece of meat on the spit, Gren whispered to Ruv, "Do you think we should set a guard, or is this section of the woods pretty empty?"

Ruv eyed the door thoughtfully. "I don't think a guard is necessary. We are likely the most dangerous predators in the Alpines tonight. Who in their right mind would bother a cabin full of wolves, panthers, a tiger, and whatever the hell Wendy's totem is? And to the casual observer, that's precisely what we smell like."

Gren snorted in disbelief. "I still don't know how you do that," he said. "All I can smell is the meat."

Chuckling softly as he laid down, Ruv remarked, "You are the Wanderer, Mari is the Dreamer, and I, apparently, am the Nose."

"Gogol would be proud."

The full moon hovered just above the western mountain range. Necria leaned out the open window and stared at it, remote, cold, a reminder of winter on a midsummer's night. The wind carried to her the scents of the first harvest, of peaches and cider, of all the fruits her family and neighbors had labored to grow throughout the previous months and all the fruits that had yet to ripen. She closed her eyes and smiled.

Her angel was coming. Her demon.

A breath of bittersweet incense cut through the fragrant wind, announcing his presence, but she continued staring out the window. She felt the familiar hands, cooling as ever, wrap around her waist. "I've brought you something," the necromancer whispered. "Two things, actually." He withdrew the necklace from a fold in his robes and fastened it around her throat.

"You always bring me gifts, yet I have nothing to give you in return." She twisted around in his grasp so she could face him, her eyes still full of the moon.

He then conjured a long, thin box from the air. "You give me more than you will ever know."

"What is it?" she asked, clutching the box to her chest but unwilling to open it just yet.

"Something nearly as rare as you," he replied. "I brought it from my homeland."

"You went home? I wonder if I could ever visit."

His gaze passed through her and settled in the distance on something she could not see. "I can't go back. I can only bring things over."

"My poor angel," she breathed. "Why can't you go home?"

"It doesn't matter." He glided to the bed, drawing her behind him. He gestured for her to open the box. "I was able, at least, to acquire this for you."

Necria untied the ribbon securing the lid. Her fingers explored the contents, feeling soft petals, leaves, a stem. She pricked a finger on a thorn. She could feel the blood beading on her skin, but gave it no mind. Instead, she brought the flower to her nose. The petals grazed her lips and left a numbness behind. The numbness spread, but after a moment it faded. She gasped. "This scent, it's so unique," she murmured. "I've never smelled anything quite so sweet, like sugar and honey and…and something else, something I can't name." She turned the bloom over in her hands, cautious lest she touch another thorn. "I can't wait to see it by the light of day. I'm sure it's beautiful."

"As I said, it's rare," he reminded her, moving the empty box aside so he could sit next to her. "This particular flower blooms only for an hour, only at midnight, and only once in a century."

"And then?"

"You already know the answer to that."

"So I'll never get to see it."

"Perhaps you will," he said. "I've picked up a new trick." He held his left palm before him, arced his right in a circle, and brought them together as if presenting a chalice. In his cupped palms flashed a spark of lavender. The spark grew into a flame, expanding, illuminating the flower as well as his face.

The flower forgotten, Necria studied the man she had only ever glimpsed by the light of moon or stars. Shadowed eyes, drops of ink suspended in ice, returned her study. His skin was white as bone; his bones, sharp as obsidian. All harsh angles and deep hollows that may as well have been carved from marble, he reminded her of a bleached deer skull she once tripped over during one of her midnight forest strolls in search of remnants she could transform into art. Yet, the one thought drowning out all others was that he was beautiful. "I knew you were an angel," she said at last. "Bringing lilies from another world. Creating fire from nothing."

"Not so," he said with a rueful smile. "But power, yes, that I have. Enough, at least."

At length, she tore her gaze from his and inspected the flower. Five silken petals, their amethyst tips descending to an ebony base, surrounded a single stamen. "I know about the power," she said. "After all, you keep visiting me. Secretly. Coming and going on the silent wind."

The flame in his palm flickered and dwindled to nothing. "One day you shall understand." He rose, gathering his cloaks around him to leave, but Necria clutched the fabric before he could fade from her grasp.

"You hold flames in your hands, but bear no burns," she pronounced, offering him the blossom. "Can you make its blooming last?"

"Maybe," he replied softly. "I will try." As his fingertips passed over the flower, a soft glow in the same shade as the snuffed flame followed, encasing the flower in light. When the light faded, the flower had turned to glass. His hand shifted to Necria, fingers brushing down the curve of her cheek just as they had brushed the thorny stem but a moment prior. "Is there anything else you wish?"

She closed her eyes and nodded. "You haven't told me what the flower's called," she urged. "If you still won't tell me your own name, at least tell me that."

"*Sife darahnthin*," he whispered.

She repeated the phrase, then asked, "What's it mean?"

He bent to press his lips against her forehead. "The necromancer's kiss."

In the next breath, he was gone.

Necria returned to the window. "My angel," she mumbled. "My demon." Despite the humid summer air, she shivered. "You're beautiful, but cold. Like a winter river. Like an avalanche. I wonder what destruction will follow in your wake?"

The indifferent moon gave her no answer.

Despite being the last to crawl in bed the night before, Ruv was the first to rise. He stoked the fire, which had died down during the few hours he actually slept, back to life. Sarah and Sam each popped an eye open at the movement but decided that waking fully could wait at least a few more minutes.

When the entirety of the group at last rose to the mingled scents of smoking venison and strong, black tea,

Mari announced that she was going to ask Laria through their fatestone link for additional details about the upcoming mission. Gren nodded, only half listening, and resumed perusing the unfinished book of songs he brought with him, a pen in one hand and a mug in the other. After Mari stepped outside the cabin, Ruv took the opportunity to give Wendy a few final pointers on the art of Sanguina before she would attempt her very first shift. "Like I told you a hundred times on Earth," he reminded her, "it is possible to shift without knowing the form you're going to take. But there's a drawback. You can't use my little rhyming chant to help you focus."

"None of you use a chant," she disputed around a mouthful of granola. She washed it down with a swallow of tea, staring defiantly back at Ruv's amused appraisal.

"That's because we have years of practice without it. Mari and Gren both used it when I first taught them."

Sarah paused between delicate sips to interject, "Sam and I learned how to shift without any kind of silly chant, so it's perfectly possible to do so."

"That said," her brother revised, his cautious look to his sister evidence of his discomfort at disagreeing with her, "we also knew the form our first shift was going to take since Kutkah told us, plus he walked us through the basics, too."

Wendy twitched her nose. "Ok. I think…I think I am going to want some privacy for this."

Ruv, his normally hazel eyes glinting gold in the firelight, said, "Then go off a bit into the woods and just do exactly what I told you to do."

Sarah drained her teacup, reached for a granola bar, and blew a kiss in Wendy's direction. "And scream if you feel threatened, darling."

Turning wide eyes toward Ruv, Wendy accused, "You never said it was dangerous here."

He rubbed the crooked bridge of his nose. At length, he replied, "No more dangerous than any other forest."

Mari returned from what her stony expression revealed had been a less than successful chat with Laria and caught the tail end of the conversation. All the same, her friendly tone exuded relaxed confidence. "You'll be fine," she assured Wendy. "Just go far enough away that you feel comfortable, but stay close enough that you feel safe."

"I take it Laria wasn't particularly forthcoming," Gren observed, stowing away his songbook.

"She won't tell me anything useful," Mari admitted with just the barest frown. "All she keeps saying is that her 'contact' will meet us at the Tipsy Turtle with the details, sometime in the vague future. She won't even give me an estimated timeline or tell me who this mysterious messenger of hers is."

"That sucks," Gren agreed. "I wonder what's with her lately? Maybe we could ask Hal, but then he'd just tell her about it. Ah, well. We'll find out soon, I guess."

After taking a deep breath to fortify herself for the coming experiment, Wendy headed toward the cabin door. However, she stopped just shy of the threshold, turned, and asked Mari, "Actually, would you mind coming with me? I don't think I want to be alone after all."

Mari surveyed the cabin. Ruv idly poked the fire with a stick, Gren was fiddling with one of his blue feathered arrows, and the twins lounged by the hearth drinking more tea. "We've still got a while before the venison is done smoking, and it doesn't look like I'm needed here right now anyway. Let's go."

After close to two hours of watching her friend's unsuccessful attempts to shapeshift into an as yet unknown totem form, Mari's encouraging platitudes had run dry. Even though the overall weather had greatly improved since the prior evening, the air remained frigid, and the snow had risen to mid-thigh during the night, so they had to clear a space before they could even begin. Reminding herself that she was dealing with a scientist, Mari decided to try a more practical approach. "Think of the cold as further incentive to make the shift quick. Then you'll have fur to keep you warm," she suggested.

"Or scales," Wendy rejoined, teeth chattering. Her eyes drifted to the pine tree right in front of her, and she reached out a hand to brush the rough bark. "I could shift into a big green crocodile for all we know."

Mari snorted a laugh. "I somehow doubt that. Odds are good you'll have fur."

"I suppose there's only one way to find out," Wendy grumbled. She closed her eyes and concentrated, following Ruv's directions to the best of her ability. She turned her thoughts inward and searched for the animal form buried within her soul. Yet she knew the tingling in her limbs was not the stirrings of magic (she had felt the difference clearly when Gren sang open the traveling circle), but rather the prickle of impending frostbite. Likewise, she knew the heat inside her chest was not indicative of an imminent transformation, but rather the mundane fire of mounting frustration.

"You can do this," Mari urged softly. "Gren is the stubbornest guy I know, and even he figured it out."

Wendy stomped one of her bare feet against the hard, frozen ground. Her skin was an alarming shade of red against the pristine snow. "It's still not working! Nothing I do is working," she lamented. In the first bit of true anger Mari had witnessed from her newest friend, Wendy punched the nearest tree trunk.

"Just trust in the magic and let your other form out," Mari advised, staring longingly in the direction where Ruv's log cabin awaited them. She shook herself and shifted her focus back to Wendy. "That's all it is. Your totem animal is already inside you. When you shift, you're just letting it roam free."

Rubbing her knuckles where the tree had done more damage to her than she had done to it, the small woman scowled. As she gathered her thoughts to turn them inward once more, she felt not even the barest breath of magic. "To hell with it," she muttered. "I'll try later. We're at the point of diminishing returns anyway." She donned her clothing as quickly as her trembling fingers would allow, and the two women trudged back through the snow.

After they arrived at the cabin, they found Sam the only one awake, lounging against his pack with his feet stretched close to the hearth. Peeling off her coat and boots, Mari asserted, "Try and get some sleep if you can. I'll keep watch over the fire."

"No arguments there," Sam said before he stretched, yawned, and settled next to his sister.

"If you don't mind," Wendy cut in before Mari could situate herself by the fire, "I'd actually like to take the watch. I'm too angry right now to sleep anyway."

Mari nodded as she curled up between Gren and Ruv and tugged the blankets over her face.

They departed the cabin in the early afternoon and reached the perimeter of Po shortly before sunset. They could see the multicolored lights lining the streets before they left the forest, flickering between the evergreens. The twinkle of gold and purple and red made a welcome sight.

Whereas the cabin had not quite lived up to Ruv's description, Po far exceeded anyone's expectations, except, of course, for Ruv, who had once been a frequent visitor to the town. Numerous buildings, some crafted of wood and others of stone, flanked each cobblestone street, and open-air markets with stalls already shuttered for the evening surrounded the central square. The town projected a warm, inviting atmosphere even though the streets and alleys stood empty, a state they concluded likely had something to do with the encroaching cold that clutched them ever more closely as the daylight died.

Nevertheless, Ruv delighted in escorting the group around the town, showing them the inn where he and his pack used to sleep during frostier nights, the massive fir tree at the heart of the square around which the residents danced during their summer festivals, the temple where they left offerings for their ancestors, and finally, the infamous tavern that featured so prominently in many of Ruv's more unbelievable tales.

With the tour complete, Ruv split his borrowed coins with Mari before heading to the inn to haggle for their rooms while the rest hurried back to the tavern.

All eyes locked upon the five humans as soon as the tavern door creaked open. In stark contrast with the streets outside, the Tipsy Turtle was a far cry from empty. Mari and Gren, who had only ever met one evrae on their first journey to Aorea, noted that many of Jack the Witchazel Wizard's features seemed to be common to the rest of his race: pointed ears, skin like polished oak, hair somewhere between pine bark and ebony, and eyes in varying shades from gold to chestnut. Jack's penchant for robes of bright orange silk, however, appeared to be unique. Instead, the tavern patrons all wore subdued furs and suede with the occasional knitted wool peeking out from a cloak.

Sam and Sarah, who had traveled between Earth and Aorea more than anyone else in their group, appeared as apathetic as ever. Wendy, having never before encountered a humanoid people who were not, in actuality, human, but at least having been warned ahead of time that Aorea was home to all manner of such beings, tried her best not to stare. By all accounts she did an admirable job.

Thankfully, the novelty of their arrival wore off before long, and the tavern's occupants resumed their previous activities, which mostly amounted to drinking, eating, and chatting with their immediate neighbors. Several tables hosted a game of ceramic tiles that, Sam observed after a few covert glances, bore a remarkable resemblance to mahjong. Most of the tavern's seats were already claimed, but a few tables along the edges, where the light from the chandeliers did not reach as well, were still available. Mari inclined her head in the direction of one such table, and Wendy and the twins took the cue while Mari and Gren approached the bar.

The grizzled barkeeper lifted his head for only a second to squint at the pair before returning his concentration to the tankard and towel in his hands. "You lot best not be any of the Old Farmer's escaped workers. I've had enough headaches on their account," he grunted.

"We're not," Mari promised, extending her hand. "Maraka Rojko. Or just Mari. Whichever you prefer. It's a pleasure to meet you."

"Hmph." The barkeeper glanced at her outstretched hand, but when he made no move to take the offered handshake, Mari put it down. "Well," he said, regarding his newest patrons, "I'm inclined to believe you're not farm hands. You don't look the type. Far too clean." After he set the tankard on a shelf behind him, he leaned over the bar to study their faces more closely. "You don't happen to be sanguines, do you? Had some trouble with a wolf pack a few years ago, too." Without waiting for their reply, he tossed them a pair of menus.

"We are sanguines, yes, but I can assure you I am the only wolf currently in your establishment," Mari stated carefully. She hoped Ruv would slip into the tavern unrecognized once he joined them.

The barkeeper, realizing belatedly that neither Mari nor Gren could decipher the script running across the menus, recited his collection of wines, meads, ciders, brews, and naturally, the spiced mulsuma for which the evrae were renowned throughout Aorea. He then described a list of stews prepared from increasingly unfamiliar combinations of ingredients.

Before the barkeeper reached the end of the list, Gren interrupted, "We'll take six bowls of that first one."

"Six? I only counted five of you."

"We've another friend joining us later," Mari explained, keeping her fingers crossed that Ruv's arrival would be uncharacteristically discreet.

The barkeeper nodded thoughtfully as he continued filling their order. While ladling substantial portions of stew into stoneware bowls, he asked, "Mari, huh? That name sounds oddly familiar."

"I'm not sure where you could recognize us from. We've never been this far north before," she replied, rubbing the back of her neck. "We've really only ever been to southern Faerie, and then the woods around the Spinner's sanctuary."

At the mention of the Spinner, the barkeeper's eyes grew wide, and his wrinkled face broke into a triumphant grin. "You're the Destined, aintcha?"

Gren shuffled his feet and looked around to see if anyone else had heard the excited declaration, but Mari just blushed. "Er, some call us that, yes," she said. "I'm the Dreamer, and Gren is the Wanderer."

"Should've recognized that jade moon you've got around your neck. Not sure how I missed it. And a sword to match, will you look at that! Anyway, the name's Therese," the barkeeper said with a dip of his graying brow. "What brings the Destined to the humble village of Po? No one comes this far north at midwinter. Not by choice, anyway."

Mari winked at Gren and said, "We've heard good things about this Tipsy Turtle and decided to give it a go."

"Is that so?" Therese beamed. However, the warmth of his smile was tempered by the slightest narrowing of his eyes and the twitch of an eyelid. Suddenly he snapped, "Kanella! Get over here and help these fine folk carry their food back to their table." He hunched over the bar, wiping down the counter with a damp towel. "Twelve daughters I've had serve here over the years," he grumbled, "and she's by far the worst."

"I heard that, you know," Kanella quipped with a feigned smile at another customer as she meandered through the crowd, weaving in between the packed tables with grace. "If you'd just hire someone else to help me until Kallia's old enough, maybe I wouldn't be so tired all the time."

Tactfully ignoring the familial exchange as she reached for the pouch Ruv had given her, Mari inquired, "How much do we owe you?"

Therese shook his head and shoved the trays to the edge of the bar. "This round's on the house. But don't get used to that, mind you. I've got a business to run."

Mari and Gren thanked him, then picked their way to the table. Kanella shadowed their steps with a basket of bread cradled in one arm and a beverage tray held aloft in the other. As Kanella set the tray in the table center, Mari explained to her friends, "We weren't sure what to get, so we just got one of everything."

Sarah snatched a shot of clear liquor before Kanella had even pulled her hands away from the tray. As Sarah downed the liquid, a look of pure bliss softened her features, but the fierce planes of her face resumed their usual expression of disinterest all too soon.

Witnessing the sequence, Sam's mouth tightened at the corners. "Would it have killed you to save me the quartz? Now I have to settle for mulsuma or beer," he moaned. "I hate beer."

"Then drink the mulsuma," his sister rejoined, reaching now for one of the wine glasses.

Mari took an experimental sip of an amber beer, grimaced, and shoved it toward Gren, who accepted it without argument. "It's not that bad," he said after a few of his own sips. "It actually reminds me a little of an IPA."

Wendy grabbed a heavy tankard with thick foam sloshing over the brim. She took a sip, smiled, and then chugged the beverage. Wiping the extra foam from her mouth, she said, "Stout. I love a good stout." When the others chuckled, she added, "Though I may not have room for that stew now."

By the time Ruv glided into a seat between Sam and Wendy, most of the stew was long gone and everyone had drained their drinks except Mari, who was still nursing half a glass of red wine. "Did I miss anything fun?" he quipped.

Wendy started, blinking behind her glasses. "I didn't even see you come in."

"Good," he rejoined. "That should mean old Therese missed me, too. Damn, doesn't look like many of his daughters are still serving."

Sarah, eyeing Mari's wine, commented, "You have got to be the slowest drinker I have ev—what in the seven hells is a leshii doing in the Alpines?"

The whole table followed Sarah's astonished gaze. The leshii in question stood out from the crowd even more than the humans had. Despite the winter weather, the petite woman wore nothing more than a sleeveless ivory tunic that fell in soft folds to just above her knees, secured by twisting vines entwined about her waist. Flaming red hair tangled about her shoulders, shedding bits of leaf whenever she tossed her head and revealing pointed ears just a hair smaller than that of the evrae who surrounded her. The tankard of sparkling cider she held dwarfed her hand, and her skin, white as birch bark, glowed a pale green in the scattered illumination from the chandeliers, yet she cast no shadow. When she turned and made eye contact with Mari, a bright smile of recognition flashed across her fine-boned face.

Brae's bare feet skimmed across the floor as she approached them. "Mari, Gren! What a lovely surprise!" she saluted, depositing her cider on the table and hauling over a chair between Gren and Ruv. "What brings you to the frosty north this wretched time of year?"

Perceiving no reason to hide the reason for their visit from someone who had helped them so much during their first one, Mari answered, "A mission from the Spinner. Laria's sending someone to meet us here with the details at some point in the near future. You?"

"Oh, nothing nearly so exciting," Brae said between glugs of cider. "I'm just on my way back from visiting my sister, Sale. She moved further north, testing her limits. She can stay away from her roots for a full year now."

"Roots?" Wendy echoed with a furrowed brow.

Gren nodded his head in Brae's direction. "She's a dryad. Well, a leshii, they're called, technically, but either way she's a tree spirit."

Even as Gren explained, Wendy dug through her pack for her notebook and a pen.

"Close enough," Brae said with a wave of her hand.

Ruv sniffed in the direction of the leshii's tankard. "Did you add quartz to that?" he inquired.

She looked coyly out of the side of her eyes as she responded, "But of course! It enhances the flavor. One shot is good, two is better."

"Oh, I think I'm going to like you," Ruv disclosed.

Brae flashed him a dazzling smile. "Of course you will. Everyone does." After a moment, she corrected, "Well, apart from most of my cousins."

Shortly thereafter the tavern activity picked up with many of the patrons milling about the room or acquiring additional food and drinks. "I do believe it's time for another round," Sam declared, scrutinizing the crowd. "Anyone want anything? Actually, no. You're all getting quartz, and you're all going to like it."

"I don't intend to get completely goosed, you know," Wendy said. She removed her glasses to polish them on the hem of her shirt. "Last time that happened I woke up with a tattoo I don't remember getting."

"Wait, I thought tattoo parlors didn't let drunk people get any?" Mari asked.

Wendy giggled shyly as she put her glasses back on her nose. "I never said it was a reputable establishment."

Sam released a pointed sigh as he took to his feet. "As I was saying, I believe it's time for another round."

"Hold up, this is important," Gren professed with a fierce glance at Sam, who reluctantly resumed his seat with a pointed eye roll. "We can't just ignore the fact that Wendy has a tattoo," Gren continued. "Our Wendy. Our practical, sweet, innocent scientist Wendy."

Mari, the only other person in the present company to have seen the artwork in question, rolled her eyes and apologized to Wendy, who grinned sheepishly and countered, "I could be a mad scientist, you know."

"Right, because there's a lot of evil geniuses who go into geology," Gren persisted.

Ruv tapped his fingers on the table and considered the recent revelation. "What's it of?" he eventually asked, his normally jovial expression neutral.

Wendy stared at her empty bowl. "Just a few feathers falling from my left shoulder and down my bicep. Nothing special or terribly unique, really. I liked it the next morning, so I kept it."

Gren and Ruv both dipped their heads appreciatively, but Sam just rolled his eyes. "Now that we've established our little one is all grown up—" he began.

"I'm the same age as you!" Wendy fired back.

"—I'm getting that second round before the crowd thins," he finished.

"I'll help you carry," Sarah offered as she joined him. She led the way into the throng with Sam following close behind her. Though normally lithe, it seemed Sarah had suddenly developed a case of the clumsies, bumping into the tavern's clientele right and left. Equally out of character, she also appeared to have developed an abundance of cordiality. Her victims, distracted by Sarah's gushing apologies, failed to notice Sam's quick fingers.

However, their activity did not go unnoticed by Brae. "That disreputable pair of sanguines over there," she said with a nod at the twins, "good friends of yours?"

"It's complicated," Mari sighed. "I suppose now's a good time to fill you in." She and Gren then recounted the tale of the rest of their journey to the Spinner's sanctuary—how they met Ruv and his wolf pack and then parted with Laria and Hal—as well as how they rescued the twins from Kutkah's cave and came to accidentally meet Wendy in Scotland.

Brae first listened attentively to Mari and Gren's abbreviated account of the past few years' events, then summarized her travels since she had last seen them in Vesna's cottage. Although she repeatedly assured them her adventures had not been nearly as adventurous, they listened in rapt attention. Wendy was especially enthralled, bombarding Brae with questions about Aorea and then recording every detail in her notebook.

She had fled her cousins' fury northward, Brae explained, narrowly escaping a few encounters with less than friendly tree sprites. After a few weeks, she managed to make it to her sister's farmstead. Sale had been delighted by such an extended visit, but Brae felt it was time to leave so that her sister and her husband could get on with their lives. Thus, she was on her way south to sneak into the Birch Forest, reunite with her roots, and see where the wind would take her from there.

Halfway through Brae's tale, Sarah and Sam returned to the table, their arms laden with tiny crystal glasses and a large decanter of the pungent liquid every bit as colorless and iridescent as its namesake. When they resumed their seats, no one was surprised to hear their pockets jingle. Brae arched an eyebrow and cast Sarah a knowing smile, but made no comment as she finished her story. Once she did, she asked, "So, where is this Spinner's mission of yours taking you? If it's somewhere I haven't been before, I'd like to tag along."

"You sure?" Mari searched Brae's emerald eyes. "We don't know where we're going yet, or even what exactly it is we're supposed to do. We could be gone a while, and I know you can't stay away from your roots for too long."

Brae took a sizable swallow from her quartz-spiked cider. "I could do for a bit of spontaneity," she said. "Besides, you humans always get into all kinds of fun trouble." She fluttered her lashes at Sarah before resuming her conversation with Mari. "Give me a few days to get in touch with my stationary half—it's been half a year as it is, so I really am overdue—and then, if you're still around when I return, I'd love to join your little adventure."

Mari and Gren exchanged pensive looks. "It could help to have an Aorean native with us," Gren admitted. "There's still a lot we don't know about this world."

The others nodded their accord. Noting the consensus, Mari extended a hand toward Brae and said, "Deal."

The leshii took the offered hand, downed the remainder of her cider, and dipped her head in farewell. As she made to leave, Gren inquired, "Wait, do you want me to sing you down to the Birch Forest and back?"

Brae returned the suggestion with an ambiguous smile. "No need. I can get there and back by my own means in about five days, and as I'm sure you remember, I'm not on the best of terms with my own kind. That, unfortunately, has not changed. I wouldn't want to announce my presence with a big splash of magic like circle travel would trigger." Witnessing the human's stunned expressions in response to her claim, she rolled her eyes and quoted, "I'm a leshii. I'm not bound by the laws of physics as you understand them." Refusing to elaborate further, she glided toward the tavern door and slipped into the night.

Soon after Brae's exodus, the six friends swapped the warmth of the tavern for the warmth of the inn. Ruv had secured two adjoining rooms on the upper level of the building. Each room was furnished with two beds, a desk supporting a lit candelabra, a small fireplace, and a window overlooking the forest that encircled the town. A communal bathroom at the center of the hall provided running water pumped from a well and, in a miracle most had not expected, heated by passing through pipes adjacent to the chimneys.

Mari and Gren admired the view from the window and chuckled softly as they overheard Sarah next door trying to convince Wendy to share a bed with her rather than sleep all by her lonesome, to which Wendy replied that she was quite fine on her own, thank you, and she wouldn't want to separate the inseparable siblings. But when they turned to comment on the conversation to Ruv, they found him already passed out in the bed closest to the door.

He had not even bothered to remove his boots.

The next morning they convened in the central dining area of the inn over tea and pastries fresh from the local bakery. Not one to idly lounge around due to lack of information, Mari spent most of breakfast discussing how best to go about acquiring additional members for their expedition. "From what little I have been able to squeeze out of Laria," she mumbled around a mouthful of crumbly muffin, "we might want to recruit a few more people to help out. I wish I knew where this damn mission was going to take us, but I imagine it will, at a minimum, involve a lot of hiking, so we'd only want the physically fit types." With her breakfast finished, she paused to lick the crumbs off her fingers. "Furthermore, since we can't exactly pay anyone, I'd say those with an overdeveloped sense of honor and adventure would be best."

"Sam and I might know a guy, assuming he's still lurking about these parts," Sarah offered, delicately picking a morsel from one of her canines. "Though no promises. We didn't part on the best of terms."

Mari asked bluntly, "Did you steal from him?"

"Not technically," Sarah replied. She and her brother headed upstairs to gather supplies before seeking out their likely disinclined acquaintance.

Watching their retreating forms with a wistful smile, Ruv proposed, "You know, the pack used to come up this way in the winter sometimes. Assuming their habits haven't changed too much, I bet I could track them down if you want. I could probably convince the whole lot of them to join us, even."

"I don't think the whole pack will be necessary," Mari replied, "but a few would definitely be helpful." Poking Gren in the ribs, she added, "Plus it would be nice to not be outnumbered by cats."

Ruv ambled toward the stairway, but he halted after a few steps and spun around on his heels. Narrowing his eyes at Wendy, he asked, "Why feathers?"

Wendy, who had thus far kept the entirety of her concentration on seeing precisely how much tea her stomach could hold, had to gulp down her latest mouthful before answering, "What feathers?"

"Your tattoo, I mean."

"Oh, I dunno. Just liked them, I guess."

"How do you feel about heights?" he pressed, a glimmer of enthusiasm brightening his eyes.

Wendy blanched. "They make me queasy."

Ruv grunted and resumed his trek upstairs. However, he paused once more to say, "Fear may be the key."

Wendy narrowed her eyes, but after a moment, she nodded. "That makes sense, actually," she commented. "It's a strong emotion. Might trigger some sort of instinctual reaction."

Mari just shrugged, but Gren asked with a smirk, "Do you want me to start jumping out behind corners and shouting and stuff?"

"I don't have the hiccups," Wendy rejoined, but her eyes glimmered with amusement.

Hal heaved the longsword over his head and swung at the great oak. Chips of bark and wood showered him as the blade cleaved the thin branch in two. He spun, gritting his teeth, and swung again, this time at the base of the branch. It cracked, but did not split entirely. Groaning, he yanked the sword out of the wood and prepared for one last swing, but a pointedly cleared throat stayed his hand.

"What did that poor tree ever do to you?"

He turned to find Gryndonmin skulking safely out of sword reach. He noticed the rest of the sanctuary's niethera gathered at an even safer distance. The countenances of those closest were painted in curiosity, but those further away revealed a mix of confusion and mild disdain, their tales twitching left and right with a periodically stamped hoof. "With Mickey gone, I need to keep practicing somehow," Hal replied, grinning in defiance of the silver nietheran's grim mien.

Gryndonmin released a heavy sigh while he scanned the damage to Hal's oaken opponent. Most of the branches within Hal's reach had already been felled, and the ground was littered with acorns, leaves, and twigs. "But *why* the trees?"

Hal shoved the tip of his sword in the ground and draped his forearms over the gilded, onyx-studded guard. His grin broadened. "Would you rather fill in for him?"

"Absolutely not."

"Mickey seemed to like it."

Gryndonmin shook his mane and took a step forward. Staring directly into Hal's sapphire eyes, he repeated, "Absolutely not."

Hal retrieved the water bottle he had set on a rock nearby and took a swig. "The tree it is," he pronounced.

The nietheran's tail flicked in annoyance, and he decided to try a different angle. "You'll ruin the blade."

"False," Hal quipped, "and you know it." He ran a hand through his ragged, sweat-soaked hair. "The sword is every bit as enchanted now as when it was forged. A good polish now and then, some sharpening, it's fine. Practically indestructible."

"Guardian Howard, " he began.

"Uh oh," Hal cut in, "you used my full name."

Gryndonmin released another heavy sigh. "You do realize your title—all of our titles, really—is largely nominal?" He pranced a slow, stately circle, dipping his horn at each quarter of the unbroken gold that encompassed the garden, the cottage, and the orchards to emphasize his point. "Nothing can penetrate the sanctuary's walls. The lanti ensured that long ago. The niethera maintain that magic. The Spinner does not require our protection so much as our service and our company."

"Sure, you all say that. Even Mickey said that," Hal replied, watching as the rest of the niethera, who had since lost interest when they realized the conversation would remain civil, faded into the landscape. He extracted his sword from the ground and held it in a loose grip. "But if there is even the slightest chance that someday, somehow, someone might break in, then I need to be ready." Mouth set in a hard line, he added, "I will protect her."

"As you wish," Gryndonmin conceded with a bow.

"Besides," Hal continued, voice still serious, "with everything going on right now, this shadow and all that crap on Earth, who knows what will happen here? I may be needed sooner rather than later."

"I do hope it will never be so," the gray nietheran breathed. Wryly, he added, "But could you at least stay away from the fruit trees?"

Hal chuckled and resumed hacking.

Mari, Gren, and Wendy spent their days waiting for their friends' return by exploring Po and the surrounding forest. Wendy, whenever she was not attempting to master the art of Sanguina in their room at the inn, took copious notes on every rock, tree, shrub, and nonhuman humanoid she saw. She also scraped numerous samples from the various minerals around the area. After a few days she had nearly filled the tiny plastic bags she had brought for precisely that purpose, and Mari warned that she may want to slow down on the note taking or find another book.

True to Ruv's promise, the evrae were not the only sentient species presently occupying Po. A pair of freesians, passing through from Pendra to secure new trade routes throughout the Alpines and Everfrost, spent several days in town. Wendy observed from a respectful distance as they spoke with different merchants and provided samples of vere wine fermented from a freshly cultivated strain of Pendral grape.

She marveled at their willowy limbs and the elegant robes of stretched silk that seemed to float around their bodies. Between their crystalline blue eyes and pearlescent skin, they appeared not only impervious to the cold, but a part of it, as if they were carved from the very ice of their polar homeland. Long, pointed ears and silver hair framed their sharp faces. Wendy eventually came to the realization that she could not quite tell whether the visiting freesians were male or female or something else entirely, but then decided it did not particularly matter; they were the most exquisite beings she had ever seen.

Unfortunately, she no sooner worked up the courage to approach the pair than they moved on to the next town.

After her own incessant badgering failed to elicit the desired response from Laria, Mari enlisted Gren's aid to harass Hal as well. Thus, with an exasperated sigh, Laria finally told Mari that their mission would ultimately take them to the continent of Dahrigek, located in the west of Aorea's southern hemisphere. Mari subsequently surveyed the locals about the place, and the general consensus was that Dahrigek possessed the least hospitable climate of any place in Aorea and ergo, remained unpopulated save for the less sentient species. Armed with such slivers of information, she and Gren gathered as many supplies and journey-stable food as their band could reasonably carry. Rumor also had it that Dahrigek was mostly desert once you crossed the border, but no one could say for sure. Evidently no one had bothered to wander that far south in a millennium or two at least, the locals said.

After four days, Ruv reappeared with two of his former packmates shadowing his steps. Much bulkier than they remembered and cloaked in piecemeal furs and rough suede, Derek was practically unrecognizable. His winter skin was far paler than when they had last seen him, even though the long face, playful gray eyes, and lengthy auburn braid remained much the same. In contrast, Killer's olive complexion had not changed with the seasons, though his peppering of moles showed more prominently. A scar, freshly healed, stretched across his forehead and down his right cheek, and a whole bearskin hung over his shoulders with the head serving as a hood.

The two men seized Mari and Gren in a fierce embrace. Derek even went so far as to lift Mari off her feet and swing her around in a circle. When he set her back down, she exclaimed, "It's so good to see you! How's the pack?"

Derek, beaming, said, "Miss Rojko, Mister Vandern, it's lovely to see you both, too. The pack is running well. The boys send their best."

"We figured we all want to participate," Killer added, "but Ruv said you don't need a whole slew of wolves, so we drew lots, and it'll just be us two this time."

"Who's standing in as Buddy's beta with you gone?" Gren queried, pushing an extra tankard of cider across the table to Derek.

"Hans, which caused a bit of a stir," he answered. "Everyone expected him to choose Vitya or Mitya." He shed his outer cloak and hung it over the back of his chair, revealing an oversized sweater to have been the true source of his apparent bulk. "Either way, the boys are in good hands. They can live without me and Killer for now."

Ruv snickered. "Careful, or you'll grow to love the lone wolf lifestyle," he cautioned. "There are only so many available ladies out there. I can't be sharing."

"Speaking of ladies," Derek replied with a twinkle in his eye, "you haven't introduced me to our new friend."

"Right, sorry. I'm the worst," Mari confessed before making the necessary introductions. She then turned to Killer and asked, "So how'd you get the scar?"

He fingered one of the bear's great paws hanging over his shoulder before answering, "The same way I got this nice, warm coat."

Just as she promised, Brae arrived the following day. After constant badgering for her to tell them how she could possibly run all the way to the Birch Forest and back so quickly, she agreed to a game of chance with Ruv. If he won, she would explain every minute detail. If she won, they would shut up about the whole thing and let her enjoy her cider. However, she beat him so soundly and Wendy looked so crestfallen at not having her curiosity sated, that Brae let slip the hint that certain tree species have connected root systems, and that those systems sometimes stretch a great distance. Eventually they accepted this mysterious response and continued gathering supplies from every willing farmer, baker, and blacksmith in Po.

Although she did not wish to wear out their welcome at the Tipsy Turtle, Mari nevertheless made daily trips to the tavern to see if Laria's mysterious messenger had arrived yet. Predictably, the rest happily accompanied her. Most likely due to his growing fondness for Mari, Therese ignored the presence of the same troublesome wolf sanguines whom by that point he had most certainly recognized. As for the rest of the locals, they accepted the growing population of humans in their town with aplomb, no longer staring when they saw them on the street or ducking into the nearest doorway. Some even grew quite friendly after word got around (they assumed due to either Therese or one of his daughters) about Mari and Gren's respective roles within the prophecies of the Destined.

Around midafternoon of the seventh day, Sam and Sarah returned with the largest man Mari and Gren had ever seen in tow. He was easily as tall as Hal but much broader in the chest, and what little they could see of his skin beneath the many layers of fur and leather was ruddy and laced with scars. Dark amber eyes, his softest features, made a stark contrast against the square jaw and jutting cheekbones. Black hair streaked with gray hung in limp strands to his shoulders, and a massive axe was strapped across his back.

By way of introduction, Sarah declared, "Believe me, you'll want this bloke on your side in a fight."

The big man approached the table, lighter on his feet than his size suggested. His eyes landed on each member of the group in turn, acknowledging Brae's presence with the same detachment he had acknowledged the rest. "The name's Tygyn," he said in a deep rumble, his voice hoarse from what the present party assumed must be disuse, as overuse seemed an unlikely alternative.

"Tygyn?" Sam echoed. "Here and we've been calling you Frostbite this whole time."

"On account of his chilly demeaner," Sarah elaborated with a smirk.

He acknowledged the comment with a grunt before asking, "Who leads?"

Everyone turned their faces toward Mari as she calmly met his gaze. A momentary furrowing of his brow betrayed his confusion, but he schooled his features back to neutrality. Without a word the others rose and moved to another table, dragging the protesting Sarah and Sam along with them. Gren held out a chair for him, and the big man murmured his thanks. Once he was seated in relative comfort across from Mari, for he dwarfed the chair beneath him, she asked, "So what name do you prefer, Tygyn or Frostbite?"

He rolled his shoulders in what may have been a shrug; it was difficult to discern beneath the layers he had yet to shed despite the balminess of the tavern. "I suppose Frostbite is fine. I've grown used to it."

"Frostbite it is. What do you know of the Spinner?"

"Not much," he admitted. "I know she's important, and that she watches the worlds in a magic Loom and lives in a golden garden with a herd of niethera."

"That's the nutshell. We've got a mandate straight from her," she stated. "We'll be heading to Dahrigek soon on her behalf. Are you a sanguine?" When Frostbite nodded, she continued, "Good. What's your totem?"

"Siberian tiger."

"How long have you been shifting?"

"Since I was a boy."

Mari searched his eyes, keeping her expression impartial. "How'd you find your way into Aorea?"

Frostbite returned her scrutiny before giving his answer. "I was born in Olyokminsk and abducted by the Old Farmer's lot when I'd barely seen six summers. I grew up as one of his farm hands. I escaped when I was twelve and had mastered shifting. Since then, I've been on the run, mostly hiding in the Kemdarian region. It's wild enough there that a man can disappear, if he knows how." He cleared his throat and withdrew a gargantuan horn, stoppered with a cork, from a holster at his belt. He popped off the cork and took a long swig. "I only started straying this far west again when I figured I had changed enough that Veles," he paused to spit on the floor, "wouldn't recognize me."

"And yet you'll tell your story to a stranger," Mari observed, wrinkling her nose at the scent of old whisky that wafted from the open horn.

His mouth twitched in what may have been an attempt at a smile. "You have an honest face."

"How do you know the twins?"

"They owe me money, which is why I didn't hide when they entered my territory." He took one last gulp from his horn then returned it to his belt. "They said if I came with you and helped on this mission of yours, you'd pay me back on their behalf."

Sighing, Mari replied, "Of course they said that." She shot a glare at Sarah and Sam, who grinned shamelessly back at her. "Exactly how much do they owe you, and how did they incur this debt?"

It was at this point that the twins decided to officially reenter the conversation despite threatening looks from Gren and Ruv. "He's run a job or two with us before," Sarah quipped.

"And some of the others actually pay," Sam sniffed.

Frostbite leveled a steely eye at the twins. "You double-crossed me and stole my share."

Sam came up and placed his slender hands on each of Frostbite's massive shoulders. Even standing, Sam's head reached barely higher than the seated Frostbite's. "Only because we knew you'd make it out just fine," he purred. "And look at you now! Handsome as ever. Even the new scars you've acquired just enhance your appearance."

Mari shooed the siblings away and resumed the interview. "I can't promise anything, but I'll see what I can do. How's your running?"

"Tireless."

"Alright," she concluded. "Stick around for a few days. See how you fit in with the less dishonest members of our group, and we'll take it from there." She extended her hand, and he accepted hers in a crushing grip. Fighting the urge to rub the feeling back into her squeezed fingers, she gestured for the others to reconvene and introduced each as he or she sat down. "Ruv, Derek, Killer, and me are all Eurasian grey wolves. Gren here is another tiger sanguine, only he's a Bengal. Next to Ruv is a leshii named Brae, and the tiny woman in the corner, who has yet to notice the others have left because she's too busy scribbling furiously in a notebook, is Wendy. We know she's a sanguine, but we don't know what her totem is since she hasn't made her first shift. And the twins, of course, you already met."

Frostbite nodded, committing the new names to memory and eyeing Gren in particular with interest. "Happy to make your acquaintance," he said to the group. Returning his attention to Mari, he added, "The twins said you were quite the clever fighter. I didn't believe them when I first saw you, but perhaps they spoke truth for once. You've a firm grip for someone your size."

"Is that so?" Mari rejoined, smiling despite herself. Her fingers still tingled. "I suppose I'm clever enough."

CHAPTER THREE
Some demon goddess of destruction

Therese, dropping a cup, was the first to notice the Spinner's messenger. The crash of glass shattering against stone silenced all pub chatter, and while all eyes initially turned toward the sound, they soon followed Therese's gaze to the cause of his surprise, where they were granted the incongruous spectacle of a nietheran attempting to squeeze through the front door. Since the evrae are not an especially large people, the building layout had not been designed with a robust quadruped in mind. His sides bulging around the door frame, Micaleth wheezed, "I don't suppose anyone has anything to grease this down?"

"A nietheran," Therese breathed. "In a tavern? In *my* tavern?" Recovering from the shock, he rummaged through the contents of the shelves behind and beneath the bar, eventually locating a pat of butter. He tossed it to an amused Gren. "Ancestors save us. What a week it's been," Therese muttered.

Gren and Mari, though unable to suppress their mirth, helped Micaleth complete his entrance and led him to the two corner tables where the rest of their growing group loitered. Ruv, Wendy, and Frostbite shifted some of the chairs out of the way. "Would someone be so kind as to get me some quartz?" Micaleth asked, plopping himself on the floor in between the tables and managing, just barely, not to stab anyone in the face with his alicorn. "It was a long journey from the sanctuary, and it being winter and all, I did not spy any of those delicious little common flowers along the route."

Gren snickered, saying, "Hal mentioned you had a fondness for those. He also said your uncle totally does not approve." At Micaleth's answering indignation, Gren strode to the bar, where Therese obligingly emptied half a bottle into a shallow dish and only charged for the price of a single serving. Gren set the dish on the table in front of Micaleth, who slurped it down without hesitation.

"So, Mickey, how's my girl?" Mari prompted, a wicked grin breaking across her face.

When he had finished swallowing, Micaleth rejoined, "She told you to call me that, I presume?"

"On the occasion that I ever saw you again, yes, she made it quite clear that was the only appropriate mode of address," she replied in mock solemnity before breaking into another smile.

"I am not an animated mouse," he sighed. "Not that I have yet figured out what that even means. But to answer your question, the Lady Laria is doing fine. She misses you both, as does the Guardian Hal," he said with a nod toward Mari and Gren.

"Poor Hal," Gren remarked, shaking his head. "Cooped up in the sanctuary all day, every day. I'm glad that's not my fate. I bet he's going crazy."

Micaleth let out an equine snort. "Oh, he does plenty! We have become sparring partners," he bragged as he raised a cloven hoof to point out several minute dents marring the crystalline spiral of his horn. "Unfortunately," he sniffed, "Though I would love to continue catching up, I am not here on just a social call. Laria sent me to deliver her message." He stretched and scratched a knee against a white leather satchel, which had hitherto gone unnoticed since it matched the precise shade of his fur, strapped around his back. Taking the hint, Mari flipped open the top and withdrew a folded, yellowed parchment. As she spread the paper on the table, Micaleth expounded, "I have brought a map of the land to which we will travel. Though, considering it has not exactly been populated in who knows how long and the last explorer to bother mapping the continent ventured there a millennium or two ago, it may not be accurate. Anyway, I will also be accompanying you on your journey as the Spinner's eyes and ears." After a cough, he added, "And more importantly, I was bored."

Gren scratched his chin. "Are you like, allowed?"

"Allowed?" Micaleth repeated, nostrils flaring and purple eyes twitching with indignation.

"To leave the sanctuary for so long, I mean," Gren explicated, holding up his hands in what he hoped would be a placating gesture.

"Who's going to stop me?"

"Fair point."

Micaleth turned back to Mari. "Is this everyone?" When she nodded, he continued, "Good. There is much you need to know." He tapped a hoof on the map. "This is Dahrigek, the continent just south of Evra."

"Laria told me that's where we're headed," Mari said, nodding. "We've been gathering supplies. I hear it's not exactly a pleasant place."

Micaleth returned her nod. "Evra and Dahrigek are connected by a thin strip of land—well, thin in a geographic sense; it is still several hundred miles across— but separated by a mountain range. Dahrigek has been populated by nothing save a few colonies of pixies right over the border as far back as anyone remembers, or at least, so we thought. However, recently the Lady Laria has noticed that when she seeks the western part of Dahrigek in her Loom, to include where there should be an archipelago along the coast, her vision is blocked. The Loom simply will not show it.

"We have searched through the annals of the previous Spinners, and there is no precedence for such a thing. The Loom has always obeyed the Spinner's will, and in all other ways it still does. Even when Kutkah masked the activity of his henchmen," Micaleth paused to glower at the implacable twins, "the Loom never obscured geography itself. Furthermore, it is only for this one area that she is blind. In short, she would like us to see what is to be seen, and if necessary, to fix it." His tone grew more serious as he concluded, "She fears some evil may be brewing there."

"Ok. We'll leave tomorrow." Mari studied the map, squinting her eyes at the scrolling, unintelligible script and the inked symbols of mountains, rivers, and trees. Most of the symbols were easy enough to make out, but one gave her pause. She pointed to a painted spiral just north of the border. "Is this a traveling circle?"

"Yes, and that tiny dot right next to it is a town," Micaleth indicated. "It's the only settlement between the circle and the Dahrigek border. There are no traveling circles in Dahrigek itself, for obvious reasons."

Mari continued her scrutiny. "Then we'll have to take the Alpine circle to that one in southern Evra, and I guess just walk the rest of the way. Figures." She looked around the table of old friends, new friends, and recent acquaintances. "Micaleth, can you take all eleven of us in one go, or should Gren sing us through instead?"

Micaleth puffed, "Of course I can take you all. At the previous Spinner's behest, I once brought an entire pack of wolf sanguines to Aorea without them even noticing."

Ruv, Derek, and Killer exchanged surprised glances before exclaiming in unison, "So *that's* how we got here!"

"I thought you three looked familiar," Micaleth commented, sniffing the air around them. "You are much older now, though."

"Humans age a little faster than niethera do, my friend," Ruv replied with a shrug. Killer and Derek nodded their agreement.

Mari giggled and said, "Clearly we need to make some more thorough introductions."

After calling it an early night and rising well before the sun, they completed the trek from Po back to the traveling circle. Micaleth had assured them that as the original creators of the circles, the niethera were not subject to the same laws that governed Wanderers like Gren. Micaleth could open the portal regardless of the time of day or year. Nevertheless, Mari insisted they leave the inn while it was still dark since it would take them most of the morning to reach the circle.

As they gathered within the ring of pines, Micaleth placed one of his front hooves on the trunk of the central fir and inquired, "Is everybody ready? It's best if you keep in physical contact."

"I must say," Sarah commented, "I'm curious how circle-travel works with a nietheran. We've done lanti, Wanderer's songs...collecting the set now, I suppose."

"I'm curious, too," Gren agreed, trying his best to ignore the onslaught of music echoing throughout his brain. He failed. His fingers trembled, one of his eyelids spasmed, and he could not help but tap his toes along with a beat only he could hear. "Mickey, how long does your method take?" he choked out.

The nietheran flicked his tail and stamped his other front hoof on the ground. "If you all will stop talking and just hold hands, you will see for yourselves." When they finally obeyed, he directed, "Now, Mari, if you will please just touch my mane—ouch! I said touch, not pull—there we go. And we're off!"

Without so much as a shimmer, reality dissolved around them and reformed, the surrounding evergreens replaced in a split second by a swirl of dust and heat. The vertigo caused Sarah to blanch and Wendy to lose her footing and stumble into Frostbite, who silently set her back on her feet, but most were otherwise unaffected beyond momentary disorientation except for Brae. Hit by far the worst by the sudden shift, she began emptying the contents of her stomach as soon as one circle gave way to another. As Brae's heaving continued, Ruv rushed to her side. "There, there, little dryad," he crooned, holding back her hair. "Traveling circles can be rather jarring."

"Shut up, sanguine," she coughed between bouts of dry heaving.

Micaleth joined Brae's other side. "My apologies," he said. "Traveling with one of the niethera can be a bit more abrupt than the other modes of circle-leaping. In hindsight, I should have warned you."

Brae stood, wiping her mouth with the back of her wrist. "It's been a while, is all. I don't remember the trip across planes being so violent before. I'll be fine. Any second now." The blood drained from her face again, and she fell back to her knees, dispelling what looked suspiciously like shredded leaves.

Resigning themselves to wait, the others began shedding the outer layers they would no longer require. Micaleth had advised them ahead of time that the border between Evra and Dahrigek was close to the equator, so they had left space in their respective packs to stow their coats. Killer's bearskin took extra effort to finagle, but he refused to part with a trophy whose earning nearly cost him an eye. Furthermore, he had argued, it could pull triple duty as a bedroll and even a disguise. He disregarded Sarah's suggestion that his own shapeshifting abilities provided a far more believable disguise than borrowed fur ever could.

After a few more minutes, Brae finally recovered enough to stand unassisted, and so everyone turned their attention to surveying their new location. They found themselves in a circle quite unlike the one they had left, in which snow and ice had buried the interior rings of moss and mushrooms characteristic of all traveling circles. Instead, in the Evra circle the spotted mushrooms remained visible, but the moss hid beneath the dust, disturbed by their abrupt arrival and only just beginning to settle. In place of the pine trees of the Alpines, unassuming limestone boulders marked the outer perimeter, and a cottonwood tree formed the circle's heart.

Rolling hills of grass and brush extended beyond the confines of the traveling circle. The circle itself slumbered at the top of one such hill. Distant mountains, darkened to red by the late afternoon haze, stood to the west and south. Laying a hand against one of Micaleth's flanks, Mari asked, "So, Mickey, how far is it to that settlement on the map? Maybe they know something."

"I remain a nietheran and not a mouse, my Dreamless Dreamer," he said with dignity, though the twinkle in his eye gave away his teasing intention. The loss of Mari's ability to dream, both prophetically and normally, remained a sore point, the fact of which Micaleth was perfectly aware. However, before her annoyance at the reminder could grow, he continued, "But to answer your question, the village is about twenty miles southwest."

Squinting at the clouded sky, Mari reasoned aloud, "Alright, so now which way is southwest? It should be pretty close to evening here since it was still morning when we left the Alpines, so if the sun will just poke his damn head out long enough to—oh, Frostbite. You're pointing."

Needlessly, the big man stated, "That way."

She exhaled, eyeing the direction he indicated before checking the sky one last time. "Huh. I do believe you are correct. Also, is that a road? That would be super convenient." When Micaleth nodded in response, she directed, "Alright then, we best head out while there's still enough light to see. Everybody good?" She focused especially on Brae, who forced a smile in response. Thus, Mari marched toward the path, Gren and Wendy to either side and Micaleth, Ruv, and Brae taking up the rear.

To Ruv, Micaleth mumbled, "So I am not the one leading this expedition, then?"

Ruv chuckled. "Not while she's around."

"I suppose the Dreamer always was rather assertive."

"It's for the best," Ruv replied. "Just accept your role. Packs work best when there is but one alpha. Take it from a former alpha." He tossed a glance at the twins, who either had not heard his comment or chose to ignore it.

Micaleth pondered this revelation for a few moments before responding, "So would that make me the beta?"

Ruv laughed again, loudly enough this time that Mari and Gren turned quizzical looks in his direction, which he returned with a dismissive wave. Once he was certain his friends had relocated their attention to the pathway ahead of them, he said, "No, the beta would be Gren."

Micaleth's purple eyes narrowed into the distance. "Your pack dynamics confuse me. I am the oldest and most powerful creature here. By all natural orders, I should be the ranking individual."

"You're among sanguines now—" Ruv began.

"And a leshii," Brae interjected.

"—and a leshii," Ruv continued with a bow to Brae. "It's more complicated than that."

"Hmph," Micaleth grunted. To Brae, he added, "Humans are weird."

"Indeed," she agreed, smiling.

The path led them along a meandering route through rounded peaks and valleys. The brush they had spied from the top of the hill turned out to grow much taller than they had initially surmised, and it was interspersed by small, shaggy pines, wind battered palms, and more spindly cottonwoods. Only the tip of Micaleth's horn and the crown of Frostbite's head protruded above the surrounding foliage. Not knowing how much daylight remained with the clouds still stubbornly shrouding the sun, yet wanting to make it as far as possible before the dark forced them to stop for the night, Mari set a grueling pace. Their feet and hooves devoured the dusty miles, jogging whenever the footing along the uneven road was sufficiently forgiving.

By the time the sky dimmed enough to impede their vision, they had journeyed for well over an hour. Mari slowed to a walk and instructed everyone to keep an eye out for a place to settle. The brush grew so high and the rocky ground made purchase so unreliable that Killer and Derek volunteered to shift in order to better locate a proper spot.

The pair had just finished slinging their discarded packs across Micaleth's broad, albeit reluctant, back, when Mari signaled for them to stop. "Who here has better eyes than me? I think I see something up ahead, but I can't tell if it's just shadows playing tricks or not."

Gren squinted up the path. "I dunno that my night vision's any better than yours, but yeah, I'd say there's definitely something."

Wendy stepped forward. Removing her glasses, she peered in the same direction. "Three people on horses," she announced. She polished the lenses on the hem of her shirt before returning them to her nose.

"The hell do you wear glasses for?" Gren exclaimed. "Fashion?"

"For once I'll second Gren," Sarah remarked.

"I'm just terribly far-sighted," Wendy explained. "It's only closer than twenty feet that I can't see shite."

"Three dudes on horses," Mari repeated. "Well, they still seem to be getting closer, so I suppose we'll find out what's up soon enough." She turned back to Killer and Derek. "You guys should still go find us somewhere to bed down. We'll wait here."

The two wolves had already returned, clothed, and reacquired their packs by the time the trio of riders came within speaking range. As they drew still closer, it became apparent the riders constituted one evrae man followed by two women. Clothed in rags with not a single pack or bag between them, both the riders and their mounts were emaciated. None of the horses even bore a saddle. Mari hailed the tired travelers, and the others tried to look as nonthreatening as possible, plethora of weapons notwithstanding. "Evening, friends," Mari called. "We are heading towards a village we heard was in the area. Are you coming from there?"

"I am Markos," the man rasped with a dip of his chin. "This is my wife Elonn and her sister Merynn. My advice to you would be to return as quickly as your feet will carry you to wherever it was you came from, far away from this cursed land."

Mari shared a glance with Gren and Micaleth, who had moved closer to the riders. "We are here to help if we can," Mari said. "The Spinner sent us to find out what's going on here. One of her nietheran guards has joined us. Please, tell me of your troubles."

Markos looked to his wife. When she nodded in response, he dismounted from his horse but kept a hand on the reigns. After his wife and sister-in-law followed suit, he permitted Mari to lead them to the area Derek and Killer had found.

She awoke to suffocation.

Necria strained against the hand that sealed her mouth, her eyes wide, her fingers clutching at the bedsheets. A voice, strangely soft in the face of her overwhelming dread, murmured incomprehensible words in her ear.

After a few seconds she finally recognized the hand, the voice, and her struggling ceased.

The necromancer released a sigh of relief, and the pressure lifted. "You were dreaming."

"You scared me," she coughed.

"You were starting to scream. I was trying to calm you before someone else came to find out why."

Necria propped herself up on her elbows. Her angel, her demon, sat on the edge of the bed, his spine twisted so he could look at her. She narrowed her eyes. His face remained as hidden as ever in the shadows. "Make the light again. I want to see you."

"Not this time."

Her nostrils flared and lips tightened. "Why not?" she demanded, frustration beginning to boil in her breast. "Why is tonight different than last time?"

"Because tonight you were screaming," he whispered. "If I make a light, someone might see. Someone might come and find me here with you. Someone might ask questions neither of us want answered."

"Three years," Necria said. She gripped his wrist and drew it toward her, prying the fingers open. She traced the lines of his palm; her fingertips settled on a scar. "Three years since I found you in the midnight forest, an arrow through this very hand. Bleeding. Unconscious." She released his hand and reached for his face. "Three years since I drug you back through the window, kept you unseen, kept your secrets." Her light fingers traced his bones from sharp brow ridge to sharper chin. "Three years since you woke to these hands binding your wounds, to this voice whispering every healing charm I knew and praying to the Ancestors that this stranger I happened upon would live, that he would speak."

"I know. I remember."

"I found you broken," she whispered. "And now you have broken me."

He withdrew his hand from hers and inspected the scar for himself. "Perhaps you should have left me where you found me. You should not have been wandering there in the first place."

"I have rarely done what I should have done," she said, the trace of a smile dawning across her lips. She rubbed her eyes, and her frustration returned. "Three years, and still I don't know your name."

"All in good time."

"You don't trust me, even now?"

"I trust you with my heart."

"But not your name."

"Names have power. Mine should not be spoken aloud." The necromancer stood, walked to her door, and touched the lock. Crimson light encircled the door frame, filling every crevice and crack in the wood's dark surface. As the light around the door faded to an invisible seal, locking them within the safety of black silence, he ran his fingertips across the candles atop her dresser and side table. Their candescence filled the room, and the sound of his normally silent footsteps reverberated as he returned to the bed. He threw back his hood, revealing his face to her once more in all its severe splendor. When he finally spoke, it was no longer in a whisper. The normal volume of his voice greeted her ears in a resonant tenor. "I wasn't sure if I could do that, but it seems to have worked. We should have some guarantee of privacy now, at least from your family."

Necria ran her fingers through the white threads of his hair, searching his bottomless eyes for a trace of something she was not quite certain she wanted to find. "So now will you tell me your name?"

"There are those who can listen from afar, my love." When her gaze hardened, he vowed, "Soon you will come to understand everything."

"I suppose you will tell me your name on the day you walk with me in the sunlight."

His fingers came to rest on the necklace he had given her to match the ring, its black stone gleaming against her nut brown skin. "You have not been wearing this during the day."

Necria blinked at him. "How did you know?" she breathed, pulling back. "I only wear it at night, when I can be alone."

"Why?"

"My family would surely question where I got such a thing, and there is no answer I can rightly give. A ring is one thing, but this is not something I can hide or explain away." She closed her fingers around his and drew his hand away from her neck. "I'll keep your secrets, but I will not lie to my family."

"Then I promise you will never have to."

The chosen camp site was cramped for so large gathering, but with the horses tethered to a nearby live oak, the space sufficed. Cottonwoods and more oaks surrounded a cozy hollow where the prickling brush was kept at a minimum thanks to an array of shattered stone. From the stones' arrangement, they surmised that some sort of rocky outcropping must have succumbed to time and sandy soil, and thus, given way; the fragmented slabs below were all that remained.

Markos and his family stood in silence next to the tethered horses while the humans set to work. Sam, Sarah, and Frostbite—pleased at how easily the brush and bracken caught—built a fire in the center of the camp so they would have more light than their few lanterns could supply. Wendy helped Mari and Gren rummage through their supplies to make dinner. As had become their custom, the first priority was to brew a pot of bracing tea. Ruv, Killer, and Derek hauled several fallen tree trunks around the blaze for seating, then retreated into the shadows to shift and hunt.

Once they had finished establishing their campsite, everyone but Mari, Gren, Brae, and Micaleth scattered to the edges to allow at least the semblance of privacy for the travelers, who remained reluctant to speak.

Mari coaxed the evrae into the fire's comforting glow. "You called this area cursed," she prompted as they huddled on a log on across from her. Micaleth, selecting a space between the tree trunks, folded his legs beneath him in a manner more akin to that of a deer than a horse. The move made Mari wonder if perhaps both species owed their descent to the majestic niethera, but she quickly disregarded the notion. Both deer and horses aplenty roamed Aorea, but neither appeared to harbor even a shred of the niethera's magic. Returning her attention to the evrae before her, Mari continued, "What sort of things have been happening?"

"We were living happily in the town of Orabet further south of here, about several days' journey, right along the border," Markos rasped. Gren offered him a cup of tea, but he refused, pulling out a rusted canteen instead. "My wife and I managed a bakery, and her sister was visiting from Thenet."

Merynn nodded. "I'm a traveling merchant, and my business took me to Orabet several weeks ago, so I was staying with my sister's family," she explained, her voice just as rasping as Markos's had been. He passed her the canteen, and she took a greedy swig before passing it on to her sister.

"It's been a while, you see," Elonn added.

When the canteen made its way back to Markos, he stashed it beneath a patched fold of his cloak. "It started with the crops," he said. "Soon after Merynn arrived, the crops started to fail. The whole town was hit. We tried everything, looked for every possible source, but there was nothing to be found." His eyes, shadowed despite the flickering firelight, glowered into the distance, sifting through unpleasant memories. "All our vegetables, grains, herbs, even the fruit trees. Everything just rotted in the field, and there was nothing to be done about it."

"I've always had a bit of a green thumb," Merynn interjected with a sad smile, "so I canceled the rest of my trip to stay and help."

Elonn took up the tale. "We harvested what we could before the blight claimed our entire garden, but it wasn't much. It wouldn't last us through the winter, but it was at least something."

"We made plans to seek out the nearby towns in hopes their harvest was better, but we wanted to wait for the blight to run its course," Markos added.

His wife nodded. "Without knowing the cause," she said, "we couldn't be sure it wouldn't spread."

"The plague came next," Markos grumbled. "At first, it only took the very young and the very old. It began with a cough. The cough turned into a fever, and then a rash and cramps. They died burning from the inside out. Before long, even the strong and healthy fell to the disease. It was unlike anything we'd ever seen."

"We live—lived—on the very edge of town," Elonn offered. She took a deep breath, her eyes glued to the flames. "When word of the sickness spread, we stayed away. I didn't want to risk falling ill with the...with...it's all my fault, I should have never..."

Markos took her hand and brought it to his lips. "Shh. There now, my love. No one is to blame but fate."

"But if I had only stayed inside!"

Markos kept holding his wife's hand as he resumed the narrative. "Merynn was helping me thresh the grain behind the shop while my wife was in the bakery, kneading dough. She had been keeping inside on account of the—the pregnancy." He glanced over at Elonn, who clutched her stomach protectively with her free hand, her face twisted into a stony grimace by remorse and rebellion. Markos squeezed her fingers and continued, "She heard a child crying in the street—we didn't think there were any left by then—and so without even thinking, she ran to help. She's always had such a kind heart. There was a little boy, he must've been only four or five years old, no taller than my knee. All red and gray with the rash, his skin flaking off in sheets. Elonn collapsed when she saw him."

His voice broke, and so Merynn took over, saying, "When we finished with the grain and didn't see Elonn in the bakery, we started to look around. We found her there, curled up next to the tiny corpse. He must have passed as soon as Elonn found him. We thought Elonn must surely be dead, too, but she was only in shock. She awoke once we moved her back inside. We…we left the child. We were afraid to move it, the poor, wretched thing."

Eyes still fixed on the blaze, Elonn whispered, "But it was too late to save my baby."

"It was only a few days later that the massacre happened," Merynn said, voice flat.

"Massacre?" Mari echoed. She looked over to Gren, then to Brae and Micaleth. They all kept their faces neutral, but the glint in Gren's eyes told her that he shared her confusion and concern. Massacres just did not happen in a place like Aorea.

Not for millennia.

Not since the splitting of the worlds, the war that banished humanity to the newly created Earth and its terrible aftermath. The wrath of Antiln, the sorceress from the unexpected third world of Daem, claimed one of the last Sierren cities in a single, destructive wave of revenge. Her imprisonment in the Loom guarded by a series of Spinners, of whom Laria had become the most recent, ensured—or so they thought—that such a thing would never occur again.

Markos nodded. "I was tending to my wife, and Merynn was out back, tilling the garden. Then we heard a commotion coming from the square."

Elonn finally lifted her eyes from the fire. She held Mari's gaze and said, "We managed to get away, but we had to leave everything but the horses behind."

"We were lucky," Markos muttered.

"We heard the screams first," Elonn said.

"Then we saw the smoke rising up."

"And then we saw the fire."

"And then the horde, the army of those—" she swallowed hard, "—things."

"There must have been hundreds of them," Elonn asserted. She bent to pick up a handful of dirt and crumbled it between her fingers. "These strange, small creatures, all misshapen, like clumps of mud come to life." She tossed the sandy soil into the fire, and a flurry of sparks shot up among the flames.

Markos nodded solemnly. "I have no idea what they might have been. Demons, perhaps?" He shook his head as if to dislodge the recollection. "Something from another place. I'd never seen anything like them before."

"Nor had I encountered them—whatever they were—in my travels, and I've been to every town this side of Aorea," Merynn concurred with a dry cough.

Brae and Micaleth exchanged anxious looks. Micaleth twitched his ears back and forth. When he dipped his alicorn, glistening amber in the firelight, toward the leshii, she stated, "I've never heard of anything like that in the east, either."

To the humans, Elonn asked, "Have you seen such things? Perhaps they came from the second world, brought here by some evil happenstance."

Gren blanched, and Mari's eyes shifted around the rest of the camp where the other humans listened on, barely maintaining the façade of privacy. She said, "I'd have to see them myself to say for sure, but just from your description, I don't think so. What happened next?"

"We grabbed our horses and ran," Markos replied matter-of-factly. "We ran, and we kept running until we came to the next town, the one you're headed towards now. Kalbet, it's called."

Merynn shook her head. "They didn't want to listen to us, and they didn't believe us about the horde."

"Or about the girl and the giant," Elonn added.

Mari tensed her shoulders, brow furrowed. "I'm sorry, I'm not following you. What girl? What giant?"

"I'm the one who saw her when we left," Elonn asserted. "I looked back—I shouldn't have looked back—

and she was right there amid the wreckage, spinning and dancing like some demon goddess of destruction while those *things* swirled around her, and I could have sworn I saw her laughing!"

Merynn placed a hand on her sister's shoulder, but she shrugged it off. "Now, sister," Merynn said in soothing tones, "I am sure if there really was any girl to be seen, she was just as terrified and helpless as everyone else."

"No! Her eyes were empty, soulless. She must have called the little demons in herself. I'm sure of it!"

Markos cast a glance at his distraught wife, then turned his face back to Mari. "No one could have survived such a disaster. No one."

Elonn glowered at her husband. "You didn't look back. You didn't see what I saw. She stood at the heart of it."

Micaleth cleared his throat. "You also mentioned a giant," he reminded them. "A giant what, precisely?"

Despondently, Markos said, "She doesn't know what she's talking about. She's in hysterics."

"The village was destroyed right before our eyes," Merynn granted. "We were all seeing things."

"I know what I saw! I saw the girl, and then behind her, I saw this massive creature. It was like a bull but somehow wrong, and it was all yellow and gold, like the sun come to ground, with great, glowing horns and a tail that whipped back and forth, fast as lightning. And it was so huge!" she rambled. "I saw it along the horizon, far off in the distance. But that girl...that girl...she knew something. She had to."

Mari bit her lip, Gren rubbed his temples, and Micaleth solemnly contemplated the ground, but none could formulate a fitting response. Into the silence Markos whispered, "Keep heading south if you must. We are going north and intend to keep warning every town we see."

Frowning, Mari asked, "Anything else unusual going on lately? Strange weather, maybe, or people or places disappearing, anything like that?"

"Isn't our tale strange enough?" Markos countered.

Mari cleared her throat. "Right. Yes. Thank you for sharing your story with us," she said. "I am deeply sorry for the loss of your friends and village, and...everything. You are welcome to spend the night in our camp before you continue on your journey. We would be honored to share our dinner with you, and if there is any other way we can be of further assistance, please let me know."

Markos thanked her for the offer, but averred, "We would rather keep moving until we come to the next town. I would not like to linger here longer than I must. We are too close. The memory is too fresh."

The evrae stood, shook the dust from their stained and tattered clothes, and began shuffling toward their horses. Mari followed, saying, "I wish you the best of luck, and I hope we meet again one day." After a pause, she added, "Next time, under better circumstances."

Mounting her horse, Elonn whispered, "Thank you for your hospitality. Travel safely."

"You as well." Mari trailed after the riders when they took their horses back through the brush, then watched them fade into the distance along the pathway. Gren came up behind her and put an arm around her waist. She leaned into the solid warmth of his chest, but, comforting as it was, she pulled away and said, "I'm going to talk to Laria and find out if she's seen this in that Loom of hers. If she hasn't, she definitely needs to know about it."

When Mari returned to the camp, Derek, Killer, and Ruv regaled the group with tales of their fruitless hunt. She slipped into a seat between Gren and Sam.

"Never seen anything like it," Derek was saying.

"There's nothing," Killer added. "Not for miles."

Ruv's eyes narrowed at Mari's distracted countenance. Catching his gaze, she simply shook her head in dismissal. "No game whatsoever," Ruv elucidated.

Killer bobbed his head up and down, bewildered. "Not so much as a rabbit."

"Hells," Derek cut in, "not so much as a squirrel."

"So we're the only animals around?" Gren inquired. "How far did you look?"

"Far," Ruv replied.

"Very far," Killer clarified.

"Well," Derek amended, "there were lizards, maybe a scorpion or two, but nothing warm and fuzzy and worth eating."

Wendy rubbed her nose. "Well, looks like we'll be vegetarians for a while once that dried goat meat runs out," she commented.

Ruv sighed in the direction of the fire "May as well extinguish that. No use keeping it lit if we don't have anything to cook on it, and we won't need the light much longer anyway."

"Thanks," Mari said, standing. "Micaleth, Gren, would you take a quick walk with me?" When they nodded and stood, Mari turned back to Ruv. "If anything crazy happens, you're in charge."

"Got it."

Once they were out of earshot of the camp, Mari stopped. Gren and Micaleth came around her, forming their own small circle amid the tangled brush. "Ok. So. I have a bad feeling about this," Mari declared.

"So does the Spinner," Micaleth responded. "That is why we are here."

"More than that though," Mari countered, drawing her brows together. She raked a hand through her hair, as tangled as the surrounding brush. "Markos and his family were clearly in bad shape, but when I asked Laria about it, she said there's never been a village right on the border, that there's only the one village between the traveling circle and Dahrigek, and nothing like the raid they described has ever happened here, not even before the splitting." The crease between her brows deepened. "So where did they come from?" she asked to the void of night. "On top of that, there are apparently zero animals anywhere around here. There's enough vegetation, at least, that there should be something living here. At the very least, there should be rabbits. So where did all the mammals go?"

"Both good questions," Gren concurred. "What do our four legged friends know that we don't?"

Mari nodded and turned to Micaleth. "You were weirdly silent when they mentioned this giant bull thing. Did it sound familiar?"

"You recall the history of how humanity came to be? Back before the splitting of the worlds, there were stories, passed down generation to generation," he replied. "I only know fragments, but something in their description got me reminiscing about those old stories. However, given everything else, I believe it is far more probable that she was hallucinating. She likely heard the same tales."

Folding her arms, Mari mused, "So we have a land hidden from the Spinner, a village that doesn't exist, vanishing animals, and now either ancient stories or trauma-induced hallucinations. Where's the connection? Who has that kind of power?"

"The lanti?" Gren posed.

Micaleth shook his mane. "I would not think so," he asserted. "They do not like to meddle much anymore. Furthermore, Morana, in her incarnation as Nemini, has not utilized her sway over death in many centuries."

"Nemini?" Mari and Gren repeated, their brows raised.

"Long story," Micaleth said. "Perhaps I'll tell you later. In any case, the only one among the lanti who was ever known to manipulate time and memory was Rod, and he sacrificed himself for the splitting."

"Veles?" Mari submitted. "Is this his MO?"

"No, not quite," Micaleth replied. "His powers have also weakened since his rift with Morana. Again, a long story best saved for another day. That said, I believe it is still wise to be wary of the lanti in general. I would not want to test the limits of their wrath, and, whether weakened or apathetic, they remain the most powerful beings in this, or any other, world." He paused for a moment, eyes squeezed shut in memory, then added, "Even when Kutkah veiled the twins and their actions, it was a simple binding. Veiling an entire location is unprecedented."

Mari uncrossed her arms and idly fingered her sword hilt. "Then that's neither here nor there. Maybe you should tell us about these giant bull stories."

"A giant bull would certainly scare away all the game," Gren stated. He reached a hand toward Mari, but she waved it away.

"But is that even possible?" she pressed. "Are there creatures like that here?"

Micaleth snorted. "Surely you have seen enough by now to know that anything is possible, young Dreamer, especially in Aorea."

She rolled her eyes. "Then allow me to rephrase my question: is it *probable*?"

"I do not think so," Micaleth murmured regretfully. "A much more plausible scenario is that she recalled the same legends, and so her memory fueled the nightmare."

Mari released a frustrated sigh. "I suppose we'll just have to hope for the latter." She tapped the tip of her nose as her eyes searched the darkness. "Come on, let's go back to the others. Nothing else to do now."

The morning sunlight trickled through the window as Laria studied the uncooperative Loom, her mouth in a thin line. She flicked a wrist in front of the perpetually unfinished fabric, and the threads twisted from chaos into order and revealed a perfectly clear image of a rainforest in southern Faerie, complete with pixies flitting between the massive trees. She waved another hand, trying to force an image of the masked archipelago, but the threads instead resumed their obstinate mess.

A knock at the window interrupted her thoughts. A lanky woman with a nose like a beak, all angles and sharp bones and black hair crowned in crow feathers, smiled brightly back at her. "Gamayun!" Laria saluted. "It's good to see you again! What brings you here?"

"Seeing you is always a pleasure, Summoner," Gamayun replied with a warm but fleeting smile. "Regrettably, I do not bear good news. Perun and Mokosh sent me. The lanti have held another council—the first in quite some time, you should know—and we have a message for you."

"Would you like to come inside for tea or something?" Laria offered, heading toward the door.

"No, thank you," she responded. "What I have to say is best said beneath an open sky." She disappeared from the window.

When Laria exited the cottage, Gamayun awaited her in the center of the courtyard. She still mostly wore her humanoid form, but she had acquired a set of crow wings sprouting from her shoulders, and the winged tattoos on her ankles had begun to morph into actual feathers that glistened violet and emerald. "For a while now," she began as Laria approached, "we've sensed something brewing beneath the land. Something familiar, and yet not. Mokosh picked up on it first, then Perun, and now even many of the lesser lanti can tell that something is wrong with the worlds." Feathers had begun to sprout from her wrists, creeping up her arms, and the toes of her bare feet had come to resemble talons. "Something dark, something powerful, something reminiscent of Antiln." Her limbs were nearly entirely feathered now, and her hair had begun the transition as well, leaving only her face uncovered. "We cannot tell where this power is brewing, but we can tell that it grows stronger every day."

Laria nodded, tactfully ignoring Gamayun's emergent plumage, and admitted, "The Loom has been acting strangely lately, but I'm certain Antiln's still inside."

Gamayun widened her eyes, which made her nose look even sharper. "Is the Loom not obeying your will?"

"In all ways except for one, the Loom has been perfectly obedient." Laria drew in a deep breath before continuing, "However, there's a part of northwestern Dahrigek that has been clouded from my view for maybe a month now. At least, that's when I first noticed it. I hadn't had much reason to look there, but when I happened to glance that direction on a whim, the threads just would not cooperate. In the last few days, that clouded area has gotten larger. It now reaches almost all the way to Evra."

"Interesting," the bird-woman reasoned, her voice grown more ethereal with the transformation. "Such an unpopulated continent would make an attractive home for a demon like Antiln to hide."

"I certainly hope not," Laria croaked. "I sent Mari and Gren and Ruv down there to investigate."

Gamayun looked noticeably relieved. "If the Destined are looking into it, then things may yet be salvageable. Give me a few moments. My family will want to hear about this."

Laria blinked, and then nothing but a few scattered feathers, flakes of coal drifting on the wind, remained where Gamayun had stood but a second before.

Hal sauntered up and dropped a bushel of green apples at Laria's feet. After brushing a few feathers out of his face, he plucked two apples and tossed one to her.

Catching it, she stated, "I hate it when she does that."

"I'm sure she'll be back soon," Hal mumbled around a mouthful of the tart fruit. "What'd she say, anyway?"

"Antiln," Laria whispered.

Returning to the camp, Mari, Gren, and Micaleth found everyone settled around the dimming embers, sharing the bits of dried fruit, meat, and flatbread they had brought from the Alpines. Frostbite managed to locate some wild carrots nearby and peeled them with his knife while reclining against one of the larger logs. Wendy sat huddled in a blanket, flanked by the gossiping twins. Brae, Ruv, and Killer muttered quietly to each other on the other side of the steaming coals. Derek was the only one absent.

Surveying the group, Mari said, "Well, considering all the game animals have fled to gods-only-know where, we should probably grab more supplies when we reach this town tomorrow. I thought we'd be able to hunt, at least, but that's clearly off the table." Recalling the contents of her pack, she remarked, "We've only got enough for a few weeks at most, and apparently foraging in Dahrigek will be pretty sparse."

"If the village does not pan out," Micaleth offered, "there is a pixie forest on the other side of the wall, but—"

"Wait, there's a wall here?" Ruv interrupted.

"Who in the hells built a bloody wall down here?" Sarah blurted.

Sam nodded his head along with his sister. "I can't picture the evrae building much higher than two stories."

"They don't seem to care for heights," Killer conceded.

Brae snickered. "Probably because they are so small."

Wendy turned an amused gaze toward her fellow diminutive and freckled red-head. "You're one to talk. You're scant taller than me!"

"I'm tall for a leshii, I'll have you know," she returned with a toss of her hair.

Ruv squinted at her. "But you all look identical."

Brae smacked him on the wrist. "Are you blind?"

"But you do!"

"For the record," she said, "I was talking about my tree-half. The birch I am linked with is quite tall indeed. And I'll have you know, not all leshii look the same. We tell each other apart just fine, thank you."

"How?" Ruv urged.

"...you'll laugh."

Mari, despite her unease at their overall situation, forced a smile at Brae. "We won't, I promise."

Brae sucked in a breath and said, "Our freckle patterns. Each one is unique."

Frostbite nodded appreciatively. "Like the stripes on a tiger," he said.

"Or the spots on a leopard," Sarah added.

"Point taken," Ruv granted, suppressing a laugh regardless of Mari's promise. "Still, that's an awful subtle difference to try and tell one of you from the others."

"Not if you're used to looking," Brae argued.

Mari arched a brow and turned to Micaleth, who observed the exchange with amusement. "Now that *that's* cleared up, I believe we were talking about a wall?" she reminded him.

"Yes," he replied, his mirth giving way to solemnity. "While it is called 'the wall,' no one actually built it. It is simply a very steep, very sheer cliff face that divides Evra from the northern mountains of Dahrigek," he expounded. "There is a pass that cuts through them about a hundred or so miles east of here, but that is a bit out of our way. I could easily run that distance in a day or two, but the Spinner said you could not move that quickly over such a length without expending too much energy. Having traveled with you, I can see she was correct. In any case, traversing the wall and the mountains here will position us perfectly to survey the lowlands on the other side before we actually approach them, which is fortuitous, because the northwestern coast is the part the Spinner is concerned about—mostly, anyway—as that is the part presently blocked from her sight."

Sarah regarded him coolly. "You don't expect us to scale this bloody wall on sheer guts, do you?"

"I didn't bring my climbing gear," Sam said.

"Nor would we even have supplies enough to go around if he had," Sarah added. "Not to mention the logistics of hauling a horse up a damned cliff."

Micaleth, whose particularly equine snort belied his annoyance at the accusation, snapped, "I am not a horse. And you need not bother with ropes or gear. There are stairs carved into the wall. It was a modification the evrae made long ago, back when Dahrigek was worth visiting now and then."

Spreading his blanket over the rocky ground, Ruv remarked, "I hope they've bothered with some regular maintenance on those stairs."

Sam shuddered. "I do not fancy a tumble."

Swallowing the bile rising up her throat, Wendy queried, "Exactly how high is this cliff-wall-thing?"

"Quite high," Micaleth answered. "Perhaps three or four hundred meters, I believe."

Wendy grew yet paler at the answer, and Gren whistled through his teeth. Frostbite, noting Wendy's increasing discomfort, tossed her the last of his peeled carrots. "Eat," he ordered. "This will help." She looked at him in confusion, but all the same, she obliged.

Mari inquired, "Now that you've experienced our apparently glacial pace first-hand, how long would you say we've got before we enter this blind spot of Laria's?"

Micaleth pondered the question for a few moments before making his reply. "If we keep the current pace," he reasoned, "it should take us several days to get to the wall, assuming we stop in the village for a few hours, and then another day to truly enter the mountains. Beyond that, we will just have to see. As I am sure you remember, Aorean distances can be a bit deceptive."

"Wonderful," Mari grumbled. "On that delightful note, I think it's time we try to get some sleep." She reached for her bedroll then abruptly straightened. "Wait, did anyone bother to work out a guard shift yet?"

Sarah yawned. "Already taken care of."

"Derek's running the perimeter now," Killer added. "I'm going to join him since everyone's going to sleep, and then we'll continue working in pairs until daybreak."

"We're up next," Sam and Sarah said.

Frostbite, having since stowed his knife, stated, "I'll be taking a shift with Gren."

"What?" Gren squeaked. "Says who?" Frostbite returned his surprise with indifference. Suddenly reminded that the gargantuan man would easily crush him in a fight should he take it in his head to initiate one, Gren added, "I mean, not that I don't like you or anything. I'm just wondering who came up with the rotation."

"Ruv," Frostbite grunted.

"Then who's on shift with him?"

Sarah let out a dry laugh. "I'll give you three guesses, not that you'll need them."

"...Mari."

Ruv coughed, quashing a smirk. "Well, it made sense to work in totem-pairs that were similar. Two panthers, two tigers, two wolves."

One of Gren's eyelids began to twitch, but he kept his ensuing thoughts to himself.

Wendy went through the list in her head again and frowned. "Guess I'm no good for guard until I figure out my totem, aye?"

Ruv smiled gently at her. "I'm afraid not, little one. Enjoy the extra sleep."

"And I presume you left Brae and myself off the list," Micaleth supposed.

Ruv scratched behind an ear. "I actually hadn't thought to include you in the first place," he admitted, but then with a mischievous grin he added, "But don't worry. You'll be on the next one."

Micaleth sputtered, his lips flapping in a fashion quite indecorous to a creature of his self-appointed rank, but the others—Brae included—cackled.

CHAPTER FOUR
A group of awfully brave explorers

"According to my memory of the map," Micaleth asserted, his hooves kicking up clouds of dust as he trotted alongside Mari, "we should see the village once we crest the next hill."

Mari gave him a tight nod as she tugged the buckle where sword met sword belt, which had slid annoyingly toward her midline, back into its preferred position at her hip. "Hopefully they're in better shape than wherever Markos came from," she muttered. "And at least we'll have a chance to pick up some more supplies before we head off into a damn desert."

After a few days of exposure to the equatorial sun, everyone had mostly acclimatized. Gren no longer complained of the heat, accepting that things were only likely to get worse as they continued further south. Thus, he decided to reserve his most colorful complaints for later. Mari and Ruv, although noting Gren's ostensible tolerance, made no comment lest he resume his grumbling. Killer's olive complexion remained mostly unchanged, the only notable difference being the increased fading of his new scar. Derek's winter pallor, on the other hand, had already deepened enough to reduce the harshness of the contrast of skin against auburn hair; the sun also brought forth a dusting of freckles across his nose. In turn, his freckles brought forth some gentle teasing from Wendy and Brae, even though Wendy—liberally applying sunscreen several times a day—faired far worse.

Brae, for her part, reveled in the light and heat, leaving a trail of serrated leaves in brilliant green wherever she tread. Micaleth likewise seemed to enjoy the change in climate, remarking on more than one occasion that niethera prefer warm weather and humidity over the frozen wastelands of the north, hence their large population in the rainforests of Faerie. Frostbite's only homage to the weather was to shed his outer layers, revealing a series of tiger stripe tattoos down his right arm, all the way from shoulder to wrist. The first time he spied the tattoo, Gren caught Mari's eye and mouthed "so basic," at her, which caused her to suppress a giggle. Fortunately, Frostbite missed the exchange. The twins had finally stowed their black leather (well, their vests, in any case; they maintained their leggings and boots) in their respective packs, sporting only their mesh underlayers. No one dared acknowledge the change aloud.

Just as Micaleth had predicted, they were granted their first glimpse of the settlement of Kalbet once they reached the summit of the next hill.

Mari slowed their train to a halt as they approached, and the group spread along either side so everyone had an equal chance to eye the village with a mild curiosity mixed with disappointment. Sarah was the first to break the silence. "Blimey, that is tiny," she observed with a derisive sniff. She tucked the tube of lipstick she had just reapplied in preparation for reentering civilization into a pocket. "Won't be anyone to flirt with."

Her brother squeezed her shoulder in reassurance. "There will be other towns," Sam said. "Well, eventually."

Derek, scratching his chin, asked, "Think we'll be able to get any quartz down there?"

"I doubt they even have a tavern," Killer sighed.

"Nonsense!" Ruv countered with a broad grin as he stretched his back and cracked his neck. "It's an evrae village. The first thing they build is a tavern."

Micaleth narrowed his eyes at Ruv. "Whence, precisely, did you acquire this information?"

Shrugging, he explained, "Experience, mostly. I've spent a lot of time in various evrae taverns." He swept the end of his walking stave down and caught an unsuspecting Gren on the back of his knees. When Gren whipped around to glare at him, Ruv's lopsided grin broadened. "Of course," he continued, stifling a laugh, "those taverns were all in Nomansland."

As they drew closer to the village, they realized even that humble term may be too generous a designation for the four blocks of buildings that lined two crossed streets with naught but a white fountain marking the crossroads. The buildings appeared to be hewn from the local stone and stacked in irregular rows beneath tiled roofs of diverse hues. Gardens sprawled behind each building in squares of vegetables and herbs and even a few fruit trees, and while they spied several goats munching in fenced pastures, no other livestock populated the vicinity. Eyeballing one of the goats with mistrust, Ruv declared, "I've got a bad feeling about this place, my friends."

"Don't think we'll find any supplies?" Mari asked. She stopped at the edge of the town to smile and wave at one of the village's inhabitants, who squinted at them before ducking behind a squat building.

"You could say that," Ruv drawled. "I'm mostly rethinking my assertion that there'd be a tavern."

Micaleth stared back at one of the more curious of the goats, who had wandered toward the edge of the fence to investigate the newcomers. Impervious to the glowering nietheran, the goat snatched a tuft of crabgrass and went about his munching. Micaleth turned his attention back to the town. "That is indeed a disappointing prospect," he said with a twitch of his tail. "I have not noticed any common flowers here, either, so unless they import quartz, we will be out of luck."

"For goodness sake, do you guys think of nothing else?" Mari exclaimed.

"What?" Micaleth scoffed. "It's delicious."

They left the goats in their pastures and entered the village proper. A few more of the locals worked in the gardens but paid no mind to the recent arrivals. Indicating one of the stone huts that sported a blue tiled roof, Brae said, "I believe that may be a shop of sorts, if I'm reading that sign correctly. Perhaps we can stock up there."

Micaleth nodded his agreement, and they headed toward the designated building, which, they soon realized, was far too small to accommodate the entire group. "Sam and I'll see if we can find us a place to eat a real lunch while you do the shopping," Sarah offered. Without waiting for anyone's approval, she slunk off down the other street, her brother trailing after her.

Ruv addressed Killer and Derek with overdramatic sternness. "See if you can find some more spiced mulsuma to bring with us. Surely they at least have that here." They saluted in response, which prompted an answering smirk from Ruv, and jogged off to obey.

In the end, only Mari, Gren, Ruv, Brae, and Micaleth entered the shop. Frostbite and Micaleth had reasoned that it was perhaps not the best idea for them both to attempt to squeeze into such a tiny area, especially if they wanted to leave on good terms with the owner. As it was, it would likely be tight enough just for one of them. Micaleth had then insisted upon being the one to enter, arguing that his boundless wisdom and knowledge were necessary to determine everything they should buy. However, his arguments proved entirely wasted since Frostbite agreed to remain outside without the slightest hesitation and, in fact, appeared to welcome it. As for Wendy, she asserted that she would rather scrape off a few more samples of stone for her expanding collection of Aorean minerals.

A waft of incense greeted them as they crossed the threshold, followed promptly thereafter by an enthusiastic squeal. "Why, I'll be a pumpkin harvest in spring!" the shopkeeper cried as he caught sight of his customers.

Mari recognized the one she had waved at earlier, recalculating her prior assessment that he had scurried off out of a desire *not* to make their acquaintance, but rather, to man his shop in anticipation. She smiled.

As if in confirmation of her altered assumption, he beamed at them from behind round glasses and planted his hands on either side of his equally round hips. "I don't think there's been humans in this shop since my ancestor Dendro founded the place right before the splitting! That's a portrait of him up on the wall there. Welcome, welcome! What brings you to these parts?" He barely paused a second before launching back into his allocution. "No one ever comes this far south unless they mean business, or else they're horribly lost. Oh, a leshii! Haven't had one of you down here in a while either. Aren't many birches growing around these parts," he rambled while the five friends spread out as best they could in the cramped shop, inspecting the contents. "Mostly pines and palms. Not really the right climate for your kind. And a nietheran! I didn't see you hiding back there at first. Not sure how I missed you, tall as you are. Must be needing some new glasses." He removed the spectacles in question and began to rub the lenses with a handkerchief. "So, what can I do for you today? In the market for some new scarves, knickknacks, something to remember your stay?"

Mari introduced herself and the others, then explained, "We're about to head into Dahrigek and were hoping to stock up on food, rope, spare clothing, maybe a few extra knives. Things like that. You seem to have a pretty good selection here, but I don't see any food. Do you know where we could get some more robura or flatbor, maybe, or some dried meat? Haven't had much luck hunting."

"Sure, sure!" the shopkeeper agreed. "Take a look around, and when you find everything you need, I'll give you directions to Tia's place. She's got all kinds of food that'll keep for you if you're going adventuring. I always say, Tia's biscuits don't decay! They last forever, they do. Might crack a few teeth, sure, but you won't go hungry. She keeps loads of dried mutton in stock, too." He bobbed his head toward the door, and the movement caused his recently cleaned glasses to slip down his nose. He quirked a sheepish grin as he slid them back into place. "Can't seem to keep much livestock around these parts besides goat, lately, and even the goats like to scamper off sometimes and then we just never can find them! Used to have more variety, too, but it's only been goat for a while now," the shopkeeper admitted with a shrug. "Anyway, it's chewy, but it'll feed you."

He finally paused his ramblings for a moment as he polished the rim of a tea cup, but his eyes followed everyone's meanderings. Brae browsed some books along a back shelf while Ruv and Gren collected armfuls of clothing that looked sturdy (and, thankfully, large) enough to fit their needs. Mari's fingers trailed along a shelf of flint and knives better suited to paring vegetables than combat. Micaleth, for his part, tried not to ruin the reputation of the majestic niethera by bumping into anything, an effort at which he decidedly failed.

"Dahrigek, huh? Treacherous place, that land is," the shopkeeper prattled as he set the teacup aside. "You must be a group of awfully brave explorers. No one goes down there anymore. Just a tiny forest, then desert as far as the eye can see, and a good deal further, I hear. You know, my own ancestors helped carve those stairs into the wall," he said with a remorseful look at the faded portrait of Dendro suspended above the shop entrance. "They say back before the splitting there was some talk of giving Dahrigek to the humans, but the lanti insisted that would have been a crueler exile than making you your own place. But look at you now! Venturing forth across the wall, exploring lands no sentient species has bothered to inhabit! There's the pixies, of course, but they've always been a bit wild. Why, I've half a mind to close up my shop and go with you, but adventuring is not for me, no. I'm much too old now. Maybe if I were younger, I'd brave the desert with such explorers as yourselves." He patted his large stomach. "And maybe if I were in better shape."

Mari, placing on the counter an armful of extra blankets, a spare med kit, hatchets, hooks, rope, and a few bags to contain the additional supplies, announced, "I think this should do."

"Oh, you're done shopping already?" he peeped, eyes wide behind his spectacles. He began rifling through the pile and stuffing the items into the bags as he resumed his discourse. "I feel like we've only just begun to talk! My, how time flies. Glad you found everything you need, at least. Sure I can't interest you in a few protection amulets to ease your travels? Blessed by our very own town mage!" He stuffed one of his plump hands into a pocket and withdrew a lump of rough amethyst inlaid with a silver-enameled triangle.

Eyeing the stone with feigned interest, Mari replied, "No thanks, but I will take that skillet hanging up behind you, actually. Cast iron?"

"Sure is! Seasoned it myself not too long ago, and my husband did the forge work." As he plopped the skillet on the top of the stuffed bags, he declared, "That'll bring your total to an even twenty deni."

Brae shoved past Mari to the counter. "Twenty?" she bellowed. "Holy—"

"That's absurd!" Ruv agreed, jostling his way next to Brae with complete disregard for Mari's personal space.

Micaleth, thrusting his snout over Ruv's shoulder, snorted imperiously and said, "I'm afraid I must agree with my friends. Twenty deni indeed seems high for a bit of ratty cloth and a rusty old pot."

"Ratty? Rusty!" the shopkeeper blustered. "If you think you can find a better price this close to the border, be my guest! But you won't find another shop within four days' distance that carries even half my selection."

"We'll give you ten deni," Brae stated. "Ten is fair."

"I'll go as low as seventeen, but I can accept no less with a clean conscience for my quality."

Mari pushed past her friends to reclaim her original position. "I'll give you fifteen and a warning. Pack up your shop after we leave. Tell all your friends, your neighbors, everyone, to do the same. Take your family, take anything of value you can carry, and head north. Keep going north, and don't look back."

Trembling with either rage or terror, or perhaps a mix of both, the shopkeeper sniffed, "Is that a threat? This village is my home! My family has lived here for hundreds of generations! Can you even conceive of how long that is, human? My people have lived here since time began!"

Mari placed a hand, gently as she could, on top the quaking shopkeeper's as she whispered, "There's something sinister going on in Dahrigek. We don't yet know what, but we're going down there to find out. It's no longer safe this close to the border. Surely you've heard about what happened to Orabet?" When the shopkeeper merely gave her a blank look, she continued, "Quite frankly, it's a miracle you're even still here. But in case we fail, in case we don't find what we're looking for or get caught up in whatever's going on, you need to leave."

"You can have the lot for ten," he murmured.

She deposited fifteen deni of tarnished gold on the counter. "You need to leave. All of you."

The shopkeeper nodded in response, his rambling terminated at last.

Ruv cleared his throat once they exited the shop, interrupting the ominous mood left by Mari's warning. "I wonder if our resident panther-twins have found anywhere we can eat one final meal before it's nothing but goat jerky and flatbor?"

"They did," Frostbite answered in his bass rumble. "Wendy and the others are there now."

He led them down the other street to the largest building in Kalbet they had yet observed, which sported a red tiled roof and windows of amber glass. As they entered, Sam and Sarah tossed several pears at the newcomers. "You've got to try these!" Sam asserted.

Mari, Ruv, and Gren eagerly bit into the fruit, then promptly nodded agreement at their deliciousness. Mari swallowed and inquired, "What else is on the menu?" An evrae, who she assumed must be a waiter due to the apron tied about his waist and the tray of empty dishes in his hand, offered her a stained card. She perused the unillustrated list with chagrin, turned to Brae, and said, "Glad I got a translator handy. Help a sister out, please."

Brae laughed and took the card. "What are you in the mood for? Looks like they've mostly got vegetarian options and a goat stew, but I do believe there's a poultry section." She squinted at the script then added, "Ah, never mind. Out of stock."

Before they left, Mari issued a similar warning to the restaurant owner, who gave a similar response. She repeated the warning a final time at the grocers, where they spent the remainder of their cash—Sarah and Sam's recently acquired stash included—to stock up on as many nonperishables as they could.

The necromancer paced through the dungeons past cage after cage. Some stood empty save cobwebs and bones; others held trembling captives that cowered in the shadows. He stopped in front of one, its inhabitant barely conscious. A flash of jewel-red hair, now dulled by filth, caught the torchlight. "She grows suspicious of me," he said, black eyes unfocused. His mind was fixed not on his immediate surroundings, but caught far away to the north whence his love ever called him, silent and sure. Even now he could see her in his mind's eye, could feel her warm fingers trailing across his frozen skin. "Her family ties are splitting her loyalty." With considerable effort he drew his thoughts back to the present. "Tell me, how long has this one been kept from her roots?"

Servorg held the torch closer to the metal bars so his master could better study the cell's occupant. "We captured this leshii eight months ago, master."

"And yet she clings to feeble life." He rubbed his wrist, feeling the faint, slow pulse that should and yet should not beat there. "If I bind her spirit to my will, that will give me a link to Nomansland. Perhaps not yet. I should not rush." He moved on to another cell, where a pixie darted to and fro, its face contorted. "There is time enough."

"Indeed, master."

"Soon I will have to expand, however," he mumbled. "These pixies are proving too weak to survive the change."

"All, master, will been converted," Servorg placated. "Soon they will bend only to your will."

The necromancer turned his back on the twitching sprite. Its wings beat defiantly. "I will plant the seeds, but then your next mission is to bring me Necria. Take your army and raze her village, but do not harm a single, lustrous hair on her pure head or I shall take every scar she gains threefold from your own miserable flesh."

"Yes, master," he said with a brusque bow.

"Feed her, too," he commanded. "And give her water. The living need water."

Servorg bowed once more and left.

The necromancer continued pacing the dungeon, but his thoughts had strayed elsewhere. The past drew him back as surely as her voice drew him forward. Centuries, it cost him. A millennium, two millennia, more. He was no longer certain. He had sacrificed countless lifetimes to gain the power to rip through the veils between worlds, layer after invisible layer, to create his own veil of secrecy and silence, to weave a shroud that none could penetrate by dream or magic. There was much more to his story, more than she could be told, lest he lose her forever.

Three years were but a single inhalation in eons' worth of labored breaths, yet those three years had brought him turmoil and confusion and an ache unlike any he had ever known before.

Three years of a craving that, once it gripped him, would not let go.

He had ventured forth from the caverns and caves where his minions had built his fortress, stone by jagged stone. He left his army behind, held fast in the sleep of the dead, as he traveled northward alone. A call tugged at the edge of his mind. He knew not its source, but he followed the summons as if in a dream. His kind could not dream, he reminded himself, and so the call must be real.

He retraced the path he had trod long ago when he first sought solitude in the wastelands of the south. After he left the lands of the one who had unlocked his power and shown him his magic, the one who was more than the simple face he presented to the world, he wanted only to find a haven where he could hone his skills until he grew strong enough to fulfill his destiny. He found such a place easily enough, but soon a loneliness began to creep its way into the void at his core. He may have ripped a hole in the universe, and he may have pulled his minions through the sundered veil, but still loneliness simmered in his breast.

And so he followed the call.

His steps drew him across the empty sand. His body, trained over ages and ages of deprivation, required no food nor drink nor rest; he could draw his energy from the land itself, from the lifeforce of the scuttling creatures that fled his approach but did not flee fast enough. Northward he tread, and death followed in his wake.

The call led him over the mountains and into the rolling green of Evra. He tried to dampen the void that drained the energy from all life near him, but still the emerald faded to a paler, duller shade everywhere he tread. Still the leaves hung limp from their branches, and flowers withered on their stems.

Though this forest grew on the far side of the world, it was not so unlike the one into which he had landed when his sister brought him and his brother to Aorea. This forest was younger, perhaps, and harbored more pine trees. He wandered its shadows, lost in thought, completely oblivious to all but the brown needles that crackled beneath his boots and the wind that sprinkled more in his path. They fell as a soft rain with every passing breeze. They showered his cloaked shoulders and dusted his hair. The call had drawn him to this forest, and so he would not leave until he knew its source.

So absorbed was he in a mix of memories and fantasies stirred by the midnight wood that he never heard the hunters' approach. He did not hear the twang of the bowstring, nor the whistling of the arrow. He did, however, feel the sharp pain as it pierced his palm. The injury would heal, he had no doubt of that, but being caught so off guard disturbed him deeply. It did not require particularly strong ears to hear the exclamations of the unfortunate hunters as they realized their quarry was not the stag they thought they had seen, but a man, taller and paler and fiercer than any of the residents of Orabet. "I'm so sorry!" one shouted, and, "Are you ok?" his companion called.

The necromancer did not bother to answer. He possessed the power to either speed the healing of his palm or avenge the injury, but not both. The choice was easy. He stretched his uninjured hand toward the pair even as they rushed toward him, their bows and arrows cast aside in the desire to aid one they viewed as an innocent victim to their carelessness. Soon the concern in their eyes gave way to dread, but they did not have long to contemplate that dread before their legs crumpled beneath them and their hearts ceased their drumming.

He heard a soft gasp behind him and turned, expecting to find another unfortunate hunter whose life he would extinguish just as quickly. But when he saw the girl, her slender, nut-brown hands covering her mouth, amber eyes wide and glittering in the moonlight, he stayed his hand. The call pounded louder than ever in his head. He stood as still as the towering pine at his back, then felt his knees give way. The rough bark snagged on his cloaks as he skidded down the tree trunk.

"Where are you hurt?" she breathed as she knelt by his side. He kept his eyes closed while the call drowned out all thoughts beyond the sensation of her fingers probing him for injuries. She smelled of the forest's heart, of pinecones and secret berries. At last, he opened his eyes. She offered him a hand. "Come with me. I can help with the pain."

He found himself quite unable to do anything but obey the girl's orders. Whether she had seen the hunters' fates or no, she gave no indication, and he never asked.

"Once her family is taken care of," he whispered to the stagnant dungeon air, "what remains of her heart will belong only to me."

The road they had followed from the traveling circle ended at the town, so they relied on the map and the sun to keep themselves oriented toward the proper mountain range. Fortunately the sun cooperated, remaining visible for the duration of the two and a half days it took them to reach the steep cliffs known as the wall. They ended up barely a mile off course to the east, which they discovered by sending a runner in either direction until they located the stairs. Considering the monotony of the terrain, no one mourned such a minor miscalculation.

The steps were cut lengthwise into the cliff face, climbing from left to right in a narrow trail. Regarding the roughly sculpted stairs with mingled apprehension and relief, Gren remarked, "Those don't look quite as bad as I was expecting, but yeesh!"

Ruv crossed his arms and nodded. "Would it have killed them to add a handrail?"

Sarah tightened the straps of her pack. "They definitely look like they've seen better days, but we'll manage."

"Especially now that we have some hooks and rope. Still not enough to go around, but we can adjust as we go," Sam added, withdrawing said items from an outer pocket on one side of his shoulder bag.

"How have they not crumbled entirely by now?" Derek mused as he twisted his braid into a hasty bun and checked that the laces were tucked into his boots.

"While Mari was busy chatting with that obnoxiously talkative shopkeeper," Brae replied, "I browsed some local history books. Turns out every couple decades, a handful of the bravest Kalbet residents go out and maintain the steps just in case someone should want to head over. There used to be some gold to be found in a stream that trickled down from the mountains, but either the gold or the stream dried up." She stifled a yawn. "No one's ventured beyond the forest in centuries, but every once in a while someone wants to search for more gold so they keep up with the stairs. Still, I'm certainly not going first. I'd rather pay Octavian a compliment!"

Gren wiped the sweat from his forehead as he crinkled his dark brows. "Octavian as in Augustus?"

"Oh no, some other eighth son who ruined Roman democracy. Yes, the first Emperor. Who in the hells else?"

"Just haven't heard you rant about him in a while, that's all," Gren returned. "And he wasn't all bad, you know. His reign triggered two hundred years of peace and prosperity that came to be known as the *pax ro…*"

"Let me stop you right there," Brae snapped.

"Well, he did!" Gren insisted. "Besides, he's been dead for like, two thousand years at this point. Why are you still holding a grudge?"

Brae pursed her lips. "I have my reasons. And it hasn't been that long for me, you know."

Mari released a heavy sigh. "Why am I always surrounded by nerds?" Gren shot her a knowing half-smile in response, but Brae glowered at her. "Anywho," Mari continued, chewing her lip, "there's no point in delaying the inevitable." She tugged on her backpack straps one final time then led the charge up the stairs.

As the most experienced climbers in the bunch, the twins took up the middle position so they could best advise the others on the distribution of their limited hooks and rope. As the heaviest, Frostbite and Micaleth took up the rear. Even despite the stairs, the rope, and the twins' guidance, they nevertheless experienced several setbacks during the ascent. When they had scaled halfway up the wall, one of the steps crumbled beneath Mari's feet just as she was attempting to secure the next hook. Fortuitously, Gren managed to steady her in time to prevent what would have been a decidedly nasty fall. Duly reminded of their mortality, they progressed more slowly after that.

Their final setback, however, was not so lucky.

Only a few feet remained when Wendy fell.

Killer had kicked loose a few pebbles, and before he could warn those behind him, Wendy skidded on the gravel and lost her footing. While flailing to regain her balance, she lost her grip on the rope. Frostbite reached for her, but he only succeeded in snagging the hem of her shirt, which tore away as she tumbled over the edge.

Unwilling to witness their friend's death yet unable to tear their eyes away, they watched in mute horror as she plummeted to the sand and gravel below.

Screaming.

Wendy's cries echoed in their ears until they ceased entirely, and everyone finally looked away.

Had anyone been watching, they would have seen the precise moment when their friend's terror gave way to triumph. Meters from the ground, the no longer screaming Wendy drew her limbs toward her core, forming a tight ball. Then, with a resumed cry, her arms burst into a flurry of tawny feathers and shredded fabric.

She spread gargantuan wings as she loosed a deafening hoot. Wendy succeeded in rescuing her tumbling pack in her massive, newly acquired talons just before it would have smashed. With a few thunderous flaps of her wings, she flew back up and over the wall. The others greeted the sight with first bewilderment, then elation as she soared over their heads. They caught a glimpse of bright orange eyes in place of her usual aloe green, and then Wendy-the-owl descended in a spiral behind a cluster of trees.

Everyone raced toward her, grinning and whooping, and by the time they arrived she wore her human form once more and had just finished tying the laces of a spare pair of running shoes. "You're an owl!" Gren shouted as Wendy pulled her backup glasses from her jumbled pack.

"I'm an owl!" she squealed back at him.

"What do you think your wingspan is, twenty, twenty-five feet?"

"I don't know!" she replied, still squealing with excitement. "It makes a sort of sense though. The size, I mean," she reasoned, eyes glazing over as she turned her thoughts inward to complete her assessment. Suddenly he snapped her focus to Ruv. "You take your mass with you when you shift, aye?"

He nodded, crooked grin firmly in place. "I always thought it was just your size that stayed the same, but you have proved me wrong."

"So while I'm on the wee side for a human," Wendy concluded, "I make a great big bloody owl!"

"Our 'little one' is all grown up," Sarah mused, patting Wendy on the back with a rare look of affection tempering her dark eyes.

The congratulations and exclamations continued as everyone tried to determine exactly what type of owl Wendy had shifted into, but no one could come up with a definitive answer. Wendy herself refused to even venture a guess, reminding them that she was a geologist, not an avian biologist, and she would prefer to do proper research once she had the time.

"Great gray owl?" Gren offered.

"I'm brown, not gray," Wendy countered.

"Eagle owl?" Mari tried.

"No idea what those look like besides *big*," Wendy replied, and thus ended the speculation.

When the excitement died back down, they surveyed the land before them. The plateau stretched for miles and miles before sloping into a steady, forested incline into the dark mountains. The pines crowded together so densely further up the mountainside that it gave the illusion of one great, black organism crawling over the ridge. Judging the distance until they would vanish into the opaque forest and accounting for the subsequently slowed travel, they estimated it would take them another day and a half to reach the summit.

"How is everyone feeling after that little adventure?" Mari queried.

"Certainly better than that time we scaled Kupala's waterfall without so much as a rope, but I'd still rather not come this way again," Gren replied with a shudder.

Ruv turned to peer back over the cliff. "Except that we *have* to go back," he grumbled.

Sarah accompanied Ruv in his scrutiny. "Judging from the view," she stated, "I'd say going back down will be ten times worse."

"Although that is quite a view," Sam said.

The rest followed suit and marveled at the wild land that stretched behind them, a land they had scarcely experienced before leaving it in the dust. The brush of the lowlands they had so recently walked shimmered chartreuse in the afternoon sun. The village of Kalbet was detectable only as a smudge, and beyond the lowlands, they spied another mountain range tinged a smoky blue by the vast distance between them.

"I wonder if those raiders used the same stairs as us?" Ruv breathed, leaning hard on his staff. He tore his eyes away and shook the sweat from his scraggly back curls.

"I wonder who, or what, they are," Mari whispered in return, her normal vibrance subdued.

Micaleth contemplated her stony expression before agreeing, "As do I. Things like that are not supposed to happen in Aorea, not since, well…"

"Not since you exiled all the humans to Earth," Mari finished for him. She turned her back on the abandoned land of Evra and instead faced the black mountains they would soon enter. "Come on. We've still got a lot of ground to cover before nightfall."

They heard the laughter of the pixies echoing amongst the trees well before they reached the forest's edge. Yet, as soon as they crossed the wooded threshold and the evergreens encased them in darkness, the echoing laughter vanished. However unnerving the sound of the pixies' mischievous merriment had been, the silence was worse. When the laughter rang anew as they edged further into the black wood, their unease grew greater still.

"Odd," Brae observed after a few steps. Removed from the harsh glare of the equatorial sun, she began to emit her own glow, and so Mari had graciously stepped aside so Brae could lead them through the murky maze. "The pixies sound more malevolent here than I'm used to. Normally they're a friendly bunch, if a bit on the simple side and prone to mischief."

Twitching, sneezing, and rubbing his face in response to inhaling a cobweb, Ruv remarked, "That's true, at least of the ones I encountered in Nomansland." He snorted out the remaining gossamer threads, earning a feigned gag of disgust from Sam, who was picking his way through the dense tree trunks behind him. "Maybe the pixies of Dahrigek have something of a different accent," Ruv continued, "that only makes them sound malicious to our unaccustomed ears?"

"Perhaps," Brae contemplated.

Micaleth, emitting his own faint glow from his alicorn, though subdued in comparison with Brae's glittering aura, dipped his snout in agreement. "Nonetheless," he asserted, "it may be best to keep a close eye on our supplies."

"Especially the sweets," Brae concurred. "In fact, I recommend we all sleep on top our stuff."

"Well, hells," Mari interjected. "I was going to say the trees are tight enough we can probably get away with only one guard for tonight, but now I'm thinking we still take our shifts in pairs."

"I'll second that," Gren popped.

"As do we," chimed the twins.

Mari nodded out of habit even though no one could see the gesture. "That's settled then. Let's start looking for a solid, defensible spot to bed down. The forest is dark enough as it is and it's only going to get darker. I don't want to be stumbling around, setting up camp in a black hole, twisting an ank—"

"Technically speaking," Gren interrupted after he only just managed to catch himself from tripping over a particularly bulky root, "if we run into a black hole, setting up camp will be the least of our worries. We'd have more trouble dealing with the *event* itself, right? We'd never see the horizon." He looked around excitedly, but Wendy, who broke into a fit of giggles, appeared to be the only one to find his pun even remotely humorous. "I'm so glad there's another geek on this trip," he confessed with a grin. "The last one was hell. I was mocked mercilessly."

Mari cleared her throat. "You were not. And do we still got everyone together? I can't exactly see well enough to count." A series of affirmative mumbles answered, and they continued stumbling half-blindly through the wood.

Thus it happened that they discovered their campsite for the night quite by accident.

Invisible even to the still-radiant Brae, the ground suddenly dissolved into a shallow depression carved by erosion and held together solely by a network of interwoven roots. Most were spared the indignity of tumbling headlong into the hole, but Brae, Mari, and Gren—trudging mechanically through the darkness at the front of the line—landed hard with their limbs as entangled as the tree roots that broke their fall. Thereby sufficiently warned of the obstacle, the rest had time to enter the depression voluntarily. They carved a cautious path between the intertwined trees, a feat which was particularly difficult for the broad-shouldered Frostbite and four-legged Micaleth.

"Ok, no more forest rambling at night," Mari professed as she extricated herself from the bracken. She shook out her hair. Pine needles and assorted debris she would rather not contemplate flew in every direction.

"Screw it," Gren grunted, rubbing his knee where he'd banged it against a rock. "Let's just set up here."

Since no one relished the thought of blundering yet further, everyone immediately voiced their approval of the idea. Frostbite inspected the perimeter of the depression and pronounced its defensibility acceptable, an assessment that Killer and Derek were quick to echo. "I'll take first guard," Frostbite then volunteered.

"I'll join you," Brae replied. "Still don't much like the sound of those giggling sprites."

By this point Wendy had located a lantern and set it on a rock near the bottom of the cramped depression. The lantern cast just enough light for them to perceive each other's faces, which flashed like skulls in the unsteady illumination. With the trees so crowded together and nothing to cook, they decided to forego their usual fire. When the twins began to grumble about missing their tea as a result, Mari reminded them that they had a limited supply as it was, and once they ran out they would miss it much more in the mornings.

Micaleth shrugged off one of the many packs strapped to his midsection and mumbled, "I come from a long, prestigious line of Guardians, yet, after only a few days amongst humans, I have been reduced to a pack mule."

Mari laughed as she dug through the contents of one of Micaleth's discarded packs to retrieve a dried sausage and loaf of hard, crusted bread, which she then passed around to her friends. "Cheer up, Mickey," she said with a grin. "If you haven't noticed, we're each bearing our share."

"My share appears to be the largest."

"You probably weigh, what, like twice as much as me, Gren, Ruv, and the twins put together," she commented before popping a slice of sausage into her mouth.

"I suppose I'll concede that point," Micaleth replied with a dramatic sigh. He rubbed his left side up against the bark of a nearby pine, then released his hind legs from their duty by planting his back end on the ground with a thump. The others coughed when the movement unleashed a cloud of dust and debris. "So, Gren," Micaleth began, drawing out the two syllables in a manner that instantly made Gren suspicious. "Hal has bombarded me with many tales of how you used to plague him with songs. Will you be similarly plaguing us tonight?"

Mari frowned. "Do you think it's safe?"

"I believe so," Micaleth said, glancing at Brae, who merely shrugged in response. "If Hal's stories are to be believed, Gren's voice may even scare the pixies away."

Chuckling, Gren replied, "If there are no objections, I don't mind providing the evening's entertainment. It'll keep me from getting too rusty." He glanced about their small camp, craning his neck around the interfering tree trunks to make eye contact with everyone. Apart from Frostbite, whose expression remained indecipherable, the general reaction appeared positive. Gren tapped his long fingers against his chin, eyes closed in thought. A few moments passed before he opened his eyes and said, "Alright, let's try this one. It's new, and I haven't performed it for a crowd yet, so I'd appreciate some feedback, especially on the melody."

He began drumming a beat on one of the larger of the unburied tree roots. After a few measures, he started to hum along with the rhythm, slowly building a deep melody over the tapping of his hands. After a few more measures, he opened his mouth and unleashed the words, softly at first, but rising bolder with every stanza.

> *When we were young and played with fire,*
> *Each step we took was on a wire.*
> *I took your hand, and you took me higher,*
> *But we fell into the dark.*

> *When we were young and danced all night,*
> *I kissed you by the fireside.*
> *The stars shone brighter than city lights,*
> *Then we just fell apart.*
> *Funny, how things fall apart.*

Mari shot to her feet in the middle of the second verse, hand gripping her fatestone, and picked her way between her companions until she had disappeared into the shadows beyond the depression. Gren, though noting her departure with a brief frown, did not let his voice falter.

> *I looked straight into the abyss,*
> *Picked up all the things I'd missed.*
> *I lost myself, but I found this:*
> *An ember to strike a spark.*

> *When we were young and blazed a trail,*
> *Just like a flaming phoenix's tail,*
> *We burned out, our train derailed.*
> *Our destruction became an art.*

He continued drumming long after the echoes of his voice had stilled. At last, he ceased the song entirely and sought his audience's reaction.

Mari had yet to return, and so Ruv left to find her. Of those who remained, most looked thoughtfully at Gren. Sarah, however, was grinning broadly, an unnerving spectacle by the flickering lamplight that cut the bones of her face into a skeletal mask. "Bravo, Grenny-boy!" she exclaimed. "I knew there was a reason we kept you around now even though we've got a nietheran to open the portals and a much larger tiger to do the heavy lifting. But those lyrics…trouble on the home front, love?"

"Huh? Oh, it's nothing," Gren mumbled, burying his face behind his water bottle to hide a blush, not that anyone would have been able to make out his burning cheeks by the light of their singular lamp. "Just a song."

Sarah snorted in disbelief. "Aren't you wondering what she's off to in the woods now?"

Gren's mouth grew tight, but he did not deign to reply.

Sam drew closer, threw an arm around Gren's shoulders, and winked. "You can sing for me anytime," he crooned. Gren just shook his head and wiggled out of Sam's embrace.

At that moment a frowning Mari and Ruv resumed their seats. Gren looked probingly at Ruv, but the other man simply shrugged. "Laria was just checking in," Mari explained. "Looks like nothing's changed."

Micaleth, still pondering the finished song, announced, "Hal made the prospect of listening to your voice sound painful, but that was actually quite pleasant."

"You can't believe everything Hal tells you," Mari cut in, her tone lighter, "especially where music is concerned. We drug him to all our gigs and half our practices. He never forgave us."

Micaleth's eyes sparkled with mischief as he replied, "Well, he had nothing but fond memories of your own musical talents, Mari."

"In that case," Mari began, smiling at Gren though he could not help but note that her smile did not reach her eyes. His concern at her disappearance in the middle of the song having since given way to annoyance, he aimed a light punch at her shoulder. However, Mari scooted neatly out of the way.

"Perhaps one day you will share with us the song you wrote for Kupala?" Micaleth suggested.

A muscle in Gren's cheek twitched as his annoyance grew. "I don't think that's a good idea," he mumbled.

"She did smash your guitar," Ruv reminded him.

"It was supposed to be just for her," Gren elaborated, ignoring the barb. "And I feel like she'd just know somehow if I sang it again, so I don't."

As the conversation drifted to silence, Mari asked, "Anyway, looks like pretty much everyone's ready for the night. Frostbite, Brae, you good to go?"

Frostbite nodded while Brae replied, "I'll talk to the trees and see if I can convince any to provide us with a bit of early warning, should someone, or something, approach." She arched her back in a stretch, lacing her fingers above her head, and began to subdue her phosphorescence. "I might not have much luck, though, considering this is a pixie forest, and the trees will probably want to protect their usual inhabitants. But still, I'll give it a go." However, after tightening her brow, she added, "Of course, if they scream, I'll be the only one who hears, so it may be a moot point."

"Hey, it's still worth a shot," Mari said. "Who wants second shift?"

"Killer and I can take it," Derek offered. Killer nodded his agreement.

"We can take third," Sam stated, ticking his head in his sister's direction even though everyone knew that was who he meant in the first place. Then, with a grin, he caveated, "That is, unless Gren wants to join me?"

"Er, no thanks."

"It's fine, you're not really my type anyway." Sam dismissed. He shot a wink at Frostbite, but the big man wasn't paying him any mind. Instead, his eyes stared blankly at some unseen spot just above Wendy's head. Realizing the futility of his teasing, Sam sighed.

"Gren can take the fourth shift with me," Mari announced. "That just leaves Ruv, Wendy, and Micaleth." She looked pointedly at the nietheran, who did his best to avoid her gaze. Mari rolled her eyes then twisted her neck around a particularly crooked tree trunk to see Wendy. "You want to scout ahead in your owl-form? I'm liking this new skill of yours."

Wendy beamed. "Absolutely! I'm dying to test these wings on a longer flight." She reached to extinguish the lamp. "I'll go during your shift. Moon should be up by then, so hopefully I'll see more."

In the ensuing darkness, everyone settled down to rest amid the twisted roots and twigs. After a few initial grumbles from Gren and Sarah, it wasn't long before the camp drifted into stillness. Apart from the occasional rustle or snore, the only sounds that could be heard were the echoes of the pixies' distant laughter. Frostbite shared a frown with Brae, her glow now utterly suppressed, then tightened his grip on his axe.

In a flurry of feathers, Gamayun blinked into the sanctuary courtyard and instantaneously enfolded Hal and Laria in her wings. "Cover your ears!" she commanded.

"What the hell?" Hal exclaimed, but nonetheless, they both obeyed.

No sooner had they stuffed their fingers into their eardrums than a bolt of lightning exploded nearby, the corresponding thunderclap deafening and immediate. When the boom had ceased echoing off the sanctuary walls and the sizzling had stopped, Gamayun released them from her sheltering wings before disappearing into the ether. Perun, his massive double-headed axe in hand and copper curls swirling around him in the aftermath of the lightning, stood at the heart of the scorched circle. He rumbled, "Summoner, Guardian. Good. The others will join us shortly. Where are your niethera?" He stowed the axe, its thunder-wielding purpose complete, on his back.

A silver coated nietheran approached cautiously from behind an oak. "I can assist you," Gryndonmin declared, his voice regal despite the lingering static electricity that turned his normally sleek mane and tale into frizzing knots. "What do you require?"

"Set up a table with seven chairs," Perun demanded, surveying the sanctuary. His expression gave no indication of whether or not he was pleased by what he saw, and no one pressed for clarification.

"I'm afraid we do not have any tables beyond the one in the Spinner's cottage, and it is not large enough to seat seven," Gryndonmin said with a respectful bow. "Even if it were, we do not have seven chairs."

Perun grumbled, "I'll have Radegast fix that later. Never mind for now. We shall stand."

Gryndonmin dipped his horn in one final bow, then retreated to a safe distance.

Perun tapped his toes on the grass but made no further effort to speak to either Hal or Laria, who merely exchanged wary glances and tried to maintain a courteous demeanor in the presence of the lantian Allfather.

After what felt like much longer than Perun's description of "shortly," a glowing chariot of gold and sky-blue descended from the sun itself. The arrival of the remaining lanti, born aloft in Svarog's bright vehicle, was much less abrupt than Perun's, and so Hal and Laria had time to get out of the way before the yellow flames touched down in the courtyard next to Perun's circle of smoking ground. Mokosh, Devana, and Kupala exited the chariot with deliberate care to avoid the flames emanating from the exterior. As Svarog could not be hurt by the very fire he embodied, he marched straight through.

Laria, squeezing Hal's hand, stifled a gasp at the sight of Kupala. However, the voluptuous goddess merely waved a disinterested hand and purred, "Relax, girl. I'm not here to toy with yours, or anyone else's, fate." She fluttered her dark lashes at Hal. "Not today, that is."

The lanti positioned themselves around Laria and Hal in a circle with Perun on the far side. Mokosh, dressed in a gown of emerald velvet, stood to the left of her mate. Her black hair, smoothed into a tight braid, hung straight down her back, and a skein of rosy yarn stuck out of a pocket.

Merry eyes twinkling and dressed to match his glowing chariot, Svarog stood at Perun's other side. Planting herself next to Mokosh, Devana folded her arms across her chest, her tanned skin blending in with the dyed leather.

Kupala, giggling coyly and twirling the translucent tendrils of silk that twined around her arms, slipped in between Svarog and Hal. She wandered a little closer to the latter than he would have liked. Hal narrowed his eyes every time she inched closer, but a forceful glare from Perun was enough to halt her advances permanently.

When the circle was complete, Perun rubbed his palms together, electricity arching between them, and announced, "Excellent. Let us commence." Turning toward Laria, he said, "Summoner, you were correct to send the Dreamer and the Wanderer into Dahrigek. We believe we know what is happening now, thanks to the information you provided Gamayun."

Laria swallowed, but her voice was steady. "What is it, then? What's causing my blind spot?"

It was Mokosh's gentle alto that answered: "We believe it is one of Antiln's brothers." At Laria and Hal's confusion, she explained, "One brother perished in the devastation she caused just prior to her imprisonment, but the other was never found. We thought he must have long since passed on—their kind are not immortal, you know, and of the original three, she was the only one to possess any kind of magic—but this power, this disturbance in the land, feels just the same as hers did."

"It's possible a surviving brother may have taken shelter with one who could hide him," Devana jumped in, gray eyes focusing on each of the attendees of the impromptu council in turn. "One who could teach him magic, perhaps even prolong his life, at least up until more recently. That one would have to be powerful indeed to have hidden him from all our sights for so long."

"Perhaps one of our own," Perun added ominously. He spat on the ground behind him.

"Who would have possibly hidden him?" Hal inquired, one hand laced through Laria's and the other firmly rooted by habit to the hilt of his sword.

Kupala's eyes wandered, but she settled a sultry gaze at Hal as she said, "We have some ideas, but nothing concrete." She released a bored sigh, and her eyes returned to wandering. "In any case, it's irrelevant. All that matters is where this brother is and what he is up to now."

"Knowing that the Loom is shrouding a specific area," Devana said, "where he is likely to be operating, our suspicions have been all but confirmed. Antiln, twisted as she may have been by hate and rage, would still protect her brother if it were within her power to do so."

"Even from within the Loom," Mokosh added.

Svarog, who up until this point had been silently surveying the sanctuary as the others relayed the results of their council, offered, "And then, of course, we have the prophecy of the Destined."

"Indeed," Perun confirmed.

Laria brushed a stray lock behind her ear as she considered Svarog's assertion. "But that already played out," she questioned. She sought clarification from the expressions of the gathered lanti, but their faces offered her no answers. Even Kupala's countenance was uncustomarily blank. "I'm here. I'm the Fifth Spinner."

Svarog eventually took pity on her puzzlement. "Ah, my child," he replied, "there was much more to the prophecy than that. While your journey may be complete, your story is far from over." He smiled warmly at Laria and Hal, and they could not help but notice all the heat of the summer sun sparkling behind his eyes. "And for the Dreamer, the Wanderer, even the Guardian," Svarog paused to look directly at Hal, who had started at the implication that he might leave the sanctuary. His smile broadening, he finished, "Yes, even you. Like your dear friends, your journey is just beginning."

The rumbling of panther snarls, the raking of massive claws across tree trunks, and the inharmonious twittering of pixies would have roused even the deepest of sleepers. Yet considering everyone's collective anxiety about their forthcoming mission into the unknown, no matter how repressed that anxiety may have been, all it took to get them on their feet was Sam's initial growl. Some reached for their weapons and others began to shift into their deadlier halves while the twins snarled and swiped at the sprites, yet their swift paws were not swift enough.

In a parody of the amulet that had prompted Sam's incarceration, some of the pixies rode astride shining, sapphire scarabs the size of housecats. However, most remained airborne, forming an amorphous blur of giggles and whirring wings. Gren loosed a few arrows into the cloud of pixies, but the points pierced nothing but branches. One arrow sailed straight through the canopy, lost to the sky. He then exchanged his bow for Derek's abandoned machete, but his efforts earned similar results.

Derek, meanwhile, already wore his wolf skin and raged alongside Killer and Ruv, but their jaws snapped just as unsuccessfully around empty air. Fruitless as their efforts proved, they did not let up.

125

Mari hurled her dagger at another of the beetles, but its exoskeleton proved too tough. The ineffectual blade bounced off the scarab's back to lodge in the soil between nearby roots. She barely had time to withdraw her sword before another beetle scampered between her legs and sent her stumbling backward while a pixie yanked her hair.

Frostbite, too large for the confined space on two legs let alone as a Siberian tiger, decided not to bother shifting. Instead, he roared even as he reached for his axe. He hacked with abandon, felling more than a few branches in the process but catching no more than a trace of gauze here and there from the pixies' garments.

Brae and Wendy, dodging Frostbite's mostly arborous victims, lobbed every rock, twig, and pinecone they could get their hands on. One of Brae's volleys managed to catch a fluttering wing, but only a momentary squeal rewarded her pains. The pixies, small enough to maneuver easily between the cramped tress, proved too quick.

In fact, the only one to achieve even a modicum of success in the skirmish before the pixies disappeared as quickly as they had arrived, was Micaleth. As one of the retreating beetles scampered past him, he pierced a joint in one of its segmented legs with his horn. He pinned it to the base of a trunk, but the beetle, urged on by its rider, kept straining forward until the trapped leg ripped off with a nauseating squelch.

"Those rat bastards!" Sarah bellowed as soon as she had reacquired a human mouth with which to make such pronouncements.

"And a fat lot of help the trees were!" Brae cried, kicking a root. The root's owner gave a shudder, shedding needles. "You keep your laughter to yourself," she ordered. She glared up at the tree's branches until the shuddering stilled.

Although Sam had finished shifting back to his human form, his voice retained an undercurrent of the big cat's ferocity. "Should we pursue?" he rumbled.

Mari, collecting her thoughts along with her breath, said, "That depends. How much did they take?"

"Not much," Sarah admitted, exhaling slowly through her nose as she patted down her pockets and rifled through her pack. "We were pretty quick, all in all. But they did snatch what was left of my mulsuma."

"Not that!" Ruv lamented. His lament was echoed throughout the party.

Mari squeezed her eyes shut and pinched the bridge of her nose. "Ok, not worth it," she dismissed. "We'd probably never catch them anyway. Let's do a quick check to make sure nothing *critical* was lost, then screw it, we'll just go back to bed. I don't relish the idea of chasing after a bunch of pixies and bugs in the damn dark."

Her friends nodded their assent, lit the lanterns, and rifled through their scattered supplies. Once Brae finished cataloguing her stash, she moved to assist Micaleth, who was trying in vain to dislodge the severed limb still oozing down his alicorn. "Cheer up," she whispered with a smile. "You were the only one to do any damage."

Micaleth bowed back at her, but his lavender eyes remained downcast as she cleaned off the residual slime with a leaf.

"Nothing missing on my end," Ruv called.

"Nor mine," Frostbite said.

Micaleth swallowed. "I'm afraid I'm missing some honey, a few packs of sweet peel, and a jar of quartz."

"You brought quartz with you and you didn't share with me?" Ruv shrieked, his voice pitched a full octave higher than anyone was accustomed to hearing.

Micaleth, recent melancholy forgotten, sniffed. "I was keeping it for emergencies," he professed. "In addition to being a delicious beverage, quartz also makes a powerful disinfectant."

"Well, duh," Gren said. "It's basically floral vodka."

"Indeed," Micaleth quickly agreed, plopping back down between two roots.

Mari shook her head and asked, "Is anyone else missing anything? No? Good. I'm going back to sleep."

"Actually, darling," Sarah cut in as she gently tapped the tip of Mari's pointed nose, "I'm the one who'll be going to sleep. You'll be pulling guard shift."

"Dammit," Mari and Gren grumbled in unison.

While everyone else settled back down with mutterings and grumblings, Wendy climbed up the prickling branches of an old pine. When she reached the pinnacle, the open sky, filled with unfamiliar stars, greeted her. She beamed and stretched her newfound wings.

CHAPTER FIVE
To break through a wall of cloud

Wendy returned shortly before dawn with nothing significant to report beyond a confirmation of the map's general depiction of the terrain, and so they continued their journey without delay. After a few hours of meandering through increasingly dense forest, a trend no one had thought possible given the original density, the trees finally began to thin. They were just able to walk comfortably two abreast when they came across a rivulet trickling down the mountainside.

Micaleth was the first to discover the water source, his ears twitching in the direction of the faint gurgle. Following his lead, everyone breathed a communal sigh of relief at the sight of the minute fountain where clear water spilled over a stack of stone, and so they gratefully began to refill their water bottles.

But as soon as Frostbite reached the rivulet, he froze.

Feet planted firmly on the rocky ground, he glanced back over his shoulder and motioned Mari and Gren to come forward. "That's beetle blood," he said as he indicated a dull, purplish splotch on the branch of a nearby juniper. "From the one the nietheran injured. They must have come this way."

"What about the pixies?" Mari asked in hushed tones.

Brae joined the huddled trio, whispering, "It's unlikely they'd have further use for their mounts once they finished making off with our supplies."

Frostbite knelt to inspect the purple splash more closely, rubbing his hand over the bark. He took a few steps forward, still hunched low to the ground, and stopped again at a set of mossy stones wedged between the space where the roots of one pine snarled with another. "There's more over here."

"Are these guys normally solitary or no?" Gren asked.

"No," Frostbite said, standing. "We should follow the trail to their nest."

"Wouldn't it be better to avoid them?" Mari countered. "They did enough damage to our stash as it is."

Frostbite shook his head. "Last night they were controlled. Alone, they are simple. Stupid and slow."

"How do you know so much about giant beetles?" Ruv inquired, back against a tree trunk and chin propped on his walking stick.

"There are many in the more mountainous parts of Kemdaria," he explained. "They like the elevation. And they make for good protein."

"Hold up there, mate," Sarah cut in. "You're suggesting we hunt and *eat* the blue buggers?" Sam curled his upper lip in an echo of his sister's disgust.

Deadpan, Frostbite said, "They taste better than pixie."

After a quick vote, the group agreed to follow the blood trail to what they hoped would be a nest of beetles whose winged masters remained absent. Mari, Gren, Ruv, and Frostbite worked out a hasty attack plan should their search succeed. In response to continued mutterings about eating giant insects, Frostbite also assured everyone that, prepared properly, beetle meat could almost pass for freshwater crab.

"I'll believe that one when I taste it," Gren snorted.

"Never had crab," Killer remarked with a shrug.

"Me neither," Derek agreed, "but I'll eat anything if I'm hungry enough."

The splotches of beetle ooze both diminished in size and grew in separation as they neared the summit. By the time they crested the peak, the blood trail vanished entirely. With conflicting feelings of dismay and relief, Mari called for a quick break before they began their descent, and so they perched themselves as comfortably as they could on the overgrown roots. Although the space between trees had increased significantly, at the mountain's peak the pines still grew too thick and too tall to grant a clear view of what awaited them on the other side.

They had traversed but another hundred meters down the the mountain when they heard a familiar amalgamation of chittering, scuffling, and clattering. They slackened their pace to a near standstill, clinging to tree trunks and hopping gingerly from root to exposed root to avoid stepping on the dry bracken that littered the forest floor. Despite his size, Frostbite proved quite adept at the maneuver, and Gren only lost his footing twice. For his part, Micaleth's cloven hooves made no more noise on the brittle needles than they would have on spongey moss. Yet, unable to conceal his bright white bulk behind the skinny pines and sporadic live oaks, Micaleth hung back well before they drew close enough to make out distant flashes of cobalt exoskeleton.

The group moved another few dozen paces after abandoning Micaleth. The din grew louder as they perceived a darkening of the forest ahead, where a depression, swallowing the already limited light, interrupted the gentle slope. The depression, which appeared to shift and writhe in the shadows, made it clear they had found the beetles' nest.

Killer and Derek inched toward the teeming shadow from either direction in a slow sweep while the rest came to a halt. They huddled close to the ground, weapons ready. Mari and Ruv, tracking Killer and Derek's painfully slow progress, waited until the pair were close enough to estimate the nest's population. As soon as Derek shot Mari a quick nod, she signaled the rest, and the fracas began.

As one Killer and Derek dove into the swarm with battle cries and thrashing machetes. Dozens and dozens of gleaming, oversized scarabs poured out of the hollow, scattering in every direction, crawling over one another in a flood of skittering indigo. The beetles found little refuge in flight. Many found their freedom, but more found the wrong end of knife, staff, and axe. The friends enthusiastically announced each beetle as it fell, and Wendy kept track of the overall count since they had agreed to kill only as many as they could carry.

Sam and Sarah flung blade after blade with precision, missing few and catching half a dozen in the vulnerable joints their exoskeletons did not protect. Ruv swung his staff in a flurry, managing to stun his victims so Mari and Gren could dart in with a quick knife to finish the job. Frostbite, this time not only able to maneuver more easily between the tree trunks but also to focus on the beetles below him instead of fluttering pixies above, accounted for nearly a dozen severed heads by himself. With the need for stealth at an end, Micaleth returned to the group and joined Brae on the outskirts of the fray, stomping and shouting to urge the beetles back.

The hunt was quick, if not clean. The battle ended as soon as Wendy declared their quota filled, and they let the rest of the scarabs scamper off into the forest. Mari and her friends waded through the sticky aftermath to collect their quarries. Some two dozen insect corpses made for a grizzly haul, but they were at least satisfied that they had avenged their lost supplies and replaced some to boot.

Enthusiastic as everyone had been for the fight itself, Frostbite remained the only one looking forward to that evening's supper.

They wiped off the worst of the goo that spattered their clothes and weapons. Frostbite assured them that, if they let the mess dry, the remnants would be easier to remove. All the same, no one relished the thought of walking around in congealing beetle gunk until then. Eventually they retrieved their packs, distributed the carcasses, and went on their way.

The forest faded into sparse, shrubby desert by the time they descended halfway down the far side of the mountain. As they stared across the daunting expanse of scrub brush and rocky sand interspersed by towering cacti, Gren remarked, "Well, I guess we'll be eating *sandwiches* for a while." He chuckled to himself as the rest rolled their eyes. "Also is that a sand storm down there?"

Mari tightened the messy bun on top her head and looked sidelong at a grayish, twiggy snarl bouncing toward the valley. "I don't know about a storm, but that's definitely a tumbleweed."

"I wish I brought more sunscreen," Wendy sighed.

"You know," Mari observed, "maybe it's a good thing the pixies made off with all our alcohol. It'd just dehydrate us, and we're clearly gonna have to ration our water from here on out."

"I am reluctantly inclined to agree," Ruv conceded.

Micaleth cleared his throat and stepped forward. "Ahem. In case you have forgotten, I am a nietheran."

"No one forgot," Sam drawled.

"Kinda hard to miss, what with the cloven hooves and the great big horn and all the preaching," Sarah added.

Micaleth snorted. "You are worried about running low on water, but I am a nietheran," he repeated. "Thus, you need not worry."

Gren grimaced and pushed his bangs up from his forehead. They promptly fell back into place, slick with sweat. "Dude, what are you talking about?"

"You clearly have no understanding of my species' abilities," Micaleth said with a haughty shake of his mane.

"Clearly not," Mari noted. "Do enlighten us."

"Niethera have at least a rudimentary control over all four elements, but usually we each have a specific affinity for one or two of them," Micaleth explained as if addressing a gaggle of unruly schoolchildren. "I happen to have an affinity for both Air and Water. Thus, if need be, I can pull the moisture from the very atmosphere to replenish our water stores."

Sarah tilted her head to the side. "That is certainly a neat trick," she said, "except that we are in a desert and the air here is frightful dry."

Micaleth's eyes sparkled. "Ah, but the Ocean of Memory is but several dozen miles away. I can draw from there as well."

"In that case, drink up!" Mari commanded.

They hiked for hours beneath the sun, cutting a winding path between the tumbled, wind-carved stones and thicker patches of prickling shrubbery. Though a sharp wind from the west, where the sea lie hidden beyond the ragged mountain range that curved southward from the Evra-Dahrigek border, whisked the sweat from their brows, a crust of salt developed on the humans' skin. Even Brae and Micaleth started to droop and slow. Mari periodically reminded the group that they had a lot of ground to cover and promised that in a few more miles, they could look for a place to spend the night.

As a salamander scurried past her feet to shelter beneath a boulder, Brae squinted into the cloudless sky. "I never thought I'd say this, but there apparently is such a thing as too much sun."

Trotting at the back of the pack next to her, Micaleth replied, "I am likewise beginning to understand why the majority of my kin live in shaded rainforests."

"Right? I'm photosynthesizing like nobody's business over here, but it's just so damn dry."

Ruv spun around to grin at Brae. "Suddenly I remember that you are a plant."

"The spirit of a plant, actually," Brae corrected, returning his smile with a wink.

The joviality was abruptly disturbed by Gren hightailing it in reverse and jumping onto Micaleth's back. The sudden movement knocked the packs Micaleth bore askew. "Snake!" Gren shrieked, pointing at the ground whence he fled.

"Get off of me!" Micaleth ordered, bucking and stamping, which did nothing to dislodge Gren, who wove his fingers in the nietheran's mane as tightly as a moth's new cocoon. "I am not a mount!"

"Get it away from me!" he cried. Finally, to the amusement of all present, Micaleth succeeded in bucking him loose, and Gren landed square on his rear on top a jumble of scrub.

Mari, still standing where Gren left her, squatted to inspect the subject of his tantrum while Gren bolted to his feet and hid behind Frostbite. "Gren, sweetie, you can calm down," she asserted. "This little dude isn't even venomous. See?" She picked up the slithering, black-scaled creature by the neck right behind its head. It eyed her back with equal curiosity, evidently unaccustomed to humans and therefore unsure if it should be afraid or friendly. The snake seemed to decide upon the latter, for as Mari held it, it twined its tail around her arms and returned her scrutiny, blinking slowly. She smiled down at it with closed lips.

Ruv moved next to Mari and stroked the docile serpent between the eyes. "Besides, this snake is a fraction of your size," he added, still grinning.

Able to control her derision no longer, Sarah narrowed her eyes at Gren and quipped, "You're a bloody Bengal, yet you're this scared of a little baby snake? You should be ashamed to call yourself a sanguine, let alone a big cat."

"You're a disgrace to felines everywhere," Sam agreed. "I retract my earlier offers."

"Even us wolves are a bit disappointed in you," said Derek, trying hard—and failing—not to laugh.

Gren glowered at his friends, eyes darting from one to another while he edged out from the shelter of Frostbite's shadow. "You all suck," he accused. "How the hell was I supposed to know it wasn't venomous? I'm not a freaking biologist!"

Mari rolled her eyes. "Oh, please. We learned this in, like, elementary school or something. It's all about the head shape. Round you're good, triangular you're not." She gave the snake a soft coo. "Besides, it's just a little harmless garter snake. We had these all over the damn place in Virginia."

"Mari is correct," Wendy chimed in, using the hiatus to re-braid her strawberry blonde hair, which had bleached even lighter in the constant sun. "The only pain you'll experience if it bites you is from the bite itself. An angular head is what you need to worry about."

Swallowing, Gren asked, "Are you sure? What if it's the other way around? Ever since fourth grade when the class snake got loose and—"

Frostbite clapped a massive hand on Gren's shoulder. "As they say in Kemdaria, 'Triangle head, you'll be dead!'" In a quiet aside to Killer, he explained, "There are many snakes in the steppes."

"You know, that little rhyme of yours easily fits the other way, too," Gren said, keeping his distance from Mari's newest friend. "Plus there have to be exceptions."

She returned the snake to the sand. The serpent gave her one final curious, blinking look, then slithered on its way. "Let's just keep going and never discuss this instance ever again. You are rapidly losing all the cool-points you've built up over the years," she chided.

"I still don't like snakes," he muttered.

"Get over it. We're in a giant desert. We're gonna see a ton more," Mari returned. "We should be way more concerned about what else we're going to see further south, like that clump-of-mud horde the evrae were telling us about."

Derek shook his head. "I do hope we see them before they see us."

Killer nodded solemnly. "I mostly hope their numbers have been exaggerated."

"That, too," Derek whispered.

The dryness and heat increased as they hiked ever southward across a landscape that refused to change. True to his word, Micaleth replenished their water supplies as fast as they could drink them; no one's bottle ever ran dry. By unanimous vote they decided to do the majority of their travel during the early morning and late evening, holing up for a few hours around midday and again around midnight so they could avoid the worst of the sun but still see. Wendy, her store of sunscreen rapidly diminishing, heartily supported the decision.

When several days passed with no trace of any animals that did not crawl under or slither between rocks, they counted themselves lucky for the beetle harvest. Two of the scarabs, roasted on spits for an hour and seasoned with some sage or wild onions Brae scrounged up during their travels, comprised their nightly dinner. They foraged for what other edible plants they could—mostly the occasional shepherd's purse and unripe hackberries—and dreaded the day they would have to start hunting lizards, scorpions, and other friendly snakes.

Late one evening they set up camp on the crest of a hill where a ring of saguaro provided a modicum of protection from the scouring wind. Despite the intolerable heat of day, the wind bit right through once the sun slept, so with suppressed shivers they executed their usual nightly tasks. Sam and Sarah patrolled the perimeter as the first guard shift. Killer and Derek got the fire going while Frostbite and Wendy prepared another set of beetle carcasses to roast. Brae and Micaleth foraged for edible plants, and the rest unpacked the blankets, sleeping bags, and stale bread. Once all the mundane activities were out of the way, they settled in to wait for dinner.

Gren shoveled a handful of robura in his mouth, asked Mari to wake him once the beetles were finished cooking, and then disappeared into a pile of blankets.

Mari nodded, squinting in the firelight to clean her nails with her dagger. "I can't believe I've reached a point in my life where I'm looking forward to roasted bugs for dinner," she observed with a wrinkled nose.

"And dreading the day they run out," Ruv added.

Killer nodded sagely as he reclined on his dusty bearskin. "We've eaten worse things for sure."

"I told you they were good eating," Frostbite said, stirring the coals. "They'd be even better if I had some buckleaf, but I haven't seen any growing here."

"Buckleaf?" Ruv echoed. "As in the tea?"

Frostbite shrugged. "It adds an extra kick to the meat."

Derek scratched his chin. "Never seen it used as a spice, but I can see how that might work."

Mari dug through her pack and retrieved the last uneaten bag of dried fruit. Catching Micaleth's eye, she offered, "Want some?"

"No, thank you," he replied with a bow of his great head. "I prefer my sustenance fresh."

Ruv arched a brow at him. "What have you possibly found out here that's fresh besides the leafy horrors Brae forces on us, and why haven't you been sharing?"

"I have been consuming cacti."

Mari snorted, nearly choking on a mouthful of dried papaya and banana chips. "How the hell have you been eating cacti?"

Micaleth's lips curled back in an equine smirk, and his eyes flashed. "Very carefully."

Scrying could show him many things: the endless power struggles that gradually destroyed the world he had left behind, the rare hatching of a dragon's jewel-bright egg, the secrets lovers whispered in the dark. Sometimes he could see the second world where the children of Sier had made their home, where civilizations rose and fell in but a few Aorean revolutions. Time spun on and on, faster and faster, as the three worlds met and parted and met again in the universe's complex dance. Time flowed fastest on Daem. His own people had vanished long ago, ceding the world to lesser creatures after one too many wars.

He could see, but he could not touch. He chipped away at the veil around Daem until the seal had weakened enough for him to draw matter across, though the effort always left him drained. He summoned nothing living, of course. Powerful as he had become, he could not sever the veils entirely. Even if he could, such an act would betray his activity before he was ready. He had created a small circle—a conduit, really—nothing more

Scrying could show him many things, but there were limitations. He could not see the lanti. He could not see inside the golden walls where his enemies kept his sister enslaved. Not that he particularly wanted her freed, but it was the principle of the thing that irked him. He could not control the visions without a link on the other side. He could not always tell present from past, past from future, future from possible future. His sister could tell, he remembered bitterly. She had needed no black stone, no water, no fire, to see the truth of what was, is, and would be. Antiln's visions had always come of their own accord. But where did that get her? Imprisoned. Bound to another's control. Unable to live, but unable to move on.

A fate worse than death, in his opinion.

Sometimes he felt another presence and knew that he himself was being watched in just such a way. The farmer-who-was-more-than-a-farmer kept tabs on all those his hands had molded, but such a relationship had its benefits along with its discomforts. He owed much to the farmer beyond just the skills he had learned. He knew the shroud that kept his activities hidden had been reinforced by a hand more subtle than his own, and there was only one with that kind of power. Perhaps he could not see the lanti, but he knew they could not see him, either.

And so he found his victims in the scrying bowl. Time and again he dispatched his servants to steal them, secretly, quietly, only ever in the dark of new moon. Capturing pixies was easy; they were close. Bringing his victims from further afield required careful coordination so as not to raise suspicions or leave a trail others could follow. Without the farmer's aid, his minions could not have operated the traveling circles the niethera had planted back when the worlds were new. The living could not survive passing across the veil, and so his imperfect circle was unusable except for him and his resurrected creations.

He acquired a leshii every few decades. He did not kidnap them so frequently that anyone would notice a pattern, but he now knew those birch-barked maidens well. Their weakness, their strengths. How their roots tied them to the land while the wind freed their spirits. They faded quickly, but each one brought him one step closer.

He did not expect every creature to survive the binding. In fact, so far none had. Twice, he had managed to steal away a kemdar colt who had been left unattended and strayed too close to a traveling circle, but the kemdar proved too young. Like the leshii before him, the first did not long survive after the attempted binding and became nothing more than another pile of bones cluttering up his dungeon. The other never even made it across the sands.

Yet he kept trying. He would keep trying until he knew how to bind everyone, every race, in Aorea, to his will.

One day even the lanti would bow to his control.

The necromancer turned away from the basin of black stone. If the water wanted to be silent and not show him the young woman he so desperately wished to see, then so be it. He would see her in person soon enough. Even without the aid of the water, he could picture her progress, stumbling southward to him through the desert. He hoped his witless minions remembered to give her enough food and water. Given his constant reminders before they left, surely even those fools could recall such a thing.

He hoped she was not too scared.

"Soon, my lovely one," he whispered to the empty waters of his scrying bowl. "Soon we will be together, and then when you are safe, I can finally finish what my misguided sister started."

They had just enough warning to huddle amid a tumble of boulders and cover themselves and their supplies before the sandstorm struck.

Wendy spied the darkness on the horizon first, but it was Frostbite who recognized what it meant. The wind picked up soon thereafter, urging the shadow toward them at an impossible speed. The storm ripped through the valley. It swallowed the ground and blotted out the sun in its rage. They sprinted toward the boulders, the only refuge to be found in the open desert, and snatched their cloaks from their packs. Clustered together and sealed as best they could within their cocoons, they waited for the tempest of silica to engulf them.

They did not have long to wait. The wind tugged and tore at their cloaks with a deafening keen. They clutched desperately at their imperfect shelters, coughing and sneezing, eyes squinted against the powder that sifted through. They could feel the suffocating sand collect ever deeper around their crouched bodies.

It felt like hours before the storm shattered on the mountains, though no one knew for sure. At last the wind released its grip, and the sand settled. As they carefully unburied themselves, shaking the dust off their cloaks and untying the cloths from around their faces, they realized the sun had since set. Since they had already hiked several miles before the sandstorm struck and no one fancied stumbling through the changed landscape with naught but the stars to light the way, they set up camp there among the boulders.

Derek and Killer were patrolling the perimeter when the moon had just begun to ascend over the mountains, and Wendy returned from her scouting flight. She landed with a skid and a thud, shifted back into her human form, and dashed back to the camp. Still tugging her shirt over her shoulders, she nudged Mari awake with her toe. "Where's that map Micaleth brought?" she blurted as soon as Mari sat upright.

Rubbing her face and squinting, Mari answered, "With Micaleth, I think."

Micaleth yawned at the sound of his name. "In the little pack," he said with another gaping yawn. Then, bolting to his hooves and shaking his mane, he added, "What do you need with the map? We just checked it this morning." He tossed his nose toward the pack so Mari could withdraw the map, and Gren, woken by all the noise, lit a lantern.

Wendy surveyed the aged parchment, brows crinkled in concentration. "You said this is an old map, aye?"

"At least several millennia old, yes, and possibly much more," Micaleth replied with a third yawn. "Well, not this version, that is. It is a copy of many previous copies of one that was originally drawn several millennia past. I imagine that version disintegrated ages ago."

She looked up from the map and met his confused gaze with one of excitement. "I found something that's not marked."

Gren shrugged, which caused the lamp light to flicker. "Of course you did. Geography is bound to shift over so much time."

"More than that," she asserted. At their expectant faces, she clarified, "I found a city. Bigger than any of the villages we've been to. Loads of streets, scores and scores of buildings. It practically could have been a human city. There was even an amphitheater!"

"An actual city?" Mari repeated.

"Yeah, a real, honest-to-gods, actual city," she continued. "Reminded me of Edinburgh a wee bit, except everything looked carved straight out of the bedrock instead of built up. Maybe Rome would be a better comparison, but I only ever saw that in pictures, so I can't really say. I think some of the buildings might have been damaged, but it was hard to tell." Her finger traced their previous path on the map and came to rest on the spot where the city lie. "I didn't want to get too close without telling you about it first in case it was where that horde came from," she added with less excitement.

Micaleth stared at her and twitched his nose before responding, "You must have been mistaken. There have never been any civilizations in Dahrigek and most certainly not this far south."

"Maybe it's new," Wendy offered, matching his stubborn stare with one of her own.

A tight line formed between Mari's brows. "Did you see anyone there?"

"Couldn't make out any movement from above, but I might've been too far away, or the residents might've been sleeping," she explained.

Micaleth stamped his hoof, and the others, stirring from their slumber at the increasing excitement, came to huddle around the map. "But there simply cannot be any cities down here! It's impossible!" Micaleth reiterated.

Smirking, Gren quipped, "Surely by now you know that nothing is impossible."

"How dare you throw my own words back at me, human," Micaleth replied with an imperious sniff even as his merry eyes began to glimmer with curiosity.

Mari grinned warmly at Gren before resuming her interrogation. "How far out of our way would it be?"

"Not very. It's a wee bit east of where we've been going, just beyond a crest. We'd make it there in about six, seven hours tops."

"Then we'll leave once the boys finish their shift. In the meantime, Laria should definitely hear about this." Mari walked just outside the camp, fingers already clutching the jade pendant at her throat. Micaleth trailed after her, curious what the Spinner would have to say about Wendy's recent revelation. Mari concentrated on the link between them, aiming her thoughts as well as her voice toward the sanctuary on the opposite side of the globe. "Laria!" she called, but she was met with only silence. She repeated the call, brows drawn together, but again received only silence.

"What's wrong?" Micaleth murmured.

She gave him no answer. Instead, she continued trying to reach her friend. "It should be the middle of the day for you over in the Endless Forest, so you better be awake!" she grumbled. "Laria? Can you hear me? Ok then…let's try Hal. Hal? Brother, you there?" She released her grip on her fatestone and kicked a pebble, dislodging it from the ground and sending the lizard hiding beneath it scampering into the night. "Nothing," she growled. "I get nothing. It's like trying to break through a wall of cloud! Let me try Gren." She shifted her aim from the sanctuary back to the camp nearby, then, catching an image of what happened to be running through Gren's mind at the moment, she exclaimed, "Dear gods, I thought you'd be thinking about music!"

Gren yelped, his voice as loud as his thoughts. "Jesus Fu…get the hell out of my head!"

Mari rolled her eyes, but her expression quickly grew serious again. "Ok, Gren's there, so clearly the fatestone link is still active," she stated. "I just can't reach Laria or Hal. Are we out of range? No, that's not it. It works fine when we're on Earth, so we can't possibly be out of range if all four of us are in the same freaking world."

"This just gets more and more peculiar," the nietheran observed. "We must have passed into the area the Spinner cannot see, and so whatever blocks her sight must also block your fatestone."

"We've barely crossed the border!"

"Perhaps, then, the hidden area has expanded."

Mari headed back to the camp. "I hope not, but either way, it looks like we're on our own now. I thought when we'd reached the hidden spot we'd know somehow, like there'd be a tingle or a boundary or something obvious like that." She kicked at another pebble. "Should have known we wouldn't be so lucky," she growled.

By the time Derek and Killer returned from their patrol, the moon cast just enough light for them to comfortably see their steps, and the camp was completely packed away. Wendy, flanked by Mari and Gren, guided them toward her discovery. She pointed out the ridge, beyond which the city hid, once they drew close enough to see it. The sun was beginning its ascent then, dispensing the chill as it rose, and its light scattered across the sandstone's wind-carved furrows.

Wendy bounced with anticipation as they crested the jagged ridge. Though the potential of coming face to face with a horde of unknown creatures lingered at the back of everyone's mind, curiosity outweighed apprehension. Nevertheless, they took their time, peeking cautiously over the apex before stepping fully to the top.

Just as Wendy promised, a city stretched before them, sprawling across the valley in a labyrinth hewn from the bedrock. The streets wound a gargantuan spider's web that spiraled out from the city center, where stood the largest building by far. The straight branches that formed the arms of the web stretched from the epicenter to the edges of the massive grid, and a final street circled all the way around the city itself. Countless buildings, some small enough to have served as a single dwelling or shop and some large enough to have housed hundreds, filled the spaces between the spiraling boulevards. Indeed, an open amphitheater counted among the larger constructions. Eddies of sand still swirled between parts of the abandoned metropolis, painting some of the streets in shifting gold and all but confirming Brae's suspicion that its reappearance was due to the recent sandstorm.

"I cannot believe what I am seeing," Micaleth whispered.

"I told you!" Wendy exclaimed with a triumphant grin. "A real, actual city."

Sarah's eyes darted from one sector to the other. "A city," she breathed.

"In Aorea," her twin added.

"A bloody city."

"In bloody Aorea."

Mari exhaled slowly. "It's definitely weird."

Wendy removed her glasses, sheltered her eyes with her hand, and squinted at the sprawling metropolis. "I still can't see any movement, so it must be empty."

"It does look abandoned or something," Gren agreed.

Micaleth trudged down the steep ridge toward the gigantic labyrinth. "If it is old enough to be abandoned," he obstinately maintained, "then it should be old enough to be on the map."

After a pause, Mari said, "Not necessarily. Especially if it was buried in the sand whenever the mapmaker came through, if he even came this way instead of just writing off the dunes as a bunch of dunes."

"Maybe the evrae got bold enough to venture over the wall way back when, searching for more gold maybe, and built the largest settlement Aorea's ever seen?" Ruv offered, although his tone betrayed his skepticism.

"And then what, forgot about it?" Sam countered.

Brae fidgeted with one of the vines wrapped around her waist, causing it to shed more leaves in her wake. "I don't think so. The building style is completely different— way too high—and the evrae never build beyond a village or town anyway. That's why we leshii get along so well with them; they respect the trees." After a pause she added, "Not that there are any trees around here to respect, but still. Same principle."

"Could it be sierren?" Mari queried. "I've never seen one of their cities, but I hear they used to be pretty big."

Micaleth twitched his tail and said, "The sierren empire never stretched as far as Dahrigek. And if by some odd circumstance they did happen to build this one, it would have most certainly been on the map." When he was met with thinly veiled disbelief, he clarified, "The original cartographer was sierren."

"Obviously can't be freesian, either. No ice," Brae declared. "I think we have ourselves another mystery."

"A lost city," Derek breathed.

Gren drew his brows together and tapped the tip of his nose. "Lost...maybe the myth of Atlantis has its roots in Aorea," he mused.

Brae flashed him a dazzling smile. "Oh, now that would be interesting!"

"But then *why* is it not on my map?" Micaleth persisted.

Eyeing him with mild amusement, Mari teased, "You really are having trouble letting that one go, huh?"

Micaleth continued to grumble about the impossibility of any advanced civilization existing in Dahrigek as they picked their way down the crest, winding between cacti and tumbled stones. When they had nearly reached the bottom, Mari stopped mid-stride. A remnant of visions forgotten teased at the fringes of her brain. "What is done can be undone," she murmured, "and what is lost can be remembered."

Gren rested a hand on her shoulder as she resumed walking. "Where is that from?"

Still adrift in thought, she replied, "Not sure. Maybe an old dream. I recall them sometimes, bits and pieces."

"What is lost can be remembered," Micaleth echoed.

The lanti remained circled at the heart of the sanctuary while the niethera kept to the outskirts of the orchards.

Laria cast a nervous glance at Hal. "So then what is supposed to happen to Mari? to Gren? To the others?" she demanded the glowering Ianti. "Can they defeat this, this…brother?"

"Dimeldor," Devana clarified. "The brother is called Dimeldor. Perhaps in naming him, we can find him."

"Right, but can they defeat him?" Laria repeated.

"We shall see," Svarog postulated.

"Some prophecy," Hal snorted. "I can see why prophets never bet on the lottery."

Laria squeezed Hal's hand in warning, but Svarog's answering demeanor was unperturbed. "Divination is imperfect; the picture it paints, incomplete." He caught Hal's eye with a knowing twinkle in his own. "Even for such as me."

"Tell them what you have seen, my son," Perun commanded.

When he closed his eyes to remember, a cloud covered the sun. Mechanically Svarog recited, "A black, twisted tree stands at the heart of a shadow, ringed by fire and pain. Death covers the desert. A gray storm pours forth from the sea. Chaos approaches, an army from another world, piercing the veil."

"Will you please get to the helpful part already?" Kupala whined.

Svarog cleared his throat and concluded, "The Dreamer stands, sword in hand, glowing red as an ember among the shadows. The Wanderer sings, and the twisted tree falls. The darkness fades into the ocean." Recitation complete, he opened his eyes, gaze soft as he read the feigned calm on Laria's face. The sun shone once more.

"So that's good, then," she ventured. "Mari and Gren will defeat whatever is clouding the Loom."

Svarog shook his head sadly. "I'm afraid that's not all I saw, just one of many possibilities." He looked toward Perun, who nodded his head, before continuing, "At this point, it is just as likely that they fail."

"For such a 'sunny' individual, you sure can put a damper on things," Hal observed.

"An army from another world," Laria mused. "That could be the horde those evrae travelers described."

"Horde?" Perun snapped. "What horde?"

"Evrae are involved?" Devana demanded.

"There's clearly more going on than even we have sensed," Mokosh stated, laying a hand on her mate's shoulder. She drew an arc across the circle with her other hand, emanating waves of tranquility and soothing the tension generated by the recent revelations.

Laria raised her eyes skyward as she recalled her conversation with Mari. "Shortly before they crossed the border, they met with a couple of refugees. They said their village had been raided and burned by an army—a horde, they called it—of creatures they'd never seen before."

"We have neither seen nor sensed such a thing," Mokosh said, her voice flat and eyes narrowed. "Such violence would have caused a rift in the land that I would have certainly detected."

"That's what's so weird about it. When I looked in the Loom, too, no village in that area had ever been raided," Laria added. "Nor even existed."

"And death covers the desert," Svarog repeated. "To be forgotten is to be truly dead."

"So we have an undercurrent of darkness that reeks of Antiln, a shadow in the Loom, and now a village disappearing from memory. Even from *our* memory. This may be worse than we thought," Devana remarked. She shifted on her feet, leather boots squeaking.

Perun cut off further deliberation by removing the double-bladed axe from his back and declaring, "This has been most enlightening."

"What are you going to do?" Laria asked as the rest of the lanti started toward Svarog's glimmering chariot.

"Us?" Perun returned. "Nothing."

"What?" Hal and Laria snapped in unison.

"There's nothing for us to do," he explained with forced patience, running a callused fingertip along the blade of his axe head. "We'll continue monitoring the situation, but it's up to the Destined now. Once you four are involved, all that's left is to let things play out."

"That's ridiculous!" Laria asserted. A wash of rose rushed from her chest to her cheeks, coloring her normally fair skin. "With all your power, why did you even bother coming here if you're not going to help them? They don't know what they're up against! How in the heck are they supposed to defeat an immortal sorcerer who can make entire places vanish and make everyone else forget?"

Mokosh smiled at her, but the smile did not reach her eyes. "Calm, child. You are the Spinner now. It is your fate to observe; it is theirs to act."

"Well, I can't exactly observe anything when the Loom itself refuses to cooperate."

"Perhaps now that you know what is causing the cloud," Mokosh suggested, "the cloud will clear."

Laria clenched her fists, long since having withdrawn her hand from Hal's warm grasp. Anger at the lanti's indifference continued rising in her chest, choking her throat. "I may have only been the Spinner for a few Aorean months now, but I'm reasonably certain that's not remotely how this works," she emphasized.

Devana regarded Perun steadily. "The Spinner is right. We should—" Perun glowered at her and made to interrupt, but she silenced him with a hand. "Let me finish, father. We should not interfere directly, I agree with that. But there is a small thing we can do to give them a fighting chance." She glanced pointedly at Kupala. "We can conceal them."

"Ah, I know what you have in mind," Kupala purred. "Between my mists and your stealth, we would be able to weave such a cloak. We may not be able to see them, but we still know where they are."

"You would do that?" Laria asked breathlessly.

Devana's answering nod was solemn. "The cloak will prevent their presence from being seen by scrying, dreams, or any other form of divination. If it is indeed the brother behind this, he will not see them coming."

"However," Kupala interjected, "the cloak will shatter as soon as your friends are physically seen by him or anyone associated with him through whose eyes he might be able to watch."

"Now go back to the Loom," Mokosh urged, her eyes soft as she considered Laria. "Focus on what you *can* see."

"The moment the cloud clears, call for Gamayun," Perun ordered. "She'll be listening."

Laria met his storm-gray eyes with as steely of a gaze as she could muster. "And if the cloud never clears? If the Loom never shows me Dahrigek again? If my friends don't return and I don't even get to see what happens to them?"

"Then—and only then—shall we interfere further," Perun vowed. "Come, my children. We've lingered here long enough."

"Wait!" Hal called just as Perun had started to lift his axe over his shoulder.

He released a deep sigh. "Now what, Guardian? Our answer will not change."

"Next time you visit," Hal inquired with the start of a grin, "can you bring me an axe? It turns out a sword doesn't work so great for chopping firewood."

"Why, in the name of all that is holy, would you need to chop firewood?" Perun growled.

The rest of the lanti exchanged confused glances. "When we enchanted this place, we ensured that it would stay in perpetual harvest, blooming and fruitful and a perfect paradise. You should never require a fire to warm you," Mokosh told them.

"I've noticed," Hal replied dryly. "But I need something to pass the time, and I've decided I want to get into blacksmithing. I'm a Smith in name already, might as well be a smith in fact."

Perun looked heavenward and pursed his broad lips. "Help the Guardian build a forge, will you?" he directed Svarog with another sigh, then swung his axe over his shoulder before Hal or Laria could delay his departure further. They had barely enough time to cover their ears and dive for cover before the blade struck the ground, and a bolt of lightning subsumed Perun. The electric shock reverberated throughout the sanctuary, the boom of his leaving somehow more deafening than his coming had been. Taking their cue, the rest of the lanti crept into Svarog's golden chariot and left the same way they had arrived: on an arc of sunlight.

Gryndonmin, peeking behind a singed tree, stated, "I hate it when Perun visits. We will have to completely reseed this section of the garden."

"So much for eternal paradise," Hal mumbled.

As soon as they drew near enough to the city's outskirts to confirm that it had most certainly been abandoned for centuries if not longer, they realized from the scale of the buildings that they could not have been crafted by any people with whom they were familiar. No one, neither the stately freesians nor the intimidating sierrens, stood that tall. Even Micaleth was at a loss for ideas. They marveled at the city's sheer magnitude and faded grandeur as they marched toward the center along one of the web's straight arms.

Fashioned directly from the granite bedrock, the smallest edifice towered over them, the lowest point of the windows well above Frostbite's eye level and the hole where doors once stood grand enough to match. Many of the outer buildings remained half-buried in the shifting sands, but the straight road kept them on course.

They shuffled on in silence, mouths agape, eyes never settling on one wonder for too long before moving onto the next. No writing of any kind seemed to adorn the outside of the buildings, perhaps erased by time or perhaps never present in the first place. However, traces of carven knotwork, spirals, and whorls edged some of the doorways and window openings.

The silence was broken by Gren as he ran a light hand along a wall. In a reverent whisper, he observed, "It's like a ghost town."

Ruv dodged a crumbling bit of stone, knocked loose by an especially strong gust of wind. The stone scattered a cloud of dust when it shattered at his feet, and he coughed, "So who built it? A race of giants?"

A blush visible beneath his white fur, Micaleth admitted, "I have not the faintest clue." He shook his mane and rolled his shoulders, but the movement could not dislodge his sense of foreboding.

Mari shivered despite the heat. "We need to reach the center. I feel a pull."

"What it is?" Gren probed. "Another dream memory?"

Mari shook her head, fingers tapping a silent rhythm against the hilt of her sword. "No. Maybe. I don't know. I just know we have to go there."

They followed as Mari quickened the pace, winding through the debris and smashed stone of the magnificent labyrinth. They passed countless structures in various stages of deterioration. Some appeared no more than a century abandoned, preserved by some strange blessing of fate, while the splendor of others had been reduced to rubble. The heart of the city endured in better condition than the outskirts. They could make out intricate carvings of twining vines and celestial patterns on the stone, but still they saw nothing resembling a written script to answer their ever growing collection of questions.

Finally they reached the building where each branch of the web convened. At the very core of the city, the massive structure, taller than any they had yet seen, endured. It may as well have been new but for the yawning hole left by doors long since decayed to dust. The domed roof, supported by numerous columns that girdled the building's entire circumference, extended beyond the walls of the main structure. Empty, glassless windows gaped at them from between each archway. They paused at the base of the stairs leading up to the main doors, awed, mute.

"Is it a temple?" Gren asked quietly.

"One way to find out," Mari declared, and she planted a heavy boot on the first step.

CHAPTER SIX
You've lived a charmed life

The looping hallways in the interior of the construction echoed the labyrinthine web of the city whose heart it marked. Without a word the group padded behind Mari as she led them toward the center, drawn there by a feeling she recognized but could not name. Mosaics covered the walls: myriad scenes of nature, of stars and seas, of forests and firestorms. The dust of untold centuries, resting in a fine film over the cunningly patterned tiles, could not conceal their beauty.

A collective intake of breath swept through the group as each stole across the threshold to the building's innermost chamber. Alcoves, evenly spaced along the curved walls, still bore smoke stains from the long-extinguished flames of candle and torch. They filed into the room one by one as if caught in a ritual. Their fingers trailed along the dusty walls, revealing yet more ancient mosaics, as they circumscribed the room, inspecting, admiring, wondering.

One by one they entered; one by one they traced a circle with their steps.

One by one they were drawn to the center.

A neat pyramid of sand had collected beneath what may once have harbored the most intricate stained glass skylight ever to grace the land, but was now just a circular void in the domed ceiling, its fallen shards eroded to glittering gravel. Encircling the debris presided four gargantuan statues, carved not from the bedrock like the rest of the city, including the temple itself, but from colossal slabs of quartz, each one of a different hue: soft lavender and sage green, smoke gray and marbled blush. A fifth place in the ring stood empty.

Mari, Gren, Brae, and Micaleth stepped inside the ring of effigies. Tongue-tied, they planted their feet, sunk in the sand, and gawked at each massive statue's face in turn. Minutes sped past, and still they kept their silence until a petite sneeze shattered the spell. "Sorry," Wendy sputtered with a sniff. "It's just the dust's getting to me."

With the glamour duly banished, they began to study the room with less awe and more inquiry. Each of the five statues stood completely nude and vaguely humanoid, except that in place of head and hands and feet, they possessed the parts of various animals. The original slabs of stone from which the statues were chiseled must have reared over five meters tall, yet no one had the faintest clue where such gigantic mineral specimens could be found intact, let alone mined and transported to the temple.

The first statue to receive their scrutiny depicted an androgynous figure cut from solid amethyst. Muscular yet soft, exquisite yet undefined, the figure defied easy description. From every angle, it seemed to shift and change to a new position. Straight lines would suddenly seem to curve, or a flash of sunlight would catch a striation in the bruised quartz, and the figure would appear to move. Delicate hands with empty palms rested one on top the other at the figure's waist as if waiting to either give or receive some nebulous donation. In a stark contrast against the slender fingers, the willowy legs gave way to great paws in place of the figure's feet, and a bear's head, caught in a rare moment of serenity, rested on top its shoulders. The curling horns of a ram sprouted from either side of the bear's skull, and a spiraled triskelion marked its forehead.

"Who could that be, do you think?" Mari whispered to Gren, who shrugged and frowned. The rest of their group echoed Gren's movement in a wave of confusion.

The second statue was less ambiguous, possessing no such sense of fluid motion, but it was no less magnificent. A small-breasted, muscular woman carved from pale-green prasiolite returned their gaze through the fierce eyes of a wolf on the brink of snarling. The wolf's head was adorned with the fuzzy, budding antlers of a stag in spring, and like the previous statue she bore paws in place of feet. A serpent curled around and over her clawed toes, its tail twining up her left calf. Her stance spoke of action: knees bent ever so slightly, paws ready to launch from the stone base and give chase after some unseen prey. Her left hand hung at her side and clutched three arrows; her right stretched before her, holding a twisting, snaking abstraction reminiscent of effervescent flames.

"Gotta be one of the huntresses," Gren offered.

Mari nodded. "She's certainly built like Devana."

"Yeah, it's the head that's confusing me," he replied. He glanced toward Micaleth, but the nietheran's stunned face delivered no answers.

The third statue, fashioned from smoky quartz, portrayed a wiry man with deadly talons in place of nails and the immense head of an elk. Enormous wings, each feather rendered in fantastic detail, sprang from the statue's back. His wings were folded, but it seemed as if at any moment he would spread them wide and take flight. He held one hand aloft, pointing at the empty skylight, while the other pointed toward the center of the room, where perhaps a mystery yet lurked beneath the sand.

"Any ideas?" Ruv asked, running his hand down one of the statue's wings.

"None of my mythology books ever covered this guy, either," Gren mumbled. "At least the last one looked more familiar. Somewhat."

A robust, heavily pregnant woman, cut from dusty rose quartz, made the fourth statue in the ring. She bore the head and tail of a leopard, but a line of feathers sprouted down each rounded arm, and a lozenge symbol was etched between the leopard's sparkling eyes. She held an empty basin in front of her, resting it on top of her protruding belly. The only statue without antlers or horns, her head was instead crowned with flowers, and a wreathe of flowers likewise obscured her feet.

Gren squinted at the intricate lines of fur carved into the statue's tail. "Bastet, maybe?"

Brae came to stand beside him and tilted her head to look at the statue's face. "I'm unfamiliar with that one."

"I don't know a whole lot about her," Gren admitted. "Egyptian. Something about cats."

"Ah," Brae breathed. "Never made it to Egypt. I tended to stay around Rome on the few occasions I visited Earth." She bent to retrieve a birch leaf that had shed from her hair, then placed it as an offering at the feet of the rose quartz mother-to-be. The leaf nestled among the carved flowers as if it belonged there. "But then they closed the traveling circle in Italy, and I haven't had the heart to destroy my fond memories by visiting anywhere else."

"When did it close, out of curiosity?" Gren asked.

The corner of Brae's mouth quirked in a grin. "Oh, sometime toward the end of that brat Octavian's reign."

"Ah," Gren snorted. "That explains a lot." He turned to face the rest of his friends, who were milling around the chamber in varying states of astonishment. "Anyone else have any suggestions?" At their blank stares and shrugs, he moved onto the final, empty place in the ring where Mari waited, her lips pursed.

Nothing but a mound of citrine shards endured where the fifth effigy should have stood. The shards, sparkling bright sun-gold in the light that filtered through the empty window above, varied in size, as if whatever had shattered the statue did so incompletely. Some fragments were all but ground to dust, the fine, gold powder blending in with the sand except for an inner luminosity that destruction could not banish. Others, though no one dared to defile the remnants with their touch, would have fit comfortably in a human hand. Still others revealed hints of what the statue may once have been: a curve of horn, part of a hoof, a fierce eye. However, one piece seemed to have survived whole, not so much as a chip marring its surface. Gren stepped cautiously around the scattered fragments to inspect the piece. At his feet he found a jagged blade suggestive of a thunderbolt.

Eyeing another fragment with mingled respect and amusement, Sam nudged Gren with his shoulder and intimated, "Somebody was certainly well-endowed."

Gren rolled his eyes and avoided the place where Sam was pointing, but Killer and Derek hustled over to see.

"Over here!" Wendy interrupted, beckoning her friends to join her at one of the alcoves. Standing on her tip toes, she could just peer over the ledge. "I think I found something important."

Micaleth and Brae rushed over and forced their way to the front, where Wendy indicated a large plaque, carved from clear crystal beneath a veneer of dust. It leaned against the back of the alcove, nestled among smoke stains and debris. Micaleth blew on the surface, releasing a cloud that sent those standing closest to the alcove—himself included—into bouts of coughing and sneezing.

Frostbite retrieved the plaque and passed it down to Brae, who used a fold of her tunic to rub off the remaining dust. The cleaning revealed vertical rows of swirling, looping characters carved into the quartz and inlaid with tarnished silver. The boundaries blurred between each character such that individual letters and words were nearly impossible to distinguish. Indeed, perhaps there were no boundaries to begin with. "Well, we can officially rule out the sierrens," the leshii breathed. "That is definitely not their script."

Micaleth plopped his snout over her shoulder to get a better view of the writing. "This must be wrong, surely."

"What does it say?" Mari asked before blowing the last of the dust out of her nose.

"I'm not sure," the nietheran said with a frown. "I thought I was familiar with every Aorean calligraphy there is or ever has been, but this is practically indecipherable. The script itself looks close to lantian, yet I can make no sense of what it says." He withdrew his snout from Brae's shoulder and faced Mari directly. "It is as if someone took the letters I am accustomed to, stylized them, and then transliterated something completely alien."

"Lantian, you said?" Mari repeated. Brae and Micaleth stepped aside so she could see. "Hmm…it does kinda look like what was sketched on the back of Vesna's mirror and some of the other things we saw when we poked around Kutkah's stash. Sam, Sarah, what do you think?"

The twins shouldered past her, nodded their agreement, and then retreated so the rest could see.

Gren jostled his way back to the center of the huddle surrounding the crystalline plaque. "Hey, Mickey, maybe you could try pronouncing it out loud? That used to help me a lot with Latin. Like I wouldn't always recognize the word until I heard myself say it, then it'd make sense."

"I suppose there is no harm in trying," he stated. The nietheran squinted at the fine script. "*Myljungo igani panje.*" He repeated the phrase several more times to himself. "That's what the far right line seems to say, but it still makes no sense to me whatsoever."

"And the rest of the lines?" Mari prompted.

"More complete gibberish. Whatever it is, it is most certainly not the Old Tongue."

Ruv waggled his eyebrows at the perplexed Micaleth. "Maybe it really was aliens, huh?"

"Little green men?" Sarah scoffed, hands braced on her narrow hips. "I don't think so."

Brae grinned mischievously, poking Sarah in one of her leather-clad shoulders. "Sometimes pixies are green," she quipped.

Sarah curled her upper lip in disdain. "But pixies are not aliens."

"Nor are they, to my knowledge, literate," her brother added, arms crossed.

Micaleth released an exasperated sigh. "I may not be able to decipher the words as they are written, but I believe it unlikely that this city is the product of either pixies or some sentient species from an alien world, whether that world is Earth or Daem or one as yet undiscovered," he lectured. After a pointed pause, he said, "And I am beginning to develop another theory, as it were."

Mari narrowed her eyes and asked, "Would you care to share that theory?"

"Yes, but not here." He shifted his focus to the ring of statues, eyes coming to rest on the empty spot where the fifth should stand. "There are a few more pieces to this puzzle I would like to unbury before I commit anything to words. If I am wrong, it is no great matter." He returned his attention to Mari. "The mystery will keep for now."

Mari waded toward the exit. "We should leave before it gets dark," she said without looking back.

They departed the city down a different arm of the web than along which they entered, cutting southwest toward the coast, and, dusty and tired, they stopped as soon as they found a good spot to wait for moonrise.

Necria staggered through the doorway, a goblin dragging her by either arm and another shoving her from behind. Their fetid breath surrounded her in an invisible, rancid cloud. Her demon stood before her, waiting. In the cold, black eyes that searched her own, she thought she could perceive a touch of concern, of longing, maybe even of fear, though she had not the first idea what could possibly cause a demon to be afraid.

"As you have wished," Dimeldor whispered, "we can finally meet by the light of day." He cast a glance at the barred window where starlight sprinkled through. The only true illumination in the room came from torches that lined the stone walls, their flames flickering an eerie shade of green. "Well, in a manner of speaking. Welcome to your new home, my lovely. I hope your journey was not too trying. My friends treated you well, I trust?"

"What have you done?" she seethed. The goblins released their crushing grip, but she made no effort to flee. She had nowhere to go.

The necromancer looked past her shoulder. "Leave us," he commanded. The goblins obeyed. His voice softened when he turned his words to Necria. "I've done only what I must so that we could be together, so that I could keep you safe from what is to come."

She clenched her fists. "You destroyed my village! You killed my family, my friends, everyone I've ever known! Oh Ancestors, my little sister...my little Naya..."

He hurried to her side and wrapped his arms around her. Despite the rage that coursed through her veins, making her limbs tremble, making her core vibrate like a bee's wings, she melted into his embrace. "No, my dear one," he whispered against her hair. "I have done no such thing. I was here, waiting for you! I only asked Servorg to escort you. If he went further than that, he will be punished accordingly."

"I don't believe you."

"But love! What cause have you to doubt?"

Necria forced herself away from him, her gold eyes fierce as she returned his scrutinizing gaze. "You speak of love as if you know what it means." She took another step backward. "I know now that you do not, that you cannot, love me. I always knew what you are, what you really are. You have never been an angel. I should have—"

"You're upset," Dimeldor murmured. "I'm sure you must be exhausted after traveling all this way. I would have brought you directly here, but the journey across planes would have killed you." He took a deep breath; Necria could tell how much effort it took him not to run to her and enclose her in his grasp once more. "We'll talk when you feel better. Servorg!" he called.

"Yes, master?" the goblin croaked as he lumbered into the room.

"Show Necria to her suite. See that she gets some rest," he directed. After a long breath, he added, "And some more food. She's thinner than when we last met."

"Of course, master."

Necria glared at her escort but meekly followed him down a hall and to another set of rooms, where two guards waited with weapons at the ready. They slammed the door behind her, and she heard a lock click. She found no lock on the inside. Her privacy would not be hers to control.

She surveyed the room. "My new home, he called it," she mumbled. "A prison." More torches lined the curving walls, painting the stone lime and olive. The sickly shade reminded her of the withered fields after the blight destroyed her family's crops. The mottled stone reminded her of the victims of the ensuing plague.

She reached toward one of the torches and passed a hand through the flames; her skin remained unharmed. The torches gave light, but no heat. There would be no smoking fire to provide her a way out. She could not experience the choking, suffocating death that had destroyed her village and consumed everything she ever knew, everyone she ever loved.

Everyone she loved but one.

A single window provided a view of the outside world beyond the iron bars, but it was too dark for her to see anything save the stars reflected on the sea and the jagged outline of distant mountains. The bars were too close together for her to reach her whole hand through, but her fingers were just able to brush the glass. The contact sent a shudder through her arm. She knew instantly that the window pane was enchanted, that it would not break, not that she could see anything in the room with which to attempt such a feat in the first place. Perhaps, she wondered, it was the same charm he had used to seal her door the last few times he visited her, back before her world exploded around her.

It seemed there would be no quick way out through glass shards, either.

Intricate rugs softened the floor, a riot of woven threads in violet and cerulean and gold. A grand bed, carved from some dark wood she could not identify, stood across from the window beneath a pile of lush, jewel-toned pillows and blankets. Her prison may be filled with velvet and silk, she observed with a wry smile, but it remained a prison nonetheless.

Days passed, each one feeling longer than the last though the reverse was true. Their path wound ever southward, drawing them further from the equator as well as further past the equinox. With the mountains hugging the Dahrigek coastline and nothing but clear skies above, they no longer needed Micaleth's map to keep their bearings. Thus, they trudged onward while the sporadic plant life dwindled to pale green memories, and the last of the wind-carved boulders and towers gave way to endless waves of sand that sucked at their feet and slowed their journey's progress. Realizing they traipsed through what must have been the birthplace of the sandstorm that unearthed the city, they prayed to whichever god would listen that the winds would stay asleep. The empty dunes would provide poor shelter.

Eventually their supplies ran low, and so they reduced their daily rations. Their steps faltered, and, as the air grew yet dryer and the mountains still hid the sea, Micaleth began to struggle to replenish their water. Mari turned their course sharply to the west in hopes of reaching the coast and finding some semblance of vegetation before their sustenance completely ran dry. However, with such small rations spread among so many people, they were obligated to take longer and more frequent breaks.

The coastal mountains loomed unbearably far away as they settled in for the afternoon, hiding as best they could from the worst of the sun. Ruv broke a piece of jerky in two and tossed half to Wendy before stuffing the other piece in his mouth. Once he'd succeeded in swallowing the desiccated chunk, he announced, "That's officially the last of the goat."

"Time to start hunting lizards, I guess," Killer drawled, wringing the sweat from his shirt as he crouched in the meagre shadow provided by his pack.

Derek, scrunched next to him in his own pocket of limited shade, twisted his braid into a bun at the nape of his neck. "It may be too late. Haven't seen any in a while."

Digging through his pack, Gren said, "Still got a few days of robura left, at least." He withdrew a small sack with a triumphant flourish. "And some banana chips! Hell yeah! I thought we were completely out of fruit, so that's a nice find."

Sam and Sarah glowered, half buried in the sand. "Just wonderful," Sam grumbled.

"We come all this way to starve," Sarah agreed.

Frostbite's grim expression grew yet grimmer. "We should keep moving. We are too far to turn around."

"I know," Mari exhaled, her mouth drawn into a tight line to match the crease between her brows. "Hopefully we'll make it to better foraging soon. The coast can't be that far." She gazed wistfully at the mountains whose distance defied her promise.

Brae, the only one not cowering in the limited shadow, stated, "It'll cost me more water, but I can survive off just the sunlight for a while. Save you all some food." She lay on top the dune, arms spread wide, ankles crossed, bright red hair fanning out on the golden sand. Her position, along with her calm smile, emphasized her point.

"Once we make it closer to the ocean," Micaleth assured, "I am certain drawing water will be easy again." He scratched his ear awkwardly with a hoof. Then, bashful, he added, "I apologize that I did not foresee quite such aridity."

Killer patted him on the flank. "It's ok, we know you're doing your best. We'll just have to go easy on it for now."

"Still short on protein," Sarah interjected, "which'll make shifting a lot harder to keep up."

Blushing scarlet beneath her pink freckles, Wendy stammered, "Sorry, I didn't mean to eat more than my share. I just—"

"Don't apologize," Mari ordered. "Your scouting abilities as an owl definitely outweigh the rest of us being a little hungry." She scowled at Sarah, who refused to meet her eyes, instead using the break to paint another layer of midnight lacquer on her pointed nails; the scent of ammonia filled their small camp. "Besides, you're our best bet at finding somewhere we can restock." When Wendy nodded her acknowledgement, Mari continued, "Take a few nights off. Save your energy. If we keep stretching it, we have enough for a few more days, maybe a week. By then we'll be close enough to the coast that you can fly over the mountains."

Ruv's face bore an unaccustomed seriousness as he replied, voice low enough that only Mari could hear, "Not to contradict you, but by then we'll be desperate."

"We don't have much choice," she whispered back.

It took them two more days to reach the base of the mountain range, and as they drew closer, they were dismayed to find nothing more edible than a few low, spherical cacti. It was so difficult to harvest any flesh from the thick crust, not to mention avoid the needles, that had they been any less hungry they would not have bothered. At least the ground was blessedly solid again once they left the dunes behind. Nevertheless, Ruv's warning rang true.

"I have never been hungrier in my life," Gren mumbled, his statement underscored by a loud stomach rumble. "This is torture."

Derek offered him a sad smile. "You've lived a charmed life, my friend."

"I've gone longer bouts without as much food as I'd like," Sarah snapped. Her mood had soured on pace with the diminishing supplies. "You'll survive."

"Ugh, how?" Gren whined. "I'm wasting away."

Sam left his sister's side to slide an arm around Gren's shoulder, which was more difficult than he had prepared for given their comparative heights, but he managed. Just. "You can have my portions tonight, then," Sam crooned. "Can't have you losing any of that lovely muscle. You're skinny enough as it is."

Gren gave Sam an awkward grin as he gently slipped out of his hold. "Skinny? Dude, I am twice your size," he chuckled.

Sam stepped away with a wink. "Oh, believe me, I've noticed."

"Give it a rest," Sarah drawled to her brother. "You know damn well it's a lost cause."

Gren dipped his head toward her in thanks, then to Sam he said, "While I do appreciate the offer, I'll be fine with just my own rations."

"And speaking of rations, I think it's time I go for that flight, protein or no protein," Wendy proclaimed.

Mari furrowed her brows. The line between them was becoming permanent. "In case you don't find anything, you'll definitely be starving when you get back."

"I have to do something," she argued. "I'm the only one who can."

167

Mari surveyed their group. Receiving nods all around, she urged Wendy on, and so Wendy slipped away to shift while the others continued their slow ascent. A wind stirred by her great wings swept over them, casting a wash of sand as she soared into the sky.

The Fifth Spinner halfheartedly contemplated the images transposed across the Loom's perpetually shifting fabric: a suburb outside of Chicago where a family crammed into a hatchback, a couple's argument in an underground sierren settlement on the border between Nomansland and the Kemdarian Region, a grandmother collecting eggs on a farm in Slovenia, a nietheran colt sprouting its alicorn in the Origin grove in Faerie, an artist with lime green hair painting deer in a Tennessee back yard. Laria fought the urge to try and call up an image of Dahrigek. She did not trust herself to stay calm if she saw the threads fail her again. She was the watcher of the worlds. If she could not see a single part of a single world, she still had plenty of other locations that she could be observing, that she *should* be observing.

She waved a hand over the threads and directed her thoughts toward the third world. A lifeless landscape of cratered rock greeted her. Nothing had changed since the last time she sought an image of Antiln's birthplace. The civilization that created the sorceress had succumbed to war and unrest, torn apart from the inside out by the same greed that sent her searching for another land in the first place. None after her approached her power, for the seal around the third world had remained firmly in place while subsequent civilizations rose and fell, rose and fell, until nothing remained of Daem but uninhabitable dust.

Although her primary role as the reigning Spinner was to guard the Loom and ensure the spirit of Antiln remained within, the unwritten secondary duty of each

Spinner was to watch, to remember, to record. The history contained within the innumerable volumes of the previous Spinner's journals paid worthy homage to that fact.

Tarel, her immediate predecessor, had taken the role exceptionally seriously, leaving Laria a whole wall of bookcases stuffed with scribbled writings. Tarel's section alone of the annals of Spinners past took up nearly an entire room in the small cottage. Yet Laria, however closely she forced herself to watch Earth and Aorea in the Loom, could not quite bring herself to record. Not yet. Not while her friends, the closest friends she had had in many years, the friends who had changed her life and showed her how much more there was to the universe, how much more there was to her, were in danger.

Especially not when she was the very one who sent them there.

She heard a soft shuffling sound from behind her and tore her eyes away from the Loom. Hal leaned against the door frame, brows brooding but mouth soft. "How long have you been standing there?" she asked.

"Long enough to see that you're not really seeing what you're looking at."

Laria rose, brushed a few stray threads off her skirt, and buried her face against his chest. He smelled of the sanctuary's expansive gardens: fresh herbs, moist earth, a trace of blackberry. "I can't believe I sent Mari and Gren off into Dahrigek with just Micaleth and a map," she mumbled.

Hal rested his chin on top of her head and smoothed a hand up and down her spine. "Ruv is with them, too," he reminded her. "You know he'd do anything to keep Mari safe." With a grin, he continued, "And that usually means protecting Gren as well."

"I don't want anything to happen to Ruv, either!"

"They also have the twins with them. They can get into and out of just about anything," he argued, drawing her away so he could study her face. "Plus there's that scientist girl. Geologist. Whatever. I'm sure she's smart enough to figure something out, at least. And don't forget Derek and Killer. They're in good hands."

"Still," she whispered. "What if it's not enough?"

Hal smiled at her, but Laria could tell it was affected. "Well, there's also that giant dude they picked up in the Alpines. Frosty, or whatever."

"Frostbite," Laria corrected automatically. "He has an interesting story. I've watched him a few times in the Loom, and I suppose he does know how to handle himself in a fight."

"See? They'll be fine!" he promised. "They're resourceful, and they've been through plenty of scrapes before this whole mess."

She scowled at him. "This is a bit more than a 'scrape,' Hal," she rebuked.

He chortled, wrapping his arms around her once more. "Just let me reassure you, ok? I hate seeing you so tense."

Laria nodded but pulled away, moving toward the window that overlooked the sanctuary fields. The rolling green of the perpetual summer spread out before her, herbs and flowers in continuous bloom, fruit and vegetables in eternal harvest. Yet, despite the beauty before her—and behind, she thought with warmth—the perfection felt hollow. "I don't think there is anything you can say to reassure me, at this point," she breathed. "I'll be tense until I hear something back from Mari, or I can see their fate in the Loom. Whichever comes first."

They were resting and enjoying a quick water break when Wendy-the-owl returned. Her success was clear from the excited hoot accompanying her skidding landing, but she could not contain the exclamation that tumbled from her throat as soon as she had a human mouth with which to form words. "I've found a place!" she cried. Mari tossed

Wendy her pack, and she began to re-clothe as rapidly as her shaking fingers would allow.

"No mirage?" Frostbite asked. He, along with the other men, kept his gaze respectfully averted.

"No mirage!" she beamed. "There's an oasis about another ten miles west. Right on the other side of the ridge." She knelt to lace up her running shoes. "There's a lot of vegetation."

"That sounds amazing," Mari said with a huge sigh. She fished the last of her rations out of her own pack and shoved them at Wendy, who wolfed down the paltry fare.

Under Wendy's guidance, they stumbled toward the promised salvation. The exertion of the shift had left her drained, so after a time Frostbite joined her up front and took her pack despite her heated protests. Micaleth swore he could smell the foliage as they neared the ridgetop, but it was Frostbite who spotted the first tantalizing flash of green from his position at the head of the column. Sure enough, as soon as they crested the rocky ridge, they witnessed their deliverance.

Although nowhere near as lush as the forests they were accustomed to traveling through in Nomansland or Faerie or even, as Frostbite assured them, in most parts of the Kemdarian Region, shades of peridot and aventurine sheltered several square miles of mountainside. Beyond the limits of the immediate oasis, thinner foliage continued as far as they could see. A smaller ridge obscured the ocean, but a westerly breeze carried the tell-tale scent of brine. They could even see a few trees sprouting here and there, mostly toward the center of the green where a spring bubbled. Lizards scampered out of their way as they descended on blissful steps into the shrubbery, and Ruv, to copious accusations of wishful thinking, claimed he saw rabbit droppings next to a gigantic aloe.

Their pace quickened such that they were practically jogging by the time they reached the spring. They threw themselves down amid the soft mosses and grass in the shade cast by palm trees. Yet the mere fact of lounging in the presence of abundant vegetation could not silence the complaints of their empty stomachs, and so before long they were on their feet again, foraging and hunting.

Frostbite, Brae, and Micaleth located armfuls (and, in Micaleth's case, several substantial mouthfuls) of edible tubers and wild carrots. Brae harvested tart purple berries that she promised were not toxic, even for humans, though she and Micaleth ate them first just to be sure. Killer, Derek, and Ruv indeed located a few scrawny hares, carrying them joyfully back to the spring to skin and dress. Mari, once she finally convinced the exhausted Wendy to lay down and rest, helped Gren build up a fire and get a pot of water boiling. The twins explored the longest, returning right before the rabbit and tubers had finished stewing with a few lizards, a headless rattlesnake, and another hare.

Later, reclining around the embers of the spent fire with a delightfully full belly and picking his teeth with a sliver of rabbit bone, Ruv said, "I wish we still had tea."

"Tea would be lovely," Wendy sighed, rubbing aloe juice on her sunburns with nothing short of rapture.

"We've been making good time," Mari declared. "We should rest here for a day or so. Give us a chance to restock our supplies before we head further south."

Wendy closed her eyes, succumbing to the cooling sensation as she continued her ministrations. "From what I could see, the climate definitely improves for a ways. I don't think we'll be starving anytime soon."

"If we're lucky," Gren said, "maybe it'll stay like this all the way down to the archipelago."

"Why are there rabbits down here, but not up in Evra?" Killer queried, frowning at the sky.

"Good point," Derek agreed. "Why haven't we seen any kind of game this whole time?"

Mari followed Killer's eyes heavenward and caught the tail of a shooting star. "I really don't know," she breathed.

"It is, indeed, curious," Micaleth stated, then rested his chin on his front legs and began to snore.

They found much with which to occupy themselves over the two days they spent recovering. They washed their clothes in the spring and mended what tears were worth mending. They talked, they slept, and especially, they hunted. Large, thick-scaled lizards were plentiful along with black, golden-eyed snakes and a breed of beetle akin to what they had discovered in the pixie forest, except these scarabs were smaller and wore scarlet carapaces in place of sapphire. They tasted just the same. Killer, Derek, and Ruv managed to catch several more hares, though there seemed to be few enough as it was, and they wanted to spare some for their return journey. No one wished to admit the possibility that there might not be a return. As for the field mice and other tiny, scurrying rodents, they determined the meat was not worth the trouble, and so left them mostly alone. Something had to survive their presence, after all.

During their second night in the oasis, Gren performed a few songs by request, and after some persuasion Mari would provide an alto harmony to Gren's rich baritone. The oasis seemed to them a place outside of time, where their bodies could heal and their minds could rest, and so a little entertainment did not go amiss.

Though he regretted the inability to carry his guitar with him on such journeys, Gren made do with the instruments at hand: a drum beat on backpack and stone, an impromptu rain stick of sand in an empty water bottle, and, once they found themselves unable to resist the music's call, a bass hum from both Killer and Frostbite, who it turned out possessed some musical talent as well. Once the three men found their rhythm, Mari quietly withdrew her own voice, content just to listen. They sang well into the night, and when Gren needed a brief respite, others began to offer songs and stories. Tunes half-remembered from childhood. Folktales and adventures.

Sometimes the tone of these tales was humorous, and sometimes less so, but they were entertaining nonetheless.

After much coaxing, the twins described their last venture on Earth prior to meeting Mari, Gren, and Ruv in Nomansland. "Kutkah brought us through the Scottish circle, blindfolded as always," Sam began. "Then he left us in Haringey with vague instructions to look for a scythe that supposedly belonged to Veles."

"We never did find it," Sarah said. "He was particularly put out about that."

"Quite. We expected him to return for us in a few weeks with another mission, like he usually did, but he didn't," Sam continued. "Months went by, and we began to wonder if he was so mad about the scythe that he'd left us for good."

Sarah shrugged. "So we figured we may as well finish high school," she said with a pointed wink at Mari and Gren, who pretended not to notice the barb about their interrupted education. "We were technically too old, of course, but whoever our parents may have been, they at least left us with good genes." She then went on to share a few brief anecdotes, punctuated by the occasional accusation of exaggeration, about their exploits.

"We'd just graduated—1986, it was—when Kutkah finally came back," Sam said with a remorseful sigh. "I do miss the music scene in those days."

"That's when he dragged us back to Aorea to look for more little relics to add to his collection," Sarah concluded. "That's when we met Frostbite, too, while hunting down a a stash of gems supposedly abandoned by one of the dracora up in the Alpines. You know what happened after that, more or less."

Brae whispered of the Birch Forest, of the secrets concealed within the white, peeling bark and fine-toothed leaves. Wendy spoke of her uncle the historian, whose stories about the standing stones above his estate first inspired her to pursue geology. Micaleth told them of how he acquired some of the indentations in his otherwise perfect horn by sparring with Hal, much to the chagrin of the other niethera and to the amusement of Laria.

But it was Derek's tale that they would ponder late into the night, long after the music and the stories had stilled.

Derek told of the time, shortly after Ruv and his wayward wolfpack had stumbled into Nomansland, when they discovered that humans were a rarity in Aorea. Their aimless wanderings took them northward to the Alpines where they found themselves inexplicably drawn into a feud between two neighbors. Each offered information in exchange for a bit of mischief conducted against the other. The boys heartily agreed. Some grain was stolen, a sheep or three relocated. In the end, they had learned where, and what, they were. They had listened in rapt attention as the feuding neighbors, their grievances eventually settled over a bottle of spiced apple wine, led them to an elder who answered all their questions.

Toward the end, Ruv took up the tale. "He told us about Sier, about the art of Sanguina, about how some humans could learn to shift from man to animal and back again," he said. "He even told us about the Destined. I know, now, why he thought that bit was important. But he would not, or could not, tell us why. Why we were in Aorea. Why us." Ruv's voice grew yet quieter. "Why me. He took me aside, then, before we left the village in search of another adventure. I never told the pack that part."

Derek and Killer looked at him with a mix of shock and bewilderment. Then Derek nodded and whispered, "I thought you seemed quieter after that. What did he tell you? What could he say to you but not us?"

Ruv closed his eyes. The memories bubbled just below the surface. "You and Hans were teaching little Jens how to fish in the river, and Torch was dazzling the rest of you with his newfound fire-starting abilities. 'Come with me a while,' the wise man said. 'I have seen something in my fires that you should know, but you must share this knowledge with no one, not until it is time.' I followed, though I cast a glance back at my pack. I worried constantly for my friends, the ones I had gathered here and there in Poland, in Germany, in Slovakia and Hungary and Russia. Boys who had once been cast off, adrift, lost. I worried, and I hoped that what he had to say would help me keep the pack together, keep you safe, despite that I was barely a man. But that was not so."

When he paused for breath, Killer said, "You never seemed worried. We never knew."

Ruv nodded soberly at him. "I kept it from you, to the best of my ability. A leader should not show weakness."

"Go on," Mari urged, her voice pitched low to match the shadow in her eyes. "This tale needs an ending."

"So I followed, and he took me to a room in the back of his dacha, the doorway covered by an old, fraying tapestry. The room was filled with candles, crystals, all manner of small wonders and oddities. I tried not to stare, but my curiosity was peaked. 'I am more than just a keeper of stories,' the old evrae said. 'I am a mage, albeit a weak one. I studied many years at the knee of the Witchazel Wizard. He was never able to teach me to transform one thing to another, or to walk between planes, but he was able, at last, to teach me to look into the fire and pull the truth of what may be from the jumble of what had been and what could have been. I have seen you in these truths, and I have seen what you will become.'" Ruv cleared his throat and took a sip of water; the others waited in silence. "'You will not be the alpha forever. A time will come when you will abandon your pack.'

"Never! I told him. I will never abandon them! 'You will,' he said sternly, 'and you must. For your heart will lead you down another path. A lonely path, though you will have friends who love you, who depend on you more than your pack ever did. You will know when it is time.' I thought the old man was done, but still he went on, telling me a future I did not want to hear. 'You will walk through darkness and fire, a strange fire, and you will lose everything you care about. But do not lose hope. I see you standing at a precipice. You must not jump. For though you lose everything, you must endure. In the end you will find another heart who needs you most of all.'"

"I don't like this story," Gren said gruffly, for he saw the way Ruv had fixed his gaze on Mari, the hazel eyes sparkling for once not with mischief, but with something stronger, something deeper.

"That is why I follow you," Ruv stated, and it was evident to all that his words were meant for Mari. "I knew, the moment I met the Destined, that my time as the alpha was over. My heart called me in another direction, and it calls me still. I do not know if this darkness is now, or if it will come later, but I know I must follow." And with that, it seemed his tale was over.

When they finally deserted their miniature utopia the next morning, they carried as much of it with them as they could, but their steps were somber. They walked in silence.

CHAPTER SEVEN
No way you could have known

"Mari?" Sam called. He lurked, half submerged in shadow, just outside their camp's perimeter. Several days had passed since they left the oasis, hiking parallel along the ridgeline and a quarter of the way below its crest. They kept the same pattern, stopping twice a day to snatch a few hours of sleep around midday and midnight. Wendy's prediction proved correct; the vegetation continued to provide enough sustenance for both their group as well as several small, scaled species of wildlife past the oasis, too. While nothing extraordinary had hounded this most recent leg of their journey, the anxious undercurrent in Sam's voice told Mari that was about to change.

She made her way to the edge of the perimeter where he waited. "What it is?"

"Sarah found something you might want to see."

Mari's fingers strayed absently to the hilt of her sword as she surveyed who was still conscious after their evening meal. Gren snored in the far corner outside the ring of firelight, his notebook of half-scribbled poems and lyrics spread over his face. Killer and Derek were arm wrestling

Frostbite. Despite the odds of two against one, the big man was holding his own, striped tattoos stretched across his bulging bicep. Ruv, Wendy, and Brae served as their audience, watching the spectacle with no shortage of enthusiasm while Micaleth snuffled through the shrubbery for grass. Mari managed to catch Ruv's eye and tossed him a nod. "You're in charge until I get back."

"Seriously?" Micaleth snorted, pulling his snout from the ground. "Him?"

Mari shrugged. "Well, Gren is clearly occupied."

"Aren't you forgetting anyone else?"

"Who?"

Micaleth returned to his search for fresh greenery, mumbling, "When is it my turn to be in charge?" He narrowed his eyes at Ruv's turned back. "I have more experience with magic in one hoof than this entire group has put together!"

"Your turn will come," Brae said softly, smiling at Micaleth's antics. It was not every day one got to witness a nietheran throwing a tantrum. "Besides, she's gesturing for you to go with."

"What? Oh!" Suddenly mollified, he trotted off into the night with Mari and Sam.

"It could be nothing," Sam was saying as Micaleth joined them, "but considering how little we know about what we're up against, we didn't want to take any chances." His leather boots, only recently reattached to his feet, squeaked and creaked over the rough terrain. Though he normally preferred to wear either his panther skin or his many throwing knives during a patrol, when he returned earlier he had left his knife belt back in the camp and instead borrowed Derek's machete.

Though noting the peculiarity at the time, Mari did not comment. "What'd you guys find?" she prompted.

Sam rubbed the back of his neck, and a muscle twitched in his cheek. "Well, like I said, Sarah found it. She's keeping an eye on it until we can get there."

"She didn't tell you?" she pressed. "How could she send you back without telling you what it was?"

"No," he snapped, "she didn't tell me." He took a deep breath before stopping in his tracks. "Look, it's hard to explain," he said more gently.

Mari regarded him in silence. At length she urged, "Try. Please." She glanced at Micaleth and found him staring off into the distance, his ears flicking back and forth in time with his tail.

Sam's mouth tensed. "We haven't talked about it yet," he repeated slowly. "I just know she found something, and she wanted me to bring you." He began walking again, Mari keeping pace with his long strides and Micaleth skimming behind on soundless hooves. He kept his eyes ahead as he continued, "See, my sister and I…we don't always have to use words to communicate. It's not quite like you and Gren and those other two with your fancy fatestones and full-on telepathic conversations. When we're in Aorea, the link is more pronounced than on Earth, but it's always there, this awareness of the other's mind. It's weird. We don't discuss it with others." He cast a sidelong glance at Mari. "I didn't want to tell you, but Sarah insisted we'd been through enough together now that we can tell you the big secret."

"Glad we finally earned your trust," she replied. "And that information could definitely come in handy. How strong is your link? Can you see what she sees?"

"Generally, no. We usually share only what we want to, and it's not a perfect system, but instances of strong emotion will sometimes trigger a more direct glimpse into the other's head." He grimaced as a memory better left buried flashed across his mind; Mari thought she could read a trace of it in his haunted eyes, but she would not ask. Not yet, in any case, and she held a sinking suspicion that it was not his story to tell. Before she could muse further, Sam announced, "I do believe we're close—I can feel her a bit further south."

"Finally," Sarah grumbled as they approached. "What'd you do, crawl here?"

"Blech! What's that smell?" Mari exclaimed.

"That, my dear, would be the corpse."

Mari knelt to study the decrepit pile of flesh and fabric in the dark, her nose buried in the front of her blouse. Bones stuck out sporadically, and some gross substance still seemed to be oozing from a wound on what looked like its shoulder. "Corpse of what, exactly?" she mumbled through the fabric.

"Haven't the faintest," Sarah said.

Mari kept squinting at the heap, face scrunched up as the inspection required her to draw yet closer. "It looks vaguely humanoid, but there's something wrong with its face." She stood, releasing her death grip on the collar of her shirt and breathing in a lungful of clean air. Well, relatively clean. The stench lingered. "How long do you think it's been out here? Time could explain why it's so far gone, maybe. But it doesn't seem…"

"I found it in panther-form," Sarah explained, "and based on the smell, it's definitely not human. I can at least tell you that much. I'm usually good at differentiating between a fresh death and an old one, but my nose gave me conflicting information with this. Maybe Ruv and that magical snout of his could do better." She nudged its arm with the toe of her boot and sneered with revulsion when a piece crumbled off. "Some parts of it seem newly dead—within the past day or so—but other parts have festered and rotted away already, as if it's been out here, exposed, for weeks."

Mari tugged at one of the tangles in her hair and, to her dismay, found a bit of bracken and thorn. "That's odd. Micaleth, any thoughts?"

The nietheran was cutting a steady circle around the corpse, his distaste evident in the distance he kept. "Sarah is right," he asserted, forcing himself to draw closer. "It is not human. In fact, it is not any creature I recognize."

"Really? Interesting. If it's not native to Aorea, I wonder how the hell it got here." Mari began to pace, the others' eyes following her movement. "Could it be a Wanderer, do you think, and sang open a portal by accident, then got lost and died? But no, that doesn't fit. The nearest circle is way too far away for he—she?—it to have wandered this far."

Micaleth bent his neck to sniff the unfortunate grotesque, then instantly regretted the decision. "Indeed, I do not believe it could have come through the circle. Perhaps Dahrigek has been home to a strange species all along, and since no one else bothered to come down here, no one knew. In any case, I am having the same difficulty determining the recency of death as Sarah. If it has only been a few days, there should still be a lingering aura. It would be faint, of course, but a trickle of light should still cling around the edges." He stepped another cautious circle around the corpse. "But with this, I see only darkness, so it must have been dead for a while."

"So are you saying there is no aura," Sarah queried, shifting her feet, "or that this thing has a dark aura?" Sam rested a hand on her shoulder, and they both suppressed a shudder.

The nietheran tossed his head in an ambiguous answer, his alicorn catching a stray scattering of starlight and refracting it outward. "All living things have a personal energy field, I suppose you could say. Certain beings— such as my kind, for example, or the very sensitive of other species—can perceive these fields as patterns of glowing color. The leshii have very strong auras. That is why even the less sensitive can see what they call their glow." He paused, studying his friends to assure himself their auras remained. Pleased with the confirmation, he continued, "After death the aura lingers, fading into nothingness over about the course of a week. So if this creature were recently deceased, there would still be a faint aura. But nothing is there. No light. No color. Only darkness."

Unable to suppress the urge longer, Sarah shivered. "Is it just me or did the temperature drastically drop?"

"Not just you," Mari agreed. She rubbed her hands together; she could perceive the pale tips of her frigid fingers despite the dark of the new moon. "It's definitely colder." Then, turning back to Micaleth, she added, "So, if we were to assume that this poor, disgusting thing is more recently deceased than not, what would that mean?"

"I do not know," Micaleth replied, voice strained. "I have never faced that kind of situation before, nor have I heard of such a thing. Even more disturbing, the more I think about it, the more Sarah's earlier question may be relevant. It is almost as if in place of where the fading aura should be, there is a shadow, a kind of reverse-aura. Instead of giving off light, it is stealing light away." He took a step backward, though his hooves felt slower than usual, as if they were growing roots in the ground. "Do you feel a pull? I think I feel a pull."

"Might explain the temperature drop," Mari said. She gripped her sword to keep her hand from shaking.

"Either that or we're just in a desert after dark," Sam offered, though the hint of a tremble in his voice revealed his disbelief in his own suggestion.

Mari tapped the tip of her nose with her free hand. "If it were still light out, we might be able to figure out more. We'll just leave it alone for now. Since it's dead, it's not exactly going anywhere, so we can just give it a wide berth and warn the others on guard so no one trips over a creepy corpse in the dark. Then we'll see what else we can find out once the sun rises." She marched back to the camp, Micaleth close on her heels. Without a word, Sarah and Sam faded back into the shadows to resume their patrol. "Damn, I wish I still had my dreams," Mari grumbled.

"So do I," Micaleth whispered.

When they returned to the camp, Mari and Micaleth found everyone much as they had left them. Gren still snored. Derek and Killer were still challenging Frostbite, but it was instead over a game of makeshift tic tac toe, and this time it was one on one. Derek, face scrunched up, moved a small rock while Killer waited his turn. Wendy and Brae talked quietly to each other, a dainty mirror of freckles and red hair for all their difference in species.

"Wendy? I need you to fly," Mari called, loud enough to startle Gren from his slumber and rouse the attention of the rest. "We may not have a quiet night after all."

Wendy prepared for her aerial trip while Mari relayed what she had seen with the twins. When it came to the dark aura, Micaleth took over, but still he could offer no reason for the presence of the shadow.

"So Micaleth can see auras, huh?" Gren asked, extending his arms forward in a stretch and cracking his knuckles. "I wonder what color mine is."

Mari sat down beside him. "I dunno, probably blue."

Gren glanced down at the loose sweater he wore, the sleeves rolled up over his elbows. By the firelight, the original color could just be perceived under the permanent layer of dust and grime. He gave her a half-smile. "I don't think my clothing preferences have anything to do with it."

"Yeah, but you almost always wear blue," she countered, smiling despite the nervousness gnawing at her gut. "Maybe your subconscious is trying to tell you something."

"By that logic, your aura is either green or the color of old mud," he quipped.

Mari rolled her eyes, but Gren could tell the annoyance in those flashing jade pools did not run deep. "Mickey, what color are our auras?" she queried, her tone flat.

"I will not say."

"What? Why not?" Mari and Gren cried in unison.

The nietheran shook his head, ragged mane tossing to and fro. "Because I am tired, because it is irrelevant, and furthermore, because we have more important things to be discussing, like what strange creature that corpse used to be, or why a village north of the wall was raided by an unknown horde but no one remembers, or how an entire city was built down in Dahrigek eons ago…"

"All valid points," Mari conceded with a dip of her chin, "but at the moment we can't act on any of that, so what's there to discuss? There are still too many unknowns." She frowned at the empty space in their camp that Wendy had recently occupied. "Until we have a better semblance of an idea of what we're facing, beyond roving hordes of unknown creatures—wait, do you remember what they looked like?"

"Well, no, I have not seen them yet, it was the evrae—"

Mari's eyes narrowed. "Right, do you remember what they *said* about the horde?"

Micaleth scrunched up his nose. "I am afraid I do not recall the specifics. At that particular moment there was a mosquito buzzing about my face, and I was trying to shake it off discreetly."

"I remember. They said they looked all misshapen, like clumps of mud," Gren mumbled. Then he raised his head abruptly and caught Mari's eye. "Ah, shit. I know what you're thinking."

"I'm thinking I'm an idiot," she grumbled. She stood and withdrew her sword. "Ruv, Gren, with me."

She took off at a jog to where Sarah had found the corpse, the two men keeping easy pace. But when they reached the proper location, the corpse had completely vanished. Only the stench remained.

Mari growled, her inner wolf dangerously close to the surface. "Great. So it wasn't dead. It's probably reporting back right now on our location to the rest of that horde of…undead things." She stowed her sword and ran an agitated hand over her face.

"So much for sleeping," Gren muttered.

"Clearly off the table," Ruv agreed.

"Gren, can you round up the twins?" Mari asked. Without delay he sprinted away to track them down. "Damn, I wish Wendy hadn't already left. Maybe she could've followed it from the sky," she mused as she began to jog back to camp. "We have to find a new location, unless, maybe, we can find wherever that thing went and stop it from reaching the rest of its group."

Ruv, who had been running with her, abruptly changed his direction. "I'll track the sucker."

"Thanks!" Mari called over her shoulder. "I'll send the boys after you. We have no idea how strong these things are, let alone how to kill them."

"If they can be killed," Ruv called back.

"We'll find out one way or another," she snapped. "Now go! I'll get everyone ready to leave, just in case. And Ruv...be careful."

Mari could barely make out his response. "Always am," he said.

"It's a lovely view, is it not?" her captor's voice reverberated off the stone walls of the small chamber. She had not heard him enter.

"I miss my home," Necria whispered without removing her gaze from the window.

Dimeldor moved closer. "You will get used to being here," he said, "to being with me, sooner than you think. Just keep an open mind."

She spun on her heels and stared daggers. If she had access to physical daggers, she would have loved to throw them. "I'd rather see an open sky," she hissed. "I'm nothing to you but a prisoner."

"You could not be more wrong," he said, and the sadness that shadowed the pale skin beneath his eyes appeared to be, as far as she could tell, genuine. "If you only knew how much I rely on your presence. I need you. I need you with me, always. I cannot—"

"Then why am I kept locked in this room," she interrupted as she stalked toward him, staring stubbornly at the stranger she used to think she knew, whom she used used to think she understood. "Why am I kept under guard night and day, my only visitor the very demon who ordered the slaughter of my friends and family? For all I know, you're the source of the torture they suffered even before the violence."

His face crumpled as if her accusation had been followed by an effective right hook, though she had made no move to assault him in body. He sensed, then, her latent power. The power that had drawn him to her. The power he had never before noticed, so entranced had he been by everything else she had come to represent. "It's all for your protection," he pleaded. He cleared his throat and smoothed a wrinkle from his robes. "You'll come around," he said, pushing all other thoughts aside except calming his love before she realized her own potential.

She could ruin everything.

"Until you do," he continued, "I can't have you making any rash decisions and getting yourself hurt. I couldn't bear the thought of no longer hearing your voice."

Necria unleashed a hollow laugh, and he winced. "If my voice is what you most desire," she jeered, "then you shall never hear me speak again."

He made to embrace her, but then he thought better of it. "You should not be so hasty with your vows of silence, my love," he murmured. Not wanting to wilt beneath her defiant scrutiny, he took to pacing. Each step drew him closer to a thought, one that disturbed him more deeply than his recent revelation. He ignored the golden eyes that trailed his repetitive movement and allowed himself to think on why he had brought her to his fortress, why he had wanted to save her alone of all the world, the world he wanted to burn. Eyes hard, he continued, "I have ways of forcing you to speak, should I wish to do so, but I truly do love you. Whether you believe me or not." He ceased his pacing and finally met her gaze. "I would never force you to do anything against your will."

"Except force me from my home."

When he replied, his voice was even softer than before, nearly as soft as when he used to visit her in her family's house, back when his primary concern was avoiding detection. "In time you will sing to me again. You'll see. Until then, I suppose I must be patient and reflect on the sweet memories of words already spoken and songs already sung."

As he turned to leave, Necria cast a wistful glance at the window. She grabbed an iron bar in each hand, gripping tight, anchoring herself in place. "I call upon the Ancestors, the mighty and beloved dead. My Ancestors of blood and spirit, who laid the path before me and even in this dark place ever guide my steps. Hear me, and lend me your power," she chanted. "By the sky above me, by the land beneath me, and by the sea before me, I bind my tongue to silence."

Dimeldor felt the force of her prayer looping through the room, and his eyes grew wide. She had felt her own power after all, and she was using it not against him, not against his plan, but against herself.

It was too late.

"No word shall cross my lips," Necria chanted further, "no sound shall escape my throat, no song shall fill my heart until I depart this mortal world to join You in the Summerlands. So be it."

"Oh, my sweet Necria, what have you done?"

Silent tears streamed down her cheeks.

Mari issued orders as soon as she returned to camp. At her behest, Killer and Derek shifted and took off after Ruv while Brae and Frostbite started fastening Micaleth's many totes across his back.

"I was so looking forward to a good nap," Brae muttered while pulling a strap taut.

"You are small," Frostbite observed. "If you need to sleep, I can carry you."

Brae cast him a sidelong glance. Satisfied that his offer was genuine, she replied with a warm smile, "I appreciate it, but that won't be necessary."

Sarah returned with her brother and Gren at her side. "Bloody hell," she snarled. "I can't believe the bastard scampered off on us. If I'd known he wasn't really dead, I'd've done something to change the fact."

Mari shoved a bag of roasted lizards into another pack. "None of us knew. I just hope Ruv can find him before his friends find us."

"Are we sure it was just the one?" Frostbite inquired. He and Brae had finished fastening Micaleth's packs, and so instead the big man was slipping into his own.

"At least in the immediate area," Sarah stated. "The stench permeates. If there were others about, we would've smelled them by now."

When everyone had finished arranging their supplies and removing all traces of their presence, Mari directed, "If the boys aren't back in half an hour, we're moving without them. They can follow our scent trail perfectly fine." After a deep breath, she added, "If they haven't returned by morning, then we'll go find them."

"That won't be necessary," Ruv called with a grin as he joined their circle. Killer and Derek followed close behind.

"You found it?" Mari asked, excitement raising the pitch of her voice well above its usual alto.

"Killed it," Ruv corrected, his crooked grin broadening.

"For real this time?" Gren pressed.

It was Derek who replied. "For real."

Sarah folded her arms across her narrow chest. "How can you be sure? Its scent fooled me."

At this, Killer lugged a reeking mass into the center of the gathering. With a nauseating squelch it bounced twice before rolling to a stop. "When in doubt," he said with a subsequent shrug, "take the head."

Brae flung her hand over her mouth and choked back the rising leaf matter that comprised her stomach's primary contents. "I think I'm going to hurl," she mumbled as she took a few steps away and did precisely that.

Mari wrinkled her nose. "That'll certainly do it. No sign of any others?"

"None," Ruv assured. "We caught him in time. He was moving pretty fast, but we were faster."

Derek nodded. "We had just caught up with Ruv by the time he'd found the thing."

"It looks like a zombie," Gren deadpanned.

"I was thinking goblin," Mari said with a frown, "but you have a point."

Sarah rolled her eyes. "Rubbish, there's no zombies in Aorea. It must have just been playing dead."

"There's no zombies, period," Sam agreed with a toss of his head. "They don't exist."

As if to undermine his assertion, at that very moment the decapitated head opened its eyes. One yellowed sphere and one soulless, empty socket surveyed their stunned faces as it began to cackle maniacally, though without a windpipe the laughter was nothing more than a hiss. Frostbite leapt upon the laughing head, axe hacking and smashing, until it had been thoroughly demolished. The force of his attack scattered tiny bits of goo and flesh throughout their former camp, and then the bits smoldered and vanished in puffs of sour smoke.

"It is gone," Micaleth whinnied softly. "The reverse aura is completely gone. I believe, whatever this unnatural creature was, that now it is truly dead."

"It was definitely a zombie," Gren repeated.

"Well, ok, maybe, with the whole decapitation thing not being enough to kill it," Mari conceded, "but I'm sure there's at least a semi-rational explanation for whatever the hell it was."

"Oh. My. Gods," Gren pronounced, his dark eyes glinting and the corner of his mouth quirked in mischief.

He suddenly looked much younger than his twenty one years. "You guys! It's a ZOMBLIN! A zombie-goblin!"

"I'm never calling it that," Sarah asserted.

"Me either," Mari said. "Terrible name."

"But it's perfect," Gren continued. "It fits. We're gonna fight a horde of zomblins!"

"Try not to sound so excited there, brother," Ruv said darkly, though the crooked smile that began to play across his lips betrayed a hint of enthusiasm.

Derek scowled at the stain on the ground where the cackling head had exploded after Frostbite's intervention. "Taking the bastard's head off wasn't exactly as easy as we made it sound."

"Alright," Mari interjected soberly. "I don't particularly like the idea of being snuck up on, but now that we have an idea of what's out there, we can plan off that. We're still going to move camp, because that smell sucks, but we don't have to go far. Ruv, Killer, Derek, let's go over how that thing fought. I wanna know capabilities. Decapitation may not kill them permanently, but it probably still makes them ineffective." Her eyes darted back and forth at the surrounding shadows. "Wendy will be able to find us after we move, and hopefully she'll find them first and come back with a ballpark count. If she doesn't see them, we'll just follow the scent trail and see where it leads. Maybe we'll get to the bottom of this little mystery soon."

Dawn had begun to peak its lavender brow above the horizon, but Mari and Ruv were still huddled close together, rehashing the details of the fight with the undead goblin while the rest attempted to steal what sleep they could before they moved on again.

Brae sat bolt upright from where she had dozed next to Sarah. "Did you hear something?" she asked Mari and Ruv in an urgent whisper.

"I don't think so," Mari replied. Nonetheless, she moved to her feet and quieted her breath. Over the sighing wind and the first twittering of birds, she detected a faint sound. A strained, muffled cry reached her ears from beyond a hill.

"That couldn't be—" Ruv began.

"—Wendy!" Brae finished.

Ruv roused the rest of their friends while Mari and Brae tore across the jagged ground. When they crested the knoll, they caught sight of Wendy struggling toward them. She clutched her right arm close to her chest, the wrist bent at an awkward angle, and her feet left crimson footprints on the sparse grass.

"What happened? Are you ok?" Mari implored as she reached her side, though all the evidence of her eyes informed her that Wendy was a far cry from ok.

The injured woman leaned against Mari's shoulder, still clutching her arm. Brae, seeing Mari could handle things for the time being, dashed back to the camp to retrieve Wendy's clothes and shoes. However, Sarah was one step ahead of her and was already heading their way with Wendy's pack.

"I had just found the horde, or at least part of it, when I was attacked," Wendy forced out, nearly breathless.

"Shh, it's ok, we can wait a few minutes for—"

"No, we can't!" she cried. "It's important. We need—"

Mari silenced further protests with a fierce look. "We can wait long enough to get you clothed and get that arm in a sling," she commanded. "And you need water."

Brae and Sarah finally reached them, and Wendy winced as the other women helped her dress. The soles of her feet were scraped raw, and her entire body was laced with scratches and tinted with fresh bruises. Bracken knotted in her fine hair. She swore she could walk back to the camp on her own, having already walked so far, but Mari insisted they carry her. Thus, with assistance Wendy reluctantly climbed onto Mari's back. She clung tight with her one good arm as they made their halting trek.

In the brief time between Mari and Brae's initial departure and their return to the camp, Ruv had nurtured the banked embers into a roaring blaze. Mari eased her friend onto a pile of blankets, ankles propped up on a rock. The men exchanged glances at the sight of her shredded feet. Wendy squeezed her eyes shut, gritted her teeth, and allowed Killer and Sam to cut away the ruined skin and clean what remained.

With her feet slathered in comfrey salve and wrapped in gauze, Derek held a cup of water to her lips. Frostbite, examining her arm, announced, "It's broken, but it looks like a clean fracture. We need something for a splint."

Gren fished a few arrows out of his quiver. When the big man frowned at him and began to object, Gren said, "Trust me. They'll hold."

Frostbite gave her a stick to bite down on. His hands were steady and gentle as he wrapped her arm and braced it between three of the arrows. Nevertheless, Wendy bit back a scream when he straightened and set the bone, and she could not quell her shivering when he tied the sling across her shoulders. "You are very brave," he whispered, amber eyes unreadable as he released her.

"No, I'm just Scottish," she corrected, though her cheeks flushed at the compliment. "We're a stubborn lot."

Laria found Hal on a bench outside, hunched over a slim book. "What are you reading?" she asked as she sat next to him.

"One of the novels Nemini brought last time she visited," he said. He held the pages open so she could see, and she caught a few lines of outdated prose. "Not sure where she stole it from, but I won't complain. About time we had something to read in here that wasn't a prophecy or an old Spinner's notes."

She gave him a rueful smile. "Well, I hate to interrupt, but I need you to do me a favor."

"Of course," he said brightly, shutting the worn cover.

"We have company. I'm about to summon the gates." She took the book from him and stood. "I need you to go outside once the gates are open and talk to her for me."

Hal nodded. "Of course," he repeated.

He escorted Laria to the golden wall that encircled the sanctuary. As she laid her hands against the flawless surface, a bright light arced up from the ground, and then that light turned into a crack. Next grand doors of polished oak materialized on either side of the crack, inscribed with carven figures of flowers and foliage. Laria gestured for Hal to open them, and then she turned on her heel and retreated to the cottage.

The gates sealed shut as soon as Hal stepped outside, the wall behind him smooth and unbroken, as immaculate as if no doors had ever existed. He had only a few moments to ponder who their mysterious guest would be before she arrived. He knew it could not be one of the lanti since, apart from himself and Laria's nietheran guard, they were the only ones who could enter and leave the sanctuary at will. However, he was certainly not expecting one of the dracora.

The beating of impressive wings as she slowed her descent generated a draft that, had he not braced himself against the wall in preparation, would have knocked him out of his boots. She came to rest with a thud several meters in front of him. Despite her cautious landing, her bulk still leveled several unfortunate trees. Giant, yellow eyes blinked back at him, set like drops of faceted topaz amidst sapphire scales. She was not quite as large as the previous—and, up until then, the only—dracor he had encountered, but he had no doubt she could swallow him whole should she develop such a desire.

Hal swallowed but kept his expression neutral as he bowed before her. "I am here on the Spinner's behalf since she cannot come outside herself," he said once he rose.

"I know who you are, Guardian," the dracor rumbled. "I am Ajagar, and I bear a tale of sadness and loss."

"I'll pass along your words."

She nodded. "My child is missing. He is only a hatchling, born these three years since. I left to hunt. I was gone for only half a day, but when I returned, there was no trace of my son." The end of her tail twitched, shaking the nearby trees. "All that remained was the scent of death."

Hal sucked in a breath. "I'm so sorry," he exhaled. "Could he have wandered off?"

"He is too young to fly, either in this plane or between them, yet there were no footprints."

"That is—is quite strange," Hal admitted with a frown. He thought he may have seen a tear moistening Ajagar's eyes, but it was just a glare from the sun. He wondered briefly if dragons could cry.

Her voice grew soft, to the extent that the voice of such an immense creature could ever be described as soft. "It gets stranger, I fear. I searched the world over. For weeks I sought answers. When there was no sign of him, I flew between the planes, but still I could not find him. I could sense him, faintly, but when I flew toward that sense I hit some kind of barrier. I am not sure how else to describe it to one who cannot travel in this way. I could not pass beyond that barrier, whatever it was. I sense he remains alive, but I do not know where, so I have come here to beg the Spinner to look in her Loom." She took in a deep breath and released it slowly. "Please."

"I will tell her," Hal assured. He grasped his fatestone, an onyx pendant in the shape of a sword that hung from a chain fastened perpetually around his neck, and relayed the message to Laria.

Laria's mental response was immediate. *I saw she was coming, but I didn't think it was something this bad. Ok. I will look now. Give me a few minutes.*

To Ajagar, Hal asked, "Is there anything you need while we wait?"

"All I need is to find my child and bring him home."

"I understand."

"Have you lost a child?" she bit.

Hal took a step back on instinct, but the wall stood solid behind him, halting his movement. "No, I haven't, I'm sorry," he murmured.

"Then you could not possibly understand."

"I'm sorry," he said again. "I didn't mean to offend."

Ajagar took another deep breath and replied, "I know. I am the one who should apologize." She lifted her eyes toward the sky then settled her gaze back on Hal. "That was unkind of me."

He felt the need to bow to her again, so he did.

Laria's voice interrupted his thoughts. *I can't find him,* she told Hal. Her voice in his head cracked with regret and confusion. *There's no trace of a dracor child anywhere. I can't even see the hatching. It's like the whole thing is completely shrouded.*

"Like with Dahrigek?" Hal sent back. His grip on the fatestone tightened.

I wish I could tell you no, but it's just the same. I look, and the threads tangle.

To Ajagar, he said quietly, "She can't see him."

"How can this be?" the dragon roared. "The Loom can show all!"

He rubbed his face as he sought the right words. "There is...the Loom has been acting weird." He paused, biting his lip. "There are parts of Aorea it will no longer show Laria, er, the Spinner, no matter how hard or how many times she looks. Your child must have somehow gone into one of those places."

"Dahrigek, I heard you say," she mused, the scales of her great forehead shifting as she raised her brow to look skyward again. "But there is nothing there to be seen. I flew there myself."

Hal shrugged, but he tried his best to maintain a conciliatory demeanor. After his previous blunder, he had no wish to make any misstep that might further offend the grieving mother. "It started with a set of islands along the coast, but almost the entire continent is hidden now."

Ajagar reared back on her hind legs. "It makes no sense. Why would such a desolate place be obscured?"

"We don't know," Hal stated. "She sent the Dreamer and the Wanderer to see if there's anything they can find out about it. The lanti seem to think—"

"The lanti," she growled. "Is this their doing?"

"No," he said quickly. "They think it might be some demon sorcerer, maybe. But they won't go themselves. They said it's up to the Destined now. Up to us."

A grumble rolled through her throat. "This is quite unacceptable. And disturbing."

Tentatively, Hal took a few steps forward and laid a hand on one of the massive toes of her nearest foot. The scales, surprisingly smooth, blazed hot beneath his skin. "I wish I could tell you more," he whispered, staring up at her. With some effort he pushed the thought that he might still become her lunch out of his mind. "I'm so sorry your child got caught up in this, whatever this is. If Mari and Gren find him, we'll let you know as soon as we can."

"Then I will stay here and wait."

"As you wish," Hal said, withdrawing his hand while he sent a silent thought to Laria. She had been waiting for just such a signal, because it was only a few seconds later that the gates opened up behind him. With one last bow, he withdrew into the sanctuary.

After they forced more water and a bit of food into Wendy, Mari allowed her to share her tale. "It was pixies, I think. They looked like the ones we saw in the forest," she explained gravely, "only something was wrong with their faces. In my owl form I couldn't think how to fend them off, and they were too fast for me to grab, so I tried to outfly them." She swallowed. "I managed to get lower in the sky and started to head back, but it wasn't enough. They followed me and must have knocked me unconscious or something. I don't know how, really, maybe they dropped a big rock. I just remember feeling a pain in my head and then waking up on top a rather smashed cactus. I don't know if I shifted back during or after my fall, but either way I landed on my right arm."

"Bollocks, I didn't think to check your head," Sarah muttered, scrambling behind her. She began to comb her fingers through Wendy's hair, much to the petite woman's embarrassment, who grumbled about baby chimpanzees being groomed by their mothers. Sarah extricated bits of twigs and a few cactus thorns from the jumble of strawberry blonde. At length, she released a sigh. "There's no blood. Might have a concussion, then, but at least no gaping head trauma."

"I'm just glad you're alive," Mari said quietly. "I never should have sent you out alone. I feel responsible."

Wendy forced a smile. "It's not your fault. I should have paid more attention to where I was flying."

"How could you have known pixies would leave their forest, let alone attack you?" she pressed. "Even those of us who've been to Aorea before never thought freaking pixies of all things would be capable of that."

"By that logic," Wendy countered, "There's no way you could have known either." She set her mouth in an obstinate line, which, had she not triggered such protective concern in the hearts of all those present, would have struck them as comical. "Sorry I wasn't more help."

Ruv grinned at her. "So you landed on a cactus, huh? I wonder which of you is the worse for wear."

"While I may have to pluck a few more needles out of my arse, the cactus by far bore the brunt of my landing." Wendy grinned back, but the grin changed to a grimace when she jolted her arm in an attempt to reposition herself. "I think I might've cracked a rib or two, too."

Mari pursed her lips. "Do you want us to take you back north?" she asked. "Horde or not, we can finish this journey later. Without you."

"I'm fair to keep going," Wendy claimed.

"No, really—"

"I'm going with you, and that's final." She stared doggedly back until Mari conceded with a tight nod. "I'm left handed anyway. I may not be able to fly for a while, but I can still contribute. I can show you where the horde was heading, and I can still fight. To the extent that I ever could, that is. And I want to help. Now that I've seen them, how many there are...no, I can't go back. What we're doing is too important."

"You're going to ride on Micaleth until your feet recover," Mari ordered. "You walked a long way barefoot through a freaking desert. I'd be pissed at you for not letting us take you back if I weren't so damn impressed."

"I would comment on my further demotion from pack mule to common mount, but I feel that would be inappropriate given the circumstances," Micaleth stated. "Miss Cerridwen MacEunrig," he continued with a regal nod in her direction, further emphasizing the formality with which he adorned the occasion by using her full name, "it would be an honor to carry you."

Mari took a deep breath. "Now I think it's time we hear a bit more about those pixies and that horde, if you're up to it. You said there was something off about them. How off, exactly?"

Wendy chewed her lip. "Maybe it was just my viewing them through owl eyes—things look a little different, you know—but their faces seemed distorted, almost as if they were all scrunched up in pain or fury, but their eyes seemed vacant. Distant. I'm not sure how else to describe it. They just felt *wrong*."

Sarah, who had been fidgeting with one of her knives, grew still. "I got the same sense from that undead goblin when I first found him. I couldn't put my finger on exactly why or how, but I just knew he was *wrong*."

Sam turned a sharp look at his sister then back at Wendy. "Do you think whatever is mutating the pixies might be connected to the walking corpses we're tracking?" he queried, voice flat.

"It's possible," Wendy replied. "The wee buggers attacked me almost immediately after I located the horde."

Mari's nose twitched. "Interesting."

"How many were there?" asked Ruv.

"A hundred, maybe. I'm not sure, exactly, but either way a lot more than us."

"Damn," Derek growled. "That's a lot of goblins to take on at once."

Gren could not help but smirk. "Not just any goblins," he added, "zomblins."

Mari rolled her eyes at him and let out an exasperated sigh before turning her attention back to Wendy. "Where were they going?"

"Same way we are," she stated. "There's a pass further south, and it looked like they were heading straight toward it." She paused to take another sip of water. "The pass would lead them right to the coast."

Micaleth shared a glance with Mari. "Were they going toward the islands, do you think?"

"I couldn't say," Wendy admitted. "It was dark still, so I'm not sure if there were islands beyond the pass or not. I was mostly focused on the land."

"About how far ahead of us are they?" Mari persisted.

"Assuming they keep the same pace, on four legs it would take us maybe a day and a half of solid running to catch up. On two legs, maybe add a day to that." She coughed; the movement elicited another grimace. "They weren't going very fast, and they were carrying a lot of shite with them, and dragging more. I couldn't see what specifically, though. Something big."

Mari rubbed the back of her neck and whispered, "I'm sorry to keep plaguing you with questions." When Wendy only smiled and shook her head in response, Mari continued, "Did you spot any faster routes while you were still airborne? Maybe we can intercept them or set up an ambush. Might give us at least a little bit of an advantage that way, instead of just stumbling after them. If they're ultimately heading toward the coast, I'm thinking we can split our forces, attack from both sides when they're in the pass, maybe find out what they're really up to...how wide was it?"

"The pass? Not very. They'll be bottlenecked. I don't think more than six would be able to walk abreast."

Mari's face lost some of its seriousness. "I think we've got the start of a plan. Micaleth, still got that map?"

"Of course," the nietheran sniffed.

Brae sifted through his packs. "Got it!" she announced.

They brought the unfolded parchment to Wendy's lap and huddled around it. "Ok, so we should be right about here," Mari said, pointing. "So I bet this down here is the pass you saw."

Wendy squinted at the indicated point. "Aye, that looks right, from what I could see."

"As we have already witnessed," Micaleth cautioned, "the land could have shifted since the map was drawn."

"Not terribly much as the owl flies, apparently."

Mari nodded. "Good. At any rate, Aorean distances are, as we keep being reminded, always deceptive. Ok. Here's what we're gonna do. We split in two groups. We're a smaller target that way, and we can rearrange our supplies strategically so one group travels lighter. Cover more ground." She lifted her head to study her companions and came to a decision. "The slower group will track the horde using the trail left by the one we already encountered and come up behind them once they're bottlenecked in the pass. The faster group will head southwest toward the coast and try to cut them off from the other side."

Wendy stared at her. "I should go with the fast group."

"No way," Mari said in a tone that permitted no argument. "You can't shift, and you'll be too slow riding Micaleth. You can brief the fast group on what you saw, but you need to stay with the other one. Gren, you lead the fast group. Ruv, Killer, Derek, and Sarah will go with you. Everyone else will be with me."

Sam and Sarah frowned. "Why are you separating us?" Sam inquired in a whisper.

"If something should happen to me or Gren, you and your sister will still be able to guide the groups back together and get everyone out of here."

Gren snapped his head toward the twins. "Wait, what?"

"Eh, don't worry about it," Sam dismissed.

"I'll explain later," Sarah promised.

"I don't like it," Gren disclosed, dark eyes studying Mari. "I don't think we should split up."

Mari took his hand in hers. "It's our best shot at heading them off, and we'll be less obvious in smaller groups," she said quietly. "Plus you can make better time in sanguine form, especially if you only take the bare necessities with you, and you guys may even get there fast enough to throw some obstacles together and slow them down." She released his hand and addressed the group as a whole once more. "When we come up behind them and they're all caught up in the pass, their numbers won't be such an advantage. We can pick off any stragglers along the way, too.

"The more we can attrit their forces, the better," she continued. "We need to figure out what they're after, who or what they even are, and what the hell they're doing here. I doubt the existence of an army of goblins is enough to cloak an entire part of the world from Laria's view, so there's gotta be something more to this. If we can capture one alive to interrogate, well, that could be huge."

Gren nodded, but doubt darkened his eyes. "I don't like it, but I'll concede your points."

"My group will carry the bulk of the gear," Mari stated firmly. "You guys just take the food and water you'll need to get you through the next two days or so. We'll have met back up by then."

"I still think I should go with them," Wendy murmured. "I'm a good runner, bloody feet or no."

Mari shook her head. "Not good enough to keep up with wolves and big cats. Give them a solid rundown of what terrain to look for, and that'll be enough." When Wendy nodded her grudging agreement, Mari urged, "We need to move on this quickly. Wendy, do you think the pixies that attacked you are still out there?"

"It's possible," she admitted with a thoughtful glance at the sky. "Since I was out for a while, I didn't see which direction they headed after."

Ruv cocked his head to the side. "Assuming there's a connection between them and that horde, I bet they're running an aerial screen of some sort."

"So be doubly alert, keep some distance, and check the sky often," Mari ordered. To emphasize the end of the conversation, she instructed Sam and Frostbite to start the process of reconsolidating their supplies. She left Gren, Sarah, and the wolves with Wendy to go over the landmarks they would need to look for on their journey.

Once their hurried preparations were complete, the two teams went their separate ways.

CHAPTER EIGHT
You still want to be there, too

Brae rode behind Wendy, helping her stay seated on Micaleth's broad back. At first the swaying and bouncing had made Wendy nauseous, especially combined with the herbs Brae kept forcing down her throat at regular intervals to help with the pain, but she slowly grew accustomed to the motion. Mari, Sam, and Frostbite padded along in their sanguine forms. To an outside observer, they would have made an interesting sight: a wolf, a panther, a tiger, and a stately niethera bearing two petite red-heads. They ran at a brisk pace with Mari in her copper fur at the forefront, nose to the ground, sniffing out the goblin's stale trail.

Quite unexpectedly, the scent led them southwest, but the course skirted the ridge that outlined the shore. Wendy's assessment that they were staying in the ravine until they reached the pass seemed to be accurate. The desert remained open, yet some of the scrub and spindly sage grew large enough to provide at least a modicum of concealment. Sam yawned periodically, and Frostbite trotted steadily on. As he had promised when he first walked into the Tipsy Turtle, his running was tireless.

"It's hot enough as it is," Brae complained at one point. "I can only imagine how brutal it must be wearing fur right now."

"At least we're making good time," Wendy said. A jolt shot through her arm as Micaleth leapt over a particularly ragged piece of terrain, and she gritted her teeth.

Micaleth heard her suppressed squeak. "Sorry about that," he murmured. "How are you feeling?"

"Ech, I'll live."

Brae, a thin arm securing Wendy's waist, used her other one to secure a pack that kept brushing annoyingly against her leg as Micaleth galloped. "Aren't niethera supposed to have healing abilities?" she solicited with just the slightest hint of admonition.

Micaleth replied in a tight voice, "Some, yes. I am afraid, however, that I possess no such skill." He cleared his throat, tail flicking back and forth. "I can manage astral travel, simple bindings like the trick I did to unlock the Destined's fatestones so they can use them to communicate, and I can draw water from the rocks and the air. But healing? That is not my strength. I might succeed in taking some of the pain, but it is just as likely that I would make the injuries worse."

"Well, if astral travel's in your skill set," Brae prodded, "then why didn't you offer to take over the scouting duties now that Wendy's out of commission? Seven hells, why are we even on this mission in the first place?"

The nietheran hung his head, and when his response came, it was barely above a whisper. "I tried. All the niethera tried. None of us could break through the shroud astrally any more than the Spinner could."

"You are utterly useless," Brae teased.

"Says the leshii enjoying a free ride."

"Oi!" Wendy interrupted. "This is about the spot where I woke up after I fell. That may even be the cactus I landed on." She gestured with her unbroken arm. "We should keep a look out for those pixies."

Brae whistled to their companions and called, "Well, four-legged friends, did you hear the girl?"

They each gave a quick nod without breaking stride.

Shortly thereafter, Mari halted their progress. Initially she tried to indicate via a series of enthusiastic jumps and other canine gesticulations the point at which the trail of their lone goblin corpse had broken off from the rest. Giving up when no one seemed to comprehend, she shifted back and verbally informed them of the discovery.

They spent a few minutes inspecting the former goblin camp site. It appeared the goblins were not nearly as meticulous in removing all trace of their presence before leaving as was their own group. There were footprints aplenty, and they found shreds of fabric, snagged on a cactus here or a bit of scrub brush there, to which clumps of decaying matter still clung. Most interestingly, they found a set of footprints that could not possibly have belonged to any goblin. Sam saw them first and called the others over. These prints pressed much deeper into the ground than the rest, and suggested a set of splayed, reptilian toes with even deeper indentations where claws would have scraped.

"How big can the lizards down here get?" Wendy enquired with a shudder.

"Not sure, but I'd rather not find out," Brae replied.

In a daze Necria wandered the stone halls, scattered memories tugging her mind down conflicting paths. Moments from her childhood flickered, unsought, unwanted, behind her eyes. She remembered the time she stumbled across a wounded sparrow and, more curious than concerned, watched as it floundered and died. She remembered when little Naya was born, a squalling and wrinkled thing. How could she have grown to love such a one so quickly? Yet she had. She had loved her little sister.

She remembered an argument with her mother about praying to the Ancestors. How can they hear us? Necria had insisted. They are dead. Yet, she ruminated as her fingers traced the rough outline of a stone, she had no trouble talking to the Ancestors now.

She remembered how she first met her angel.

Her demon.

With effort she forced her thoughts back to the present. She knew she must have eaten—she had not grown deathly thin, after all, and she felt no want or weakness—but she could not remember doing so. It was so much easier to lose herself in the past, to reminisce, to succumb to the mist of dreams, than to face the reality before her. Ruefully she realized she had lost all track of time. She could have been in the fortress for weeks, months even. Years, she thought uncomfortably.

Lifetimes.

Her steps carried her to the heart of the castle where Dimeldor did his scrying. She saw him hovering over the stone basin, and though she knew he must feel her presence even as she always felt his, he did not turn around. Her hand strayed to her cheek and came back wet. Her fingers settled on the jewelry she still wore. The necklace he had given her hung cold against her throat, and the ring pressed heavy against her knuckle. He had lavished her in yet more jewels upon her arrival: a bracelet, a tiara, an armband. Each piece held those same glittering, black stones that suggested the depths of the infinite void. Why did she still wear them? The answer came to her quicker than she would have liked. Though she could never forgive him, part of her still loved her angel.

Her demon.

Necria made to return to her velvet prison, but the necromancer caught her by the wrist. She had not heard his approach, but then, she rarely did. One had to live in the present to observe one's surroundings. "I wish you would talk to me," he breathed. "It has been too long."

She met his dark gaze blankly, vaguely aware of the tears still rolling down her cheeks. How long had she been crying? She could not remember.

"I thought when I brought you here that it would make everything right," Dimeldor continued, "that I would no longer feel this emptiness. Your silence wounds me. Please, just tell me what you want." When she continued to stare without any indication of comprehension, he disclosed, "I should spend more time with you. I know that. I have been so busy, too busy, but I must continue, you understand? My destiny calls me, even as you once called me." He whispered so softly that, had any of his minions been in the vicinity, only Necria would have heard. "Even as you still call me."

She yanked her wrist away, and this time he let her go.

Servorg rounded the corner and cleared his throat.

"How could you let this happen?" the necromancer snapped at Servorg, not removing his fixation from the retreating form of his love.

"The journey was too long. She couldn't surv—"

"You have failed me."

"Yes, master," the goblin agreed, bowing his head. "But at least we brought you the bones."

Dimeldor growled low in his throat. "I know. I saw." He turned on his heel to glower at the goblin. "But now you must correct this oversight."

"Of course, master. Next time—"

"No. Now is not the time. We were lucky with the first two. They wandered off from the herd." The necromancer curled his lip in a dismissive sneer. Another thought rose unbidden to his mind. He also could not risk losing more of his army in the process, and none of the other creatures he acquired had proven resilient enough to survive for long in his study, nor to withstand reanimation. More disappointing still, though his minions were stronger than the weak species of Aorea, still they could not last forever.

The dead crumbled eventually.

The ranks of his army grew thin alongside his patience, and he could no longer draw goblins forth from Daem; their kind was just as extinct now as his own. Dimeldor let these thoughts remain unspoken. Better, he decided, to not let his minions know they were less disposable now than they once were. "Yet even those primitive fools," he continued, "would surely notice another of their own disappearing so soon, and I am not yet ready to reveal myself." He cast a disgusted glance at Servorg. "Leave."

The goblin obeyed.

Dimeldor's black eyes came to rest on the empty space down the hall where Necria had disappeared around the corner. "We've been through so much together, you and I," he whispered to the nothingness. "But I suppose you wouldn't remember. Not anymore." He swept back into the scrying room to consult the waters. Perhaps this time they would show him what he wished to see. Perhaps this time he would be able to control the visions.

"What do you guys think of this spot?" Gren asked as they navigated one of the larger patches of the spindly bushes with short, sharp needles that clung to the fabric of their dusty clothes.

Sarah fumbled with her vest's zipper after her recent return to human form as she quipped, "All these bloody spots look the bloody same."

Ruv grunted. "I think we can do better. There's not much protection here."

"There's not much protection anywhere," Sarah grumbled. "We're in a freaking desert!" She twirled in a circle, arms spread wide, to emphasize her point. "Freaking...ugh, I've spent too much time with you lot. I'm starting to talk like you."

Gren chuckled. "We must be growing on you. Anyway, I guess we'll keep looking." He took a few more paces, started to stumble, and grabbed at a nearby branch to keep from falling. His calluses did little to protect his palm from the branch's thorns. "I really need to crash," he admitted, drawing his hand back. "I'm dead on my feet."

"You look it," Ruv agreed. "Not that the rest of us are faring any better."

Derek pointed ahead. "Maybe there's a good spot on the other side of that hillock."

"I freaking hope so," Gren mumbled.

"See?" Sarah shrilled. "I got that word from you!"

They crested the hillock and determined it was as good a place as any to bed down for a few hours. "Man, I miss trees," Gren remarked.

Killer pulled out a knife and cut a few slices of juicy cactus, its needles removed before he had stowed it in his pack. "It's a lot easier to hide in forests, for sure." He tossed a piece of the cactus to each of his companions.

"I'll scope out the perimeter and see how visible our footprint is," Derek offered, already on his way to do so.

"As long as we don't start a fire," Ruv reasoned, "we should be fine."

Gren leaned his back against a rock and stifled a yawn. "We don't exactly have anything to cook." Suddenly his fingers twisted around his sapphire fatestone as he heard Mari reaching for his mind. "Yeah, we're ok," he told her.

Any sign of the horde?

"Nah, doesn't look like they came this way. We're stopping for a few, but we should reach the pass well before dawn."

Good. You sound exhausted. Get some sleep.

"Yes, mother," he snickered. He could almost hear her desire to smack him through the link.

When it was apparent that Gren was no longer conversing with Mari, Ruv asked, "Before dawn, you say?"

"Well, we already passed the rock that looks like a giant gorilla," he reasoned, "and that was the last big landmark. Soon we'll be right at the exit of this pass."

Derek returned from his brief patrol. A toe caught on a protruding rock, and he fumbled for purchase but managed to keep his feet. "Our perimeter looks good," he announced, dropping eagerly to the ground. "If I didn't know where to go, I wouldn't have found my way back. That horde would have to literally stumble over us to know we're here, and a few good gusts of wind will wipe out our footprints."

"It's unlikely they would stumble over us anyway, I'd think, since we definitely would have passed them by now. Plus I haven't smelled any heading this way," Gren mused. "Now if only there was something we could do about our aerial exposure."

Ruv frowned. "What are the odds of the pixies tracking us? I haven't noticed any flyovers. Besides, we're pretty small, unlike Wendy's great big owl form. We can scatter some of that prickly shrubbery over us while we sleep if you're worried. Hells, we can bury ourselves in gravel."

Sarah rolled her eyes. "That'll only be mildly uncomfortable."

"I suppose you're right," Gren acknowledged. "I'm probably overthinking things."

"I'll take first watch. Half hour shifts?" Killer asked.

"Sounds good. We won't be here very long."

"All of you, please shut up," Sarah snapped. "I need what little beauty sleep I'm likely to get."

Ruv's turn on guard was nearly complete when he heard a branch snap somewhere to his left, far enough away to give him a few moments to react, but too close to ignore. He moved slowly, quietly waking the others. They managed to secure their weapons just in time to see that they were completely surrounded.

"Everyone about ready?" Mari inquired, surveying her group. Sunrise was still two hours away, and Sam and

Frostbite had already shifted. Brae tugged the final strap that held Frostbite's many packs in place then shoved Wendy onto Micaleth's back before sliding behind her. Once the women were situated, Mari shifted, and they resumed their journey.

They smelled them long before they saw them.

Mari, Sam, and Frostbite each shifted abruptly into their human forms, retching as they reached for the first available tunics to pull over their shoulders. Brae and Wendy, whose sense of smell was not as keen as that of wolf or panther or tiger, were less affected by the scent of putrefaction washing over them on a sudden wind. Nonetheless, their faces twisted in revulsion as the odor hit them. Mari, wiping her forearm across her mouth, pronounced, "I don't know what we're about to walk into, but I know it won't be pretty."

Sam shook his head. His eyes watered from the damage the overwhelming stench had wrought to his nose. "I don't think it's the zombie-goblin horde, at least. The scent is even fouler, somehow—which, for the record, I did not believe possible—and there's a weird…I don't know how to describe it. Sweetness?"

Mari nodded, a pallor greying her sun-browned skin. "I picked up on that, too. Almost like cotton candy or something." She swallowed the bile that threatened to spill out of her throat. "I'm never eating cotton candy again."

"I'll go first," Frostbite volunteered with admirable stoicism. He pulled the collar of his shirt over his nose, crouched low, and crept over the knoll whence the wind had blown. After he peered down the other side, he stood, all the while keeping his nose covered. From the tight expression marring his face, the rest surmised that the flimsy fabric of his tunic did little to help.

Joining Frostbite on the crest of the hill, Micaleth said, "I suppose we know what happened to the pixies."

A grotesque scene spread before them. Small, brightly colored carcasses littered the vale. The breeze stirred the broken wings, making it appear as if they retained the power to fly despite the sprites' fractured and, in some cases, utterly destroyed bodies. Some looked as if they had been torn asunder, limbs scattered here and there, while others appeared to have exploded entirely, leaving only a filament of wing or a few fine bones intact. Multihued goo painted the ground in a rainbow of gore.

Exchanging dumbfounded looks, they silently and unanimously agreed to skirt the outside of the massacre instead of charging straight through even though it would add another half hour to their journey. To reduce the effects of the lingering stench, Mari, Sam, and Frostbite walked on two legs until the carnage was far behind them. Only then, once they were certain they were out of range of even the strongest wind, did they shift.

They had traveled several more miles before Mari halted the train and reclaimed her human form. Kneeling on the ground, brows furrowed, she announced, "We've got another problem."

"What's up this time?" Brae asked.

"The trail splits again." Sam and Frostbite came over to inspect with their own noses; they quickly nodded their confirmation. "One part kept going south toward the pass, and it looks like that giant lizard went with them. But the other half cut straight west."

"That's odd," Wendy remarked.

Micaleth shook himself, jostling his two passengers. "Why would they head right across the mountains when they have been avoiding them this whole time?" He stared down the shadowed rift that lay between the ridge they had recently crossed and the final crest that separated them from the Ocean of Memory. "It makes no sense."

Mari's frown deepened. "Surely they wouldn't know about us? We killed that one before he could make his way back to the rest." Just then, she gasped and clutched her fatestone, listening to Gren's updated circumstances. "Shit, ok," she muttered back to him. "Hold tight."

"What is it?" Wendy inquired in a wavering voice. "Is everyone ok?"

As she released her grip on the faceted jade pendant, Mari announced, "Change of plans. I'll fill you guys in on the way."

"These buggers smell even worse *en masse*," Sarah grumbled as she scraped the back of her head against the prickly trunk of the small tree to which she was tied. Fifty odd goblins tarried nearby, though none appeared to be paying significant attention to their captives. The horde had dragged them back into the valley that lie between the two ridges. Kicking and thrashing against their bindings the entire journey, it appeared they had finally worn their captors' patience thin. Thus, as soon as they had reached a relatively green area where a few trees struggled up through the dry ground, the goblins bound their arms behind them and fastened them to the trunks.

"We just need to put up with them a little bit longer," Gren assured her. "Mari's crew should be here soon enough, and then they'll create a diversion while we escape." In spite of his hopeful words, his brow crinkled in a frown. "In the meantime, at least I still have my bow. If I can get free, maybe we can use that somehow."

Ruv twisted his neck around to regard Gren. "Did Mari say what kind of diversion?" After a thoughtful pause, he added, "Also what, exactly, is our escape plan?"

A muscle in Gren's jaw twitched along with a lower eyelid. "I didn't ask. As for the escape plan, I'm working on that one."

Still scratching the back of her head against the tree, Sarah jeered, "You really are an idiot sometimes."

"Hopefully they don't gut us before then," Derek offered in a tone incongruously light given their present circumstances. "I rather like having my bowels intact."

"I mean, they seem to want us alive so far," Gren commented. "There's gotta be a reason."

Killer let out a disillusioned laugh. "Unless they're just keeping the meat fresh before they eat us for dinner."

"Undead or not," Ruv posited, "I don't think they're quite *that* kind of zombie. I haven't seen them eat anything at all, actually."

Gren narrowed his eyes at the horde. A wrestling match had broken out between two goblins while the rest watched on, shouting and stamping their feet. "They don't seem very smart, all in all."

"Agreed," Ruv said. "I'm not sure how they managed to find us in the first place. Must have had some help."

Derek sniffed, then scowled as the activity brought a sharp whiff of death to his nose. "I have been wondering the same thing. I mean, they tied us up on the edge of their camp—which, quite frankly, I am not complaining about, but it wasn't exactly a good decision on their part—and left us with only two guards."

"Who are not even doing that thorough of a job," Killer drawled, eying the ostensible sentries, who were busy arguing over which one of them would get to keep the staff they had stolen from Ruv.

Then, as if finally remembering their assigned task, the pair whirled around and stalked toward them. Sarah ceased her scratching at once. "Pipe down, chatty humans!" the first one rasped.

"Don't make us gag you!" the other threatened.

"But the master said—"

"I don't care what the master said!"

"The necromancer will have your head!"

The second cackled, a choking, rattling sound. "He'd have to leave his safe little castle to come take it!"

The first goblin dove headlong at the second, tackling him in a muddle of creaking bone and peeling flesh. The brawl was short lived. Within moments, the first guard had decapitated his partner, twisting his head off with his bony hands and launching the trophy well outside the perimeter of their camp. He gave the now headless corpse a good kick in the ribs. "I'll deliver your head myself!" he growled. Then, wandering off toward the rest of the horde, who did not even seem to have noticed the skirmish, shouted, "Get me another guard over here!"

Sarah, having resumed her movement as soon as the goblins' attentions had strayed, commented, "Well, that was certainly brutal."

Gren raised a brow at her. "What are you even doing over there?"

"Contributing to our eventual escape."

"By what, rubbing your pheromones all over that tree?"

Her normally sleek black hair had been snagged into a frizzing halo, the ends sticking out at all angles and clinging to the bark. "Try not to draw attention to me unless you want those buggers to steal my last knife."

Gren's eyes grew serious. "Wait, you managed to keep a knife on you?"

She paused her scratching to flash him a haughty grin. "I always keep one strapped up under my hair," she explained with thinly veiled superiority. "No one ever thinks to search there."

"How, exactly?" Ruv asked with a slight frown. "You don't have much hair to hide it under."

"I don't have to share all my secrets, you know."

"Fair enough," he conceded. "But I'd like to learn your trick. Our hair's about the same length, after all. And mine's a lot thicker. Maybe it'll work for me, too."

Sarah shrugged, a gesture limited by the ropes pinning her arms around the trunk at her back. "I'll warn you, it can be a bit uncomfortable if you forget to take it out before you sleep. Nicked my ear once that way when it popped loose from its sheath." She changed the direction of her scratching, eyes squeezed shut in concentration. "Almost...and...got it!" She beamed triumphantly as a faint click and flash of steel accompanied her announcement. She managed to catch the handle between her thumb and forefinger then set about sawing at the ropes around her wrists.

Gren cleared his throat. "Hold still," he coughed.

Sarah froze at the warning and eyed the goblin approaching them.

"What are you plotting, chatty humans?" he snapped. They could not tell if he was the same guard as before or a new one entirely. Between the shapeless gray rags, shoddy leather armor, and scraps of decaying muscle, the shambling corpses all looked much the same.

"Your demise, of course," Ruv mumbled.

"What about my eyes?"

"Never mind."

The goblin began to growl, shuffling close enough to cause their noses to wrinkle at the smell. "Easy now!" Gren called. "Wouldn't want to anger the necromancer."

"What do you know about the master?"

Gren's eyes darted quickly from side to side settling back on the goblin's misshapen face. "Only that he's, uh, he's our master, too. So if you hurt us, he'll be very angry."

"Wrathful, even," Ruv chimed in.

The goblin squinted his yellowed eyes. "Then why did the master send us to fetch you?"

"To provide an escort, of course," Gren said with his best imitation of one of Micaleth's imperious sniffs. "There are enemies out there, you know."

The goblin's mouth twisted as he considered the new information. "Then what was your mission? Are you bringing a tribute?"

"Help me out here, guys," Gren muttered.

"The weapons!" Derek chimed in.

"Yes, the weapons," Gren repeated. "The ones you took away from us—that's our tribute."

"And what would the master need with more weapons? He has us."

"Magic!" Ruv offered.

Gren nodded heartily. "That's right. They're not just any weapons, they're magic weapons. Just like how you couldn't take my bow away, yeah? It only works for me. The other ones are enchanted, too."

"But we could take those."

"It's a different enchantment, one that can work for anyone," Sarah purred. "If you bring them back, we can show you how."

"I don't believe you," the goblin grumbled. "But perhaps we will see." He regarded them for another moment before lumbering toward the main camp. "Bring me those weapons!"

Ruv flashed his lopsided grin at Gren. "Good thinking," he said under his breath.

Gren allowed himself an answering smirk. "I'm really just making this up as I go along." He closed his eyes and concentrated. Without a free hand to grasp his sapphire fatestone, his link to Mari was more difficult to summon, but he caught her thoughts nonetheless. "How much longer?" he asked as soon as he could feel her mind turned toward him.

Her response was faint. *We're close*, she sent back, along with a brief glimpse of her present location. Her group spread out along the hills on the far side overlooking the horde. *How many are with you right now?*

"Just the one, and he's back and forth." He updated her quietly on the rest of their situation. Then, addressing his fellow captives, he asked, "Sarah, how close are you to getting those knots undone?"

"Oh, I finished that ages ago," she bragged. "Just waiting for the right moment to slip free."

"Good stuff. Now act normal, everyone. Looks like boss-zomblin and his henchmen are returning."

Three goblins limped toward the cluster of trees, burdened with armfuls of the stolen knives, machetes, and staves. "Now you will tell me how your magic weapons work," the head goblin commanded. "If I am pleased, your lives may be spared for now. At least until the master decides what to do with you."

"Of course," Gren granted with a solicitous dip of his head. "If you just untie me, I can sh—"

A commotion on the opposite side of the camp interrupted him. Shouting and the clashing of metal could be heard as the horde scrambled to react, and wisps of smoke curled toward the sky. "What's this?" one goblin cried, rushing into the fray. The others dropped their burdens and hobbled after him.

"You!" the leader snarled, pointing at no one in particular. "Give me a report!"

"That guy makes a terrible alpha," Ruv observed.

Sarah slid out of her bonds in a single fluid motion before snatching a larger knife from the pile discarded by the otherwise preoccupied goblins. With it she began to hack and saw at Derek's bindings, tugging on the rope until it loosened enough for him to slide his hands out. He rubbed his wrists appreciatively. "I must say," he murmured, "you're quite pretty when you're in action."

"Thanks, but I'm afraid you're not my type. If you could convince Mari or Wendy to swing my way, however, I would be eternally grateful." She gave him a friendly wink then moved on to the next tree where Killer waited.

Derek was still retrieving his own collection of blades when Wendy appeared behind Gren, who craned his neck to look at her. "So glad you're here!" he sighed. "Where are the others?"

Wendy charily sawed at the ropes restraining his wrists. Hindered by the use of a single hand, hers was a much slower process than Sarah's had been. "They're all off causing the ruckus," she said, tugging at a particularly stubborn knot. She bent to use her teeth, but the putrid taste made her gag. "Brae lit some fires to distract them," she choked after she finished spitting. "Sam's gone full-panther, and Mari's in wolf form, too. Frostbite hurled a few of the zombie-goblins into the flames." Blushing, she glanced to her right, where Killer was already shaking loose of his own restraints, then to the left, where Derek was nearly done releasing Ruv. She turned her full attention back to the knots. "Turns out fire kills them a lot faster than anything else."

"Good to know," Gren remarked. "What's Micaleth's role in all this?" Finally free, he stepped out of the loosened ropes and surveyed the scene, but he could not see the nietheran in the immediate vicinity, nor did he spy a flash of white amid the haze enveloping the horde.

"He's hiding just back that way. Watching the rear," she indicated with a toss of her head.

A dozen goblins burst out of the smoke and began hustling toward the now entirely unbound humans. Gren shoved Wendy behind him. "Get back to Micaleth and get out of here," he hissed.

"I can—"

"Go!"

Wendy scrunched up her nose and glared at him, but she obeyed.

Sarah crouched, brandishing one of her longer knives with a toothed blade, as she waited for the goblins to reach her. Ruv, standing to her left, held his staff at the ready. Derek and Killer bore a machete in each hand. When Gren joined the line, he withdrew the dagger their adversaries had been unable to remove from his person thanks to the ancient charm that bound it to his fate.

One blink, two, and the goblins were on them.

Sarah sprang at the first to enter her range, plunging her knife into its eye socket and jerking the blade downward. She pinned her victim to the ground, knees pressed firmly on either arm, while she wrenched the knife from the cheek bone where it had lodged. The goblin spat black ooze at her face. She choked, but she did not loosen her hold as she sawed through the rotting neck.

Another one headed toward Sarah while she was still engaged with the first, so Ruv swept the newcomer off his feet then swung the metal tip of his staff downward in an arc to make direct contact with the goblin's head. He could not generate enough momentum to shatter the skull entirely with the first blow, but a few good wallops did sufficient damage to render his enemy ineffective. As more arrived, Gren used his blade to finish those Ruv sent flying. Sarah joined them shortly thereafter once she put her original enemy out of commission.

Between Derek and Killer and their four whirling machetes, the rest of the goblins were dispatched in short order. Unfortunately, no sooner had they defeated the first wave than a second hurtled toward them. They gritted their teeth and continued the fight. Outnumbered as the humans were, the disorganized swarm—confronted on both sides by Mari and Gren's respective teams and lacking the element of surprise that had allowed them to apprehend Gren's group in the first place—succumbed quickly. The entire battle, from the moment Brae lit the first fire until the last goblin twitched headless on the ground, took less than half an hour.

The cleanup, however, was another matter.

Hal sat across from Laria at dinner. In addition to their usual fare of bread, cheese, and fruit, a platter of roasted beef sat half-eaten in the center of the table. "She's still outside, you know," Hal stated, mouth full of raspberries.

Much to the dismay of the niethera, who were patently herbivorous, every few days Ajagar dropped off an entire cow, a deer, or sometimes a goat, outside the sanctuary. Gryndonmin would grudgingly send a few of his brethren to help Hal drag the carcass inside, but the skinning and carving were left up to human hands. Since Laria had neither the time nor the stomach to assist, Hal learned the butchering process mostly through trial and error. Fortunately, Ajagar did them the favor of charring the meat with her fiery breath before knocking politely on the sanctuary walls with a gargantuan talon.

"I know," Laria said, eyes cast downward. "I feel terrible. I wish there was something more I could do."

Hal swallowed the raspberries. "It's not your fault."

"How could it not be? I'm the Spinner. I'm the watcher of the worlds!" she exclaimed. "The one thing I am supposed to be able to do is control the damn images on the damn Loom, and I can barely do that anymore." She slammed a fist on the table; their waterglasses rattled. "It's not supposed to be this way."

"Sure, but there is more to this," Hal whispered, taking one of her delicate hands in his own. "It has nothing to do with your ability or inability. The Loom was working just fine before, and it will work just fine again. Whatever is hiding Dahrigek, whether Antiln or her brother or someone else, isn't something you could have predicted or controlled." He released her hand and speared a slab of charred beef.

Laria shook her head. "I should have noticed sooner. I should have called in the lanti earlier, instead of sending Mari and Gren to their doom." She rubbed at one of her eyes with a pale knuckle. "Then maybe the lanti would have actually done something instead of just sitting there."

"They've veiled them," Hal pointed out. "At least that's something."

"I've been trying to see if they survive and what happens after, but whatever's hiding Dahrigek in the present is now hiding the future, too." She worried at a hangnail. "I'll see flashes now and then, but nothing concrete."

Hal breathed heavily through his nose, eyes fierce, brows furrowed. "Well, then I guess it's the same as with Ajagar's missing hatchling. Their fates must be hidden right along with that stupid freaking desert."

Softly, she asked, "You wish you could be with them, don't you?"

"I belong here," he asserted, for what he thought must be the thousandth time. "With you."

"But you still want to be there, too."

Hal hung his head. "I just...they've been my best friends for so long. We grew up together. We spent every summer racing through the woods and climbing trees and wrestling and shit." His eyes lightened for a moment, and he laughed. "I remember back in like, sixth or seventh grade when Gren tried to learn how to skateboard, so of course he made me and Mari try, too. We were terrible at it. Well, I was pretty good, but Gren was terrible at it. Mari was ok, too, but she didn't want to make Gren feel bad. So we both just faked falling all the time." His eyes, formerly lost in memory, returned to Laria as his tale came to a close. "Eventually Gren gave up, and that's about the same time he picked up the guitar."

She smiled, but all too quickly her countenance grew despondent. "I'm sorry," she murmured. "I wish things were different. I want you to stay, of course. I want you here. But I want you to have them, too."

Hal forced a grin. "Who knows? Maybe they'll swing by for a visit when all this is done."

"I'm not sure if there will be a 'done,'" she said, voice choked. "I can't see one."

"Keep looking. You're bound to see something eventually."

Laria twirled her fork in her fingers. She had barely touched her plate. "Well, I do see things now and then," she mused, "but it's nothing certain. I get these glimpses. Small images. Nothing I can really understand." She stabbed a strawberry, but she did not bring it to her mouth. "I can see Mari, sometimes, and I can see Gren here and there. Hazy glimpses. But when I look forward, I never see them together."

Hal fought to keep his voice and his expression calm as he replied, "All we can do is keep trying. One day at a time." He took her fork from her and started to bring it toward her mouth. "Come on, eat," he urged. "You're no good to anyone if you're passing out from hunger. Can't spin your magic thread or see into your magic Loom if you're unconscious."

"Thank gods you're ok!" Mari breathed as she collided with Gren and wrapped her arms around his torso. "I was really worried about you."

He chuckled as he returned the embrace. "Why, didn't think we could take care of ourselves?"

"No, you idiot," she murmured before brushing his lips in a quick kiss, then pulled away with a grimace. "Ugh. We're gross. We smell like them," she said, indicating the scattered corpses with her thumb. To the rest she called, "Let's get these disgusting little dudes in a pile and light them up."

The adrenaline high did not last long. Though brief, the battle had taken its toll; its aftermath, doubly so, especially combined with their erstwhile chronically insufficient sleep. Thus, they saved further conversation until after they had ensured every corpse deserved that particular label, which made for arduous work.

When they finally departed the smoking remains of the goblin camp, they did not travel far. Everyone was near dropping from exhaustion after stumbling no more than a few miles. No one complained when Mari decided it was time to stop and recoup. Micaleth gratefully plopped himself on the hard ground, allowing Brae and Wendy to dismount and remove his many burdens. Even the ever-stoic Frostbite admitted his relief.

Since no one had the energy to hunt, let alone cook, they decided to forego the fire and share a simple meal of whatever they grabbed from their packs first. The rest of the usual tasks were completed automatically and silently. In fact, no one spoke much at all until they were gathered in a loose circle, reclining on blankets and propped against packs. However, now that the opportunity had presented itself at last, no one could surrender to sleep.

"So we found the pixies," Mari stated flatly into the silence. "Well, what's left of them." With periodic comments from those who had likewise witnessed the carnage, she proceeded to fill in the others.

"The smell was different than the zombie-goblins, but there was that same wrongness about it," Sam added, nose wrinkled in memory.

Sarah squinted thoughtfully at her brother, then glanced at Wendy. "You said the pixies that attacked you looked wrong. Faces all twisted up."

Wendy nodded, but it was Brae who answered. "They smelled wrong, and they looked wrong. But however changed, they were definitely pixies."

"I wonder," Gren postulated, "if this master that's controlling the zomblins might have been controlling the pixies, too."

Micaleth scraped at the rocky ground with a hoof. "It seems the most likely explanation. Now we just need to figure out who this master is. And, I wager, he'll be found on those islands."

"Pixies are delicate creatures, for all their mischief," Brae reasoned. "Perhaps they could not survive the—and I can't believe I'm using this word—*zombification* process as well as whatever those goblins used to be."

Micaleth ceased his scratching and nodded sagely.

As the night descended and still no one seemed able to sleep, they lit a few lanterns and continued talking in hushed tones while tending to their various cuts and bruises. No one suffered any serious damage, and they scoured with sand wherever goblin goo had made contact with their skin.

Wendy, inspecting a snag on the side of her pants by the dim light, grumbled, "This was my last clean pair." Frostbite rummaged through his pack, withdrew a small box, and tossed it to her. As she opened it to reveal a collection of thread and variously sized needles, she confessed, "Er, thank you, but I'm afraid I never learned to sew properly."

He came to settle beside her as Wendy's cheeks burned red. "It is not difficult. I will teach you."

"You can sew?" Mari asked with amusement. "Good on you, man."

Frostbite shrugged. "It is harder to find clothes that fit than to make my own."

CHAPTER NINE
With all the intensity of a star

Though they were eager to press onward now that they were closer to the coast, Mari made them stay put until the next afternoon. "We need time to rest and recover before we take on another horde," she had argued in her most commanding tone, which, considering her default tone was assertive at the least, bore quite a bit of force. Grudgingly they agreed, and so they caught up on as much sleep as they could in between guard shifts. No one fancied the thought of the other half of the horde sneaking up on them, too.

By the time they crested the final ridge, it was too dark to fully appreciate the ocean view. A scattered reflection of the waxing moon danced across the waters, but all they could see of the islands were foggy outlines against the stars. In case more goblins awaited them on the beach below, they pulled back toward the landward side to set up their next camp rather than linger on top of the ridge where they, too, could be silhouetted. "We'll move just before sunrise," Mari decided. "Then we can scout ahead and make sure no one is ready for us."

The twins shifted to hunt. They returned with only a few small lizards and half of a snake. "I accidently ate the other half while still a panther," Sam admitted with a shrug. His mischievous eyes revealed no remorse. Micaleth found a few edible tubers; Frostbite, some wild onions. Brae brewed both into a thin stew along with the lizard and snake meat. Still drained from recent events, there was little conversation as they ate, and none once they tried to sleep. Although there had been no sign of the other half of the horde, no one wanted to take any undue risks. Thus, they alternated two teams with two persons each, one of which maintained a static guard in the camp while the other patrolled the perimeter.

It was during Ruv and Brae's turn on the perimeter that the general monotony was broken.

"You need to see this," Ruv urged, breathless, after he sprinted back into the camp and shook Mari awake.

She stifled a yawn and smacked Gren on the shoulder. He sat up with a start. "What'd you find?" Mari queried with another yawn.

"I have no idea," he admitted, "but I promise you it's not a goblin. And you. Need. To. See. This." He punctuated each word by poking Mari in the arm. She glared at him. "Actually, everyone should see this," he declared, voice loud enough to wake them.

They stumbled to their feet and followed Ruv into the dark, picking their way carefully between the sharp rocks and shrubs. Only Frostbite had stayed behind to keep watch over their supplies. Keeping a slow enough pace that Wendy could hobble along on her ruined feet, Ruv led them to a giant depression scooped out of the uneven slope. Easily fifty feet in diameter, the sides of the depression cut away so steeply that, had Ruv not warned them ahead of time, at least a few would have blundered right over the edge.

They peered down. The nearly full moon illuminated clean lines curving off to either side, so clean as to make them suspect the depression was not entirely natural in origin. That suspicion only increased when they noted the way the rocks at the bottom of the depression had been completely pulverized, crushed and ground into pebbles and dust and that the cacti and shrubbery had been squashed almost beyond recognition. Were it not for the splotches of green, visible even in the night, they would have thought the depression barren of any vegetation.

"What the hell is this?" Mari murmured.

"I swear that wasn't there when we were hunting," Sarah said, disbelief apparent in her tone.

Sam turned wide eyes first toward the depression, then his sister, then back to the depression. "We were right here. Just a few hours ago. I was standing *right here*."

"And there was nothing," Sarah whispered.

"Up here!" Brae called, motioning for everyone to join her. She had scrambled up a rocky outcropping that overlooked the depression and now sat at the top with her white legs dangling over the side.

"This whole journey is bringing up more questions than it's answered," Mari grumbled as she began to climb.

"Don't worry," Wendy said, "I've been keeping meticulous notes."

Mari smiled at her. To Gren, she asked, "What do you think made that? An explosion? But no, we would have heard an explosion."

Gren shook his head. "Can't have been, not even a silent one. There's no charring. The plants were still green, just completely smushed."

"It's like someone hurled a great big rock from the top of the ridge," Derek observed. "A very quiet rock."

"Then made the rock disappear," Killer added.

"At this point," Mari conceded, "that seems as likely an explanation as any."

Once they joined Brae at the top of the ledge, they noticed she was even paler than usual, and for good reason. From the higher vantage point, they could make out the shape of the depression. Gren linked his fingers through Mari's. Ruv took her other hand and gave it a nervous squeeze. Derek and Killer glanced downward then frowned and back away. Wendy huddled close to Micaleth's flank. Even the normally unflappable twins, still having difficulty processing that such a thing could appear, unheard and unseen so soon after they had passed through that very area, remained in shock.

"It's…" Mari began, face drained of blood.

"…A hoofprint," Gren finished.

"Whatever could leave a print that size is not something I want to meet face to face," Ruv muttered. "We should get out of here."

As they made their way back to Frostbite, Micaleth sidled next to Mari. "You recall what I said in the lost city," he presumed.

"About something from ancient stories?"

Micaleth nodded. "I believed, or perhaps merely wanted to believe, that those stories were irrelevant. That the similarities with the statues were merely a coincidence." He swallowed hard then breathed out through his teeth. "But now I believe it is time to share what I have heard."

After they filled in Frostbite on the impossible discovery, everyone gathered around to listen to Micaleth. They no longer bothered setting a guard. Micaleth cleared his throat. "Before I begin, allow me to pose a question." He looked pointedly around the group; they returned his gaze with rapt attention colored by confusion. "Whom do the gods worship?"

"Easy," Sarah quipped. "No one."

"They're bloody gods," Sam agreed.

Micaleth curled his lips in a knowing smile, all too happy to play the role of pedant. "Suspend that assumption for the time being. Whom do the gods worship?" he repeated.

"Other gods?" Killer tried.

Gren's dark eyes grew darker, his voice unusually hoarse. "Older gods."

Micaleth dipped his alicorn in Gren's direction. "I believe the city we found was built by the lanti, and I believe we need to reassess our understanding of them."

Mari frowned. "I mean, I know they're powerful and all, but having met a few...I dunno, I feel like they would have told someone if they built a giant city way down in Dahrigek, of all places. They don't exactly have any qualms about bragging."

"Plus they seem rather cozy in their various domains," Ruv added.

"Ah, but long ago, Dahrigek may not have been so remote," Micaleth countered. "Back when the world was new and the Ancients reigned—"

"But I thought those were just myths?" Brae cut in. "Everyone knows the dracora are the first."

"Not according to the dracora."

Brae furrowed her brows. "Well, what about the 'Song of Words,' then?" she prodded.

Mari turned her glance from one to the other. "What are you guys talking about?" she asked. "Songs? Ancients? Sure, we're not Aorean natives here, but I feel like we still would have heard of some Ancients or whatever by now."

"The 'Song of Words' tells the story of how the Old Tongue came to be," Brae elucidated. "Each verse relates to the contributions of the first five species to populate Aorea, from the dracora to the freesians. Well, the first five sentient species, that is. Naturally, we don't count the amoebae swimming in the primordial ooze."

"Interesting," Gren commented. "How's it go?"

The leshii waved a hand in dismissal. "I'm no bard."

"Liar," Ruv said, a teasing glint in his hazel eyes. "You've a beautiful voice. I've heard you humming."

Brae tossed her hair, the fiery tresses glowing orange in the dim light of her suppressed aura. "Fine, but later. I need time to try and remember the proper verses. I haven't bothered with it since I was just a sprout, and that was quite a long time before any of you were born."

"Deal," Gren said with a grin. "And if you could teach it to me afterward, that'd be awesome. It'd be cool to finally add some Aorean songs to my repertoire."

"If you insist. I don't understand your human musical notation, but I'm sure between the two of us we'll figure it out," Brae granted.

Gren nodded, enthusiasm at the prospect of any sort of musical activity banishing his disquiet. "It's ok, I don't quite have perfect pitch, but I have an excellent memory for things like this."

"I would certainly hope so," Ruv quipped.

"Shove it," Gren retorted.

Mari released a pointed sigh. "I swear, I don't know how I put up with the two of you."

Ruv gave her a crooked grin. "It's our dashing good looks and easy charm."

Rolling her eyes, Sarah said, "You're a bloody saint, that's how."

Gren lightly punched Mari in the shoulder and said with a wink, "Hardly! Anywho, back to the topic at hand."

"How Gren's scared of snakes?" Derek jested.

"Dude, that was forever ago," Gren rejoined. "I meant what Micaleth was saying before we got sidetracked: what, or who, I guess, are the Ancients?"

"I was beginning to think we would never retreat from that tangent," Micaleth chided with a sniff. "Now, there are two competing theories about the first species in Aorea. The most commonly held belief is that the dracora, who were born out of the Fire Mountains in the Olde Isles, were the first creatures who could think and speak, followed shortly thereafter by their close cousins the sea serpents. This belief is so common, in fact, that the oldest among the dracora—the Great Dracor himself, in fact—is often referred to as the 'last of the first,' because he is the only remaining dracor who was born directly from the Fire

Mountains. The rest of the dracora population are either his descendants, or else the descendants of one of his siblings who have since passed on from this realm. That is the first theory."

"What's the second?" Mari interjected.

Micaleth sniffed again. "I'm getting to that! You humans are so impatient. That must be why your lives are so brief." He cleared his throat and continued his account. "Some of the niethera in the Spinner's sanctuary have been around far longer than I. Most, actually. And some were lucky enough to be able to speak with the elder dracora while their memories could still recall their youth. According to my uncle Gryndonmin, some of the oldest dracora once recalled a time when Aorea was home to ancient beings of immense size, who each held a unique form and ruled a unique territory. These creatures were so gargantuan, in fact, that they made the massive dracora themselves appear small, as if they were but insignificant sparrows fluttering next to a thunderbird.

"It was when I saw the statues in the temple that I thought, perhaps, there was some truth to the legends, though I hoped otherwise," he admitted with an apologetic glance around the circle. "Not much is known, but my uncle told me of it when I was a colt, as his father told him, and his father before that, stretching back through the generations. You must understand, this was billions, trillions of years ago—long before the niethera came to be, not to mention the sierrens and you, their unwilling offspring. I remember his descriptions of the Ancients well, as that was what always fascinated me. Thus, however little else I may know, I can say there are certainly some correspondences between the legends and the statues." Micaleth glanced around the group again. Apart from Wendy scribbling in her notebook, everyone's eyes were glued to him. "If, indeed, the Ancients were real, and if the lanti built the lost temple in their honor, then the lanti are far older, and far more, than they appear.

"Just imagine, at the beginning of time, what Aorea may have been like, primordial and wild, with giant beings of immeasurable power, each ruling over a continental territory. The dracora could not have built that city, for what need have they for walls? And if a race of simple giants once populated Aorea, there would be other remnants. No. Perhaps, just maybe, the lanti walked Aorea during the time of the Ancients, and, for reasons known only to them, they have concealed that knowledge and likely, much of that power."

Mari drummed her fingers across her knee. "From my old dreams," she said, "and from what Laria's told me, the whole reason Antiln found Aorea in the first place was by following the trace of power left behind by one of the lanti. That might give them a reason to hide the extent of their power now, but that wouldn't apply to back then."

"We can speculate all we want," Sarah interposed, "but it won't affect our present situation. I would much rather hear what could have left that print."

Micaleth inclined his head first in Mari's direction, then Sarah's. "Indeed. So. The Ancients. The icy continent of Pendra was home to Ursu, the bringer of winter storms, of blizzards and avalanches. Ursu was a giant, white bear with the curving horns of a ram and a long, feathered tail. The flick of his tail was so powerful that it would cause the snowy drifts to slide right off the frozen mountains. Ursu was so large that the den where he slept created the valley in which the freesians would later build their greatest city: the Veil of Uhrsual. If you ask my uncle, the veil is named for its creator, who slept there in times long forgotten."

"Was there an Ancient on each continent?" Frostbite inquired, scratching his stubbled chin.

"Yes," the nietheran replied. "Back then, there was even less of a distinction between Kemdaria and Nomansland, for the Serpent Sea had yet to form, and so both territories were home to a single Ancient. The Kemdarian plains were walked by Cervu, the bringer of strong winds and harsh currents. Cervu was a winged, red elk, but although he possessed the wings of a falcon, his elk-form was too massive for him to leave the ground. Instead of touching the sky when he beat his wings, he created a wind so strong that tornados ravaged the planes, leaving a wake of destruction wherever he trod. To this day, the Kemdarian Region is known for being a land of unforgiving air."

Frostbite pursed his lips. "The wind in the steppes bites, but I have seen no tornados."

Micaleth shook his mane. "Cervu no longer roams there," he said as if that were all the explanation required. "Sarah, Sam, you should enjoy this next one. The rainforests of Faerie were ruled by Pardu, the bringer of floods, of hurricanes and humidity. Pardu was a giant panther, with a black, feathered crown and a tail so large he could not raise it, and so it dragged behind him for miles, soaking up water from the damp soil and releasing it in a great tide once his fur could retain no more. The path he cut through the forests became the great rivers, which is why (at least, if you ask my uncle) the niethera named the largest river in Faerie the Parduana."

Sarah tilted her head to the side as she regarded Micaleth. "If there's a correlation between these Ancients of yours and the statues we found, you might want to check your gender there."

"My apologies," he replied. "I do recall the statues. I was simply retelling the legend as it was told to me. For all we know, the Ancients had no gender. They were each one of a kind, after all."

"Fair enough," she granted.

"My dear wolf sanguines, the fourth Ancient may interest you." He looked at Ruv, Mari, Killer, and Derek in turn. "The continent we now call Evra was roamed by Lupu, the bringer of draughts and wildfires. Lupu was a giant wolf, covered all in amber fur, with the great antlers of a stag. His—or, I suppose, her—tail was wreathed in flames, and whenever she brushed against the vegetation, a raging wildfire would ensue, sweeping across the dry forests of the west. Lupu made a den for herself among the northwestern mountains, and the lakes in which she cooled her burning tail became the hot springs that now bubble there."

Derek smirked. "I can picture ole' Killer here with a rack, but I think I'm happy in my regular wolf-skin."

"Really?" Killer returned, touching the empty air above his head thoughtfully as if antlers in fact grew there. "I feel like they would get in the way."

"They'd accentuate your tiny head," Ruv joked.

Derek's smirk broadened, and he poked Killer in the ribs. "Or they'd make your tiny head look normal-sized."

"May I continue?" Micaleth solicited, voice firm.

The three men shuffled their feet and grumbled various conciliatory statements.

"And finally," Micaleth pronounced, "the land in which we currently find ourselves—the unruly, desert continent of Dahrigek—was home to the largest of all the Ancients: Tauru, bringer of swift death. Tauru was a great, golden bull, with arched horns that burned with all the intensity of a star and four sharp hooves that gleamed like burnished copper. His tail was said to be made not from flesh, but from lightning, so that thunder followed his steps and death hid in his shadow. The ground shook and split beneath his weight, swallowing whole mountains and transforming tiny valleys into gaping canyons. That is why Dahrigek remains such a treacherous and deserted land, because it was once home to Tauru the Bull, the mountain-eater, the death-bringer. His presence here left a stain, a memory buried in the land itself."

Brae tilted her head to the side, emerald eyes flashing. "*Cur mundi aedificatores repente exstiterint, innumerabilia saecla dormierint,*" she recited under her breath.

"Wait, what'd you say?" Gren inquired. "I swear I've heard that before."

"Of anyone here, you're the only one who may have," the leshii returned. "It's from Cicero's *De Natura Deorum*."

"On the nature of the gods," Gren translated automatically. "It's been a long time. I always liked Cicero, but I'm more familiar with his orations."

Sarah flung a rock at Gren's feet. "Quit yapping about dead Romans and translate, will you?"

It was Brae who fulfilled the request. "Cicero asks, 'Why did the builders of the world suddenly awake after they slept for countless ages?' Or at least, that's close. My Latin is admittedly a little rusty, but it felt relevant."

Ruv tapped his chin. "Any link between Tauru and the Old Farmer's golden cattle? I mean, how many different types of glowing yellow bovines can there be?"

Micaleth started. "You know, I never thought of that."

"That does seem like a helluva coincidence," Gren offered, recalling the golden cow he helped steal to trade for Mari's life. "I guess we're lucky that his don't grow as big as Tauru."

The necromancer stood at the foot of Necria's tower. With mixed longing and remorse he conjured the memory of the last time they had shared a night. Her touch warmed him then; now her touch was as cold as his own. She descended the spiraling stairs on silent toes, the face that greeted him devoid of expression. When she reached him, he cupped her cheek in his palm. She closed her eyes against the contact and breathed shallowly, but when he tried to draw her closer, she pulled just out of arm's reach. "After all this time," he whispered, "still you do not forgive me?" As her face retained its stubborn obscurity, he continued, "All I ever wanted was you. To keep you with me, to keep you safe. If I'd left you there—"

"I have news, master," interrupted Servorg.

"It can wait."

The goblin bowed and shuffled out of sight.

"Necria," Dimeldor breathed. "Oh, my Necria. This shade you have become breaks my heart."

Her blank expression morphed then. He could read her response in her eyes. He knew that if she could speak, she would have mocked him, asking, *what heart?*

He snatched her wrist and held it to his breast, where, sure enough, she could just perceive a slow, painfully slow, beat. "There used to be nothing. For so long there was nothing. But you...you brought me to life." He released her hand, but to both his pain and delight, she did not pull it away. When she met his gaze once more, he could discern a trace of sympathy. "If I had left you there, you would have grown old. You would have, one day, withered and faded, and I would have been alone." She did back away then, but she made no move to flee his presence entirely. "Alone again," he concluded.

She tilted her head, frowned, and tried to convey a response without her voice. She gestured slowly, and her eyes seemed to say, *That is the way of things. We are born, we live, we die, we are born again. The cycle goes on.*

"I had to break the cycle," he replied. "Don't you see? Even now, can you still not see?" He searched her eyes, but this time they gave him no silent words. His hands fell limply to his sides. Necria took a step forward, braced her hands on either side of his face, and kissed him. It was the lightest brush, so light he could barely feel it. All too soon, she released him and slipped away.

"Master?" came Servorg's tentative voice.

The necromancer raised a hand to his eye where, much to his surprise, he felt a leak. He inspected the moistened fingertip with bewilderment. When he spoke, his voice was choked. "Not now." After a few breaths he turned to face his servant, and his eyes had resumed their standard detachment. "I will call you when I want your news. For now, I must consult the waters. We have guests approaching, after all."

He followed Servorg away from the tower then left the goblin outside the scrying room. Bent over the still waters, he searched for an image and, thankfully, he found what he sought. "Greetings, my old friend," he said to the face that shimmered before him. "I wanted to thank you for your gifts. They will be a great help in keeping my latest acquisition fed."

"So what happened to the Ancients?" Wendy asked tremulously. "Why has no one seen them except the dracora and possibly the lanti?"

Micaleth rolled his shoulders in an awkward movement that resembled a shrug. "According to my uncle, the Ancients simply went to sleep one day, hidden away in their dens. Ursu buried himself beneath a glacier at the heart of Pendra. Cervu retreated into a deep cavern below the Kemdarian steppes. Pardu slumbers in one of Faerie's many secret caves, its only entrance hidden underwater. Lupu retreated into a mountain den, her tail causing the hot springs to keep bubbling." He paused to look down at his hooves, which made subtle indentations in the ground. "As for Tauru, he is said to have fallen into one of the chasms created by his own hooves, swallowed up just like a mountain.

"It is also said that at the end of time, when the reign of order has finished and chaos makes its inevitable return, the Ancients will awaken and roam the lands of Aorea once more, and thus will be the demise of all of our civilizations. Perhaps the great sea serpents will remain, slithering beneath the waves, and perhaps the dracora will take to the skies and survive among the clouds as they once did. But the niethera, the kemdar, the freesians and sierrens and evrae and leshii, and yes, especially any humans…none of us will be safe. We are too small, our lives too finite, our bones too brittle."

Gren let out a long breath through his nose. "So the waking of the Ancients basically means Ragnarök for Aorea. Got it."

"Speaking of the doom of the gods," Mari said, picking up the thread of Gren's thoughts, "how do the lanti fit into all this?"

Micaleth frowned and answered slowly, "The lanti are separate, I now believe."

"How so?"

"Well, as far as anyone knows, they don't seem to have an origin," he said with a repeat of the awkward shrug. "They have just always been here, always been a part of things, always meddled. The common theory is that they came sometime after the dracora and sea serpents, but before the birth of the niethera, but I now have my doubts. Considering the lantian ability to change their forms, their names, their faces, they could very well predate all the species on Aorea. Perhaps no one has seen their true forms. Perhaps the lanti are descended from the titanic Ancients, or perhaps something else entirely.

"Now, the niethera are no strangers to magic, but even we have our limits. As for the lanti, well, some can pass between worlds without the aid of a traveling circle. They can control the forces of nature. Some can bend reality. It is said that once, some could even bend time. Perhaps they simply always were and always will be." His voice was a bare whisper when he postulated, "Perhaps the lanti are the Ancients themselves, their current incarnations merely an elaborate illusion."

Ruv raked his fingers through his scraggly black hair. "This is getting a bit too existential for me."

Gren folded his arms across his chest. "This is a fascinating mythology lesson," he remarked, "but it seems very much like just that: a myth. A symbolic explanation in an attempt to control an otherwise uncontrollable world."

Micaleth returned his scrutinizing gaze with a somber one. "Maybe you are correct, and they're just old stories, and we'll have nothing to worry about except a horde of undead goblins and this master of theirs. But if that woman indeed saw a giant bull, stomping across the horizon, its horns encircling the sun, and if it was a statue of Tauru that lay shattered inside that temple, and if that hoofprint was rendered by the bull himself...then we may have to prepare ourselves for a much worse fate, and the prophecy of the Destined will remain forever unfulfilled. Because if even one of the Ancients has reawakened, there is nothing mere mortals can do."

"Aren't niethera immortal?" Killer murmured.

"I suppose by human standards, near enough," Micaleth acknowledged. "Our natural lifespan is similar to that of the freesians. We'll live for a few millennia if we're lucky, but not quite as long as the dracora or the sea serpents, and certainly not as long as the lanti, who may very well outlive us all. As far as I know, only one of the lanti has ever left this realm for the next."

"Rod," Mari interjected softly. "keeper of time. I dreamed of him once, of the sacrifice that split the worlds and ended the war between humans and sierrens."

"Yes, Rod," Micaleth repeated.

"He's the same as Saturn, right?" Gren queried. "And Chronos?"

"He goes by many names, as is the way with the lanti."

Gren's expression lightened. "Hey, Brae, how comes that song you're trying to remember?"

Startled out of her thoughts, the leshii said, "I think I've got it all in my head again. It's been a long time. How best would you like to go about it?"

"Sing it through once for me so I can get the general idea," Gren directed, "and then we'll go over the melody and lyrics afterword so I can record them."

Brae nodded and began to tap out a measured, stately rhythm on her lap. Her voice, once she started singing, was clear and bright, weaving a hymn that leaned more toward chant than melody:

Words flew out of the smoke and the fire;
Upon leather wings the First came from the isles.
They witnessed the world, yet they wrote nothing down.
Still, the Words, they scattered all around.

Words rained down from heavens' dreams;
With their glittering scales they claimed the seas.
They witnessed the world, and they named every sound,
Yet the Second wrote nothing down.

Words gathered 'round the forest springs;
With their shining horns they hailed the breeze.
Like the First in the sky, and the Second in sea,
The Third witnessed the world and began to sing.

Words leapt up from the ashes of old,
And they tended the fires of the stories told.
They played and they fought and they made such a sound;
But the Fourth, they wrote nothing down.

Words danced forth from the northern snows;
In crystal and ice they embraced the cold.
The Fifth wrote of all the world they could see;
Thus, immortal Words came to be.

"See? I knew you had a lovely voice," Ruv said with a coy smile, slipping closer to Brae.

She returned his remark with a flutter of her eyelashes and then a derisive giggle. "Flattery will get you nowhere with me, wolfie. I've sworn off humans since that mess with the field hand. Adame, I think it was."

A memory flashed in Gren's eyes. "Do you still have his heart?" he asked in a murmur.

The leshii frowned. "Not quite. I never gave it back, but by the time I returned to the Alpines, it had disappeared." She shrugged her narrow shoulders and fidgeted with the hem of her tunic. "I must have lost it somewhere along the way. I couldn't find him either, though, so I suppose it doesn't matter in the end."

Mari and Gren shared a glance. Softly, Mari pressed, "What would happen to his heart if he were, um, dead?"

"Why do you ask?"

Gren took a deep breath before replying, "When we met some of the other guys at the Old Farm, they implied that something may have happened to him."

Brae blanched. "Then perhaps I didn't drop it after all."

"Where did you meet this Adame?" Frostbite asked Brae, his face furrowed in a heavy frown.

"In the Alpines at a tavern," she stated. "He was recently escaped. Still smelled a bit like the cows."

Gren regarded the big man with curiosity. "When we were hijacking one of those golden cows, one of the dudes we fought said Adame came back to the farm. He said some other things, too, but I can't remember."

"Then he is dead," Frostbite replied under his breath. He would not meet their eyes. "Who did you fight?"

Mari swallowed, and Gren shuffled his feet. Neither liked where this conversation was headed, but both felt obligated to explain. "I'm afraid I don't remember their names, only their faces. There were three. One was very tall, almost as tall as you, but not quite so—" she eyed his broad shoulders and heavy muscle, formidable even after surviving off such low rations for such a long time, then swallowed once more. "They left him behind to guard the barn. He fought Hal. The other two chased after me and Gren. The one I faced was bigger, too, with curly hair and a beard. Black hair, I think. Dark eyes. He seemed to be the leader. I would have lost if he hadn't been bowled over by Nemini's giant mortar."

"Bolen, I bet," Frostbite mumbled. "He could be a bully, but at heart, he was a good man."

Softly, Gren explained, "The one I fought was about my size, I guess, and his eyes...they struck me as young. Younger than the rest of him. He used a mace."

"Erick, or maybe Greg. Whoever it was you fought, they are also dead now," Frostbite stated.

Wendy reached out a hand and timidly placed it on Frostbite's forearm. "Did you know them well?"

"They were friends."

There was a collective exhale, and then Frostbite silently left. Once outside the circle of firelight, he shifted, the stripes tattooed down his arm stretching into furred stripes over the entirety of his massive form. At first Sam made to follow, shedding his leather jacket, but Sarah cut him off. "Let him be," she ordered. "He needs time."

When Frostbite had fully disappeared into the shadows, Gren pulled out his notebook and gestured for Brae to join him. "Thanks for sharing," he murmured as they ambled toward the edge of the camp. "And sorry about Adame—it wasn't your fault. But if I could just steal you for a minute and we can nail down that melody…"

In a lighter tone than anyone had ventured to use in some time, Ruv observed, "What a woman. Beautiful, clever, talented."

"I see you've quite moved on," Mari teased with one eyebrow arched.

Pouring as much charm as he could into his crooked smile, Ruv declared, "From you? Never."

"Join the club," Sarah mumbled.

"Pretty sure I'm the founding member," Ruv returned.

Rolling her eyes dramatically, Mari quipped, "You're both wrong. The founding member would be Matt Johnson in fourth grade. He used to pull my ponytail." Quelling further banter with a fierce look, she directed, "We should get some rest. We've got a lot to think about."

The niethera watched from a wary distance as Hal hacked at the trunk of his wooden opponent, now felled entirely, courtesy of his new axe. He had struck a deal with

Gryndonmin that he would plant a tree for every one he took down, and he had promised not to touch the fruit trees or the oldest of the oaks. On the ground nearby sat Svarog, legs crossed and back straight between the roots of another tree. Unlike the niethera, he watched Hal's activity with amusement rather than disdain.

"You know," Hal said, leaning the axe against the fallen trunk as he took a break, "this would go a lot quicker if I had another set of hands."

Svarog's lips quirked in a wry smile, and his merry blue eyes twinkled. "This is all your work, Guardian. I have plenty to occupy my time in my own forge. I am merely here to ensure you don't burn down the whole sanctuary in your enthusiasm to become a smith."

"I'm already a Smith," Hal jested, then took a sip of water. "But yeah, I suppose there's no rush either way. I'm just bored. I mean, the whole point of this is to occupy my time, you know? There's only so many laps around the gardens I can run."

"What sharpens the body, sharpens the mind," Svarog stated soberly.

Hal chugged the rest of his water bottle. "Growing up, I never believed in any gods or magic or anything like that. Seemed like a load of mystical jumbo to me. And now, here I am, conversing with a deity like it's no big deal."

Svarog inclined his head in Hal's direction. "There are many who would think this is, in fact, a 'big deal,' as you phrased it."

"So you're saying I should watch my tongue a bit more around you guys, huh?"

"You need not concern yourself with offending me," Svarog replied with a knowing grin. "We are kindred spirits, you and I. Of a sort. But perhaps next time you request a favor from, say, my father…"

Chuckling at the memory of Perun's reaction when he had asked him for an axe, Hal said, "Gotcha. Next time I'll grovel appropriately."

Svarog got to his feet and stretched. "We lanti are not quite what you imagine us, I believe."

"No, probably not," Hal admitted. When Svarog made to leave, however, Hal grabbed him by the bicep. Realizing that was undoubtedly inappropriate, he blushed and released his grip, asking, "Hey, so what other prophecies have you seen?"

"Prophecies can be misleading," the god warned, his countenance suddenly serious.

"Yeah, yeah, I know," Hal said with a shrug. "You've said that before. But you have to tell us something. Laria's really worried, and the Loom still hasn't been much help." He began to pace, the axe and the tree since forgotten. "She's too busy trying to force a vision of Mari and Gren's current state to bother looking elsewhere for very long. Earth could be burning in a nuclear holocaust right now for all we know."

Svarog set a warm hand on Hal's shoulder, and Hal's pacing ceased. Tall as Hal was, every lanti he had encountered seemed to match him for height. "I can at least tell you that Earth is not undergoing any sort of extinction event," Svarog said softly. "Well, not right at this moment, that is."

"Cryptic as always," Hal grumbled. Switching tactics, he tried his best for a pleading pout, a feat at which he failed miserably.

Nevertheless, Svarog granted him an amenable sigh and pinched the bridge of his nose. "Fine," he said. "I will tell you some—but only some!—of what I have seen, and you must not, under any circumstances, tell the Summoner."

Hal jerked back. "What? I'd have to tell her."

Svarog shook his head, his generous mouth set in an uncharacteristically stern line. "What I have seen is unpleasant. It will be difficult enough for you to hear. I would not wish to alarm the Summoner in case these things do not come to pass. The Loom shows her enough darkness as it is."

Hal counted his breaths for a few moments, weighing whether or not he wanted to hear such a truth, and whether he should, or even could, keep such a secret from Laria. Eventually, he whispered, "Tell me."

In the dim light of pre-dawn, Mari and her friends clustered at the top of the ridge overlooking the ocean. They inched forward on their elbows, slowly moving the scrubby branches and bracken aside so they could see. Even Micaleth did his best to remain inconspicuous, although scooting along the ground did not come naturally to a nietheran. The islands that had been but hazy outlines by moonlight were now clearly visible. A humble scattering of stony pillars and atolls jutting out of the waves, they did not look any more hospitable than the mainland, and the gray palette painting each one did not imply much vegetation. The archipelago stretched south as far as they could see, but only a few islets dotted the sea to the north.

Gren cursed softly. "I didn't think there'd be so many to choose from."

They watched, mute, as the rising sunlight struck the eastern face of the islands. As the light crept across the waves, they could perceive a series of shadows skimming across the water. "Wendy, can you make out anything with that awesome distance vision of yours?" Mari urged.

She removed her glasses and crawled forward a few more inches. "There's a whole load of boats," she whispered, pointing at the shadows that glided over the waves. "And it looks like they're making for that one over there. The big one."

"You think that's the other part of the group we met?" Sam whispered to his sister.

"Hard to say," she replied.

Gren brushed his hair out of his eyes. "I wonder how many of them there really are?"

"Can't give you a number from this far away," Wendy confessed. "Especially with them bobbing all over the place. But I can tell you that's a damn big fleet."

"Hmm," Ruv grunted. "I bet there's more boats on this side. We took out half of them, after all. Maybe in a hidden cove or something."

Derek rolled on his side to regard his former alpha. "Are you thinking what I'm thinking?"

"That we don our wolfskins and get a closer look?"

Already undressing, Derek replied, "See what they've left behind?"

Joining Ruv and Derek, Killer added, "Secure ourselves some transportation?"

"Let's go, boys!" Ruv urged, right before he shifted into a scraggly, black-furred wolf. He gave a nod to Mari and then loped away, Derek and Killer hot on his heels with their clothes and machetes clutched in their jaws.

"I will follow after them from a distance," Frostbite pronounced. "Perhaps there is a goblin or two remaining on this side that I could interrogate."

Mari considered him with an ambiguous expression. "You've experience in that field, huh?"

Frostbite's countenance broke into a rare grin. The effect was terrifying. "Ask the twins," he suggested before stealing quietly after the wolves.

Mari turned a quizzical eye to Sarah, who stated flatly, "You don't want to know. Trust me."

"For once, I'll believe you," Mari said. "Either way, if we can capture one of these suckers alive—well, as alive as they get, I suppose—it could definitely be helpful. Maybe we could get some answers finally. I suppose that should have occurred to me earlier."

"It would be nice to know what we're walking into on yonder island. I tried to get what I could out of them while we were captured, but I didn't have much luck," Gren admitted. "Just something about a necromancer and bringing tribute."

Mari nodded. "A necromancer makes sense, considering the whole zombie thing."

They stayed were they were, hiding among the sparse, wiry foliage as the dawn gave way to morning. Mari kept a steady watch while the rest gradually drifted into a light sleep. After a few hours, Mari saw Ruv ambling up the mountainside alone. Since he made no attempt to conceal his presence, she rose to her feet, dusted off her leggings and tunic, and roused the others. When Ruv drew close enough for her to make out his expression, she was pleased to see him beaming triumphantly.

CHAPTER TEN
See a monster that needs slaying

Ruv updated his friends as he escorted them down the steep, rocky hillside toward the place where he, Derek, and Killer had located a cave. Even by daylight the route was treacherous, with loose sand slipping readily from beneath their feet as they skimmed along the wind-scoured rocks, and so they counted themselves lucky that they had not attempted such a trek in the dark.

"Just about a dozen total of them," Ruv explained, offering an arm to steady Brae as she faltered at a particularly slippery section. "Luckily, they were split up into smaller groups, so it was easy pickings. Killer and Derek are still clearing the rest of the caverns—there's a whole network down there—to make sure there aren't any of the bastards left. There's a bunch of boats in the bay, and we think they were left to guard them until the rest of the hoard caught up, which, obviously, won't be happening now. Oh, and we were able to keep one alive, albeit it's short a few limbs. Frostbite was just beginning his interrogation when I left."

"Does this seem too easy to you?" Mari asked quietly.

Ruv shrugged. "They are not intelligent creatures, to be sure. The more I meet, the more I wonder how the hell they got the jump on us in the first place. Perhaps we will survive this after all."

A single entrance, half concealed by the spindly shrubbery, awaited them at the bottom of the hill. They stopped outside to light a few lanterns before entering. Though Ruv's team in their sanguine forms had seen well enough through the dark, no one wanted to bother shifting. The entrance to the cave was so small that even Wendy and Brae had to duck to pass under, but once inside, the cave opened up substantially. The stone floor sloped downward, twisting and winding beneath the hillside. Their steps echoed off the damp walls as Ruv led them deeper and deeper by the flickering lantern light.

Eventually the tunnel widened into a spacious chamber with a chimney open to the sky. Multiple tunnels extended off in each direction, some of which continued to descend toward the sea. Others cut dark paths back toward the heart of the mountain. Killer and Derek waited in the center of the chamber below the chimney, watching over a pile of assorted body parts that included heads that glared and hissed at the observers, their mouthed threats rendered ineffectual by a lack of lungs. A second pile of ragged cloaks and stinking leather was shoved inside one of the nooks that indented the cavern wall. They deposited their supplies along the chamber's circumference, as far from the stench as they could get.

"And I just got that smell out of my nose," Brae groaned.

"Now that you're here with the rest of our supplies," Derek said with a merry grin, "we can get the fire going."

Gren obligingly fished around his pack in search of his lighter. He tossed it to Derek, and the pile ignited in a matter of seconds. Clinging to the bones, the greasy flesh provided plenty of fuel on its own. Greenish smoke stung their eyes as it curled and coiled up through the chimney opening. They gathered around the fire and watched, as mute as the screaming skulls. The disassembled goblins burned hot, and they burned quickly.

"The rest of the caves are all clear, I take it?" Mari asked as the hungry flames died down to a steady smolder. Apart from a few divots in the walls and floor, the dark stone was mostly smooth, carved and polished by the sea. Stains around the cavern ceiling implied they were not the first to light a fire in that particular location. "And how high does the tide reach?"

Ruv shrugged. "Not to this chamber, it seems, or at least not in a long time. There's a clear tideline down in the cove where we found the boats."

"At least I can check 'drowning in my sleep' off the list of shit to worry about," she mumbled, cracking her neck. "Where's Frostbite?"

Killer gestured toward one of the other tunnels branching off from the chamber. "Down that way a bit, but he said not to approach."

"Something about messing up the flow of the interrogation or what-have-you," Derek added. "Don't worry. He'll fill you in when he's done."

Mari shrugged. "Then I guess there's nothing else to do for now but check out those boats."

Wendy stifled a yawn. "I'll sit this one out."

"We'll keep you company," Sarah replied.

Ruv led Mari and Gren down another dark tunnel. They could hear the sea before they saw it. As they rounded a corner, the tunnel suddenly gave way to an expansive, covered inlet, where a handful of wooden rowboats were moored on the sand, tied to stakes just below the tidemark. The skiffs were large enough to accommodate six or seven people, but each held only three sets of oars.

Mari vaulted into the nearest one. Inspecting the wood, she commented, "You know, these little things actually look surprisingly seaworthy." She hopped up and down.

The wood creaked, but no cracks appeared. "Should be sturdy enough for a trip to the island, at least."

"A round trip, you mean," Gren corrected.

She leapt out of the boat. "We'll cross that bridge when we come to it," she dismissed. "Or burn it, more likely."

"Mari—" Gren and Ruv started.

"What?" she snapped. "I'm just being realistic. We're walking into a hornets' nest with no clue how many hornets there actually are. What we *do* know is these undead bastards are being controlled by a necromancer, and there's probably a lot more under the surface that we haven't even scratched yet." She stared at them, breathing through her nose. "But we're here," she continued in a softer tone. "And something has to be done."

They returned to the main chamber to find Frostbite pacing on the far side of the dimming embers while the others engaged in quiet conversations. Wendy was showing Killer and Derek how to fold a paper crane with one of last empty pages ripped from the back of her notebook. Brae and Micaleth were debating whether or not the dracora were truly the eldest Aorean species. The twins were whispering to each other, their voices pitched too low for anyone else to hear.

Mari studied Frostbite's urgent pacing. "Are you done with the interrogation?"

"Not quite," he rumbled without ceasing his march. "But I believe I am near a breakthrough. I am letting him stew in his choices."

Sam cleared his throat; all eyes turned his way. "So Sarah and I have been talking," he announced.

Gren gave him a lopsided grin. "Hadn't realized you'd ever stopped."

Sam returned the grin with a dismissive wave. "You know what I mean. Anyway, it's been a while since any of us had a proper bath, and the sea is right there."

"It's not perfect," Sarah granted, "but it's a helluva lot better than scrubbing ourselves with sand."

"That is a fine point," Ruv observed.

"We could wash our clothes, too," Derek said, sniffing one of his sleeves with a grimace.

Killer slung his overstuffed pack over his shoulder. "My bearskin is rather rank," he admitted.

Derek snorted. "It was always rather rank, brother."

"Sold," Gren affirmed. "Let's go."

"I see the boys have first dibs, then," Brae commented.

"Fine by me," Mari returned. "They smell far worse."

As the men—Micaleth included—headed toward the cove, Sam pulled a razor out of his pocket and winked at no one in particular. "If we're going to die," he crooned, "we may as well die pretty."

Frostbite started to follow them but stopped after a few steps. "The interrogation is incomplete. The next part will be...messy." The other men shrugged and continued on their way.

When they returned, fresh-faced and smelling pleasantly of the sea, the women greeted them with a chorus of whistles before heading to the cove themselves.

"Master, we lost Caivah's group on the mainland," the goblin groveled, his face smushed against the stone floor as he prostrated himself at Dimeldor's feet. When he rose, he left behind a rancid puddle. "They are more formidable than we believed."

Dimeldor ground his teeth, right eye twitching and his mouth pulled thin. "Are you implying that my assessment was incorrect?" When Servorg shook his head violently, he added, "Sending Caivah was a test, nothing more."

"What would you have us do now, master?"

"Nothing."

"Is that wise, master?"

The necromancer clutched the goblin by his malformed throat and held him aloft. "Again you question me," he seethed. "You may be the first among my children, but do not forget that you are as disposable as the rest. If I say 'do nothing,' then you shall do nothing." He released his grip abruptly, and Servorg tumbled to the floor.

Trembling and rubbing his neck, the goblin coughed, "I apologize, master. You are the wisest of all."

"Let them come. We owe our very existence to the children of Sier, after all. If not for their rebellion, the worlds would never have been split." He pondered then if Servorg even knew the history he referenced, but concluded in the next breath that it did not matter. "It would be rude not to invite them in now that they've traveled so far just to meet me."

"Yes, master."

Dimeldor's cold eyes dared his minion to move; Servorg offered no challenge. "The experiments with the leshii keep failing. The pixies have proven too fragile for my purposes. The kemdar, too." Dimeldor ticked off each point on a long, pale, bony finger. "You and your brethren remain a disappointment. Perhaps these ones will prove strong enough to withstand the process," he muttered to himself, turning his back on his henchman. Disposable, he had called him. Perhaps once. Too many he had lost, succumbing to decay and deterioration and the very in-fighting that left them extinct on their home world. Powerful as he had become, he could not reverse the damage of time. That Servorg, his oldest creation, had survived this long was nothing short of miraculous.

Now, in one fell wave, he lost nearly half of those who remained. A blessing in disguise, he thought. The goblins made for poor company, and ever since Necria had bound her voice...

Necria.

An emotion he refused to name settled in his chest.

He spun back around, intending to see what could be seen in his scrying bowl, only to instead see Servorg still standing there. Realizing that his minion had not understood the dismissal, Dimeldor massaged his temples and instructed, "Ensure Necria is safe, then set a guard at the front gate. We can't make this too easy for them, after all, or they may become suspicious. But still, they must be allowed to enter."

Servorg bobbed his head in acquiescence, but he hesitated at the threshold. When Dimeldor did not immediately chastise him for lingering again, he asked, "Why do you not just destroy them, master?"

"My reasons are my own."

"Yes, master."

As the goblin bowed and hurried off to obey his orders, the necromancer changed his mind and headed toward the dungeons. The waters could wait. "My secrets are already out, it would appear, if they have managed to get so close before I saw them," he mused to himself as he reached the top stair. "So let them come. Let them find what they came to find." His steps reverberated off the stone as he spiraled down into the dank, stagnant air. A cold breeze hailed him from below, and he felt a breath of anticipation bubbling in his belly. He would have to move faster after this. With a stronger army, fortified with this fresh new blood and the magic of a nietheran, victory would soon be within his grasp.

"Sister, if you could but see me now," he whispered with a smile.

Frostbite tossed the last dismantled corpse amid the blackened bones and glowing embers. He stayed only long enough to ensure the oily flesh caught fire before leaving without a word. When he returned again, his hair dripped sea water and his last few weeks' worth of beard was cropped close. His eyes defied anyone to comment; no one did. "I have some information that will greatly help our plan," he announced.

Mari stretched. "Excellent. Let's hear it."

"These undead creatures belong to an army, controlled by some sorcerer. A necromancer. That much we already knew," he summarized, crouching in the center as the rest gathered around him. "Both the creatures and their master come from another world. Their master has been hiding here for quite a while, but only recently began building his army. That said, these creatures' sense of time is rather skewed, if not absent altogether. I could not make it understand the difference between a year, a day, a week. He only seemed to grasp 'then,' 'now,' and 'later.' Nothing more concrete."

"Do we know this master's endgame?"

"No," he replied with a shrug. "He tells them little beyond their next target. When they are not on a mission, they go to sleep."

Gren tapped his foot. "Like real sleep? Or like, how a computer sleeps?"

Frostbite gave him a blank look. "What is a computer?"

"Er, never mind."

"I was able to extract a basic layout of the fortress from him as well," the big man continued.

"Sweet!" Ruv and Gren exclaimed simultaneously as they high fived.

"Do not be too excited," Frostbite cautioned. "It is rudimentary at best, and we have no way of testing the accuracy until we see the fortress for ourselves."

"Still, even a basic layout would give us something to work with," Mari rejoined. "At this point, I'll take whatever I can get."

Frostbite nodded, but the thin line of his lips revealed his reservations. "I got out of him what I could, but they are like feral children."

"Bloody ugly, smelly, strong, and unnaturally fast feral children," Sarah corrected. "Apart from the limping."

Mari shuddered. "And now I'm remembering every zombie movie I've ever seen. Thanks for that." She noticed Frostbite had begun sketching the outlines of a building on the cavern floor, his finger tracing neat lines in the accumulated salt and dust. "I appreciate your hard work, by the way," she remarked. "Once we're done planning, you should try to get some rest. It looks like we've got about five hours or so before the sun sets, and I imagine we'll have another long night ahead of us."

Frostbite's only acknowledgement of her praise was to take a step back from his completed drawing so the rest could see. "Like I said, rudimentary."

"This will do," Mari replied brightly. "Let's see what we've got here…"

In the end, there was little to plan besides who would go where once they entered the fortress. They intended to eat something resembling lunch while they discussed their options, but the odor of smoldering rot proved less than appetizing. Thus, once they had memorized Frostbite's hasty map, they secured a lantern, grabbed some of their dwindling food supplies, and retreated to another section of the extensive caves. When the basics had been decided and the food had been eaten, Mari sent everyone but Ruv and Gren back to the central chamber so they could snatch a few hours of sleep while she and her chosen strategists refined the details. They were all too eager to oblige.

With their final planning complete, Mari, Gren, and Ruv arrived at the central chamber to find their friends already deep in slumber. Only Killer remained awake, his gaze fixed on the play of smoke and sunbeams dancing through the cave's natural vent. He gave them a nod as they entered.

Gren and Ruv fell asleep quickly enough, and Killer eventually joined them. However, Mari found that, so close to the finish line—for she knew in her bones, even without the aid of her once prophetic dreams, that one way or another their journey was nearing its end—her mind would not stop spinning. She replayed their brief battle with the goblins. She sifted through the various options they had discussed for approaching the island fortress. She counted the divots in the cavern ceiling. She pondered the origin of the necromancer and his horde. Daem, she guessed. The third world.

Unable to keep still any longer, she slipped down to the cove where she found the tide lapping closer to the edge of the moored boats. The rhythm of the waves soothed her mind, but fleetingly. Before long her brain was whirring once more with old memories and new questions. Possibility after possibility flitted through her thoughts, and so engrossed was she that she did not hear Gren's approach until he was right behind her.

He slid his arms around her waist and rested his chin on her shoulder. "You know, we could just run," he murmured in her ear. "Take everyone back north. Make someone else deal with all this."

"Who else could?" she asked, eyes still fixed on the waves. "Besides, we've come too far now to go back." She shrugged out of his grasp and faced him. "I can't believe you're even suggesting this. What's with you?"

"Nothing's with me," he bit. "I'm the same. You're the one who's drifting." Despite the edge in his tone, his touch was gentle as he stretched to brush her cheek.

"Drifting?" she scoffed, pulling just beyond his reach. "I know we haven't exactly had time to ourselves in, like, months, but this mission is important. There's something sinister going on here, and dammit, somebody needs to get to the bottom of it before Laria's Loom stops working altogether." She shook her head. "As far as we know, her blind spot is still growing. All we can say for sure is that it started right here. On those islands. We're almost done, Gren. And then, assuming we defeat this necromancer and his horde of zombie-goblins, *then* we'll have some time to ourselves again. We can ditch Ruv in a tavern somewhere for a few days and reconnect, if it makes you happy. But we have to finish this first."

"Do you even hear yourself?" Gren muttered.

Mari intended to snap at him again, but the sorrow written in his dark eyes gave her pause. Softly, she said, "What else is there to say? We'll do what has to be done, and I'll be leading the charge."

"But why does it always have to be you? You're so eager to just throw yourself into the center of the fight."

"The mission comes first. I thought you understood."

Gren opened his mouth to argue further, changed his mind, and seized her wrists instead. In a hoarse whisper, he said, "You're right. I just forget sometimes that you don't see the world the way I do. You see a problem that needs fixing, so you solve it. You see a monster that needs slaying, so you reach for your sword." He paused, searching her face; it gave nothing away. When he continued, his words were barely audible. "But me? All I ever see is you."

"I never go into the fray alone. I have you with me." Mari closed her eyes and exhaled slowly. "I've always had you with me."

Gren released her wrists and raked a hand through his hair, still damp from the sea. "I guess we should get back."

She tilted her head and regarded him for a few seconds, and then her face broke into a coy smile. "I think we have some time," she declared. She grabbed him by the collar and shoved him against the wall. It was not long until they were pressed close together, her lips against his, his fingers in her hair, all previous arguments forgotten.

They fell to the cavern floor in a tangle of limbs and partially removed clothing. Mari winced when the bare skin of her back made contact with the cold stone. Gren lifted her bodily from the floor to slide his own shirt beneath her, then laid her back down gently. "You're always so sweet," she giggled, tracing the strong line of his jaw. "I don't deserve you."

He kissed a trail down her throat and along her collar bone. Despite their heat, his lips left goosebumps in their wake. "Somebody has to take care of you while you're taking care of the worlds." His dark eyes blazed with a sudden intensity as he vowed, "I wouldn't let the job to fall to anybody else."

"The fate of the worlds balances on the edge of a cliff, you must understand," Svarog professed, "and the chances of survival for both the Dreamer and the Wanderer are slim. If even one of them should perish at this time, it would doom everything." Hal stared back at him, unblinking. "Both are needed," Svarog continued in a low voice lest the niethera wandering in the fields should hear him and carry his words back to the Spinner. "And both are in danger."

"What kind of danger?" Hal whispered. "From Antiln's brother?"

Svarog nodded, his eyes sparking with the sun he embodied. "From him, and from others." He began to measure a slow circle around the fallen oak, pretending to study the wood Hal had already chopped and split. Hal kept close to him. "I still cannot see Dimeldor himself," Svarog continued, "nor Dahrigek. Their present fate is as shrouded against me as it is for the Lady Laria. But I have seen many visions over the eternities of my existence, long before Antiln and her brothers came to be, and it is those visions I reference now. We have been waiting a very, very long time for the arrival of the Destined. Rod knew before the splitting of the worlds what role you would come to play, and he sacrificed himself not only to bring peace, but to preserve *you*. The legacy of the Destined will last beyond even this Spinner's lifetime." His voice grew yet quieter. "Beyond the last Spinner's lifetime. For better or worse, you four will change the fate of Aorea forever."

"And yet no one will tell us what the hell it is we're supposed to actually do," Hal spat. Then, remembering belatedly that he was, in fact, conversing with a god, he strove for a more respectful tone. "It would be helpful, I mean, if we knew what these prophecies say."

Svarog looked pointedly at him, clearly more amused than offended by Hal's continued irreverence. "Prophecies are best fulfilled by innocents."

"And speaking of prophecies…?"

Svarog sighed. "None of us foresaw Antiln's brother surviving her destruction, let alone becoming a sorcerer in his own right, but we—myself and a few others of my kin—did see a possible future in which the Destined walk heedlessly into darkness and never return. A future in which the prophecy remains unfulfilled."

Hal's golden brows drew together in a tight frown. "And this is that shadow."

"I believe so."

"Are there possible futures where they do come back?"

"There are many timelines, many more possibilities than even I could ever hope to see," Svarog admitted. "In a select few of those timelines, a shadow arises from the West and consumes all. The other lanti would not wish me to tell you, but I believe there is more to this shadow than just the one sorcerer." He paused, eyes darting in every direction, taking in the sky, the ground, the surrounding green, unsure if he should continue. At a pressing glance from Hal, Svarog finally resumed speaking. "There are those who once walked this world before ever the dracora were born from the fire, who walked this world even before my kin. Such titanic forces could not exist in the same world as those we wished to bring about—"

"Wait, what?" Hal interrupted.

"No. I have said too much already, it seems," he declared with a frown. Svarog's eyes came to rest on Hal's fatestone pendant, which had fallen out of his shirt collar sometime during his exertions. He blinked and looked away. "All I am trying to tell you is that there may be forces at work who are stronger than me, stronger than Perun and Mokosh and all of us combined. We thought we banished those forces when we split the worlds, but they may be returning." He took several paces back and raised his arms heavenward. As he drew them down in a slow arc, his flaming chariot appeared from the sky and descended in line with his hands. When the chariot had finished its descent, he added, "Earlier than anticipated."

"And what would that mean?"

Hal could barely hear Svarog's response as he stepped through the flames. "It would mean that, Destined or no, we are all doomed. Even the lanti."

Mari and Gren crept into the central chamber only to realize their efforts to remain quiet had been entirely wasted, for their friends were already wide awake. Derek and Killer were engaged in an unusually solemn discussion with Frostbite, to which Wendy was listening with rapt attention and reddened cheeks. Micaleth scratched incessantly at one of his ears, his long face wrinkled in intense concentration. Brae exchanged odd looks with Sarah while they both picked at their nails. Sam and Ruv, sitting closest to the tunnel exit, watched the newly arrived pair with identical, impish half-smiles.

"Why is everyone being weird?" Gren queried. At the sound of his voice, Wendy's eyes grew wide just as her cheeks grew even redder.

Mari scanned the room, frowning. "Did something happen while we were gone?"

"Funny thing about caves, my friends," Ruv said, his crooked smile taking on a particularly roguish air, "they tend to echo."

All the blood drained from Gren's face, and he froze where he stood. "Oh, dear gods, kill me now."

Ruv took to his feet and clapped a hand on his friend's broad shoulder. Gren remained too mortified to react. "Sounds like you resolved your, uh, issues there."

"You needed that," Sam added, still smirking.

Mari tried to retreat into the shadows of the tunnel, muttering, "I'm going to go drown myself now, thanks."

Brae rolled her eyes. "Oh, for heavens' sakes!" she cried. "It's nothing. We've all heard worse."

"Except for Wendy, I'd wager, judging by the shade of those rosy round cheeks," Sarah said with a wink. When Wendy buried her face in her hands, Sarah cackled.

Gren stayed, face alarmingly pale and blank of all expression, in the entrance while Ruv snickered at his side. Mari took a deep breath and flopped down next to her bedroll and blankets. "Well," she mumbled, staring at her fidgeting fingers, "the tide is in, and the boats at least seem not to have sprung any leaks. So assuming the weather holds, so should they."

Micaleth sniffed the air thoughtfully, no longer feigning interest in an itchy ear. "It does not feel like a storm is brewing anytime soon," he observed. "Plus Dahrigek is still in its dry season."

"Good," Mari sighed. She took another deep breath, still unwilling to meet anyone's eyes. "Sorry for waking you guys. We really should try to get some actual rest. We've had a lot of long nights—"

"Some longer than others," Ruv quipped.

"—and tonight's going to be another," she finished, glaring at the floor, her own burning cheeks rivaling Wendy's bright shade. "And shut up, Ruv."

At last Gren relinquished the shelter of the tunnel and shuffled toward his pack. Collecting his things and redepositing them as far from Mari as possible, he grumbled, "So this is what it feels like to die of shame."

Ruv settled by Sam again, and neither man could suppress a chuckle. Reclining against the cave wall, fingers laced behind his head and long legs crossed at the ankles, Ruv divulged, "If it makes you feel any better, at least four among the present crowd wished they could have joined in the fun."

"Don't tell me anymore. Please."

"I mean, the tw—"

"Seriously," Gren interrupted him with a raised hand and a pointed scowl. "Don't." He yanked his blanket over his head and refused to interact further with anyone in spite of Ruv, Sam, and even Brae's persistent teasing. Eventually they lost interest in their silent subject, and so one by one the group resumed dozing.

Whether or not Mari and Gren continued to blush beneath their respective blankets, no one could say.

Just before dusk Mari, Ruv, and Gren roused everyone but Wendy. In silence they departed the chamber, abandoning their cache of supplies but retaining their myriad weapons. It was with much reluctance that Killer parted with his hard-won bearskin and much exuberance that Micaleth discarded his many burdens. Yet, one thing upon which they all agreed, was the necessity of the threadbare cloaks and decrepit armor they had salvaged from their erstwhile enemies. No one wanted to bring the reeking articles along, but everyone knew they would need them on the other side.

They watched the sun sink below the horizon from the shelter of the stone, their palms wound tightly in cloth to ward off blisters once they started to row. Calluses they already possessed, but after listening to a few horror stories from the twins about ill-prepared boating ventures, they decided not to test those calluses on a new activity. Once the crimson sky deepened to violet, they hauled three of the better preserved boats forward and prepared to board. Mari was just about to step inside the first skiff alongside Sam and Brae when she felt a tap on her shoulder. She whipped around to find Wendy, arms crossed and eyes blazing. "If you don't put me in a boat," she announced, "I'll swim."

"I told you this would happen," Sam muttered.

Mari took a step toward her. Though only of average height, she still towered over her diminutive friend. "Be realistic," she commanded, poking Wendy's makeshift cast to emphasize her point. "You can't swim with one arm."

"The only way to make me stay here is to break my legs or knock me unconscious. You choose which."

Mari's nostrils flared. "Wendy, you know I admire the hell out of your brains, and you have absolutely proven yourself as brave and stubborn as anyone, so please don't take this the wrong way." She studied Wendy's posture, her squared shoulders, her set jaw. "Right now, no matter how stubborn you are, you'll only slow us down."

"I won't."

"You will. You're a liability, and you know it."

Wendy narrowed her eyes, calculating. "If you leave me here," she pressed, "and something happens to the rest of you, I'll have no way of knowing unless I swim over there anyway." The corner of Mari's mouth twitched, so Wendy continued her argument. "I can't talk telepathically with any of you, and you know you won't leave yourself or Gren or one of the twins behind."

"Right, but—"

"I'll have no way back home," Wendy added, ignoring Mari's attempted arguments. The rest of their friends were dismounting the boats as well, but no one moved to take one side or the other, content merely to watch the increasingly heated exchange. "Even if, by some miracle, I make it all the way back to Evra on my own, I can't exactly operate the traveling circles." Wendy moved closer to Mari and poked her in the chest in an echo of Mari's earlier action. "You want to keep me alive? My best chance is with the rest of you."

"Wendy, I—"

"Besides, you mentioned my brains. Maybe I'll see a solution you miss."

Any further assertions were interrupted by Frostbite, who strode behind Wendy and rested a hand on her good shoulder. His massive fingers swallowed her shoulder whole. "I'll protect her," he rumbled.

Mari met his eyes, set every bit as stubbornly as Wendy's. Grudgingly, she snapped, "Fine." She kept grumbling as she hopped into the boat. "I suppose leaving our supplies unattended is the least of our worries. If we can't make it back, it's a moot point anyway."

Sarah unbuckled one of the knives attached to her thigh and thrust it at Wendy hilt first. "You'll have to tighten the strap, but it should fit," she said by means of explanation. Wendy nodded and buckled the knife around her own thigh. Scrutinizing her, Sarah added quietly, "Try not to stab yourself, little owl. I've become rather fond of you—it'd be a shame to lose you now."

CHAPTER ELEVEN
What do you have to wager

"Not too much farther," Mari called, pulling her set of oars in time with Sam and Brae, who were seated behind her in the creaking skiff. The shore of the main island drew closer, pull by steady pull, as they bobbed over the waves. Derek, Killer, and Sarah navigated the second skiff that glided along to their left. They maintained just enough distance to keep the oars from tangling. Bearing the most weight and accordingly slowest in the water regardless of Frostbite's powerful arms on the oars, Gren's craft trailed behind. Micaleth, meanwhile, pedaled his four legs furiously to keep pace with Mari's boat.

Sam whistled through his teeth. "Good," he groaned. "I'm sick of rowing."

"We all are," Brae drawled. "And you know, I'm probably the first leshii in the history of leshii to ever set a freckled foot in a boat, let alone help row one."

Micaleth, his head barely held above the water line, puffed, "At least you are dry. This water is freezing!"

Mari scoffed. "For the love of…you're the one who *wanted* to swim."

"You should have tried harder to talk me out of it!"

She affected the nietheran's haughty tone as she recited, "'It'll be good for me,' he said. 'The water will feel nice after this desert,' he said. 'I can replenish some of my magic.' All direct quotes."

Sam snickered. "You forgot one: 'Never in my life will I set hoof in a rickety old boat when I am perfectly capable of swimming.'"

"You humans crack me up," Brae commented with a broad smile. "I'm glad I decided to tag along. I'll have all kinds of stories to spread after this."

"On a serious note," Mari began after a few more pulls on the oars, "at least it doesn't look like there's any activity on the island right now."

"That or the bloody bastards can see in the dark."

"Maybe it's a good thing Wendy talked her way into a boat," Mari mused. She looked pointedly at Micaleth. "She may be able to see something with those owl eyes of hers."

Micaleth snorted, the seawater gurgling beneath his nose. "Fine. I will swim over and ask her," he griped. "First I am a pack mule, then I am a mount, and now I am a measly messenger. At least the current is easy here."

"I swear, he is the grumpiest nietheran I've ever met," Brae remarked, watching his white head float backwards to the overburdened boat.

"He's the only one for me," Mari said. "I've got nothing to compare him to."

Brae chuckled. "They normally don't complain nearly this much. Stoic, peaceful Zen-types, if a bit judgmental."

"Yeah?"

"Of course," she replied with a dip of her head. "Always spouting off bits of wisdom, working magic on the weather, making flowers bloom and such." They paused their rowing to let their craft skim over a particularly large wave, the water sloshing over the sides.

When they had settled back into their rhythm, she added, "They do have a slight pretentious streak, I suppose, but they generally don't deign to express discomfort in front of us lowly bipedal folk."

"I think I prefer the grumpy version we have," Sam observed. "Ah, speak of the devil."

Micaleth spluttered as he lurched out of the water and rested his front hooves and chin on the side of the boat. The movement nearly capsized the little skiff, but the occupants leaned hard just in time to balance the weight. "Wendy confirmed the lack of activity on shore," Micaleth panted, his face showing not the slightest remorse for nearly drowning his friends. "I believe it will be safe to approach." Mari acknowledged the information with a nod, and after a count of three the nietheran slipped into the water while Mari, Sam, and Brae rebalanced the boat.

The main island loomed over them as they drifted just off shore. Concealed in the shadow cast by the island itself, they studied the rocky shoreline. They saw no beach on which to safely land the boats. Instead, the island jutted out of the ocean in a mountain of jagged stone and clinging barnacles. As they rowed around the coast, they found hundreds of other boats in various states of seaworthiness secured by rusted chains, which were attached directly to the rock. From what they had seen on their approach as well as what they could see from their present vantage point, they assumed the rock began to level off near the top of the secured chains. Only a fraction hung empty, and they wondered exactly how many more goblins awaited them on the land. Much to their dismay, the number of boats they had watched cross the bay accounted for less than a quarter of the fleet presently moored before them.

Unseasoned sailors at best, it took multiple attempts to successfully maneuver the three skiffs close enough to the empty cables to hitch them. Once they finally managed to do so, they realized the only way up to safe ground was to climb the chains. The rock itself, bathed in sea spray and coated with slick weed, was far too slippery to provide stable handholds for anything beyond the most dexterous of crabs and seagulls. Sarah offered to climb first to test the footing above the line of rusted cables, and upon her return she was delighted to report that their assumption was correct. The stony terrain, though still rather treacherous and uneven, was at least traversable by foot.

While such a climb was easy enough for the two-legged members of their party to manage, provided Wendy had a bit of assistance to account for her broken arm, it proved quite impossible for poor Micaleth. Thus, after a quick discussion (to include a few wry remarks from Brae and no shortage of laments from Micaleth himself), they looped two empty chains around the nietheran's torso and fastened them together with a length of thick rope. Micaleth, balancing precariously on one of the boats, waited semi-patiently while the rest scurried up the rock face. However, once he was actually dangling in the wind and bouncing against the stone, his patience ran dry.

"Next time the Spinner initiates an adventure," he squeaked, panicked eyes darting to and fro, "I am declining to participate." His left flank ricocheted off the rock wall, and he flinched. "I am never, ever, ever doing this again."

"First of all, you're not doing a damn thing but hanging there while we do all the work," Gren taunted from above, muscles straining alongside the rest as they heaved on the chains. "And secondly, didn't you volunteer for this?"

"Irrelevant," Micaleth grumbled. He continued listing his grievances between dramatic breaths, and as soon as he was close enough to scramble over the edge, he collapsed gratefully on the ground.

While they unwound the cloths that had protected their palms throughout the rowing and hauling, they scanned the rest of the island. Most of the rough landscape resembled what they traversed on the mainland: perilous footing and sharp rocks, loose pebbles that crumbled at the slightest disturbance, and jagged plants that indiscriminately deposited barbed gifts in clothing and skin alike. Though where the mainland had been left to its own devices to develop an austere beauty and wildness, the island bore outward signs of cultivation. Sheltered in a hollow from the biting ocean winds, they found a small orchard, where walnuts and maples grew in overgrown rows next to lemons and figs. As they made their way across another dip in the terrain, they discovered another garden overflowing with vegetables.

They stood just outside the patch, wary to break the threshold between sand and soil. "How in the hells do they manage to grow tomatoes here?" Ruv whispered. "And do we even want to know where they get their fertilizer?"

"And why would they need to eat?" Gren added. "I guess it's all for their master. It looks a little neglected, though. I bet zomblins are shitty gardeners."

The moon rose steadily, illuminating the path as they continued the slow journey between the jagged rocks. Some stood large enough that they could not see beyond until they had circumnavigated them. Others were small enough to skip over without difficulty. They cut a trail vaguely north toward the center of the island, where stood the fortress they glimpsed now and then whenever they crested a hill.

Eventually, after rounding the final corner of an exceptionally sizable collection of stones, they came face to face with the outer wall. There was a collective intake of breath as they retreated, thankful that the gap between stones had not deposited them directly in front of the gates and thereby invalidated their plan. Regrouping safely behind the boulders, they discussed in hushed voices how best to pinpoint the gates. Since they had already assessed the approximate size of the fortress and deemed it small enough to circle in less than twenty minutes even at a slow pace, they determined to stay together as they skirted the wall. They held little doubt, based on their previous encounters with the goblins, that they would hear them before they were heard in turn, and so they headed east to search for the gates.

They had not been walking long before Wendy felt herself yanked backward, her squeal silenced by a large hand. When she recognized the owner of the hand, she relaxed, and the arms restraining her released. Apart from Brae who tossed a glance backward and nodded encouragingly at Frostbite, the rest of the group continued their journey, unaware of the silent activity.

"May I speak with you?" he whispered.

Wendy pursed her lips. "It better be quick or we'll lose the group."

Frostbite's lips curved in a rare smile. "We will catch up," he promised.

"Then go ahead."

"I wanted to say this while we still had the chance, in case there is—is no opportunity later." He took a deep breath, and Wendy realized the big man, who had never before revealed the slightest hesitation, was nervous. "I admire you greatly," he said, voice rough. "Your courage, your cleverness." He took another deep breath, steeling himself for the rest of his prepared statement. "I have never met a woman like you in all my life."

Wendy, cheeks burning so red they were visible by the faint moonlight, found she could not reply.

"I know you plan on going back to Earth, but I wanted to ask you," he continued with great effort, "if maybe you would consider staying in Aorea? It is too late for me to go back, I know that, but I—" When her eyes grew wide and still she did not speak, Frostbite hung his head. "I'm sorry. This distresses you. Please forget I ever asked."

She sucked in her own deep breath and released it slowly. "Are you saying," she forced herself to ask, "that you want me to stay...with you?"

Frostbite froze and swallowed hard. "Yes," he choked out. "I would very much like that."

"Must've been something in that cave," she giggled.

"What?"

"Never mind." Then, standing on her toes as tall as she could manage, she extended her good hand to grasp the back of his neck; she could barely reach. His eyes searched hers, now as wide as her own, as she dragged his head down. Shocked into immobility, he held perfectly still while she brushed her lips against his. As she pulled away, she murmured, "Ask me again when this is over."

He nodded, and hand in hand they darted to catch up with the rest of their friends. This time it was Sarah who noted their return, and she waggled her eyebrows questioningly at Wendy. The woman's ensuing blush was all the answer required.

Soon enough they found the gates, and so they snuck away to hide among the boulders. They crawled, one inch at a time, to the top of a jutting rock where they could finally study the fortress in its entirety without being seen by the hapless gate guards. Like the abandoned city revealed by the sandstorm, the fortress was hewn straight from the bedrock. Unlike that city, the fortress was of plain, sturdy build, clearly constructed for functionality over splendor. They faced windowless walls several stories high with a central tower overlooking the island. A set of iron gates, barely wide enough to accommodate four walking abreast, were guarded by a pair of goblins with spears. The only light they saw came from the top of the tower, where a single window exposed a flickering, greenish illumination.

"Well, looks like at least someone's awake in there," Gren observed under his breath.

"It's a lot bigger than I was expecting," Mari muttered. "I have the feeling our rudimentary building plans only covered, like, a third of that thing."

"I stand by my techniques," Frostbite growled.

"No one is doubting you there, big guy," Gren replied, an eyebrow raised when he noticed Frostbite and Wendy's laced fingers. "And giving the poor zomblin the benefit of the doubt, maybe that's all he ever saw."

They skated down the ledge. Without a word they shrugged into the stolen cloaks. Adequately disguised, Mari breathed, "It's go time."

Derek and Killer, with hoods up and crouching to conceal their true height, led a stumbling Micaleth toward the gates. The guards nodded and stepped aside to allow them entry. As soon as Micaleth's twitching tail had passed them, machetes flashed and the guards were each short a head. As one the men stowed their blades and chucked the heads as far from the fortress as they could. They bounced revoltingly over the rocky ground.

First phase of their plan complete, the rest of the group scurried forward. The twins dragged the guards' useless bodies away from the gates. "So gross," Sarah whined, wiping her palms on her pants as she returned.

"Can we take off these awful cloaks yet?" Sam inquired with a sneer. "I'm not sure how much more of this dreadful scent I can stomach. My nostrils are burning."

Mari glowered at him, but softened when she realized he was teasing her. Nevertheless, she reminded him, "We talked about this. We've got to see what's inside first. From a distance they should help us blend in, and what we just saw confirmed it."

"If you say so," Sarah grumbled, but she was grinning.

"I am taking ten baths when we finish this," Sam said.

"Only ten?" his sister asked.

"You're right. Let's make it an even twenty."

"With rose petals to boot."

"And plenty of wine."

Mari cut off further exchanges with a hiss. "Time to split up. Reassemble here in an hour. If shit goes sideways, well, you know the signal: scream."

And so they stepped across the threshold.

They were immediately plunged into darkness with not a single torch lining the walls. Brae, who had held her aura strictly in check throughout their approach, allowed herself to emit the tiniest glow. Nevertheless, it took them a few moments for their eyes to adjust, and, once they confirmed they were alone, they risked lighting two small lanterns.

Axes and spears, some new and some corroded by age, lined the walls of the antechamber. Three passageways opened at the far end. Mari, Derek, and Killer took one lantern and moved toward the central passage, which they believed led to a set of spiraling stairs that would take them to the upper level. A few paces down the hallway proved it. Gren, Sam, Frostbite, and Wendy tiptoed toward the hallway on the left, which should, according to their rudimentary layout, allow them to explore the chambers on the ground level. Led by Ruv with their steps lit by Brae's soft glow, the final group entered the third hallway, which took them to another staircase that spiraled down to the dungeons.

As they reached the bottom of the staircase, Ruv muttered, "Lucky for us, this place appears to be not too heavily guarded."

"Unlucky for us, we got the shit detail," Sarah returned. "Literally. These dungeons reek."

Ruv's forehead crinkled in a frown as they cautiously turned the corner to find a row of barred cells devoid of any goblins. "It's strange, though. You'd think they'd at least have one guard posted down here."

"Perhaps they assume since the prisoners are already locked up, they're not a threat," Sarah proposed, trailing a finger along the wall. When she withdrew her hand, a grey smudge coated her fingertip. She grimaced.

Ruv peered inside the first cell. Apart from a pile of dust and old bones, it stood empty. "Or perhaps there's no one down here after all." Then, he heard a small noise, just the softest rustle, at the far end of the corridor. He stopped in his tracks. "I guess I was wrong."

"I sense one of my cousins!" Brae gasped as she raced down the hallway past cell after cell without a glance.

"Here," came the faint reply.

Brae stopped outside the final cell on the left. Clutching the bars with both hands, she sunk to her knees. "Oh, my poor cousin," she murmured, her eyes searching the dark cell for a trace of another leshii's glow. "What did those monsters do to you?" A mess of twigs and dead leaves, crumbling on top a mound of dust, stood in one corner of the cell. In the debris she recognized the remnants of leshii past, in death reduced to the litter of the forest that had once sustained them.

In the other corner huddled a pale figure, her tunic in tatters, her hair a limp knot of faded red. The vines at her waist were brittle and brown. "Water," she coughed, scrambling toward Brae's light.

Micaleth stepped forward. "Hold out your hands," he instructed. When she obliged, he closed his eyes, and her hands slowly filled with water drawn and purified from the dank air of the dungeons. After she had drained her cupped hands, he refilled them, and she drank again.

"There you go, cousin," Brae said softly. "We'll get you out of here. You'll be just fine." She stood and motioned Ruv to follow her as she retreated toward the center of the corridor. "She's dangerously close to the edge," Brae whispered. "We need to return her to her roots as soon as possible. I don't know if she'd survive the whole journey—all that way—but we have to try."

"Of course," he whispered back. "Is there anything we can do to give her a fighting chance?"

"More water. Sunlight." Her white face twisted in sympathetic pain. "We get her outside, she might be able to speak almost normally. For a time, at least. She's fading fast. It may be too late even now."

Ruv pursed his lips, studying her. "Would that happen to you, too, if you spent too long away from your roots?" he asked gently.

"Eventually, yes." She returned to the other leshii's cell. "How long have you been down here?"

"I don't...know..."

Sarah's hushed voice interrupted their conversation. She stood outside one of the cells on the right that they had ignored in their haste to locate the leshii. "Found that giant lizard we were curious about."

Brae remained slumped on the floor outside her cousin's cell, quietly trying to draw answers from her, while Micaleth and Ruv joined Sarah. "Practically a newborn," Micaleth breathed. The dracor stared back at them, golden eyes wide and glossy with fear. His pale blue scales were dull with dirt and grime, and his delicate wings were folded protectively around his shivering body. "He can't be more than a few years old."

"Can they fly at that age?" Sarah asked. "Breathe fire?"

"They can't even speak. I'd be surprised if he were even properly weaned."

Ruv glanced from the dracor to the leshii. "Poor things. Sarah, think you can pick these locks?"

"Already tried. These are beyond me."

"So many bones," Brae murmured, voice thick. "Cousin, who else was down here with you?"

"Other leshii," she coughed. "Faded before I arrived, but there are traces of many." Her words came slow, strained. Micaleth refilled her cupped hands once more. "Talk of others," she continued, thirst temporarily slaked, "but I never saw."

"I'm so sorry, I shouldn't keep making you speak," Brae said. "You need to conserve your strength. I'm Brae, and this is Ruv, Sarah, and Micaleth. We have more friends here in the fortress, too. We'll get you out."

The imprisoned leshii's face cracked into what might have been a smile. "Brae? I know you," she managed before being racked with coughs. "I voted on the council to have you sacrificed."

Brae affected a warm smile. "As you can see, I escaped." She reached a hand through the bars and laid it on the other leshii's arm. "Soon I'll help you do the same."

"My name is Faro," she choked out before collapsing in a faint.

"She ok?" Sarah whispered.

"She's not remotely ok," Brae snapped. "But she's not dead yet. If we can get her outside before morning, she just might make it after all. But we need those keys!"

Sarah nodded and, to the extent that she could manage through images and impressions, passed what they witnessed to her brother. "I think I got through to him," she said at length. "At least partially, anyway."

"Right," Ruv replied. "Come on. These two aren't going anywhere, and we should keep looking around, maybe find the keys ourselves."

"I can't abandon her!" Brae cried.

Ruv took her hand and drew her to her feet. "We'll come back. We won't leave without her, but we also can't leave you hear alone."

With a lingering backward glance, she followed.

Gren's team waited at a turn in the hallway with their backs pressed against the wall. They had already looked through three rooms, two of which stood empty except for more stockpiled weapons and armor in suboptimal condition. The middle room, on the other hand, had housed a jumble of inanimate goblins, all slumped together as if their brains (or at least whatever they possessed in place of brains, Gren suggested with a bitter laugh) had ceased functioning at the same moment. Unwilling to test whether they were truly dead or just sleeping, they quickly retreated from the room and bolted the door.

Sam dropped to his knees to peek around the next corner, and when he gave the all clear, they snuck into the hall. As they did so, a strong odor wafted over them. "Did we somehow end up near the dungeons?" Sam asked, his words muffled by the fabric he yanked over his nose.

Unfortunately, the fabric he had casually grabbed to cover his face came from the goblin cloak he wore, and so he promptly released it. "Bloody hell, that's bad."

Gren shook his head. "Entrance to that was at the other end."

"I know that smell," Frostbite whispered, pushing his way toward the front of the group. "It's the smell of cow filth and stale hay. The Old Farm."

"Cows? Here?" Gren echoed as he swiveled his head around to check their rear.

"This is why my sister and I prefer cities. No livestock, no smell."

"Just pollution, then, huh?" Gren quipped. He then dipped his brow in acquiescence to Frostbite, who had gestured toward a barred door at the far end of the corridor. They saw no other rooms in the short hall. "Couldn't hurt to get an idea of their food stores. If they're keeping cattle, I bet they've got some other things, too."

Wendy, peering around Gren's shoulder, said, "I see a bit of a light ahead from under that door. Sun couldn't be rising already, could it?"

Gren turned her a ponderous look. "Having once walked through a wizard's cottage, I can say with confidence that time tricks aren't completely out of the realm of possibility." He looked back toward the door and curled his fingers around one of the iron bars that reinforced the heavy wood. "But I don't think that's the dawn," he breathed. "I recognize that glow."

"As do I," Frostbite sighed. He swallowed and shared a glance with Gren.

"But it couldn't be, could it?"

"What are you two mumbling about?" Sam cut in. "What the bleeding hell kind of cattle do you think we'll find behind those bars?"

Gren ignored him. "I thought only Veles raises them?"

Frostbite, finally unbolting and shoving open the door, declared quietly, "And yet, here they are."

Sure enough, the Old Farmer's golden cattle greeted them with soft lows. Another set of iron bars stood on the opposite side of the door, preventing the cattle from trampling through the opening. They were crowded so closely that none could shuffle from side to side without bumping into a neighbor. A ceiling of old rafters and moldy thatch hid the sky, and the only ventilation was provided by narrow windows on either side of the stable.

Reaching a hand through the iron to stroke one of the cows between the eyes, Frostbite said, "Gentle creatures. They deserve to be out in a pasture, not locked up here in this fetid stable."

"They're food, not pets," Sam rejoined.

"It is nighttime, though," Gren said with a shrug. "Maybe they're just spending it indoors."

"No," Frostbite asserted, voice fierce as he continued stroking. "See how dull their eyes are? And their glow is faint as well. These beauties haven't seen the sun for weeks, let alone grazed on fresh grass."

Sam arched an eyebrow. "For a predator with your particular reputation, you sure have a soft spot for prey."

"Cattle are not prey," he growled. "They are herd animals." Softly, he added, "My earliest memories are from a farm. What you see now is merely respect."

"Wait up," Sam ordered as he held up a finger. "My sister is trying to tell me something."

Frostbite stepped aside to let Wendy approach the cows. "There's a good coo," she murmured, "stay calm, sweet lass. Or maybe lad...both could have horns."

"Yes," Frostbite replied, his expression softening yet further. "But this one is a cow, not a bull."

"They've found a young dragon and another leshii in the dungeons, both in bad shape. Neither will be able to help us," Sam recounted.

"But they need our help, then. And I thought you guys couldn't communicate with words?" Gren inquired, black brows furrowed.

"We can't," Sam confirmed quickly. "She showed me. It was hazy, but I still saw." He slipped past Gren to resume his position at point. "Which means she's pretty shook up about the whole thing," he added in a whisper.

Pretending not to hear the last part, Gren directed, "Alright. Time to move on. I'm gonna fill in Mari."

Mari opened the door an inch and peered through the crack. When nothing rushed to confront her, she held up her lantern. The dim light illuminated a sparse room full of catatonic goblins. She immediately backed up, closing the door as quietly as she could and motioning for Killer and Derek to retreat. "At least a dozen in there," she mouthed when they had gone a few steps.

"I guess the undead really do need their beauty sleep," Killer offered.

"Ugly bastards could stand to get a bit more of it," Derek hissed in response.

Killer narrowed his eyes at the door and tapped his chin. "Seem to be deep sleepers."

Mari chewed on her thumb while she calculated their next move. "Maybe Gren's computer reference wasn't far off. Anywho, I saw another door on the far side of the room," she mumbled. "Let's explore a little more, then if we don't find anything else, we'll just pull up our hoods and try to sneak past them." She sighed and added, "If they wake up, well, we'll fight our way back out. That's kinda what we came here to do anyway." The men nodded their accord, and they went on their way.

Mari did not need her lantern to see inside the next room they came across. The door was already cracked open, and the remnants of a fire glowed in a hearth on the wall to the left while a table in the center hosted a collection of lit candles. They heard gruff voices echoing down the hall from behind and recognized the dragging steps. They had just enough time to duck into the room and press their backs against the wall before the guards passed the open door.

After the footsteps had faded to silence, Killer poked his head outside for a moment and, finding nothing, motioned for the others to move. They were about to exit when Mari, glancing behind her on a whim, noticed another open door, which had been concealed by a thick curtain and only revealed once their movement caused the fabric to flutter aside. She tapped Killer and Derek on the shoulder, then indicated her discovery with a toss of her head. In silence they agreed to investigate.

Peeking behind the curtain, they found an even larger room with another hearth, this time stoked to a warm blaze. Sconces lined the walls, emitting the same green glow they had spied flickering in the tower and illuminating shelves lined with books, bottles of powders and potions, and assorted bones. Skulls of creatures they could not recognize stared back at them with empty eyes. But it was the far side of the room that caught and held their attention. There they discovered a tall figure in robes of black with silvery white hair flowing to his shoulders. Seeing him, Mari's team froze, but the figure gave no indication of noticing their presence. Instead, he remained hunched over a large, shallow basin supported by a table of stacked stone, his pallid, bony hands gripping either side as he muttered quietly to himself.

The basin was filled to the brim with water. Mari caught the candlelight reflected in its still surface between the gap of his arm and torso, but she could not make out his words. She felt a strange gravity dragging her toward him, toward the bowl, toward the water, but Killer grabbed her shoulder and hauled her back before she even realized that she had taken a step forward.

She shook her head as they slunk to safety behind the curtain and into the other room. "That must be the necromancer," Mari mouthed. The men shared a glance, the corners of their lips turned down in twin scowls. "I'm not sure what he was doing," she continued as they retreated toward the hallway. "Using that bowl to communicate maybe? He was saying something, but I couldn't hear what."

"Ruv could probably tell you more," Derek said as they scooted quietly along the corridor. "I've heard about *cigany* using bowls of water sometimes to tell the future, kinda like a crystal ball. Never seen it myself, though."

Mari took a deep breath. "There was something off about him," she mumbled. "I felt something weird coming from that bowl of—" She twitched and stifled a squeak as she heard Gren's voice intruding on her thoughts. No matter how often they used the fatestone link, the abrupt addition of another's internal voice remained startling. Gren recited what his and Ruv's respective groups had found. "Interesting," she replied quietly, gripping her jade pendant. "What would he possibly want with a leshii, a dragon, and a bunch of golden cows? You think the Old Farmer himself is involved?"

Veles does have a nasty rep, Gren replied, *but I can't see why he'd bother with an army of zomblins. He's a lanti. Why would he need a freaking army?*

"True. And we found the necromancer, by the way," she explained. "He was staring at some big, black bowl."

Why?

"Hell if I know." She looked back and forth at her companions, then nodded once she came to a decision. "We're going back to keep an eye on him," she asserted. "I need to learn more."

She perceived Gren's hesitation through their connection, but nevertheless, he replied, *We'll keep exploring the ground levels.*

Mari's team returned to the room in which the necromancer lurked. Derek stayed just inside the door, hiding in the shadow cast by the door itself, a naked machete concealed in the folds of his stolen cloak. Mari and Killer peeked behind the curtain to find the situation unchanged. Still the necromancer gave no sign of any awareness beyond his pool of water.

This time the gravity tugging at her was even stronger, and it was only Killer's firm grip on either arm that prevented Mari from bursting past the curtain and rushing toward the black basin that had likewise captured the necromancer's attention. Killer did his best to restrain her as the gravity grew stronger and stronger, calling her, drawing her consciousness down into the hazy visions dancing across the water's surface, the same visions captivating the necromancer.

He races to keep up with his sister. He is older, but somehow she is always stronger. He and his other brother follow her across the smoking, barren lands of Daem, from ruin to ruin, from war to war.

Always the three of them.

He hates her, but he cannot help but follow. He follows her across the veil to a forested land, rich in resources but peopled by lesser beings, slower beings, stupid beings.

They search the world for power. They find none. From ruin to ruin, from war to war. This time they bring the ruin. They bring the war.

He follows her to Aorea. They find what they seek.

Another ruin, another war.

He crawls from the ashes in the dark of midnight, the smoke clinging to his charred flesh. He crawls from the wreckage into the cover of the forest, inch by painful inch. He crawls until he sees a pair of boots blocking his path. The boots stink of dung and hay. A brown, wrinkled hand reaches out to him. He stands. His flesh heals.

His memories spin out of him. He has no control. Something is wrong. Something is different.

Someone else is there.

A dozen goblins, his goblins, his children, pour forth from the traveling circle in the Birch Forest. He stays inside the circle, watching them. A leshii, curious, comes to investigate the disturbance. They snatch her and disappear in a flash of crimson before she can scream. Another leshii is drawn by the magic. She finds nothing.

A girl stands amid rubble and smoke, black hair streaming in the wind, amber eyes vacant. She sings. She cries. Her cries wound him. He does not know why.

He knows why.

A group trudges across the desert. Humans. Why did he not see them sooner? They are coming for him. He lets them come. They will be his new children, his better children. Stronger children.

A monster lumbers across the sky, stardust trailing in its wake, dark matter clinging to its hooves. This is not a memory. What is this? Why can he not control it? Its horns are bright, too bright to look at, as bright as a sun. Its hooves come to rest on the bottom of a ravine. Its tail flicks, and the sand stirs. Someone is calling, beckoning, but it is too soon. It is still alone.

Mari jolted back to reality and stumbled into Killer as he dragged her away from the doorway. He kept dragging her until they were out in the hallway with Derek. "He was starting to turn around," Killer hissed as Mari tried to go back. "Jesus, will you stop fighting me?"

She shuddered. "I'm ok now, sorry."

"We gotta move," Derek urged. He took off in the direction they had originally been heading before they found the necromancer, and Mari and Killer shadowed him with hurried but quiet steps. They slowed when they reached a corner, rounding it cautiously. There was no sign of the guards who had passed them earlier, and they were too thankful to ponder why.

"I was in his head," Mari whispered as they hurried through the winding halls. "He knew we were coming, but now I know his plan."

They stopped at a window that overlooked a courtyard. Beyond the barred glass they spied a stunted, twisted, spindly tree, its bark blackened and shredded. Not a single leaf adorned its coiling branches, and its gangly roots cracked the dry ground. The tree grew at the heart of a ring of unnaturally tall mushrooms. Wrinkled caps of scarlet crowned withered, shriveled stalks. Nine stones, crusted over with dusky moss, encircled the mushrooms.

"Is that what I think it is?" breathed Derek.

"A circle," said Killer. "Here."

"A dead circle, looks like," muttered Mari. "I am liking this less and less."

On the other side of the courtyard reared the tower they had seen from outside the fortress. Another window drew Mari's eyes upward, and she saw a figure silhouetted in the light. The figure looked back at her with amber eyes.

She recognized the girl from the vision, the dancing, crying girl amid the smoke and chaos.

"New plan," she stated.

Mari filled in Gren while her team hurried down the next hallway, which led to the stairs that would in turn lead them to the tower. Gren told her that his group had one corridor left to explore on the ground level, and then they intended to meet back up with Ruv's group and follow Mari to the tower. She anxiously agreed.

"We've gotta be almost there by now," Derek panted as they rounded another turn. "One, two flights at most."

"My money's on two," Killer quipped.

"What do you have to wager?"

"Same as you, I imagine."

"So nothing, then."

Mari shushed them. "I think I hear voices at the top," she exhaled. "Sounds like there's two or maybe three."

They slowed for the final ascension, keeping close to the wall. When his head was in line with the last step, Derek took a peek around the corner. "We're in luck," he mouthed, and he held up two fingers. He motioned for Killer to join him, and they slowly withdrew their machetes.

Mari made to draw her sword as well, but Killer shook his head. "No need," he said. "We got this."

"Practically an art at this point," Derek whispered in her other ear as he slunk past.

Mari rolled her eyes and sighed. "I'll keep watch."

The two men leapt from the stairwell and decapitated the goblins before they could even sound an alarm. Without a fire in which to dispose of the heads, they settled for slicing them down the center so the mouths—which kept trying to summon their comrades regardless of the futility of speaking without breath—would at least stop hissing at them. They kicked the bodies out of the way while Mari rapped on the door.

When a returning knock was the only response, Mari furrowed her brows. Then, noticing that the door was locked from the outside, she slid open the bolt and knocked again. This time the door opened slowly, and she found herself face to face with the girl from the vision.

"It's ok," she said. "We're friends. You're the girl who was taken from that village up north, right? Necria? Is that your name?" The girl nodded but gave no other response. "You're safe now," Mari continued.

"Well, almost safe," Derek amended with an incongruously merry smirk. "There's still a necromancer and his henchman running about."

Mari glared at him, then turned her attention back to the waif hesitating in the door jam. "Well, safer, yes. We're here to help. I'm Mari. This is Derek and, uh, Killer. Don't worry, he's nice. The name's ironic. Anyway, we'll get you out of here and away from this awful place, but some information could help us do that. That traveling circle in the courtyard—you know if it works?" Necria shrugged her shoulders, but still she offered no verbal response. "Ok, then about your captor himself. I know things are, er, complicated, but does he have any weaknesses or anything that you know of?" When she was met with nothing but a blank stare, Mari cursed under her breath.

Derek, growing more serious, stepped forward and adopted the face he often used as Buddy's beta to calm the younger members of the pack. "You don't need to be scared of us. We really are friends." In an aside to Killer, he ordered, "Smile!"

Killer bared his teeth in an awkward grin.

"I should have divided the groups differently," Mari moaned. She studied Necria's blank face, the shadowed golden eyes, the translucent skin that had once been the color of ripe acorns. "Look, Necria—am I saying that right?—Great. I mean, do you want to come with us? I know you don't know us, but it's not a trick, I promise. We're here to fix things. Part of that is freeing the captives held here, you included," she rambled. No change in emotion crossed Necria's face. "Ok, we're gonna go now to take care of the necromancer himself, and then we'll come back for you. You don't need to be afraid anymore. Just wait here." Necria finally gave her a tight nod in response, and Mari sighed in relief. "Alright. As soon as we defeat this guy, we'll be back."

However, Necria's only answer was to slam the door.

"And how is it you plan on defeating me?" a flat voice came from behind them.

They whipped around to find the necromancer standing not one foot away, black eyes calm and hands folded in front of his waist. He nodded once, and a dozen goblins spilled out of the stairwell. Mari spat at his feet. "You'll find out soon enough," she avowed. She held his eyes, jaw set firm, while Derek and Killer pressed close and angled their shoulders in front of her. However, they soon discovered they could not move further.

Their limbs had frozen in place, bound under the necromancer's mocking gaze.

"Seize them," he commanded without taking his eyes off Mari. A small smile played across his lips. "I've let these little games go on long enough. Lock them in the dungeon and find the rest." As his minions restrained their wrists and stripped their weapons—all but Mari's sword and dagger, which, bound by their own magic, could not be removed from her side by another's hand—his smile grew. "Think I didn't sense you poking about my memories and forcing your visions upon me?" he scoffed. "I hope you enjoyed your little intrusion."

Mari's eyes narrowed, but she otherwise kept her expression in check. "You're going down, necromancer, no matter what you do to me. Just like your sister."

He backhanded her hard across the mouth; a drop of blood trickled down her chin. He wiped his thumb over the red and brought it to his lips, leering. "What could you possibly know of Antiln?" he scoffed. "She's been useless for millennia, and I'm far more powerful now than she ever was."

"Ah," Mari snickered, "but unlike her, you're mortal."

He sucked the remainder of Mari's blood off his thumb. "Not as mortal as you."

As the goblins dragged them away, Mari shouted, "Then why are you so afraid, huh? I was in your mind! You can't hide your fear from me!"

"Gag her, too. I'll deal with that tongue of hers later."

Laria planted herself before the loom, willing the threads to untangle. At length they obeyed, weaving into a new pattern and revealing an image she thought might finally assuage her doubts. She hoped it would show her, if not the present, then the future. A possible future. Anything at all that would allow her the faintest glimmer of hope that all would be well, that her friends would return to her whole and sound.

She was wrong.

The woven filaments on the Loom depicted a scene she had watched before. The location of the scene would change from vision to vision, but the action remained the same. Gren wandering alone with his guitar, no bag, no backpack, not so much as a spare jacket, just a wooden instrument with broken strings. Gren with an unkempt beard. Gren haggard, thin, too thin, with shadows beneath lifeless eyes.

The image flickered, faded, and changed. Now she saw Mari crying uncontrollably, eyes and nose streaming, beating Ruv's chest with her fists while he tries to comfort her, though all the while his own tears flow. Another flicker, another change, and now she saw Gren ripping the fatestone from his neck and dropping it into a sea. He turns his back on the waves.

She could see Mari. She could see Gren. She could see one or the other of them with Ruv, or one of the twins, or Wendy. Sometimes Brae. But in every vision of the future she called to the loom, she never saw Mari and Gren in the same frame.

She turned away from the loom, blinking back the tears that threatened to spill down her own cheeks. She took a deep breath. In, out. In, out, and repeat. When she felt calmer, she faced the Loom. Perhaps this time it would show her something other than misery.

Laria set a hand on either bar of the frame and squeezed her eyes shut. She focused on her breathing until there was no thought in her brain but the steady rise and fall of her own chest. She let herself fall into a meditative trance, then she pulled a ray of hope from her core. Show Mari, she begged silently. Show Mari and Gren.

Show the one chance.

She opened her eyes. The Loom portrayed an ancient, tangled wood. The trees clustered close together, with black moss draping their branches and the shadows between them thick and heavy. A girl, perhaps five or six years old, sat cross legged on a flat stone. Her hair was a crown of mahogany curls, coiled tightly about her round, tanned face and pointed fae chin. Mari's chin. Her eyes were shut, the lashes dark and long, and her expression held a preternatural calm. A pool spread before her with not so much as a ripple disturbing the mirrored surface.

It must be her past, Laria thought. Disappointed, she tried to dismiss the image and look elsewhere, somewhere in Faerie, perhaps, but the image clung stubbornly in place. Whatever glimpse into Mari's childhood the vision offered, the Loom insisted Laria see it.

Behind the girl one of the shadows stirred. "You are being watched," the shadow said in a low, husky voice. Laria willed the trees to part so she could see who was speaking, but she could no more control the trees in the image than she could control the image itself.

"I know," said the girl. She did not turn to look at the shadow but remained motionless.

The shadow moved, yet Laria still could not see who it was. "Good. What else do you know?"

A line came between the girl's brows, a strange sight on one so young. "The watcher is not of this time," she asserted. Her voice was so much like Mari's. It had to be Mari. "Not of this world."

"Where is the watcher from?"

"The second world. The world of men."

"Not for much longer," the shadow commented quietly. "What else?"

"I—I don't know," the girl admitted, a trace of a whine in her voice, revealing that she was, in fact, a young child and not a miniature adult. She turned around to face the woods where the shadow lurked.

"I will give you no answers," the shadow stated as the girl turned back to the pool, eyes squeezed shut once more. "Look inward. See beyond. Your enemies will be many, my child," the shadow continued. "You must learn to see them."

"This isn't an enemy," the girl insisted.

The shadow did not immediately respond, but when the response came, it was in an even lower tone. "Why do you think so?"

The line between the girl's brows deepened, but then suddenly, her face relaxed. A small smile played across her lips. "The watcher is kind. A friend," she answered with conviction.

"Do you know, now, who is the watcher?"

The girl opened her eyes and looked upward, as if seeing Laria straight through the Loom. "The Summoner," the girl declared.

Laria shuddered and pulled away from the frame. The threads, no longer holding her attention, faded to a swirling pattern of blues and purples, stars in a foreign sky. The vision left her unsettled. She wanted Hal.

She found him, arms laden with split logs, walking toward the bones of the forge Svarog was helping him build. "I saw Mari's past," she announced when she was close enough for him to hear. "I was looking for her future, but I must have seen her past instead."

"Yeah? Nice," Hal said, dropping the sticks on top of the pile. He clapped the dust off his hands. "Was I there?"

"No, she was very young. It would have been before she moved to Virginia," Laria explained.

Hal wiped a wrist across his sweaty forehead. "Ah, ok. What was she up to? I've always wondered about little Romani Mari." He grinned. "She never really told me or Gren much about it. Then again, she was only like, seven when she left."

"She was meditating, I think," Laria said with a slight frown. "Sitting on a rock in the woods."

Hal snorted a laugh, then the laugh turned into a guffaw. When he could breathe again, he said, "I have never in my life seen—or heard of—Mari sitting still long enough to meditate, except maybe when she's asleep, and I don't think that counts. Are you sure it was her?"

"It had to be. The girl looked exactly like her!"

Though Laria's hands were on her hips, Hal noted a trace of doubt in her pursed lips and furrowed brow. "I feel like there's a 'but' coming," he prompted softly.

Laria took a deep breath and searched Hal's face. "What color are Mari's eyes?" she asked in a whisper.

"Green," he replied automatically. "Or maybe grey. I dunno. But light, I remember that." He shrugged sheepishly. "This is definitely something I should know, hold on." He paused, looked thoughtful for a moment, and then his face lit up in memory as a wry smile flashed across his face. "Yeah, they're definitely green. I remember listening to Gren ramble on and on about how they remind him of 'the end of summer, right before the leaves turn gold,' blah blah blah. Nauseating."

Laria's shoulders drooped. "Then it can't have been Mari. This girl's eyes were very dark. It was weird. She stared right at me, like she could see me. She even named me." She started to head back to the cottage where the Loom awaited her attention, but then stopped, the spark of an idea working its way through her thoughts. "I thought I got it wrong," she said slowly as Hal stared at her expectantly, "but what if I actually did see her future?"

"Gren has dark eyes," he breathed.

"That should teach you," one of the goblins taunted as they tossed Mari, Derek, and Killer into the cell across from Faro. The leshii, conscious once more, gripped the bars and watched. "Sneaking around our castle."

"Ha! The master will take care of you soon enough, filthy shapeshifter," another said as he bolted and locked the cell door. "Yes, we know who you are. Our army knows all about the little beasts that got away." His decrepit face twisted into a mockery of a smile. "Well, you won't escape so easily this time." He cackled and stormed off, taking the keys and most of the other goblins with him. Only two remained behind to guard the prisoners.

Able to move again now that they were out of the necromancer's sight, Derek and Killer slipped out of their bonds. Mari, on the other hand, seemed too distracted to move, so the two men shared a concerned glance. Derek gently removed her gag and wiped the remaining blood off her cheek. "You ok?"

"I'm fine," she growled, at last wiggling out of the ties around her wrists. Then, after sucking in a deep breath to calm herself, she added, "I was able to fill in the others while they took us here. Ruv's team should show up soon. Gren said they didn't go far."

It turned out they did not have long to wait. Shortly thereafter Sarah stepped out of the shadows with a long knife in hand. "Only two?" she purred.

The first guard raised his own knife, the blade better preserved than most they had seen, but he was not fast enough to dodge Sarah's strike. The second tried to flee, but Ruv tripped him with a swing of his stave. "And where do you think you're going?"

Sarah leapt on top of Ruv's felled quarry and finished the job with relish.

The brief battle thus concluded, Mari said, "Their leader took the keys."

"We saw," Ruv replied. "Brae and Micaleth are tailing him now."

"And I'm about to help," Sarah added as she faded back into the shadows.

Ruv knelt outside their cell. "So, met the necromancer himself, did you?"

"Worse," Mari said with a grimace. "Been inside the dude's brain."

"And how was that?"

"Dreadful."

Killer gave his former alpha a rueful smile. "I thought I'd never see the view from this side of the bars again. Isn't that what you promised me?"

Ruv's hazel eyes moistened as he returned the look. "I believe it was, my friend. But just like last time, you won't be there for long."

Killer nodded solemnly. "I know."

Less than ten minutes passed before Brae, Micaleth, and Sarah returned with the keys as well as a fresh layer of viscera. Even Micaleth's white coat was stained with ooze and rot. Sarah tossed the key ring to Ruv, who began trying key after key in the lock. "Not that one, ugh...not that one either...how many damn keys are on this stupid ring?" He jiggled several more before one clicked.

Gratefully they fled the cell. "We should try to go back to that tower," Mari stressed. "Gren's group should be there soon, too, though I told them to be more careful since it looks like our new friends are finally awake. Hopefully they get more out of Necria than we did. I think she's the key to all this."

"Speaking of keys," Ruv groused as he fumbled with the lock to Faro's cell, "would it have killed them to label these things?" He finally managed to open it, and Derek and Brae rushed in to help the leshii stand. Too weak to walk on her own, she smiled wanly as Micaleth kneeled to let her mount. Brae skipped up behind her to keep the wilted leshii upright.

Mari placed a light hand against Micaleth's neck. "There's some kind of traveling circle in the courtyard," she told him. "I want you to take them both back to the Birch Forest immediately. We'll take care of everything else, then Gren can sing us through."

Micaleth started. "There is a circle here? How?"

She shrugged. "I don't know for sure, but I think the necromancer must have planted it."

His large nostrils flared. "We should wait for you. The Spinner—"

"We can do this," Mari interjected. "You have to get that leshii out of here now. And Brae, you have to help her find her roots." She watched as Micaleth nodded his acquiescence and trotted toward the dungeon stairs. "Now we just gotta figure out what to do about a baby dragon. He seems too scared still to follow Micaleth."

"He's awful cute for a scaly fellow," Sarah commented.

"Can't we just take him back with us when we leave?" Derek inquired. "Maybe he'll warm up to us by then."

"Of course we will," Mari said, "but I meant now. We still have to defeat that necromancer asshole—who any minute will figure out his zombie-goblins make horrendous guards—and—"

"So don't unlock the dragon's cell, is what you're saying," Ruv cut in, withdrawing the key he had been fumbling with and stowing the ring in a pocket.

Mari nodded. "He'll be safe enough here for the time being. I'm going to get in touch with—"

Sarah's sharp intake of breath interrupted her. "Sam!" she gasped as she clutched at her heart, her violet eyes wide with horror. "He's gone!" She cast one glance around their small group then bolted.

Mari cursed, fingers laced around her jade crescent. She turned a stunned face to Ruv. Her breath caught. "Gren is, too," she choked. "The connection just broke."

CHAPTER TWELVE
None of the stories the elders tell

"Well, shit," Gren mumbled as he rounded a corner to find a slew of previously catatonic goblins spilling out of a room, rusted weapons at the ready.

Sam withdrew two of his knives and launched himself at the gaggle. Gren and Frostbite dove into the fray behind him, and Wendy kept her distance, though she gripped Sarah's gifted knife tight. In such narrow quarters, dispatching their enemies was more complicated than in the open field when they had room to maneuver and could outpace the limping creatures, even though those in less decrepit condition could move nearly as quickly as they. Nevertheless, they would have succeeded in the endeavor if not for the necromancer's interference.

Summoned from his scrying chamber by the clamor in the hallway, Dimeldor seized an unsuspecting Wendy by the throat. Her knife, unused, clattered to the floor. "If you wish your friend to live," the necromancer stated calmly, "you best cease your struggles."

Frostbite growled low in his throat. He clutched the head of one unlucky goblin in both hands, and in less than a second he wrenched its head from its shoulders.

Congealed fluids spattered everywhere, flecking the stone walls as well as his companions in dripping black. Without a thought Frostbite rushed toward Dimeldor, but a throttled squeak from Wendy as the necromancer tightened his hold halted the big man in his tracks.

Gren and Sam stowed their respective weapons. The surviving goblins moved in and bound their wrists behind them. Jaw set hard, Gren snapped, "What do you want?"

"Only your compliance, for now," the necromancer replied with a half-smile. "Follow me."

He released his grip on Wendy, but in place of his hand, a crimson glow encircled her neck. A rope of the same glowing red bound her to him, and so she stumbled helplessly in his wake as he strode past the curtain into his scrying chambers. Coming to a stop in the center of the room, he gestured for his captives to sit along the wall. "Make yourselves comfortable. Well, as comfortable as you can," he instructed. "You must conserve your strength if you are to survive the process."

"What process?" Sam echoed with a scowl. He writhed his hands behind him, but the knots held.

"You'll see," was Dimeldor's only reply. He dipped his head at his henchman, and they took up positions on the other side of the curtain, leaving them alone.

The necromancer casually raised his right hand, palm up, and the scarlet light around Wendy's neck spread until it enclosed her entire body. He raised his other hand, and she began to hover. Toes skimming a few inches above the floor, Wendy tried to wriggle out of her ethereal cage to no avail. The necromancer sniggered at her efforts, but his laugh soon gave way to a grimace. The light binding Wendy's limbs wavered and began to fade.

"Running out of juice, are you?" Gren goaded.

Dimeldor pierced him with a glare, commenting, "You're as mouthy as your little friend. You will learn better, even as she did." Smoothing his features to impassivity, he stepped gingerly to one of the shelves lining the room. He withdrew a faceted turquoise gem the size of his palm. Squeezing the gem until the facets cut into his skin, he leveled his gaze at Wendy, and the confining glow strengthened once more. "We'll start with the little one," he announced. "Cerridwen, isn't it? No, you prefer Wendy, I believe." At the sight of Wendy's widened eyes, he added, "Yes, the great tawny owl. I know all about you. I have been watching you since you met with that unfortunate straggler. Well, unfortunate for him. It was certainly fortunate for me."

The men twisted their fingers and rolled their wrists, trying to loosen their bonds without betraying the movement while the necromancer's attention was focused on Wendy. Gren shared a pointed glance with Sam and Frostbite, and the two men nodded back at him, a nearly imperceptible gesture. "So you knew we were coming for a while now, then?" Gren prompted in an effort to stall until the rest of their friends could escape the dungeon and join them. Based on what Mari had told him through the link, he assumed they must be close. "How? And why?"

"What, do you expect me to reveal my whole plan to you, is that it?" Dimeldor sneered, rounding on him.

"That's how it happens in the movies," Gren quipped with a shrug. The movement strained his shoulders but allowed him to stretch the ropes around his wrists a touch looser. "Sure, you've been dropping hints, but now's the part where the villain—that would be you, if you didn't know—tells the heroes—that would be us, obviously—why he did what he did, what he's doing next, blah blah blah. I'm just trying to help you fulfil your role, my dude, so the audience knows what's going on."

The necromancer narrowed his black eyes at the remark, but otherwise his expression did not change. Instead, he snapped his fingers, and six goblins answered the summons. Dimeldor instructed them to tighten the ropes on his captives' wrists. As an afterthought, he added, "And bind their ankles, while you're at it."

When the goblins were two paces away, the three men leapt to their feet and barreled into them. Gren and Sam managed to slip out of their bonds in the process, but Frostbite's bulk left him not quite flexible enough to succeed. Thus, while the other two drew their knives and dashed for the necromancer, Frostbite thrashed and headbutted his way through the swarm.

Dimeldor roared and flung the turquoise crystal at the approaching men. Wendy loosed a scream, but it was cut short when the crystal exploded into a fine blue mist, engulfing them all. The humans coughed and choked, unable to breathe, unable to see. Frostbite fell to his knees, gasping for air but taking in none. Blinded, Gren and Sam stumbled onward, but each threw the other off balance. They found themselves gasping on the floor next to Frostbite as the crystalline dust scored their lungs.

The necromancer's sharp laugh cut through the haze, and soon thereafter the dust cleared. The men could breathe again, though the clean air stung the microtears throughout their respiratory systems. Frostbite rolled onto his side only to be pinned down before he could get his bearings. Goblins pressed him back to the floor, using their collective weight to hold him down while they wound thick rope around his ankles and tied his ankles to the bindings that secured his wrists. Although the big man continued to struggle, his efforts proved futile. Grunting, the goblins shoved him back toward the wall.

While the goblins were occupied keeping Frostbite under control, Gren and Sam struggled to their feet. They made to rush Dimeldor again, but he moved faster. Dimeldor whipped his arm forward, and a streak of black lightning burst from his extended fingers. The force of the blow propelled Gren and Sam backward. Their shocked cries ended abruptly with the crunch of bone shattering against granite.

"Pity," Dimeldor remarked as they slumped to the floor in a heap next to Frostbite, who shuddered and breathed heavily through his nose. "They would have made excellent additions to my army." The necromancer sauntered over to the fallen men, and a flash of blue at Gren's collar caught his eye. He knelt, reaching a pale finger toward Gren's sapphire star. His face lit up as he recognized the spark of magic in the fatestone, and he murmured, "Now that would certainly help replenish what this little skirmish has cost me."

Frostbite grunted a hollow laugh. "So Gren was right. You are running out of power."

"I have power enough for this," the necromancer hissed. He yanked on Gren's fatestone, and the delicate silver chain gave way, releasing the sapphire star to its new master. Dimeldor gave one last look at his fallen enemies, then released a sigh and returned his attention to the imprisoned Wendy. "Ah, well. With them gone, you'll just have to do for now. Surely if you survive the transformation, the rest will."

Suppressed sobs shook her chest as Wendy eyed the fresh smear of red running down the wall.

Drawn by her final sense of her twin before the link severed, Sarah dashed up the stairs and through the halls to the scrying room. A handful of goblins guarded the door to the outer chamber. Sarah and Mari cut straight through, sliding under and between them, the guards' weapons too slow to hinder the women's advance. Ruv, Derek, and Killer cleaned up the grim aftermath.

They burst beyond the curtain to find Frostbite shuddering and bound like livestock for slaughter, but at least conscious. His eyes were cemented on Wendy, whom the necromancer held immobile in a cocoon of light that shifted between indigo and lime and crimson. Only her head remained exposed. Sam and Gren, backs slumped together and mouths slack, lay unmoving on the floor.

The necromancer looked over his shoulder as Sarah sprinted toward him. He aimed a bolt of crackling violet at her, but she rolled out of the way and skidded to a halt behind her brother's body. Instead, the bolt caught the empty sheath of Mari's sword and knocked her aside. She tumbled into Ruv and Derek, and the three of them landed on top of Frostbite in a jumble.

Sarah, crouched between Sam and Gren with a finger pressed against either man's wrist, heaved a sigh of relief. "There's a pulse," she cried. "Faint, but there."

The necromancer laughed as Killer helped his tumbled comrades to their feet. He kept laughing as the glowing cocoon around Wendy constricted, and she screamed. "Leave her alone!" Mari thundered, leveling her sword at him. "Try me instead!"

"Why, afraid the owl might get hurt?" He snapped his fingers, and Wendy's already broken arm twisted behind her, more bones splintering in a stomach-churning crack. She screamed again before mercifully passing out.

Stirred to semi-consciousness by the force of Wendy's cry, Sam let out a soft moan. Sarah cradled his head on her lap, stroking his bloodied hair. "You bastard," she muttered over and over. "You bastard."

Dimeldor surveyed the humans arrayed around him, his lips twisted in a cruel smile. "I see you have realized the futility of your efforts. Best just stand there and do as you're told, for as much as I am enjoying playing with you miserable—" A blinding flash interrupted his speech by destroying the window, fragments of glass scattering at his feet and lacerating the hem of his robes. His smile vanished. "What's this?"

"That," said Ruv, leaning against his staff, "would be a grumpy nietheran and two leshii."

"Really, the security here's a joke," Mari added. "You should have used smarter minions."

The cruel smile returned. "Why, precisely, do you think I allowed you to get this close?"

Mari, determined to distract him while Sarah tried to coax her brother and Gren back to consciousness, commented, "For a four thousand-and-whatever-year-old demon sorcerer, you sure can be dense."

"I'm no more demon than you are, as you well know," he seethed. "My world was far more advanced millennia ago than yours will ever be."

Sarah, unable to withhold her tongue, thundered, "Then why the bloody hell did you leave?"

"Ah, but what is any world compared to this bright, shining Aorea?" He swept his arms around him. "Magic flowing everywhere, woven into the land itself, ripe for the taking. Magic coursing through such simple objects as mirrors and books and..." He paused to twirl the stolen fatestone in his fingers. The torchlight caught the facets, painting the walls in a shimmering dance, as he continued, "...Stones. I just had to learn to see it the way my sister could. And oh, the things I've seen!" There was another flash of light from outside, weaker than the last, and he strode to the shattered window. Peering over the ledge, he observed, "It would appear your nietheran is not as adept at operating circles as you thought."

Mari's brow crinkled. "What?" she bit.

Dimeldor parted his thin lips to retort, but then his eyes darted to the curtain. The humans followed his gaze to find Necria hovering there in a gown of lavender silk. The necromancer stood rooted to the floor as she approached him, his eyes following her every gliding step. "Darling, you shouldn't be here. It's not safe," he murmured. She stopped in front of him. "You should go back to your room," he added gently, caressing her cheek. "How did you even get out? Those worthless idiots must have forgotten the lock. But you should return. I will come get you once I have finished dealing with these intruders."

In the split second of his distraction, Mari made eye contact with Derek and gave a tight nod toward the window, mouthing, "Go."

Derek grabbed Killer, and the two fled the room.

All the while Dimeldor's attention lingered on Necria. As Mari took a step toward him, raising her sword, he acknowledged her presence at last. But with his back turned on Necria, he did not notice the maiden reach into her bodice to retrieve something; what it was, no one saw.

Dimeldor kept his attention fixed on Mari for no more than a few seconds, for Necria twined the fingers of one hand into his hair and drew him toward her. At first he tried to wrench away, but soon he succumbed to her lips against his. As the kiss deepened, she raised her other hand, and silver flashed in the torchlight. Necria thrust the knife into his chest, the point slipping between two ribs to pierce a lung.

Shocked, Dimeldor stumbled backward, his finger's fluttering toward the hand that still held the knife. His haughty expression melted to grief. "Why?" he breathed. Necria dropped her arm, and he gritted his teeth while he extracted the blade. The air rushed out of the collapsing lung with a hiss.

"You should have just let her choose," Mari whispered. "She would have chosen you." Mari bobbed her head to Ruv, and he knelt by Frostbite to untie his restraints. Once released, Frostbite rolled his shoulders, cracked his neck, and rubbed his wrists appreciatively as he took to his feet. Ruv then moved to Gren, who was blinking slowly and massaging his own temples, eyes unfocused. As the necromancer's life began to wane, the cocoon of light encasing and supporting Wendy winked out, causing her to drop to the floor. Frostbite was able to break her fall just in time. He set about trying to set the freshly broken bones while she remained unconscious.

Dimeldor braced himself against the wall, but he could not prevent his knees from crumpling beneath him. Necria caught him as he fell and lowered him gently, stroking his forehead with one hand as the other came to rest over his heart. A faint purple glow surrounded them both, wavering in time with the necromancer's weakening pulse. He laid a hand on top of Necria's. "Why?" he repeated, his words wet as a wash of black bubbled up from his throat.

"It's nearly finished," Mari said, sheathing her sword.

The necromancer gurgled a laugh. "Not quite." With great effort he sat up and propped himself on his elbows, leaning against the wall for more support. Necria stayed by his side, her arm now draped about his shoulders. Cold tears ran down her cheeks and spattered Dimeldor's face where they mingled with his.

Mari felt the tiniest pull, a thread tugging at her core, that made her suddenly desire to take a step toward the pair. The same kind of pull that had drawn her into his visions in the scrying bowl, or perhaps, she thought, drew him into hers as he said. Breath by breath, she felt the thread draining her energy. Her eyes grew wide, and she addressed her friends, "We gotta get everyone out of here! I think he's using us to heal himself."

Sarah forced her brother to his feet. Shoving her shoulder under his armpit, she dragged him away, thankful that her own slight build found a mirror in his. With Frostbite's aid, Ruv managed to get Gren upright, but in doing so they realized his left ankle had been broken. The pain of putting his weight on the useless foot shocked him into full consciousness. Gren subsequently released a flood of curses as he hobbled along, leaning heavily on Ruv. Frostbite scooped Wendy up in his arms, cradling her against his chest with her arm pinned tight.

Unburdened in comparison, Mari led the charge to the courtyard. Her sword found little use on the way. The goblins they encountered roved in a state of chaos, as liable to attack each other as her. Dismembered corpses littered the hallway. It seemed as the necromancer's power lessened, so did his control over his feral minions.

They found Micaleth, pearlescent horn stained a dark gray, standing within the ring of withered mushrooms. Brae and Faro crouched behind him against the tree's hard roots, while Killer and Derek were hacking through any of the goblins who strayed too close to the leshii in their violent confusion. Mari's group wound through the frenzy, dodging flying limbs and heads at random. When they made it to the traveling circle, Sarah, Ruv, and Frostbite eased their companions to the ground and joined Derek and Killer's whirling machetes.

"Why didn't you leave?" Mari asked Micaleth. She tore a shred of cloth from her tunic and wiped the worst of the goo from his horn.

"This circle is unnatural," he responded with a heavy frown. "Corrupted."

"But it's still a circle, right?"

Micaleth let out a long breath. "Yes and no. There is death here." He gave her a hard look. "The living cannot use it and survive. He ripped the veil, but incompletely."

Brae looked up at him. "We think we can fix it," she stated. "He's a nietheran, after all, and I'm a tree."

Mari nodded at her. "We have to try. That leshii won't survive for much longer, and we have to get Gren and Sam and Wendy out of here. Not to mention the rest of us."

"Fixing the circle would take a great act of healing, a subtle control over powerful forces far beyond anything I have ever attempted," Micaleth cautioned, shuffling his hooves. "The heart is wrong. It must be undone and rewoven. Such healing would take a lifetime."

"The heart," Mari mused. "You mean the tree?"

Brae stood as Micaleth gave a solemn nod. "I can help with that part," she said.

"Even then, this is deep magic. It took three niethera together to plant each circle. On my own I could never—"

Mari interrupted him with a fierce glance. "But you're not on your own," she said, then called, "Frostbite!" He turned at the sound of his name. "Take down this tree!"

He decapitated the goblin he had been fighting in a smooth arc of his axe, and then without a word he rushed over and began hacking at the base of the twisted tree. As he did so, Mari and Brae moved the injured safely out of the circle's perimeter. Once they had been moved, Mari shouted to Micaleth over the din, "I'll be back. There's something I still have to do."

"But what if—" the nietheran started.

"Just try!" she ordered before racing inside the fortress, dodging the stumbling attacks of the last goblins who remained upright.

She raced past the curtain to find Necria and Dimeldor precisely where she had left them, surrounded by the odd light that flickered in and out like a dying candle. "Necria?" she called softly. "You need to let him go now."

The maiden shook her head fiercely. Mari noticed the elaborate jewelry suspended from her earlobes, around her neck, at her wrists: smooth, unnaturally black stones, so black they seemed to swallow the very light from the surrounding torches. Mari's eyes strayed to the necromancer's collar, where his robes were pinned with a similarly designed broach. She glanced at the great basin resting on a table of stacked rocks and found the same smooth, unnaturally black stone.

A connection twitched in her brain.

"I'm not dead yet," he coughed. The wet, gurgling breath came slow and ragged, and specks of black blood patterned his chin and neck, but a taunting leer curled his lips. "I may yet heal."

"You won't," she promised in a whisper.

The necromancer watched her heave the stone basin from its table. His eyes followed her as she hauled it toward the window, and they widened with horror as she shoved it over the edge. When Mari leaned out the window to confirm the smooth, gleaming stone had been reduced to dust, he remarked, "He'll be angry about that, you know."

She ignored him and knelt next to Necria. "You need to let him go," she repeated, her voice kind. "He's draining us to save himself. He's draining *you*."

Dimeldor choked on a bitter laugh. "There is nothing left to drain."

He watched, but did not struggle when Mari removed the broach from his collar, nor did Necria make any move to interfere. Instead, unprompted, Necria removed her gifted jewels one by one. She unhooked her earrings and placed them delicately in Mari's outstretched palm. Next she unfastened her necklace, the intricately twining threads of gold flashing pink in the pulsating aura. She slid the bracelets off her wrists. Finally, she slipped off her ring. She held it to her heart for a few breaths, eyes squeezed shut, before relinquishing it to Mari's care.

Necria placed her newly unadorned hands in Dimeldor's, and with his waning strength he brought them to his lips. "It won't be long now, my love," he murmured. He sucked in another painful breath and coughed up more blood. The dark glow of the aura that had once encompassed both him and Necria drew inward, fainter and fainter with every heartbeat, but still present. Necria planted a kiss on his forehead.

Mari strode toward the hearth where the fire blazed. The stones cracked and popped as she tossed them into the flames. The flames flashed green, blue, then green again, then disappeared entirely, taking the torches with them. The only illumination in the room came from Dimeldor and Necria's lingering aura.

Mari's brows furrowed in confusion. "But that should have severed the last connection!" she protested. Then, remembering the stolen fatestone, she marched back over. Her fingers probed his robes for the jewel, eventually finding it in a fold of fabric. "This doesn't belong to you any more than she does," she snarled as she took it.

There was a sharp intake of breath from Necria, and then she collapsed on top of Dimeldor's chest with a cry.

The necromancer choked out a laugh, his chest shaking. "Surely you did not think it would be so...simple..." his voice trailed off into another fit of coughs, "...to save her? All you've done is help her...to follow me..."

Necria forced herself up, the glow around her banished. "Thank you," she whispered. Her voice was dry from disuse. Then her eyes rolled back, and she fell. Before she even hit the ground, both she and the necromancer had disintegrated into dust.

Mari sank to her knees. "We failed," she murmured. "I failed. I couldn't save her."

An unexpected arm draped about her shoulders. "Come, love," Ruv said softly. She had not noticed his arrival. "It's over. There's nothing more to be done." He gathered Mari in his arms, and he held her while she sobbed, shocked, against his chest. She kept sobbing until the tree's fall shook the building beneath them and the consequent thud hit their ears.

She pulled herself together, wiped her eyes, and headed toward the door. "Yes, there is," she asserted. "There is something to be done, just not here."

Mari and Ruv returned to the courtyard, where they found Frostbite, Derek, and Killer hauling away the felled tree. Gren and Sam sat back to back to prop each other up while Sarah squatted next to them, keeping an eye on the men as well as the unresponsive Wendy. As for the corpses of their erstwhile enemies, no trace remained but for ash and dust and a few rusted weapons.

Micaleth, Brae, and Faro stood inside the traveling circle, deep in concentration. Micaleth stretched his neck so the tip of his horn pierced the heart of the dead stump. Brae held both hands outstretched toward the same, and Faro, bracing herself against the other's shoulder, extended her free hand as well. A hush fell over the courtyard as their concentration deepened.

Eventually a tiny speck of green sprouted from the center of the stump. The sprout grew, slowly at first, in barely perceptible millimeters of development. But then the sprout became a white-barked sapling, and the dead wood buckled and split around its burgeoning roots. The sapling grew branches. The branches grew delicate, toothed leaves. The white bark split and peeled, and the sapling kept growing.

When the birch tree was barely as high as Micaleth's shoulder, he stumbled backward, and the two leshii fell prostrate. Frostbite and Ruv rushed to their sides, announced with relief that they lived, and began to carry them outside the circle. However, Brae shook them off as her senses returned to her. "It's not enough," she panted. "We're not done yet."

Micaleth, regaining his balance, agreed with her assertion. "We must continue to root the magic," he urged.

Reluctantly, the men helped Brae and Faro stagger back toward the young tree. They propped the wilted leshii against Micaleth's left shoulder, Faro braced between Brae and the nietheran. Brae smiled wanly at them as they left the circle once more.

Before the trio resumed their efforts, Mari regarded Gren. "Music is magic," she mused, tugging the thread of an idea that had gradually built in her brain. "Is this something a Wanderer could help with?"

Gren returned her scrutiny, his dark brows drawn together in confusion. "How? I can't even stand."

Micaleth pondered the proposition carefully. At length, he said, "Possibly. He can touch the heart of the circles. Maybe he could help create one."

"Yeah, but that doesn't mean I know what to do," Gren protested, swallowing hard.

Mari drew him to his feet. He leaned on her shoulder as she helped him limp toward the center. "You always hear the music," she reminded him him in a soft voice. When he hesitated, the rest urged him on with various statements of confidence and assurance.

"Place your hand on the trunk with me," Micaleth instructed as he arrived, gesturing for Gren to lean against his flank. "We will find the song together."

Gren shot Mari a panicked look, which she returned with an assertive nod. She supported him against Micaleth, and he threw one arm around the nietheran's neck. Faro, sighing, laced her fingers through Gren's. They were cold and fragile as an autumn leaf.

Brae twisted her head around to view her companions standing just outside the circle's perimeter. She looked each one in the eye and smiled. "It's been one hell of journey," she called. To Gren, she recited, *"Durate, et vosmet rebus servate secundis."* With that, she squeezed Faro on the shoulder, nodded to Micaleth and Gren, and so the magic began anew.

They closed their eyes and started to hum. Gren's honeyed baritone underscored Brae and Faro's soprano harmonies over Micaleth's deep bass. Urged by the power of their eerie song, the tree recommenced growing. More branches sprouted from its crown, and leaves, loosed by a newly stirring wind, spiraled and swirled about the circle. The humming deepened, spread, and grew louder. The humming reverberated throughout the courtyard. The flagstones vibrated with it, and the fortress walls shook. A pale blue light began to slowly encompass the tree, then crawled from the tree along invisible roots to the ring of mushrooms, then crept all the way to the ring of stones.

Suddenly the pale blue light swelled to a blinding flood, hurling Gren and Micaleth outside the circle and knocking everyone else to the ground. Their ears rang with the echo of magic. When at last the ringing ceased and they could open their eyes, they saw the circle pulsating in and out with a weak, violet radiance.

"Something's wrong," Micaleth stammered. He wobbled to his hooves and picked his way slowly toward the young tree. "Something's wrong," he repeated. As soon as he crossed the circle's stone perimeter, the light went out entirely. The tree at its heart stood lifeless, its branches black and bent, its leaves skeletal.

Brae and Faro were nowhere to be found.

"It didn't work," Gren coughed, knuckles white as he balled his fists around empty air.

Micaleth shuddered and paced the inside of the dead circle, his nose pressed to the ground as if to sniff out a trace of the missing leshii. Eyes dark with anguish, he cried, "They're gone."

"Micaleth," Mari called, trying to pry his attention away from the dead tree and empty circle. "What happened? Where are Brae and Faro?"

"They're gone," he said once more.

"Ok," Mari placated, "but where?"

It was Gren who answered her. "Nowhere. They're just gone," he stated plainly.

"And for nothing," Micaleth added in a ragged whisper. "They sacrificed themselves to complete the tree, the circle, but it didn't work. It wasn't enough."

"We failed," Gren choked, head in his hands. "They gave everything. Everything. They let themselves fade, but we still failed. It was all for nothing." Had he enough strength left to cry, his tears could have washed the dirt and grime and viscera from them all.

Silence rippled through the group as the realization hit. Ruv, numb, stared at the empty space where Brae should be, stared at his empty hands, stared at the black sky. Killer and Derek moved to Ruv's side and laid tentative hands on either shoulder. He gave no indication of awareness. Sarah hunched next to her brother, squeezing his hand as he blinked back more emotion than he had let himself feel in years. Frostbite remained with Wendy, cradling her limp form. At least she still breathed, he thought.

Everyone replayed the scene over and over. The loss of Faro made sense, though they were all saddened by it. Too long away from her roots and starved of sunlight, she had little energy to begin with, yet she had been willing to use all that remained of her lifeforce to give them a chance to escape. They would never survive the journey back, that was understood by all. But Brae...

Mari drew a steadying breath, wishing to offer some modicum of comfort to her friends, but she realized she could not speak. She had no words. Instead, she studied her companions, searching for something concrete to distract her while she processed. Injuries, that would work. There were plenty of injuries to catalogue. Sam and Gren could not stand unassisted, and both sported a dangerous pallor. Gren had gone even paler after his exertions in the circle. Circle. Brae.

Her father.

No. Injuries.

Wendy, whose shattered arm might never heal properly even if she were granted proper medical attention, remained insentient. The scrapes and bruises born by the rest of their band may be minor in comparison, but they were all thinner than they should be, all exhausted by the journey and the battle and the weight of every discovery they had made along the way.

And now, Brae...

"We honor them." Derek's voice rang clear, cutting through everyone's scattered thoughts as he took to his feet. "We honor who they were and what they have done."

"We honor them," Killer echoed. "Before we do anything else. It's what's right."

"There's nothing to bury," Gren murmured. "There's no bodies to burn. What can we do but remember?"

"We honor them," Ruv repeated. He swallowed the dry lump in his throat and stood, nodding solemnly to Derek and Killer. "We honor them with those memories."

With Micaleth leading the way, those who could walk stepped inside the broken circle, helping—and, in Wendy's case, carrying—those who could not. They gathered around the wasted tree. Sarah plucked a leaf, a small speck of green that had survived the tragedy, from off the hard ground. She passed it around to her companions, and one by one they shared their stories, calling forth memories of their fallen friend. They talked until their voices ran dry.

"She knew," Gren said when it was his turn. "She gave me a message for everyone."

Micaleth sniffed, for once not imperiously. "I heard, but I did not understand. What did she say?"

Gren swallowed. "I've been racking my brain trying to place it. I think I finally have it figured out. It was from *The Aeneid*. We covered—we went over that in my fourth year of Latin."

"Do you remember?" Mari urged.

"I think so, yes. *Durate*," he repeated. "Endure." After a steadying breath, he continued, "Endure, and save yourselves for happier days."

As the first rays of the sun touched the fortress walls, Ruv asked, "So now what?" He rubbed the bridge of his crooked nose and watched the play of light.

"Now we endure, as Brae said. We rest," Mari answered. She helped Gren limp away from the group to a pile of crumbling stones. Sitting down beside him and gripping his hand, his skin cooler than she would have liked, she said, "I saw things again. Just for a few moments, when I shared the necromancer's visions while he was scrying in that bowl, when I got inside his head...or, I guess, when he got inside mine. That was what he told me, that they were my visions, not his."

"What did you see?"

"Tauru," she said breathlessly. "I saw Tauru, and I saw where he's going. We need to find him. We need to send him back to sleep."

"But how?" he enquired, pressing her fingers tighter. "We're not in any shape to be facing a giant bull with lightning for a tail. Sam can barely stand, I certainly won't be running any marathons anytime soon, Wendy won't be able to fly for a hell of a long time, assuming she ever even wakes up, and for all we know, Laria still can't see us in the Loom. How do—"

"Laria!" Mari exclaimed. Her free hand shot to her fatestone. "Dahrigek to the sanctuary! Can you hear me?"

Laria's response was immediate: *Even better. I can see you!*

Gren sighed through his nose as Mari bolted to her feet and began communicating enthusiastically with her distant friend. She wandered aimlessly around the wreckage of the courtyard, clasping her fatestone.

The ambulatory sifted through the rubble for anything worth salvaging. They found a blade here, a mostly whole strip of leather there. Growing bored after only a cursory search, Ruv came to sit next to Gren in Mari's vacant seat.

"Don't worry," Ruv said with forced lightness, "I won't try to hold your hand."

"What was her name?" Gren asked suddenly.

"Who?"

"Brae's sister," he explained. "She needs to know."

Ruv smiled sadly. "Sale, I think. We'll find her."

Once the necromancer died, I could see everything, Laria was telling Mari. *I'm so glad you guys are safe! Well—*

"Not all of us," Mari softly corrected. She puffed out her cheeks and blew. "We're terribly low on supplies, and it's a long journey back north."

You've got something else to do, first. Go back to the dungeons and bring Baby Blue Eyes outside.

"Baby Blue Eyes?" Mari echoed, brows raised as her curiosity temporarily got the better of her grief. "You mean the little dragon?"

Yeah, that's what he's called, apparently. His mom's already on the way to pick him up.

Mari blanched. "Ok. An adult dragon. We can deal with an adult dragon." She released her grip on her fatestone and let her link to Laria fade to the back of her mind, thankful that this time, it would not fade entirely. "Hopefully this one's nicer than the Great Dracor," she mumbled to herself before beckoning to her friends.

To keep everyone from dwelling on the potential outcomes of a gargantuan, winged reptile heading their way, but at least thankful for the distraction, she began to issue instructions. "Ruv, you and Frostbite go release those golden cows. Let them roam loose. They deserve their freedom, no matter how short lived, and hopefully a herd of cattle will look a lot tastier than a band of ragged humans. They're certainly cleaner at this point. Derek, Killer, Mickie, keep an eye on our less mobile comrades."

"I don't need watching," Sam snapped, "I just need the feeling to return in my legs."

"Nothing we can do about that now," Mari returned. "Besides, if Wendy wakes up and needs something, which she eventually will, you're no help. Anyway, Sarah, try to look less menacing, and let's go see if we can convince the little blue dude to come outside."

They set about their assigned tasks. Frostbite and Ruv, sporting twin frowns, discussed how best to break down the walls of a mostly stone and iron stable on such short notice. Derek and Killer distributed water and jokes as needed, while Micaleth mostly sat with his legs folded beneath him and his nose pointed toward the ground, allowing an unconscious Wendy to lean against him. Every once in a while he would glance toward the brightening sky, but he said little.

"There's something you're not telling us yet," Sarah commented to Mari, her voice unusually kind, as they descended the dungeon stairs. The keys jingled at her hip.

"That's because I'm not sure how to put it in words yet," returned Mari, picking at a dried splotch of unknown origin stuck to her belt.

Sarah touched her shoulder lightly, the black nails chipped to their natural state by the recent skirmish. "The words will come in time," she said.

"I hope so."

"And when you're ready, we're here," Sarah added. "Goodness knows we're all going to need some time unpacking this over a round or three."

Mari forced a smile. "I know. It's just...there's a connection still that I'm not seeing, between my dreams and the necromancer. Or rather, I *see* the connection, but I don't yet understand it." She lifted the lantern high as she reached the bottom step, illuminating the cells full of bones. "A piece is still missing."

Kneeling to work the lock, Sarah cooed softly at the young dracor, who they found shaking and whimpering with his wings wrapped tightly around himself. "Hey there, Baby Blue Eyes," she crooned. "Your mama's almost here. Do you want to come with us?"

The dracor blinked at them and tilted his head, but he offered no sign of comprehension, let alone immanent obedience.

Mari and Sarah shared a tight-lipped glance. The two women heaved the door open and crouched low by the cell's exit. They kept cooing and talking gently to him while attempting to mime what they wanted. They pointed toward the stairs and at the ceiling, and some measure of recognition seemed to glimmer in his eyes. Sarah mimicked cradling a child, then flapped her arms as if soaring. They repeated their gestures over and over until the young dracor finally unwrapped his wings. He took one hesitant, wobbling step, then another, then suddenly he was waddling as fast as he could and bowled them over in his zeal. They could not help but giggle as he nuzzled and licked their faces, the rough tongue dragging uncomfortably across their skin.

Eventually they regained their feet and led him out of the dungeon. He toddled along behind them, making tiny squeaks of excitement. "I wonder why the bastard kept him locked up down here in the first place?" Sarah mused. "I mean, what use would a bloody necromancer have for him? Can't fly, can't breathe fire, can't even talk."

"But I bet he sure eats a lot."

"Must explain the cattle."

Mari sighed. "Well, he wouldn't stay a baby forever, so maybe for the same reason he seemed to want us." She looked reflectively at the sky as they reentered the courtyard. "But I suppose we'll never know the whole story. It's not like Dimeldor's going to reveal the rest of his master plan now."

"But you were in his head, yeah? Surely you've got some idea."

"I only saw bits and pieces. And apparently he knew I was there the whole time," she admitted with a shrug. "I don't think I saw anything he didn't want me to see."

Sarah rolled her eyes. "Oh, come on, girl! You have to at least have a theory."

She swept her arms over the wreckage of the courtyard and said quietly, "Part of me wonders if *this* was his plan, or at least, if it became his plan, once he met her."

"So you think he wanted to what, die?"

"Not necessarily to die, but…" she hesitated, frowning. When she at last worked out what she wanted to say, she continued, "To prove something, though, yes. How else could a demon love, except through pain and obsession and sacrifice? So that's what he did, because she made him feel. For the first time in millennia, Necria made him feel. And that feeling made him mortal again."

"And so he loved her for it," Gren finished as they reached their reclining friends. Wendy, finally sentient, moaned in the corner, pressed against Micaleth's flank. Derek spoke quietly to her while Killer forced her to drink some water.

Mari gave Gren a melancholy smile. "And hated her, too, a little bit." She reached out a hand to draw him to his feet, and he winced as his weight landed on his bad ankle. "Come on, let's get everyone outside this damn fortress. I've had enough of this courtyard."

Ruv and Frostbite joined them outside shortly thereafter, a herd of cattle rumbling behind them. The cows began to mill about the island, blinking in the sunlight and munching on the sparse vegetation. Mari hoped the cows would not find the gardens, or at least not until her own group had the opportunity to restock their minimal rations for the return journey.

"I'm going to check in with Laria again," she announced, "and see about how long we have to wait for Mama Dracor to join us."

While they waited, Mari summarized the rest of their journey: the sandstorm, the city, the pixies. She omitted most of the grosser details of their undead opponents, not wishing to disturb her friend's delicate stomach. Also not wishing to relive recent embarrassments, she omitted certain events in the cave as well. She did not think she could survive the inevitable teasing.

In turn Laria recounted everything she could see in the Loom now that the fog had been lifted, though she had no answers for how Dimeldor had created that fog in the first place. *He really was mortal,* she agreed with Mari's assessment. *He had gained unbelievable abilities over the years, but he was never able to make his body invulnerable, even though he was able to hide himself and all his activities. That's why our fatestones couldn't reach you once you passed into his territory. You guys were brilliant, Mari.*

"I don't know about that," she said sorrowfully, choking out the words as the battle replayed in her mind. "We did very little, in the end. Necria did all the work, but I still couldn't save her." She forced herself to confront the image of the empty, broken circle. "Or Brae."

Laria hesitated for a few seconds before she replied, *Necria had been dead a long time before you met her.*

"No she wasn't. She'd only just been taken from the village a few months ago—we talked to Markos and his family, the survivors said—"

Mari, no one but Necria survived the burning village.

"But we saw them! We talked to them!"

They were shades, she explained gently. *They were on a loop. The village raid happened more than three hundred years ago. Necria …she lived, for a while, at least. But she wasted away in the fortress not long after she arrived there. You did save her, just not the way you thought. You freed her soul.*

"But—"

Dimeldor was a necromancer, Mari. He had no power over the living. Go back with the others. I've got company now—of course as soon as you contacted me, Gamayun came to tell me the rest of the lanti would be showing up any minute. Mari felt Laria's exasperated sigh through the link, and she imagined she could hear her guests arguing in the background. *Anyway, the baby's mother will be there soon enough.*

Laria struggled to her feet, brushing off the bracken that clung to her dress from diving to the ground to avoid being electrocuted by Perun's dramatic exit. "Why can't he just use the chariot with everyone else?" she grumbled as she drew a piece of grass from her frizzing hair.

"Probably a dominance thing," Hal replied.

Gryndonmin surveyed the fried seedlings he had planted only a few days before. "Lady Laria, I must say, yours has by far been the most eventful reign of any Spinner," he commented, "and yet it has barely begun."

Grinning, she said, "You say that like it's a bad thing."

"Well, I would not call it good, either." The silver nietheran snorted and trotted away.

Hal watched his retreating form, one corner of his mouth quirked upward. "I think I see the family resemblance, now."

"I suppose," she said. Hal escorted her to the cottage where the Loom, as ever, waited. "Though Mickey isn't quite that grumpy yet. I'm looking forward to having him back. The rest of the niethera are always so serious."

"And I'm excited I won't have to fight trees anymore," Hal agreed.

Laria laughed brightly. "That part will make Gryndonmin happy."

"And you are happy you can see everything again."

She forced a smile. "Yeah, it's definitely a relief."

He stopped in his tracks. "Now what's wrong?"

"Nothing, it's fine," she dismissed a little too quickly. "I can see Dahrigek. I can go back and see everything Dimeldor was up to. And we can talk to Mari and Gren again, which is awesome. She sounds really good, all things considered."

"But?"

"But there's...I still feel like there's someone pulling strings somewhere," she whispered. "I just can't figure out who or what or why. I can see the city they found, but I can't see its origins, or how it ended up abandoned and buried in sand." Laria looked down at her feet, shuffling as she paused at the threshold to the weaving room. "I see nothing of the city until it was unburied. And even then, I can't see how it was unburied, only the way they found it."

Hal placed a hand on either of her shoulders and studied her face. "Why didn't you bring that up with Perun and company?"

"It just didn't feel right. This whole time, everyone has been saying Dahrigek is uninhabitable, that there was no reason to go there. Why?"

"I could ask Svarog, maybe," he offered, scratching his chin. "He seems to be a little more forthcoming. And I think he really does want to help us, regardless of what the rest may or may not want."

"So you get the same feeling about them that I do," she commented in a whisper. "We shouldn't discuss it here." She took a deep breath. "Ok. Back to the Loom I go," she affirmed as she strode toward the object in question, its unfinished fabric weaving itself into a new pattern even as she made her approach. "I have a job to do, after all."

Wendy, her back propped against a rock and still gravely pale, pointed north with her good arm. She grew, somehow, even paler. "Hey lads?" she squeaked. "How many dragons, exactly, are we expecting?"

They followed her gaze north to see a flurry of small, dark specks in the sky. The specks increased in size, and soon they could count the swarm approaching them faster than anyone—except, of course, for Baby Blue Eyes, who had begun trumpeting, flapping his fragile wings, and dancing around on his wobbly legs—would have liked.

"Oh my various gods," Sam muttered.

Sarah spit out the water she had been sipping. "How confident are we that we're not on the menu?"

Ruv let out a long breath. "Can't see how we could be with all these tasty bovines about, but all the same."

"Calm down," Micaleth puffed. "Dracora have never been known to eat niethera."

"That only makes you safe," Derek pointed out, "not the rest of us."

The humans watched in awe and not a small amount of fear as the recent arrivals circled overhead. One of the dracora, resplendent in a coat of sapphire scales, roared as she broke away from the rest of the group. From the similarity in color to the child they sheltered, they assumed she must be the mother.

The blue dracor descended first, landing a few dozen meters from them. A great wind swept over them as her wings pumped to slow her descent. Her child waddled toward her. They greeted each other with soft noises and the rubbing of noses while the rest of the dracora came to join the sapphire-scaled pair. Fortunately, they, too, kept their distance, perching on parts of the fortress or the many hilltops and rockpiles in the vicinity.

With a mix of wonder and trepidation, they counted twenty-four dracora in all.

"Thank you for saving my child," the mother hailed, her voice resounding against the stone walls. "Our entire clan has come to meet you and repay the debt. You may call me Ajagar."

Mari bowed, and the rest of her friends echoed the gesture. "It was nothing, really," she called out, her fingers clutching the hilt of her sword in an attempt to keep the trembling at bay. Her last and only encounter with one of the dracora had been more than a little stressful. "We just did what we could."

"You've done more than you know, little one," Ajagar rumbled. Her topaz eyes remained kind. "I would like to take my child far from this evil place at once. Are you ready to leave?"

Mari's mouth dropped open. "Leave? With you?"

Ajagar nodded her gargantuan head. "It would be an honor to deliver you to a place of comfort where you can rest and heal your wounds."

"Not all of us will be able to hold on," she said with a gulp. "We're in pretty bad shape."

Sniffing the death that covered the land, she replied, "It seems you have earned that shape through a long battle. Not to worry. We can carry the injured in our talons. The nietheran, too. We'll be gentle. Come—those who are strong enough to ride may climb onto our backs." At these words, ten of her brethren strode forward and bowed their heads to the ground. "We've each two ridges that you may cling to at the base of our necks. That's how our children first take to the skies when their wings are yet too fragile to bear their own weight. Baby Blue Eyes can show you." She bent her neck, and the tiny dracor scrambled up her shoulder and, wings folded, clutched the ridges with his front talons while his back legs braced against a smaller set located further down her spine.

Mari nodded her thanks. "Before we leave for good, could you maybe take us over to the mainland? We have some supplies we need to collect."

"Of course, little Dreamer."

They led the injured forward first. Though they could not control their thudding hearts and shaking fingers, each managed to keep a brave face. Micaleth clopped forward first, intending to lead by example and prove the dracora truly meant them no harm. He dipped his horn to a coppery scaled dracor, who returned the bow with dignity before extending a massive arm toward the nietheran so he could climb aboard with mincing steps. Despite his assurances, he could not conceal a tremble as he did so. The rest pretended not to notice.

Gren was claimed by a dragon of navy blue with golden ridges, and Ruv climbed atop one with a forest green back and amber underbelly. Sarah led her hobbling brother to a burgundy dracor, who nodded low as he clutched Sam (who did an excellent job maintaining his composure and even managed to look rather arrogant) in his talons. The dracor Sarah subsequently mounted was painted a frosty white with just a hint of silvery sheen. Frostbite set Wendy gently in the outstretched claws of a dracor with scales of dark fuchsia before climbing onto another of charcoal gray. Derek and Killer, taking to the situation with as much joviality as they always did, climbed atop dracora of lavender blue and daisy yellow, respectively.

Waiting until the rest of her friends were safely in position, whether that meant holding onto or being held by a member of Ajagar's family, Mari was the last to mount. She climbed up the shoulder of an orange dracor, who tranquilly introduced himself as Ogonh. Without further ado, the jewel-bright dracora flapped their gargantuan wings and took to the clouds.

For their part, the humans did a commendable job quelling their screams.

Although flight made their return journey significantly swifter, Ajagar warned them that it would still be several days before they reached the traveling circle in Evra, for with passengers the dracora could not travel between the planes as they had on their way south to the island. To do so would most certainly further injure their human riders, and would quite probably kill them, she had explained. Only the dracora could pass through the void unscathed. Their armored scales and sheer bulk protected them from the absolute cold, and their ability to hold their breath for hours on end steeled them against the vacuum itself. In his youth such a journey would be dangerous, if not deadly, even for Baby Blue Eyes.

And so above the desert they soared.

On the second day they passed alongside a deep ravine that, traveling by foot, they had not encountered on the voyage south. Mari shielded her eyes from the wind and looked eastward where a tempest ravaged the far side of the jagged chasm, the sand whipped into a frenzy by the raging wind and scores of lightning flashing amid the dusky clouds. One bolt struck the heart of the ravine, and the resultant thunderclap reached her ears after no more than a count of five. A spark of recognition teased at the back of her mind. "Ogonh," she shouted, "can you take me closer?"

"I don't think that's wise. That is no normal storm."

"I know," she yelled back. "It's Tauru."

She felt the jolt of the dracor's surprise undulate down his spine. "How do you know of Tauru? The Ancients are beyond us," he returned.

"Please! I need to get closer." Mari could find no reason for her certainty, yet she felt the truth in her own words as they spilled out of her. "He's saying something," she explained with fervor.

Another jolt of surprise coursed through the dracor's body. "In none of the stories the elders tell," Ogonh said, his words measured as he banked his wings to steady himself, "have any of the Ancients ever uttered a single word. It is understood that we were the first to speak."

"But I can understand him," she insisted. "I need to know why."

At last Ogonh relented. He trumpeted an announcement of his forthcoming actions to his clan before he cut eastward, bearing Mari closer to the chasm.

Torrents battered them as they drew nearer, and Mari gripped her mount so tightly her knuckles blanched. Flying along the western edge of the ravine, the thunder overwhelmed her ears, and she could feel it pounding in her chest in time with her heart. "Closer!" she shouted. Reluctantly, Ogonh complied.

She saw the mammoth bull standing at the eye of the storm. She could not look directly at him, so brightly did he burn, but the electricity emanating from him was palpable. Her hair frizzed out in its own static cloud, and sparks jumped wherever her clothing and skin rubbed. Still she urged Ogonh further, but he refused to bear her into the storm itself regardless of her protests. It was all he could manage to stay airborne at the edge of the swirling winds. Mari forced herself to look at Tauru though it nearly blinded her. Amid the white hot intensity, two eyes, pinpoints of ebony, met hers. She focused on those ebony eyes, blinking back the tears that built in response to the wind and light.

In those eyes, she saw his journey.

He spoke to her not in words, but in shifting realities, in the fluctuations of space-time, in gravity and energy and the balance between life and death.

He spoke to her in dreams.

Galaxies he had crossed, crawling his way back across dimensions, galloping from one black hole to the next, swimming through rivers of dark matter and churning nebulae. The splitting of the worlds had scattered his family to the limits of the universe, but he was home again. Summoned by so much death and destruction, he was home again.

She saw through Tauru's eyes as he awoke, imprisoned in gold. She saw through his eyes as he shattered his crystal prison. She saw when he tried to wake his brethren, and then when he raged at discovering their idols were yet empty, awaiting their arrival. She saw when he searched the continent for the death that summoned him home, fading in and out of corporeality as he traveled.

As a torrent she felt his frustration when he discovered that the deathly call had ceased.

Soon, he promised, his kin would return. When they did, Aorea would also return to its primordial splendor, reunited in a great collision with its daughters Earth and Daem. Whether or not the three worlds were ready, the Ancients were coming home.

In a matter of seconds the winds abated, the lightning crackled and faded, and all that remained of Tauru's star was a scorched canyon. "Are you alright, child?" Ogonh asked as he cut back to the east where his clan waited.

However, Mari did not hear him. Her eyes rolled back, and she lost her grip. Sliding off his shoulder, she plummeted to the desert below. With a roar he folded his wings and dove after her, managing to recover his lost rider before she reached the ground. Mari safely gripped in his talons, he sped back to his clan.

EPILOGUE
Ah, but the burden is great

A sense of déjà vu overwhelmed her when she found herself in the bright, open parlor of the Witchazel Wizard's cottage. Familiar faces drifted around her, but it took a few moments to sort through her memories for their names. A tall, wiry man with a crooked smile and even crookeder nose: Ruv. A beautiful, ageless woman with kind turquoise eyes and hair like a river at midnight: Vesna, the Lady of the Wood and the younger sister of Nemini. An evrae with a merry face who always dressed in obnoxiously orange robes: Jack, the Witchazel Wizard himself. All three were smiling at her, but she could not help but notice that their smiles did not reach their eyes.

She glanced to her left, where she saw a floating table upon which slept someone whose name she could never lose. "Gren," Mari croaked, trying to sit up.

Jack forced her back to a horizontal position. "Not yet," he ordered cheerfully.

"Is he—"

"He is fine," Vesna cut her off. When Mari tried to speak again, Vesna silenced her with a stern look.

Mari nodded, then cast another worried glance toward the sleeping Gren. She tried to sit up again, and this time, Jack allowed it. He motioned for Ruv to assist, and Mari was soon propped against a stack of pillows with a cup of hot tea in her hands.

"And before you stress yourself further," Vesna continued, staring down Mari as she grudgingly swallowed the pungent brew, "Your other friends are also safe. Wendy lies in the next room, guarded by that big man with the striped tattoos. He refuses to leave her unattended. It is a painful process to reconnect bones in such a manner, so it is better they remain unconscious for it, as the Wanderer is. Yet her injuries were far worse, and despite the induced slumber, she still cries out upon occasion. Thus, we felt it prudent to keep her separate from you both for now. Didn't want the noise distressing you." When Mari opened her mouth to protest, Vesna's delicate nostrils flared. "My goodness, child. Will you just accept help for once? It is imperative that you gather your strength as soon as possible."

"What about Sam?" she pushed before Vesna could silence her again.

This time it was Jack who answered. "Sam refused my aid at first, but his sister talked him into it. When you can walk—get back down, you're not ready—you will find them in the room next door. The other two left to seek their pack."

"They'll bring the boys back here once they find them," Ruv said as he laid a warm hand on her shoulder. His face grew serious. "Mari, why did Ogonh break away from the group? He wouldn't tell us anything."

"I saw Tauru. He spoke to me."

Vesna froze. Schooling her expression to neutrality, she asserted, "The Ancients do not speak."

Mari shook her head. "They do," she retorted. "It was the same as when I shared Dimeldor's visions in the scrying bowl. Or he shared mine. Whatever. He seemed to think what we saw somehow came from me, not him. But I wonder, now, if those visions came from someone else."

The Lady of the Wood massaged her temples. By the time she spoke again, her face and voice had both adopted a peculiar calm. "What did Tauru say?"

Mari began to reply, but then hesitated. "It's—I'm not sure if I can put it into actual words," she admitted. "But I'll try." She furrowed her brow as she concentrated, bit her lip, and then at last ventured an answer. "He showed me where he was, clawing and struggling and fighting his way back. He's not even really here, not yet, but he's close. Dimeldor's work drew him to Aorea. The violence, the death. The magic."

No longer maintaining her mask of tranquility, Vesna's voice was strained as she asked, "Do the others come?"

"Yes," Mari replied quickly. Then, after a moment, she added, "But they're still far away."

Jack regarded Vesna with a frown. "Darling, you told me the Ancients slept beneath the land?"

"They did," she whispered, tucking a lock of black hair behind a perfect ear. "Once." Vesna turned to stare at the forest beyond the open window. She stretched out her hand, and a responding breeze stirred among the trees, sprinkling new leaves and early blossoms into her palm. She inhaled the spring scent with a soft smile, then crumpled the fragile petals onto the floor. "It appears we did not scatter them far enough."

Mari swallowed another mouthful of tea. "Tauru isn't evil," she insisted. "I don't think. Not inherently, anyway. He's just...he's a force of destruction. That's his nature."

Vesna pursed her lips as she took the empty cup from Mari's outstretched hands and held it before Jack. With a flick of his wrist, the teacup disappeared. "We must continue to act as if the prophecy will unfold as planned."

Mari turned a pleading glance to Ruv. He hovered around Gren's shoulder. He lifted the hem of his shirt—a new one, judging from its cleanliness—and polished one of the sapphires on the sleeping man's quiver. He grinned at Mari's scrutiny, but he did not take his eyes off the task.

Still no sound nor motion came from Gren.

"Soon, I think, one of you lanti should tell us what exactly that damn prophecy says," Mari grumbled to the Lady of the Wood. She slid one of the pillows out from behind her and tossed it on the floor so she could lie back. The others started to go. Mari was just about to close her eyes when she bolted upright again. "Vesna, wait!" she called to her hostess's retreating form. "Does anybody besides the Old Farmer raise golden cows?"

Two figures, wreathed all in shadows, watched the sun descend over the water. The waves swirled around their ankles, yet the hems of dress and robe remained dry, unstained by the waters. Solemnly they stood, hand in hand, as the breeze blew straight through them and the shades of their lives rippled across the surface of the water, a reflection of their memories given to the ocean that bore the same name.

In a mirror of the seaside pair, two women perched atop the fortress roof. Devana, clad in hunting leathers darkened by the blood of her prey, surveyed the remnants of the previous night's battle, or at least, what remnants there were to survey. The wind had already dispersed the ashes of the fallen army, and the sand had mostly buried the rusted weapons they left behind. In time, the island would reclaim its former state. Moss and lichen would grow over the cracked flagstones. Salt and brine would erode the obsolete navy, chains and all. The fortress itself would crumble. The visiting dracora had begun the process; the ocean would take care of the rest.

Devana knelt to inspect a stone that had been loosened by a massive reptilian talon. "The time approaches sooner than anticipated," she announced as she straightened.

"So Svarog tells me," her companion replied, her honeyed voice at odds with her demure garb. A shapeless coat concealed her curves as its hood concealed her face. However, no disguise could hide the voice of Kupala.

"As he told, apparently, the Guardian," Devana added.

"That was unwise of him. Uncharacteristically unwise."

"Perhaps." A quiver materialized from the air behind her shoulder, and the huntress withdrew an arrow. She stretched her left hand before her, gripping a bow that appeared in her fingers even as she moved. She aimed at the vale where the vegetable garden hid. The arrow flew. From its tip leapt mice and voles, fleet-footed rabbits and sure-footed goats. "We shall see, I suppose," she said as she lowered the bow.

"It is too soon," Kupala purred. "They are not ready. *She* is not ready."

"They must be."

Kupala sighed and let down her hood. "Sometimes I wonder if we made the right call."

"No point in doubting Rod now. It is too late to rewrite the past, even if we could do such a thing without him." Devana aimed at the sky and let fly a second arrow, and from its fletching flew rock doves and hawks, gulls and pigeons.

"Stribog denies sending the wind," Kupala remarked, her beautiful face distorted by a frown, "but who else could have called forth such a storm? Who would?"

The huntress loosed a third arrow, and from its tip sprang geckos and iguanas, snakes and tortoises. "Our uncle has been quiet in all of this," she stated. The bow and arrows vanished back into the ether.

"Father seems to think he is too diminished to act."

"He is as diminished as the Yaga. No more, and certainly no less."

Kupala laughed bitterly. "Two sides of a coin."

"The duality endures, the same as we," Devana said.

"Duality, opposition," she echoed. "Chance, destiny."

Kupala dropped her cloak and spun in a slow circle, arms making elegant arcs through the air. Mists trailed after her hands. The mists spiraled out from her and encased the island in a sheltering fog. The fog settled over the land, clinging to the rocks and blanketing the moss. "We circle one another as surely as the stars in the heavens."

"And so the dance continues."

"*But what if we were wrong?*"

A frown creased Devana's brown forehead. "Time is short. The child must be brought sooner rather than later."

Sighing, Kupala said, "I will unlock her womb, but not yet. It is too soon. She needs time to recover."

"She is strong. She can bear this burden."

"Ah, but the burden is great."

"Sacrifice always is," the huntress whispered. "Send her to me. It must be within the year, or else too soon will become too late."

They watched as another figure, clothed in rippling seawater with hair and a beard of dark weed, rose above the waves. A trident gripped tight in one hand, he beckoned to the shore with the other. Hand in hand, the shades of Necria and Dimeldor walked into the waves. Hand in hand, they disappeared into the west, swallowed by the Ocean of Memory.

GLOSSARY OF CHARACTERS

Ajagar: dracor; mother of Baby Blue Eyes

Antiln: zheverin; prophet and sorceress, currently imprisoned in the Loom and the source of its power, sister of Dimeldor and Derrien

Baby Blue Eyes: dracor; Ajagar's hatchling

Brae: leshii; sister of Sale, exiled from the Birch Forest, used to visit Rome on Earth before the traveling circle was closed

Buddy (Yuri): human, Eurasian grey wolf sanguine; current alpha of the wolfpack, former beta to Ruv, born 1838 on Earth (Slovakia)

Caivah: undead goblin; second in command after Servorg

Dendro: evrae; the shopkeeper's ancestor

Derek Wilk: human, Eurasian grey wolf sanguine; currently Buddy's beta, born 1839 on Earth (Poland)

Derrien: zheverin; brother of Antiln and Dimeldor

Devana: lanti; goddess of the hunt and moon

Dimeldor (the necromancer): zheverin; sorcerer, Antiln's elder brother, lover of Necria

Elonn: evrae; refugee, sister of Merynn and wife of Markos

Faro: leshii; kidnapped and imprisoned by Dimeldor

Frostbite (Tygyn Chakar): human, Siberian tiger sanguine; escaped worker from the Old Farm, born in 1704 on Earth (Siberia)

Gamayun: lanti, the messenger crow

Great Dracor, the: dracor; the last surviving member of the first generation of dracora

Gren Vandern (the Wanderer): human, Bengal tiger sanguine; bearer of the Wanderer's bow, sapphire star fatestone, born 1986 on Earth (Virginia)

Gryndonmin: nietheran; one of the Spinner's guardians in the sanctuary, Micaleth's uncle

Hal (Howard Smith, the Guardian): sierren; bearer of the Guardian's sword, onyx sword fatestone, a changeling born on Aorea and raised on Earth (Virginia)

Hans Mueler: human, Eurasian grey wolf sanguine; member of Ruv's former wolfpack, Jens's older brother, born in 1840 on Earth (Germany)

Ilya Rojko: human; Mari's father, born in 1963 on Earth (Slovakia)

Jack (The Witchazel Wizard): evrae; sorcerer and diviner, lover of Vesna

Jens Mueler: human, Eurasian grey wolf sanguine; member of Ruv's former wolfpack, Hans's younger brother, born 1843, Germany

Kallia: evrae; younger sister of Kanella and daughter of Therese

Kanella: evrae; waitress at the Tipsy Turtle, older sister of Kallia and daughter of Therese

Killer (Fyodor Petrov): human, Eurasian grey wolf sanguine; member of Ruv's former wolfpack, born 1839 on Earth (Russia)

Kupala: lanti; goddess of love and fertility

Kutkah: lanti; trickster god, former employer of Sarah and Sam, currently imprisoned

Laria Sumner (the Summoner): human, nietheran sanguine; the reigning Fifth Spinner, watcher of the worlds, bearer of the Summoner's knives, chalcedony teardrop fatestone, born 1987 on Earth (North Carolina)

Mari (Maraka Rojko, the Dreamer): human, Eurasian grey wolf sanguine; bearer of the Dreamer's sword, jade moon fatestone, daughter of Ilya, born in 1987 on Earth (Slovakia)

Markos: evrae; refugee, husband of Elonn

Merynn: evrae; refugee, sister of Elonn

Micaleth (Mickie): nietheran; one of the guardians to the Spinner, Gryndonmin's nephew

Mitya (Dmitri Wolak): human, Eurasian grey wolf sanguine; younger member of Ruv's former wolfpack, brother of Vitya, born in 1842 on Earth (Slovakia)

Mokosh: lanti, goddess of crafts and motherhood, Perun's mate

Naya: evrae; younger sister of Necria

Necria: evrae; a jeweler, lover of Dimeldor and older sister of Naya

Nemini (Morana, the Yaga): lanti, goddess of death and rebirth, older sister of Vesna and former mate of Veles

Ogonh: dracor; member of Ajagar's clan

337

Perun: lanti; the Allfather, god of thunder, mate of Mokosh

Radegast: lanti; god of hospitality

Rod: lanti; the progenitor of the gods, sacrificed himself to split the worlds, which created Earth and Daem

Ruv: human, Eurasian grey wolf sanguine; former alpha of the wolfpack, born 1838 on Earth (Slovakia)

Sale: leshii; one of Brae's sisters, exiled from the Birch Forest, wife of an evrae in the Alpines

Sam Kuroneko: human, black panther sanguine; twin brother of Sarah, born in 1911 on Earth (London)

Sarah Kuroneko: human, black panther sanguine: twin sister of Sam, born in 1911 on Earth (London)

Servorg: goblin; commander of Dimeldor's army, first to be resurrected

Stribog: lanti; god of winds

Svarog: lanti; god of the sun and prophecy

Therese: evrae; owner of the Tipsy Turtle, father of Kallia and Kanella, among many other daughters

Torch (Andor Farkas): human, Eurasian grey wolf sanguine; member of Ruv's former wolfpack, born in 1840 on Earth (Hungary)

Veles (the Old Farmer): lanti, god of cattle, agriculture and the underworld, former mate of Morana (Nemini)

Vesna (the Lady of the Wood): lanti; goddess of spring, younger sister of Nemini and lover of Jack

Vitya (Viktor Wolak): human, Eurasian grey wolf sanguine; member of Ruv's former wolfpack, brother of Mitya, born 1843 on Earth (Slovakia)

Wendy (Cerridwen MacEunrig): human, sanguine totem unknown; PhD candidate in geology, born 1998 on Earth (Scotland)

ABOUT THE AUTHOR

Melissa A. Ivanco-Murray is a writer, artist, musician, and grumpy Army veteran who resides in Virginia with her husband Sean and their pack of both furred and feathered children. Melissa is currently working on the next companion novella, *Frosted,* as well as the third full length novel in the *Circle* series, *Vanished.*

For more information about Melissa and her many past and future works, go to www.maimurray.com.